OFF COURSE

SARAH CRICHTON BOOKS

FARRAR, STRAUS AND GIROUX

NEW YORK

OFF COURSE

MICHELLE HUNEVEN

Sarah Crichton Books
Farrar, Straus and Giroux
18 West 18th Street, New York 10011

Library of Congress Cataloging-in-Publication Data
Huneven, Michelle, 1953–
    Off course : a novel / Michelle Huneven. — First edition.
      pages   cm
    ISBN 978-0-374-22447-9 (hardback) — ISBN 978-0-374-71053-8 (ebook)
    1. Doctoral students—Fiction.   2. Single women—Fiction.   3. Man-
woman relationships—Fiction.   4. Mountain life—Fiction.   I. Title.

    PS3558 . U4662 O38 2014
    813'.54—dc23

                                                        2013036858

Designed by Jonathan D. Lippincott

Farrar, Straus and Giroux books may be purchased for educational, business, or
promotional use. For information on bulk purchases, please contact the Macmillan
Corporate and Premium Sales Department at 1-800-221-7945, extension 5442,
or write to specialmarkets@macmillan.com.

www.fsgbooks.com
www.twitter.com/fsgbooks • www.facebook.com/fsgbooks

10   9   8   7   6   5   4   3   2   1

For Dorée Huneven

If a woman in her late twenties hasn't found an absorbing occupation, and if, restless or adventurous, she begins to drift, she flirts with peril; for this is a vulnerable age, when demons present, singly and in droves, often taking the form of men.

—Dr. Beverly Cheswick

Love is trauma.   —Donna Pall

PART I

THE MOUNTAIN

One

Cressida Hartley moved up to her parents' mountain cabin to finish her dissertation. She would *not* become one of the aging lurkers around the Econ Department who hoped for sections of Intro to teach while the tenure track shimmered eternally on the far side of two hundred pages.

Her friend Tillie thought of the cabin. "Tell your folks you need three months free and clear and just bang it out up there."

As it happened, Sam and Sylvia Hartley were building a new cabin behind the old A-frame and they liked the idea of Cress being around to keep an eye on the construction; they even offered to make her student-loan payments for the duration. Her mother, with uncharacteristic restraint, didn't mention that, historically, Cress hated the cabin and had never once gone up willingly.

Cress had never driven to the cabin on her own, either, but she'd remembered the turnoffs—north of Bakersfield onto a two-lane blacktop through the oil fields; then, just before the small agricultural city of Sparkville, a ninety-degree right turn due east toward the cloud-scarved Sierras; and finally, beyond the tiny, sad foothill town of Sawyer, a veer to the right of a huge red barn. The road began to climb then, twisting through oaks, back and forth, the blur of foliage alternating with glimpses into the ravine where the south fork of the Hapsaw River, low in August, formed green pools in biscuit-colored rock.

Being tossed around in the car for an hour was one reason Cress had hated going to the cabin. But it was better to be driving. And lovelier than she remembered, with glossy-leaved oak limbs draped over the road, river views, and dramatic granite outcroppings. Scenery, she thought, was wasted on children, or had been on her. In no time she was in the pines, then passing the Hapsaw Lodge—halfway already! At 5,500 feet, cedars proliferated, and by 6,500 feet, the hundred-foot ponderosa and lodgepole pines prevailed, along with the odd cluster of red-trunked giant sequoias.

The Hartleys' cabin was in the Meadows, a small private development surrounded by National Forest. Her parents had just left, and their housekeeper had come in, made the beds, and laid a fire, match-ready, in the freestanding Danish fireplace. Even in August, a fire at night was a pleasure.

But how ugly the A-frame was—she could see that now: its party-hat pointyness and spindly deck! And inside: the cheap pressboard paneling, the battered cast-off furniture, and ill-fitting venetian blinds. The fireplace, its blue enamel now blackened and chipped around the mouth, seemed a misguided effusion of the sixties, the Scandinavian design a prop for consciousness-raising and wife-swapping sessions—not that her parents went in for either.

A sugar bowl pinned down a note on the wood-grained Formica table: *Upstairs shower stall cracked, use downstairs. Rick and Julie Garsh (contractor + wife) want to have you over. Enjoy. Love, Mom.*

Below that, in her father's slanted scrawl: *Enter high/low temp in log 8 a.m. and 8 p.m.*

The sun had already slid behind Shale Mountain when she arrived, though another hour of light remained. She set up her typewriter on a card table in the living room. The air was warm and dusty, heat still shimmered off the deck. Outside, with her feet on the railing, she enjoyed a small portion of her mother's bourbon until the mosquitoes found her.

Another reason she'd hated the cabin: no comfortable place

to settle in. A wicker love seat was too hard. The built-in window seat was better—at least she could stretch out—but narrow, and also hard, its cushion degraded from years of direct sun. She grabbed the top issue from a two-foot stack of *New Yorkers*, then couldn't stay awake. At eight, ignoring the thermometer and temperature log, she went to her usual room, the enclosed loft with an ultra-firm queen-sized bed that nobody else would sleep on. The day's warmth had collected in a familiar stuffiness. She wrestled the window open along its corroded aluminum track. Wind soughed through the trees, bearing the scent of pine and mineral dust. The moon cast a blue glow. As a child, alone in this room, she'd often heard a distant chorus singing in the highest registers. She knew that the singing came from her own mind, that it was a response to silence and often the prelude to a headache.

She stretched out on the unforgiving bed and closed her eyes. There, at the very edge of hearing, far far away, a thousand voices labored, a cappella.

And so it was on familiar roads, in her family's other home, with the blessings of those closest to her, that she veered off course, into the woods.

Morning brought still more reminders of why she'd hated the cabin: a panging headache, a weird gluey lethargy, small wheeling prisms in her vision. Her mother had attributed these symptoms to Cress's attitude, admittedly rotten. But Sylvia Hartley was off by a letter, as Cress had discovered camping in the Tetons and skiing in Utah. Anywhere above 6,000 feet, she was a poor adapter.

She phoned Tillie in Pasadena at 7:40 a.m. "My head's like an old hangover cartoon," she said. "With little devils pitchforking my eyeballs."

"Why are you calling so early?" said Tillie.

"The rates go up at eight."

They got off the phone a minute before. Cress squinted at the clock. The thermometer hung on the porch sight unseen.

She took three aspirin, then chopped carrots, onions, and celery, and made enough lentil soup for a week, possibly a lifetime. She stuffed a man's large red mitten with ice and, stretching out on the window seat, placed it over her eyes.

The aroma of the soup must have carried outside. The porch creaked and Cress lifted the mitten. A very large dog nosed the sliding glass door as if waiting to be let in. She stood—too fast, setting the prisms into a frenzied whirl—and the creature too rose up on his hind legs. A bear.

He stood like a man, his arms hanging, his head cocked so that his long, whitened snout slanted upward against the glass. One eye—displeasingly small, yellowish, not intelligent—squinted in at her. The visible ear, round at the top and pinched at the stem, lent him a comical stuffed-toy look. He was definitely a he—in the sparser fur of the low belly was a hairier, vertical thicket, with something stuck on it—a dry leaf? A bit of bark? His own crustiness?

Perhaps overconfident of the Thermopane, Cress moved closer. Her heart, which recognized danger, began to race. But when had she ever been so close? She knew from childhood admonitions, *Mustn't meet his eye.*

He was not a handsome or hygienic bear, no, his coat dirty, clumped, its dull brown bleached unevenly on the ends.

His black nostrils quivered, steamed the glass, and slid against it in dark, shiny adhesions, leaving smears. The claws, translucent black crescents, looked like plastic.

She moved closer yet, and he dropped back to all fours. Doglike again, he lumbered down the steps, shoulders rolling. The whole cabin shuddered.

She noticed then other smears, at the same heights, high and low, all along the sliding glass doors, the front set and the side ones.

Her hands shook as she phoned her nearest neighbors, the

retired couple a quarter mile up the hill. "I just had a bear on my porch," she told Florence Orliss. "Big old shaggy brown one."

"Him, yes. He's by here almost every day. Neville squirts him with a hose or bangs pans at him. You want to discourage familiarity."

"It's Thursday, you should go to Family Night at the lodge." Her mother was calling for the third time in as many days. "Jakey puts out a decent buffet. Charge your dinner to our tab. You can buy your own drinks. How's the writing?"

"Marvelous." Cress eyed the sealed box of research notes. "I'm on fire."

"Have you met the Garshes yet?"

"No, Mom, not yet."

"They'll be there. Be sure and introduce yourself."

Cress put on black cigarette pants, a velvet opera coat she'd bought in a Bakersfield thrift store on the way up, and lipstick. She brushed her straight fine hair, but by the time she'd walked the 1.2 miles to the Meadows Lodge, it had separated into strings again. She entered the log building through the bar, and the three dirt-blackened workmen hunched over beers turned as one. "Hey hey! Look at *you*! Can we buy you a drink, darling?"

"That's okay," she whispered, regretting the velvet, the lipstick. "No thanks, no. Thanks, though."

A few steps more and she was in the large, open room. The usual Meadows retirees were out in force, and older; she hadn't seen most of them since she'd been a regular visitor in high school, ten, twelve years ago. The Orlisses. Jim and Sandy Green. Abe and Belinda Johnson. That was Jakey Yates, the lodge owner, hauling a steel tub of broccoli to the steam table. Brian Crittenden waved to her from a booth—she was pretty sure it was Brian, whom she also hadn't seen in ten years, but her mother said he was at his family's chalet recovering from a divorce. Grateful to know anyone under seventy, Cress went over. A small, big-eyed young woman curled under Brian's arm.

"Join us," Brian said. "Heard you were up." His cheerleader good looks—blue eyes, snub nose, wide mouth—had thickened, gone bleary. When Cress was eleven, he'd told her he was "SAE at U.S.C.," and the rhyme still bounced in her brain. "This here's Franny." Brian jostled the slight waif, who had a delicate sharp jaw, those outsized eyes, and long mole-colored hair, shagged.

"I clean your folkses cabin." Franny spoke with a lavish twang.

The buffet opened and they got in line for ketchup-bathed meat loaf, mashed potatoes, broccoli. Cress had never seen the lodge so bustling. Then again, when she was growing up, her family rarely patronized the place, her parents offended that the hamburgers cost what steak did down below.

Brian knew everyone: the retirees, the pack station cowboys. Those dirty guys at the bar were loggers. The men by the fireplace were his fellow carpenters—he'd taken a job on Rick Garsh's crew to pass the time.

"Who's the New Age squaw?" Cress nodded toward a stout blond woman with long braids who'd piled on the fringe, beads, and feather jewelry. "With the tubercular-looking guy there—in the far booth?"

"You don't know? That's who's building your parents' new place! Rick and Julie Garsh. Come on, I'll introduce you." Brian started to stand.

Yipes. "No. Um. Not right now."

Brian had been at the Meadows since June. Decompressing, he said. Banging nails for Rick. Taking a break from the stock market. Catching his breath in the big trees. "Ole Franny and I are having a grand old time."

Rejostled, Ole Franny did not smile, but the sly, inward look that slid over her face made Cress like her.

A heavyset waitress gathered their plates with a clatter, then slammed down small dishes of peach cobbler. "Oh, now cheer up, DeeDee," Brian said.

"Go bleep yourself," she said.

As people ate cobbler, an old guy took to the tiny plywood stage, amped a guitar, and sang "We'll Sing in the Sunshine," then "Embraceable You." He motioned to a young woman standing by with her guitar. "Ladies and gentlemen," he said. "Put your hands together for the Sawyer Songbird."

The Songbird sang "I Fall to Pieces," deftly navigating the octaves and sometimes hiding behind, and sometimes shaking back her long brown hair. She in turn called to a banjo player in the audience. "Mason, you lazy egg sucker. Git up here and start pickin'. And I don't mean your nose."

The loggers hooted.

"Charming," said Brian Crittenden.

"My sister and her's friends," said Franny.

Together, the old guy and the Songbird sang "Hello Stranger," with the banjo plunking along. Franny and Brian got up to dance. Cress went to the bar for another beer. As she waited for the bartender, Jakey Yates slid onto the stool beside her. A big burly laugher in his late forties, Jakey had owned the lodge for a decade. Cress had been such an infrequent visitor during his reign, she knew him only by sight. He had thick salt-and-pepper hair, a full beard, and blue eyes full of movement and humor. "Hartley girl—right?" he said. "Would that be Sharon or Cressida?"

"B," she said.

Her beer came, and he pushed back her dollar. "On me," he told the bartender. "And give her a shot of whatever she wants."

Cress ordered a Dickel and Jakey had one too. "Hear you had a bear on your deck," he said.

"News travels fast."

"Welcome to the Meadows. I was out tracking him this morning."

"You're not going to kill him."

"Naw, naw. I just like to see where he goes. Learn his habits. I'm a student of animal behavior."

He had something of the bear in his frank, sidelong glance.

"How are your folks?" he said. "Starting construction this week?"

"You tell me," she said.

"And you?" He nudged her arm. "What're you up to these days?"

"Sketching a little," she said, not wanting to describe her academic purgatory on such short acquaintance, and because she no longer said dissertation so easily. "Charcoal, pastels."

Jakey leaned into her then—snuggled, really—and somehow got a thick forearm against her ribs. "You've gone and grown up," he said. "One day you're a skinny kid buying Popsicles, now you're a full-grown glamorous woman."

She'd never bought a Popsicle from Jakey. He'd only owned the lodge for ten years, and she was twenty-eight.

As for the glamour, that was the thrift-store velvet, and some red lipstick Tillie had left in the Saab.

Her folks, Cress knew, preferred Jakey, if slightly, to the lodge's original owner, the Meadows' drunken developer who'd sold them their property. Jakey, her mother said, had made the lodge a growing concern. Cress also knew that Jakey was divorced—her mother must have mentioned this too—and that his wife had left him.

Jakey petted Cress's velvet sleeve, nudged. "Do you show in a gallery?" he asked. "Do you sell? Drawing, painting—now that's a tough life.

"I know," he went on. "I did my grad work in landscape design, which is not unlike painting"—nudge—"only the canvas is bigger and the pigments far less stable!" He laughed with joy at his own joke, looked her in the eye, clamped his big paw on her thigh, and squeezed, setting off a blinding, bourbon-tinted flash. Cress missed whatever he said next.

"Pardon me?" she said, perhaps too loudly. "Do I want to what?"

He glanced about with a comic cringe, as if to check who'd overheard; then he came in close again, squeezing anew. "Come on, Cressida Hartley," he said. "Let's beat it out of here."

How quickly had the air cracked and from the fissure come a large laughing woodsman to carry her into the wilderness.

Brian and Franny were still rotating slowly across the dance floor. Cress caught Brian's eye, waved.

In Jakey's old green truck, a former Forest Service vehicle scrubbed of logos, they bumped along a logging road through stands of ponderosa and Jeffrey pines, and hundred-foot Doug firs. In a flat open space, Jakey parked and started kissing her. His body heat and mass were memorable. She had never kissed a man so large, or so much older—twenty-one years, almost to the day—and never had one ever shown such an interest in her.

"Good stars," he said. "Shouldn't waste 'em."

So they climbed out of the truck. The moon, oblong and coolly bright, lit the landscape so that every leaf and rock was distinct as in a nighttime diorama. "What's that?" she asked about a messy pink dust cloud.

"That? The Milky damn Way," Jakey said, and tugged her down onto a slippery bed of needles. In no time, he was at her buttons. Well, what did I expect? she thought, and went along. They made love urgently, sweetly, ending a few yards down from where they started.

A little precipitous, thought Cress. But Jakey was so affectionate and grateful. God knows when he'd last had sex.

She was a bit rusty herself in that department.

Jakey tugged her jeans back up and kissed her so lovingly, she felt selfless, exalted, as if she'd answered a prayer. The deep dark sky, spattered, no, silted with stars, spread its faint eternal light. Slowly she grew aware of pine needles pricking through her clothes.

Jakey unlocked the lodge and they had a nightcap at the bar

in the dark. And another. He dropped her off at the foot of her driveway. Trembling, as if freshly anointed—he was the first adult she'd known from her parents' world to desire her—she walked up to the A-frame.

The next morning, hanging up the velvet coat, Cress saw, on the back, flattened spots of resin with bits of pine needles and grit ground in, small dirty galaxies. She never could get them off and had to throw the coat away.

Two

Cress's sister, Sharon, was thirteen when Carl Abajanian, a pale, skinny boy with black hair, asked her to go steady and gave her a Saint Christopher medal. What awoke embarrassed pleasure in Sharon changed the family's life forever. "Nobody is going on a date, let alone *going steady* until they are at least sixteen," Sylvia Hartley declared. "If then." The cheap white enameled disk was returned, and weekly camping trips commenced in a steady rotation of mountains, desert, and beach. The Chevy wagon was soon replaced by a black-and-red VW van, outfitted—to save money—by Sam himself with a tiny fridge and a hip-bruising table-with-benches that folded into beds. Every Friday afternoon, Sylvia stowed duffels and groceries in the van and ordered the girls in after; they drove for hours, pitching camp in darkness and waking up to Joshua trees, pines, or thundering surf. Sylvia Hartley had a small inheritance from her mother and wherever they went—Arrowhead, Anza-Borrego, Gaviota—she and Sam looked at vacation property. Cress learned to read and to draw in a moving car, and how to pull in deep, so time would pass in a blip.

On a Sunday morning in early June, they were breaking camp on the banks of the Kern River when Sylvia, always fond of a map, spotted a little-known pass over the Sierras. They took it east to west, switchbacking through red-limbed manzanita and white-flowering elderberry. The only vehicles they met were logging trucks that downshifted with terrible roars, their hydraulic brakes gasping and spitting. Mosaics of bark on the transported logs smeared past the van's windows only a few feet from Cress's face.

After an hour of climbing, the road straightened out along a high ridge with tall pines and granite boulders. In a few miles, just where the road began its westerly descent, a large new log building stood on the left, its pale wood still raw and shiny with shellac. A banner hung from the rafters: THE MEADOWS LODGE GRAND OPENING. Below that, stuck in the dirt at a jaunty angle, a red-and-white placard: LOTS FOR SALE. "What do you think?" said Sam.

"No harm in looking," said Sylvia.

"You girls want to come in?"

The sisters did not glance up from their books. The parents climbed out, smoothed themselves, and disappeared into the log building.

Cress put down *Hawaii* and, wobbly from the drive, stepped squinting into the sun. The air was clean and thin. The parking lot, recently scraped from the woods, had high clumps of churned mud and brush at its edges. Windshields, car chrome, mica in stones bristled with sharp white slivers of light. A mean little headache began pulsing behind her eyes. Her parents emerged from the lodge with a small, bandy-legged man. "Girls!" they called. "Let's go!"

Reggie Thornton, land developer and lodge owner, wore blue jeans with a crisp white Western shirt. He had a meaty pink face, a spaniel's woozy brown eyes, and a sculptural, milk-white pompadour. "Sam and Sylvia, you're in front with me," he said, pointing to a mud-spattered yellow Coupe de Ville. "Girls, in the back. That's it, that's it. Watch your head there, Sylvia."

He drove through the development with one hand; the other held a cigarette outside the car window. He was the first man Cress had ever met who wore a bracelet! A thick gold one. "You a skier, Sylvia?" he said. "We're surveying for a rope lift, Syl, just across the road there."

"You play tennis, Sam? Clay courts are what we have in mind—what do you think, Sam? We're afraid concrete will crack."

A few glass-faced A-frames hid amid the trees, and one modernist box of stained wood and Thermopane, but the sprawling, ranch-style log home was most popular. Three of these log ranchers were spec homes and for sale, but Cress's parents demurred, preferring a buildable lot. Reggie Thornton duly drove them first to a buggy hollow where a cabin might be tucked, then to a hillside view lot, and finally to a flat half-acre of scrub brush.

"Got mostly retired folks so far, Sylvia, but once the ski slope and tennis courts go in, families'll be on this mountain like a rash. Best get in early, Sam, before land prices skyrocket and all the prime lots sell."

His cologne fed Cress's headache. She disdained, as her parents normally would, the inflated hair and 14-karat curb links, the pimply ostrich cowboy boots. She willed her parents to exchange that look, her father's cue to say, *Thank you, sir, we've seen enough,* and liberate them from the Caddy's stiff upholstery. But neither parent displayed impatience: apparently home sites in the big pines for under 5K eclipsed all their usual snobberies.

Sam and Sylvia, whispering, settled on the view lot, Sylvia insisting, although it cost five hundred dollars more. The three-quarters acre of decomposed granite and car-sized boulders had seven tall pines, clusters of young spruce, and a long switchbacked driveway. The house site was graded, an electric pole already planted and strung.

"You've got a real eye for property, Sylvia—you know the best."

Solemn, and in palpable terror, her parents wrote a check for the deposit.

"Fully refundable, Syl, don't you worry.

"Sylvia, Sam, girls. A pleasure."

Then came the rest of the road. On the map it was only thirty miles downhill to the tiny town of Sawyer, but the red squiggle glossed the steepness and tightness of the curves hugging the Hapsaw's ravine. This road was far slower and more perilous than the way up from the Kern. Her father braked, downshifted, swung them back and forth. A pencil and a plastic cup rolled from one side of the van to the other. Halfway, Sharon roared for him to stop and burst from the van to vomit on the shoulder. Far below, the foam-white Hapsaw gushed with spring runoff. It took them an hour and fifteen minutes to reach Sawyer and a straightaway. Surely, Cress thought, the drive would chill their ardor: Would her parents really want to drive it every weekend? (Yes. Yes, they would. They would happily drive it forty, fifty times a year, up and back.)

Their check cleared instantly. When Reggie Thornton didn't return her father's calls for three weeks, her parents grew frantic, certain they'd been swindled. But Reggie Thornton was not a con man or a thief; he was a garden-variety drunk. He sobered up, resurfaced, and called back as if nothing had happened. Eventually, despite several such lapses, inspections took place, the title cleared, more money changed hands, and escrow closed.

Thus, their fates were sealed: Sharon and Cress Hartley would not go to parties or school dances or spend Saturdays at the beach or at the movies with friends. All sleepovers and make-out sessions would take place without them. They would not have boyfriends or be the popular girls. They would be *at the cabin.*

Sam Hartley built the A-frame's shell from a kit he found on sale in a catalogue, 40 percent off. Sylvia and Cress both lobbied for something more rustic and charming, a board-and-batten redwood cottage with shutters, say, or a modest log cabin stained dark; Sam insisted that the A-frame would give them more room and a panoramic view—for significantly less. Having been a union carpenter when younger, he managed the nailing, plumbing, electrical, and finish work by himself, to his own relaxed standards. For paneling, flooring, and fixtures, he haunted salvage yards and a warehouse by the Los Angeles rail-yards that sold unclaimed and damaged freight.

Friday afternoons, when Cress and her sister got home from school, anxiety shivered their mother's voice. "Get your coat, Sharon, your *parka* . . . Cressida, where are those new snow boots I bought you? . . . Sam, I *told* you we needed ice for the cooler!"

Sylvia exhorted her friends, colleagues, even her students to *come up to the cabin.* Her closest friends were under steady pressure. Cress heard her mother on the phone: *You haven't been up for a year, Barbara. That's right. More than a year. Nope, nope. I'm sure. I have my calendar right here.*

All Cress wanted was to stay home with her friends—Tillie and Rochelle Boyer and the Ellis twins—and loll in each other's bedroom or take the bus downtown in a gang. That was her real life, and it was forbidden to her. When she was fourteen, Cress called the A-frame Auschwitz to her mother's face. And was slapped across the mouth.

Tillie had once tried to intervene on Cress's behalf. "Please, Mrs. Hartley, can't Cress stay home a couple weekends and do stuff with us? These are her *high-school years!* She should have fun!"

For days afterward, Cress heard her mother on the phone: *Cressida's friend thinks I'm a terrible mother because I won't let her run wild every weekend.*

Cressida's friend informed me that Cress should be able to do whatever she wants.

Apparently, our having a beautiful vacation home has ruined Cressida's whole high-school experience. So I've been told.

Once at the cabin, the sisters could come and go as they pleased, as long as they were home by dark. Sharon stuffed a backpack with books and food and disappeared until dinner. Cress stayed in bed, exhausted, her head throbbing, until her father started hammering or her mother put a Mahler symphony on the stereo. Taking a book, Cress wandered down to the epony-mous meadows, alluring green expanses that were deceptively boggy; she hopped hummock to hummock; a misstep and she sank to her shins in muck. A narrow, deep trout stream meandered through the middle and led to a slumping, shuttered log cabin. The Bauer family, who had owned the whole private parcel before the Meadows was developed, had held on to this ancient cabin and the two meadows. (In fact, there were no meadows in The Meadows, Inc.) Cress spent weekend afternoons on the cabin's shady porch, technically trespassing, but she never ran into any Bauer—or anyone at all. She stretched out on a waney-edged wooden bench to read and daydream and doze until the bugs or the rising cold or the sinking sun sent her home. Such was her teenage wilderness experience: hours alone on a bench.

Sylvia Hartley's strategy to keep her girls away from boys, booze, and drugs so easily could have backfired. For all the attention Sylvia and Sam actually paid to their daughters up in the Meadows, Cress and Sharon might have spent their days joyriding on borrowed snowmobiles, smoking pot, losing their virginities on the warm smooth granite slabs by Spearmint Creek. Had there been any Meadows boys, or even naughty girls. But the Meadows never prospered as Reggie Thornton predicted. Rope tow and clubhouse, tennis courts and skating rink never materialized; families never swarmed the mountain, nor did land prices skyrocket. Around the time Cress started college, Reggie Thornton was forced to sell the Meadows Lodge and Land Company. Cress was in grad school when her mother reported that Reggie was in prison for killing a young couple in a head-on collision while driving drunk.

Jakey Yates came over on Saturday afternoon and left the A-frame once that night for thirty minutes, when he went to check on the lodge. They ate and drank in bed. He brought steaks and a stack of LPs and sang along with George Jones and Lefty Frizzell, clamping her under his hot arm.

He rolled his big overheated body right on top of her, and she gasped with laughter, then for breath.

The next day, she and Jakey hiked to the fire lookout on Camel Crags; he'd packed sandwiches and wine, and he gave the firewatcher twenty bucks to go for a shower and a beer at the lodge while they borrowed his bed, with its three-hundred-degree view. They laughed and grabbed their clothes when they heard hikers clomping up the wooden stairs from below.

He had been single now for two years, Jakey told her in that tiny glass hut. His wife had waited until the day their youngest graduated from high school to move out. In fact, they were driving between the graduation ceremony in Sparkville and the celebratory dinner at the Sawyer Inn when his wife said that she was filing for divorce, and even as they spoke, a moving company was in their home taking everything she'd tagged. He'd noticed that morning yellow confetti dots on a lamp, the back of the rocking chair, a pillow. Vaguely, he'd blamed the grandkids and in the flurry and excitement of the day forgot about it.

"She hated it up here," Jakey told Cress.

From where they reclined, looking out on ridge after ridge, to the far escarpments and white glaciers of the Sierra Nevada, not one squiggle of smoke drifted upward. Jakey admitted that he had played the field some since his wife left, but he was losing his taste for it. "Enough diversion," he said, and added, thrillingly, "I'm ready for some real company."

They took long drives in his battered green truck down logging and fire roads deep into backcountry to check for grouse or deer or cougar, whatever was on his mind. (Cougar. Who knew she'd ever track cougar?) They drank hard liquor and talked. They used beds in various cabins whose owners had entrusted their keys to Jakey, and sometimes the cool banks of streams. One night, he took her to a canvas tent alongside Spearmint Creek, just outside the campground limits; the inside was furnished with a small woodstove, Persian carpets (fake, but still charming), and a real bed on a frame, with a tufted chenille spread that left stripe marks on Cress's backside, as if she'd been tied up or caned.

Jakey wasn't keen to have her at his place; although he lived alone, his two youngest sons lived nearby and often dropped in without warning. A few times, Jakey took the risk anyway, showing Cress where to park in the aspen grove, where her old Saab couldn't be seen.

He cooked dinner at the lodge, then came to the A-frame smelling of wood and cigarette smoke, alcohol, grilled meat. He held an ice pack to her temples, snuggled against her, a fleshy furnace, comfort incarnate.

"It's a shame I'm so damn old," he said. But Cress didn't miss the athletics, often tedious, of her former, younger lovers.

"Cressida." His voice was graveled after sex. "What kind of name is that?"

Well. Her mother had come to Los Angeles as a young actress and landed a role in an equity waiver production of *Troilus and Cressida*. "By Shakespeare?" said Cress. "Not his best. It's long and draws these obscure parallels between Elizabethan England and the Trojan Wars." But her mother had received wonderful reviews: *Sylvia Hartley plays Cressida with crackling hauteur.* "So basically, I'm named for her best role. Her finest hour."

"That's unique." Jakey bit her arm. "Kind of sweet."

"Except Cressida is this scheming nympho who flirts with everyone and sleeps with the enemy. Even in Shakespeare's time, her name was synonymous with *prostitute*. So thanks a lot, Mom. Why not just name me Whore Hartley?"

"Oh now." Jakey rolled all his weight on top of her. "I'm sure she didn't mean it that way."

—

Cress ducked into the lodge for milk or eggs, which Jakey sold to her for pennies. He poured her coffee or drinks, made her lunch, no charge. He sat her in a booth where he could see her as he cooked.

He'd loose a roar when someone he knew came through the door, and he knew legions: the Meadows' full-time and part-time residents, of course, but also the campers, hikers, hunters, fishermen, cross-country skiers, and snowmobilers who returned year after year—and the camp rangers, loggers, fire crews, and Cal Trans workers who cycled through in shifts. Men jockeyed for Jakey's attention, became heartier, gruffer in his presence. Jakey bought drinks for friends, and to woo strangers; he cozied up to the shy, the elderly, the disapproving, the worshipful; he plied them with Yukon Jack (his liquor salesman left a promotional case); he spiked their hot chocolate, no charge. He nudged with knee, forearm, and shoulder, until his subject relaxed, capitulated, fell under his spell.

"Now *you*, Hartley—*you* I can talk to," he said. "You're a good listener."

"He's how old, again?" said Tillie.

"But I like that," said Cress. "He's the first real grown-up I've been with."

"And the diss?"

"I've opened the boxes. That's more than I did at Braithway."

Braithway Court in Pasadena was a pretty, U-shaped complex of ham-pink tourist cottages from the Arts and Crafts era. Cress had stayed there with Tillie and Edgar for three months after her orals, with the idea that she would move into the next available one-bedroom unit—Tillie was the manager. While Cress was in college and graduate school, Tillie had wandered through Europe, India, and the Middle East, then come home to

Pasadena, where she found the Braithway job in the classifieds. The position came with a large second-floor apartment that had a commanding view of the court. It happened that Edgar Copperud from Karachi, post-doc in climate physics at Caltech, lived in #6. *Three with one blow*, Tillie liked to say: *Home, job, and husband landed in a day.*

Before Cress saw Braithway for the first time, she had planned to move to Minneapolis with her grad-school boyfriend, John Bird. She and John both had internships at the Fed that would turn into real jobs once their dissertations were done. But after visiting Tillie's architecturally beguiling pink home over Christmas break (when the daytime temperature stayed steady in the high sixties/low seventies), Cress found the Midwestern winter intolerable. Why live where the temperature did not rise above freezing for six weeks straight? Why not return to her sunny hometown and dwell among the very friends off-limits to her in high school? John Bird took her defection well enough; he moped, but never tried to talk her out of it. Who can argue with homesickness?

Only then she had to find work. She took a CETA job in a university art gallery, but her boss kept forgetting to file the necessary paperwork to pay her. She finally quit to be a waitress at the Dinner Plate, an upscale coffee shop in South Pasadena. But waitressing took so much energy, she had little left for the diss. Writing on her own—without her advisor's prompts, without John Bird modeling discipline in the same room, and without a firm deadline—was like doing jumping jacks at home: in aerobics class, jumping jacks were as easy as skipping; at home, her arms felt leaden and she soon lost all bounce.

By the time she moved to the A-frame, all she had was an ambitious prospectus, a rough introduction, and detailed outlines of the first two chapters.

On his day off, Jakey took her to the Kern River to fish and swim in the warm, low, late-summer water. He stood up to his thighs, his thick chest pinkening in the sun, and hollered: "Any happier, I'd need a tail to wag."

Back when he had his own landscaping firm in the San Fernando Valley, a client had offered him the use of a Meadows cabin. With two days of trout fishing and the alpine air fizzing his blood, he saw the FOR SALE sign on the Meadows Lodge and all interest in hardscape and nursery plants deserted him. Now he grew one box of petunias on the lodge's deck each summer.

He and his wife had envisioned lodge life as a family-run business: living above the store, kids doing homework in booths, all pulling together to make it work like the family in a TV show. *Little Lodge on the Mountain.*

They put in eighty-, sometimes a hundred-hour workweeks. The bar, restaurant, grocery, and gas pumps didn't generate a living, so they added caretaking services, housecleaning, a realty office. "I loved every minute," Jakey told Cress, "but she isn't such a people person. The public wore her out. She missed her sisters in Northridge. I built her a big house across the way there, but the kids took school buses down the mountain every day, two hours each way; in winter, we never saw them in the daylight. Then they started graduating and leaving. She struggled over that."

Even so, Jakey said, he was shocked—no, *devastated*—when she left. "A cannonball to the head," he said. "Then my back went out. For four days, I crawled around on all fours like a damn baby. The lowest of the low."

His two younger boys, Kevin and Derek, shared a cabin by the Meadows' back entrance. The oldest boy and two girls lived down the hill in Sawyer and Sparkville. They were in and out of each other's home all the time.

Among the full-time residents, Jakey, Abe Johnson, Barry Sypes, and now Rick Garsh jockeyed for what money and status could be eked from the small community. Each offered caretaking

services and patrolled the development, checking the homes on
their lists. They opened and shut cabins, they monitored water
pipes in the winter, hired housecleaners, often their own wives
and daughters. They shoveled decks and stairs. The snowplow-
ing franchise with its small state stipend and aging, orange
Oshkosh plow rotated among them.

Owning the lodge made Jakey the undisputed king of the
mountain. He talked to the most people. He saw who came in
and out; he knew who was up for the weekend, whose house was
empty, who'd gone down the hill for the day. He held keys to the
most cabins, he hired the most housecleaners and snow shovel-
ers, brokered the most rentals. He was consulted about local history, the weather, hunting, fishing, snow conditions, property
values, and high-altitude baking.

For all his stature in the community, Jakey could be beauti-
fully unself-conscious. He sported cheap cotton-poly shirts from
Sears and wore his hound's-tooth polyester cook's pants out on
dates. He cut his own hair indifferently when it fell into his
eyes. In a community where men were vain about the beauty
and structure of their fires—Abe Johnson was the one to beat:
he sawed logs to a uniform twenty-four inches and stacked them
so flames licked up six tiers just so—Jakey tossed logs atop
barely crumpled newspaper, squirted everything with barbecue
starter fluid, and threw on a lit match. *Fahwumph!*

The only book in his living room was a Bible with a cro-
cheted cover on a swirly wrought-iron stand.

Three

Cress awoke to men talking outside her bedroom window. Trucks filled the driveway behind the A-frame. Stacks of lumber were off-loaded. Strings demarcated the new cabin's foundation. In the next week, wood replaced the string, plumbing was stubbed in, and a cement truck churned steadily for two days, leaving a powdery gray platform in the pines. Cress finally spoke to wan Rick Garsh, shook his bony hand, met the crew.

"So far so good," she reported to her parents. "Moving right along."

"Talented man, that Rick," her father said. "Keen mind. I like how he's determined to make a life up there. Reminds me of myself when I was young."

"You were never so scrawny," said Cress.

"Hear the mornings are cool," her father said. "How low's it going?"

"I don't know, Dad. The fifties? The forties?"

"Julie Garsh wants us for dinner tomorrow," Jakey said. "You free?"

"I'll check my calendar." They were in Cress's bed. "You want to go?"

"She's a helluva cook."

"They just don't seem like anyone my parents would be friends with," Cress said. "How Rick talked my dad into building this cabin is a mystery. My dad's always built everything himself, on the cheap cheap cheap."

"Rick has big plans for all of us up here," said Jakey. "He's going to build a hundred homes. Spend all our money. She's got her eye on my little real estate office in the lodge. Who knows, maybe I'll let her have it. Good to see some ambition on the mountain. I hope they get something out of it."

Jakey picked her up; together they drove the quarter mile to a line of vehicles parked along the road: two pickups, a battered Bobcat, a Subaru station wagon. The large circular house had thick concrete pilings and wraparound windows tinted dark, which gave it the look of a spaceship or a ski slope bar.

Rick led them inside. The sunken living room was built around a jagged stone fireplace in whose enormous black hearth burned a tidy, tiered, triangular stack of logs—possibly the most photogenic fire Cress had ever seen.

Julie, in braids and full fringe, waved a knife from the kitchen. "Come in! Come in!" She stepped forward to hug. Silver earrings in the shape of feathers clanked against Cress's glasses.

"The boys want Scotch." Julie's tone was low and confidential. "Join me in white wine?"

"Please," Cress said, wanting the Scotch.

The living room had spoked beams, a semicircular sectional. A yellowing philodendron ran laps along the walls. "Did you build this?" said Cress.

"God, no," said Rick. "We just needed a base when construction season started. This was a repo, we got it for a song. If I ever have time, I'll knock it down to a nub, start over from the ground up."

"Here's to that day!" Julie handed drinks all around.

The men drank in front of the fire; Cress caught scraps of Meadows politics: whom they wanted on the community council, who wouldn't pay half for repaving a shared driveway. Julie had Cress tear romaine for the salad, then sprinkle on croutons, dried cranberries, sunflower seeds, alfalfa sprouts. Thick blue cheese dressing held the scoop's shape like ice cream.

"I'm so glad you're here," said Julie. "The weeks get long and awfully short on intellect, if you know what I mean." She came closer, bowed her head. "I hear you need a job—and Rick needs a gofer." She pronounced it like the rodent. "You'd run to Sparkville once or twice a week."

"I'd love that," Cress said, thinking with dread of the road.

"I've heard such marvelous things about you," Julie murmured into Cress's shoulder. "From your folks. And him."

How could that be true? Her parents didn't think she was so marvelous. And what did Jakey know? "Yeah, but I've only been seeing him a few weeks."

"You two click. I can tell. Rick and I clicked like that, too." Julie kept her voice low. "From the moment we laid eyes on one another."

They'd only been married for a year, Julie went on, and together for a year before that. This was the second marriage for both. They'd met at a seminar on creative entrepreneurship. Both knew instantly. "Rick was still married. But he was emotionally and spiritually disconnected from his wife. By our first official date, he had a divorce lawyer. That was my condition." Julie pressed her arm into Cress's. "I'm so glad Jakey found you. You're just what he needs."

Julie knew nothing about her. But it was hard not to be flattered.

Dinner was oxtails braised in bourbon and scalloped potatoes. That multitudinous salad. Rick, Cress noticed, took small portions that didn't touch on the plate—he was like a character she remembered in a children's book: a slow eater, tiny bite taker. He systematically cut off and left all bits of fat.

"Tell you what," Jakey said to Rick. "We should build a chapel by the pond—some nondenominational interfaith wee-kirk-of-the-woods sort of thing. Get some retired preacher in there on Sundays."

"I could build a beautiful little church," said Rick. "A jewel box."

"You could," said Julie. "But who needs a church up here? Nature is the greatest cathedral. Just to walk in the tall trees is a sacrament . . ."

"I'm thinking of the after-church brunch crowd," said Jakey. "And weddings, anniversaries, christenings, funerals—with catered receptions."

"Bar mitzvahs," Cress said.

"Hell, why not?" said Jakey. "I could do kosher."

"When my parents bought their lot in '65, there were plans for an ice-skating rink and tennis courts," said Cress. "A swimming pool and clubhouse."

"All pending," said Jakey. "Still in the works."

For hot fudge sundaes, they moved to the living room, around the fire.

A signal flickered between Julie and Rick. "Cress, may we be frank with you?" Julie said. "We're crazy about your folks, but we could use some advice about how best to work with them."

"Your father has his own ideas about building," said Rick. "Sometimes we don't see eye to eye."

"I'm amazed my dad hired you," said Cress. "He's built all his homes himself. The house in Pasadena. The A-frame. The new place in Oxnard."

"Your mom I adore," said Rick. "She's open to everything. But your dad—I adore him, too—but he . . . he finds it hard to give himself the better things in life."

"My dad? He's as tight as the skin on an apple!" Cress cried, using her father's own phrase. "A child of the Great Depression!"

"It's so good Rick's building him a house," Julie said. "Some people need help forging an enjoyable relationship with their wealth. We can help with that."

The room was very warm. Beside her, Jakey breathed through his mouth, his lids fluttering. "I wouldn't say my folks have *wealth*," Cress said.

"What your dad doesn't understand," said Rick, "is that even slightly higher construction values make for a sturdier, more comfortable home—to say nothing of higher resale values."

"Is he cheaping out on you?" said Cress.

"That's what I don't understand!" cried Julie. "Why deprive himself of the better things in life if he can afford them! It's spiritual starvation! Everybody says we should give generously to the poor—and we should. But we need to give generously to ourselves first. Because if we come from abundance we don't begrudge anyone anything—we give freely from the overflow."

"Not sure my dad thinks that way," said Cress, wishing Jakey would rally and rescue her. And he did. He startled himself awake with a big snore, then bustled them out.

Julie called from the door, proposing a hike the next day. "Just us girls."

"Sure, great," Cress called back, not knowing how to refuse.

"*Overflow?*" Cress said to Jakey as they crawled into her bed. "*Abundance?* They sound like televangelists. Or Republicans. I have a terrible feeling they voted for Reagan."

"What's wrong with voting for Reagan?"

She sat up. "Oh my God." She snatched at the sheets. "You?" She scooted away from him, wailed. "I can't believe I've had sex with a Republican."

"I'm not a Republican," said Jakey. "I just hated Carter. So lily-livered and ineffectual. And at least we got the hostages back."

"You can't seriously believe Reagan had a single thing to do with that." Cress swung her feet out of bed. "I need water."

What have I done? she asked the pressboard walls as she thudded downstairs. A Reagan Democrat—the worst! How had politics never come up before? She drank a long cold cup of water, nabbed the bourbon bottle.

"I'm a small businessman," Jakey said. They were sitting up now, facing forward, passing the bottle. "You can't believe the permits and fees and inspections I pay for. The disability, the unemployment, the social security. I'd probably still be married if I hadn't had to work thousands of extra hours just to keep the government off my back."

She didn't know where to start. How could he object to such basic entitlements? "Careful, sweetie pie," she said. "You're in bed with a Keynesian."

He laughed and reached for her.

"And furthermore"—she squirmed away—"maybe a lodge at the top of the world with a seasonal clientele is not the most economically viable business. And that, more than governmental policy, may be the real issue."

"I'm remote, yes, but that's not taken into consideration. Tulare County told me this week I need a new grease trap. That's five, eight thousand bucks, easy, and for what? I'm not on a sewer line. And all you have to do is watch the Forestry Service up here to know that government shouldn't manage these lands. They have no idea what they're doing."

"Oh yeah, turn the forests over to private interests. Great idea, Jakey. They'll shave this mountain bald as a boulder. Not a tree left standing. That'll give your business a big boost."

Jakey took a long swig of whiskey and handed her the bottle. "How 'bout this? How 'bout you be my personal economics advisor?" He poked her thigh. "You can give me a full economic evaluation. Seriously. I'd pay you for that."

He slid down, kissed the side of her breast.

In fact, she'd already ascertained that Jakey had his own private economy. At the register, he ignored the price list stored under the counter and charged whatever he felt the customer could bear; a bag of marshmallows for her (or some kid) would be a dime; for Dr. Peterson of Thousand Oaks, a buck and a dime. Jakey ran his restaurant, bar, and market by self-interest, but not the kind that fit any rational model. There was no maximizing of any profits. God knows what his books looked like— fiction of some ilk, no doubt. Often, she noticed, he didn't even ring something up, just opened the cash drawer and made change. If someone squawked over a high price, Jakey would say, "Fine, fine, go buy it at the bodega across the street."

Of course, the nearest competition was the Hapsaw Lodge, sixteen twisting miles down the hill.

Julie arrived ten minutes early with a wooden walking stick. Having feared a slow pious trek through the woods, Cress was disappointed to be led down the familiar looping asphalt roads to the lodge. Tap tap tap, they went, Julie keeping close, often brushing against her. Cress had never been nudged and brushed against as much as she had here in the Meadows. But she'd never spent as much time so close to older people, who might be hard of hearing.

"You should know," Julie said, "Jakey went a little nuts after his wife left. A little frantic for company. Terrified of being alone. But he's been looking for a special someone for a while now. And you"—here, her arm collided with Cress's—"you're so different from all the women up here. I have to give him credit. He's surprised us by making an exceptional choice."

"We'll see how it goes," Cress said. "It's only been a few weeks."

Tap tap tap. "I'd love to give you a little advice," Julie said. "May I?"

Julie knew an equation that applied to divorced men: Take how many years they were married and divide it by two: that's how many years before they're actually ready for another relationship—how long before they're out from under their old marriage and can be fully present for a new one.

Cress did the math: if Jakey was married for twenty-four years, he'd need twelve years of recovery time, two of which had elapsed. "Ten more years!" she yelped. "He'll be really old then."

"But you should snag him now," said Julie. "Men don't wait around. Ready or not, they find someone new right away. Rick wasn't over his marriage when we got together. But he's worth all the Sturm und Drang."

"Sturm und Drang, like what?"

"He gets moody, won't talk for a whole day. Rick can be very dark. But I wasn't getting any younger. I knew I better grab on and fasten my seat belt."

Jakey seemed incapable of moodiness, even grumpiness. Distraction, maybe. Jakey could be distracted.

"I like Jakey," Cress said. "But I don't know about the long run."

"Jakey's super!" Julie shoulder-bumped Cress. "Friendly, good business head. Big heart. So lovable. He's worth it, I can promise you that."

Why would Julie promise her anything? Cress wasn't used to making friends this way: assuming the best, and leaping ahead as if they knew each other. And Julie was so much older, so far outside Cress's circle, so fond of Native American accessories.

"Don't let Jakey's age put you off," said Julie. "Some of the happiest marriages I know are May–Decembers."

Marriage! Cress hadn't gone to Minneapolis with John Bird in part because she'd wanted to avoid the courtship-leads-to-marriage track. Wasn't there romance that flowered differently, that didn't morph right into marriage, pregnancy, childrearing, and monogamy for its own sake? What was the sexual revolution for, if not to allow for more varied experiences, a wider range of happiness? Cress was in no hurry to re-create family life—at least not as she'd known it. How surprised she'd been when Tillie—the fastest girl in high school, the first of their group to move out of her parents' house into her own apartment, the first to live with a man—was also the first to turn up married. Was that where Tillie's sexual curiosity, energy, and naughty laughter were pointed all along? Why? Women no longer had to pick one man, set up house, and reproduce. Though setting up house with Jakey might be fun. For a while, anyway.

"By the way, I haven't told my parents I'm seeing Jakey yet," said Cress.

"They won't hear a peep from me."

A small, late lunch rush was in progress at the lodge. Jakey came out to pour them each a glass of white wine. "You gals set the world straight yet?" He nipped Cress's neck, went back to the grill.

A man at the end of the bar stood and walked over. "Is that Sharon Hartley, all grown up?"

"Cressida," she said, as an older, rheumy-eyed Reggie Thornton toasted her with his coffee cup. His pompadour had deflated, his white hair sat close to his skull, in perfect waves.

"Cressida Hartley. I'll be darned. You up for the weekend, Cressida?"

"A couple months, actually. And you? Visiting old friends?"

"Still have my place by the pond," he said.

A convicted killer—that made her shy. But Reggie was cheerful and friendly; he asked about her parents, her sister, about the new cabin going up. "I knew Cressida when she was a skinny little sprout about yea high," he told Julie as he walked behind the bar. He filled his coffee cup with bourbon from the well, then grabbed the wine bottle and topped off their glasses to the brims.

"How do you kill two people driving drunk and still drink?" Cress asked Julie on their way home.

"He's not supposed to," said Julie. "The coffee cup's so the sheriff and rangers won't catch him violating parole."

Cress herself was drunk. A nasty Chablis-yellow ache pulsed behind her eyes, and all she wanted was a dark room, ice on her face, and a gallon of water. Julie had left her walking stick against the bar, and Cress, noticing, was so grateful not to have its metronomic accompaniment all the way home, she said nothing. She walked quickly, to get there, and she talked, too, to distract herself from her headache. Art, she told Julie, had been her first major, but so damn hard. Then economics had come so easily. Her boyfriend in college was an econ major, and she'd just taken an intro class so they could talk. But the first econ paper she wrote won the department's yearly essay prize—her boyfriend never forgave her for that. She'd entered his territory and bested him. It broke them up. But who knew she'd had a talent for economic theory? Even before she graduated, she'd had a paper published—when she was still a fine-arts major. Only when she was applying to grad school did her painting professor sit her down. Maybe think twice, he said. Frankly, he—her teacher— didn't think she had the temperament for life in the art world. (He said temperament, but she knew he meant talent.)

"If art's your calling," Julie said, "it doesn't matter what anyone says."

"I don't know about calling," Cress said. "I just liked making it." She'd applied to Pratt and Cal Arts, anyway, she said, and got into Cal Arts, but without any financial aid. In econ, she got into all four places she'd applied, probably because female applicants were so scarce. Iowa gave her a three-year fellowship. Her boyfriend there, John Bird, was also an economist. But that's it. No more economists for her. And once she was done with the diss, no more econ either.

"So you'll go back to painting?"

"I don't know." For her dissertation, she planned to write about the economics of art, how the work accrues value. She'd posed certain questions, then tried to answer them: for example, what brings more value, a good review or a sold-out show? A major prize or a museum purchase? A museum retrospective or the artist's death? She'd spent last summer in Chicago talking to gallery owners and museum directors, who were as interested as she was in the answers. The market realities were sobering and could chill any artist's ardor. "The best thing an artist can do is die," Cress told Julie. "Nothing raises prices more than death."

The death line usually made people laugh, but Julie Garsh

had no discernible sense of humor. She pursed her thin lips. Then, panting as she trotted to keep up, she said to Cress pretty much what everyone else did: "Just finish the dissertation. Then you can do whatever you want."

In the morning, waiflike Franny appeared at the A-frame's sliding glass doors with a vacuum cleaner. The top of her head didn't reach the standing bear's nose smears. "Your mom says I have to clean, 'cause her and your dad's coming up."

"I guess she doesn't trust my housekeeping."

"That's what she said." Franny hauled the hose and canister inside.

Cress didn't want to lie around reading *New Yorker*s while Franny worked, so she sat at the card table and took out a file, scrolled a sheet of paper into the Selectric. CHAPTER ONE, she wrote at the top of the page, and under that *The Problem of Value in Art.* Okay now. Start. *Determining the utility of visual art has always been a difficult discussion.* Too much, too vague, and she probably shouldn't begin with a term like "utility," which means something different in econo-talk than in English—not if she ever wanted to publish this as a popular (as opposed to an academic) book. She yanked out the paper, balled it up, tossed it into the fireplace, and twirled in a fresh sheet. *The intrinsic value of art may be incalculable, but the price of art tends to be linked directly to market realities.* Nope. Too big a bite. Yank, crumple, and toss. *How art accrues value in the marketplace is only subjective at the beginning.* Better, more grabbing. But soft, soft. Into the flames!

"Bingo," said Franny, who'd been watching from the loft.

Four

"Oh Cress. What have you done?"

In seventeen years, the cabin had filled up. Sylvia Hartley had a reputation, well deserved, for being a gourmet cook—an achievement, given her famously cheap husband—and people bore that in mind when buying her a gift. Her refrain for every too-specialized gewgaw or arcane gadget was *We'll take it to the cabin!* In the packed drawers and cupboards of the A-frame's kitchen—itself just a small corner of the front room—could be found tortoiseshell caviar spoons, a shuddery electric knife, a tortilla press, clay butter molds, a fish poacher, three pedestal cake plates, an ebelskiver skillet, an oven mitt in the shape of a salmon, and linen dish towels from Stratford-upon-Avon and the San Diego Zoo. Crowding the space was an enormous pickling crock holding a decade-old arrangement of dried artichokes, an old-fashioned grocer's scale swinging from a canted beam, and a slumping stack of place mats on the table that periodically, with no provocation, slid to the floor in a splay of raffia, chintz, and plastic.

Cress had carried many of these items to the guest room's closet. She'd also removed someone's attempt at macramé that sagged on the bathroom door and the faded family photographs on the one stretch of unslanted wall by the fridge, replacing the photos with five small colorful street scenes that Tillie had painted in Tehran.

Sylvia made Cress bring back the photographs, the grocer's scale, the macramé. "Cindy Hazzard made that for me," she said.

Whoever Cindy Hazzard was.

"It's not your house," her mother said.

"I know, I know."

"And another thing," Sylvia said. "Your phone bill was through the roof.

"Through the roof," she repeated.

Cress muttered, promising to pay. The problem was, you could call New York late at night and talk for hours for what a ten-minute call to Tillie cost midday.

Cress walked by the lodge to warn Jakey that her parents were up, lest he barrel into the A-frame at midnight. "Saw 'em drive in!" he said, and bustled her into his office for sex on the rug.

The next day, he waved her down. "Sneak over to my house later." His hand crept under her gingham shirt, right there on the lodge's porch.

After her parents went to bed, she slid open the door, and her mother called her name. "Just getting another log, Mom," Cress said, and went back inside.

She and her mother peeled vegetables for a stew. "So you know, Mom, I've been out a couple times with Jakey."

"Jakey? Jakey up here?"

"The very one."

"Oh Cress. He's way too old."

"He's a lot more fun than most guys my age."

Orange ribbons unscrolled from her mother's carrot. "Be careful, Cress," she said quietly.

"Why? What makes you say that?"

"It's just . . . Jakey hurts people without trying."

"Like who?" Cress asked. "Who has he hurt?"

"I don't know of any one incident," Sylvia said. "Just stuff I've heard."

—

Her parents left, and she phoned the lodge. "Free at last!"

"My kids are coming up," Jakey said. "Any minute."

"Come by after," said Cress.

"The oldest will stay," he said. "She always does."

"Will I ever get to meet them?" she said.

"You already know Kevin." His youngest, a big, blushing kid, helped out at the lodge; introductions had been hollered across the dining room.

Cress spent that night by herself. The next night, Jakey came roaring into the A-frame after ten. "I miss you, Hartley, in spite of my damn self."

At Family Night she said, "Coming up later?"

"Worn out. Need to catch up on my sleep."

Another night alone. Then he had to get up early—another. Thus they settled into a more workaday routine, found a more reasonable pitch.

She was now driving to Sparkville for Rick once or twice a week. For a load of lumber or pipe, she took his truck; otherwise, she took her own car. Rick paid her thirty dollars a run, and he let her fill up at Jakey's pump on his tab. "Is he also remunerating you for wear and tear on the Saab?" her father said. "That road is hell on clutches, brakes, and transmissions."

No. Rick was not paying for wear and tear, but she would not tell her father that.

"I'll check," she said.

Rick had three jobs going. A Fresno optician and his wife, Tom and Ondine Streeter, had bought one of Reggie Thornton's log homes and hired Rick to remodel it. He had also taken over from a bankrupt contractor a six-thousand-square-foot folly owned by a Tulare businessman named Rodinger. The Hartleys' new cabin would be his first custom home at the Meadows—or anywhere.

After running Rick's errands, Cress shopped for Julie (and herself) at Younts supermarket, where local produce was set out in field crates: blushing Bartlett pears, leathery pomegranates, frilly bouquets of chard and kale, late-season melons still dusty from the melon patch.

On her way back up the hill, she spotted Jakey's truck at the Hapsaw Lodge and found him in the restaurant eating. The woman across from him was a good ten years his senior—glasses, loose neck, dyed-dark pageboy.

"Ah, Cress," he said. "Meet Honor. She owns this joint."

Honor gave Cress's hand a dry, indifferent shake and went back to her steak. Jakey's hands hovered above his silverware.

"Well, bye, I guess." Suddenly embarrassed, Cress scratched the air in a silly little wave.

"Like any professionals," Jakey told her later, "lodge owners have a need for collegiality."

He'd stop by, he said, before going to town on Friday, or afterward if he was pressed for time. When he hadn't shown up by eight that night, she called the lodge and spoke to his answering machine. "It's me. You coming up or what? I mean, uh, don't heat the oven if you've got nothing to bake."

Half an hour later, he was in her bed. She liked his heft. A chest she could barely reach around. His ruddy skin and strong legs, his readiness to be amused. He was such a large man, big arms, big laugh, big personality. Yet he blushed at compliments and frank sexual suggestions. Cress didn't push for more than he freely gave. There'd be no point in pushing a man like Jakey, who did all things for the joy in them.

Time opened up all around her, free time, empty time, chasms of time. Time to take stock of the light hour by hour, the syrupy sunrises and blanching noons, the wan starlight on moonless

nights. Time to gauge the nip of fall, chart the yellowing of aspen leaves, note the close of fishing season and the first cracks
of shotguns aimed at quail and doves. Time to drift about the
house to George Jones and Lefty Frizzell—Jakey's favorites—
and to Beethoven's late quartets and Glenn Gould playing the
Goldberg Variations straight through. Time to talk for hours
late at night to Tillie, and to read—finally!—faded back issues
of *The New Yorker.* Here in the shortening days, time was vast
and all her own; no more lunch shifts at the Dinner Plate, no
more spongy white uniforms and orthopedic clompers, or tainting
disapproval from moronic male managers.

Into the yawning hours also came sudden drops and voids,
onrushes of anxiety. She was alone at 7,300 feet. The man she
thought about slipped in and out of sight. The typewriter, whenever she approached, made her sleepy. In the A-frame's basement
she found her old easel, a Christmas present in high school; she
set it up and started sketching in charcoal: rocks and a cluster of
spruce. Her powers felt thin in that high air. But they'd felt thin
in Pasadena, too.

Afternoons, she took the same four-mile loop she'd devised
as a teenager, tramping overland to the Bauer cabin. The meadows had dried out sufficiently so she could cross them without
sinking into slime. She checked the deep channel for trout—
Jakey said there were native goldens in there—then followed its
oxbows to the log cabin. Even on weekends, she rarely encoun-
tered another soul. Once, a man was balanced on the cabin's
porch railing. The owner, she thought, but closer, with a propri-
etary pang, she recognized one of Rick's finish carpenters, the
older, less friendly of two brothers working at the Rodinger
house. His misshapen leather hat gave him the look of a
nineteenth-century prospector, so appropriate to the slumping
cabin. To avoid him, she veered off the trail and climbed cross-
country up a ridge all the way to the saddle. There, the whole
Spearmint watershed spread out below her, a vast bowl of pines
standing as they had for centuries, a soft wind ruffling their

nap, like a hand over velvet. Ah, but the trees' days were numbered. The president had increased harvest levels, and local men, grateful and defiantly happy for work, had begun clearcutting. A pale swath of raw stumps and debris piles already encroached from the west.

As she walked, she made a frame with her hands, imposed her own geometry on the landscape, composing scenes of trees and rocks, moving water, bushes and grasses, the interplay of shadows and the soft late-summer light.

She stuck her nose in bark; Jeffrey pines smelled like vanilla, lodgepoles like retsina.

Woodpeckers hammered at the trees, their red heads a blur; the whole forest rattled from them; were they the same birds she saw day after day?

On the fishermen's path along Spearmint Creek one afternoon, she saw a bush thrashing up ahead, and a deer's spindly, split-hoofed leg striking the water. Closer, Cress saw the animal full on: a doe, who continued to paw the shallows until, backing up, she drew a curling and flopping trout onto a sandbank. The deer struck until the fish, dredged in sand, grew listless. Pinning it with her cloven toe, then stretching her long neck, the doe closed her mouth over the fat V of the tail and, tugging as if at grass, she bit it off. She chewed fixedly, head low, protecting her prize. More pawing ensued—and still the fish twitched and tried to flop—until the doe pinned it again for a second bite. Blood, and a bright ocher organ flashed.

The deer's nonchalance disturbed and thrilled, as did her indifference to suffering. Cress rehearsed descriptions for Jakey, that student of animal behavior. *Like a cat with a mouse!* She would tell Julie Garsh, too, of the violence and cruelty in her outdoor cathedral. The utter lack of mercy.

Jakey, behind the grill, saluted her with his spatula. Cress stood at the bar; she assumed he'd finish cooking and come talk to her. Only one table waited for food, a mother and daughter. The grumpy blond waitress delivered their burgers, but Jakey didn't emerge. Cress feigned interest in the sports section but soon, afraid of being a pest, she left the lodge and walked home.

"Something is chilling Jakey's ardor," she told Tillie.

"And yours?"

"That's what worries me. I used to be the less interested party."

"Just hurry up and finish your thingy," said Tillie. "Number 12 should be open by Thanksgiving. Old Fiona's moving to the Scripps Retirement Home."

On supply runs, Cress explored the small, uncharming city of Sparkville. Once a railroad hub for farming, ranching, and logging, the downtown now had the depleted anachronistic ambience of a backwater with its scantly stocked dime store and dowdy private department store, its windowless bars. The handsome brick hotel by the old station had long been lodging for seasonal farmworkers. Off the main drag, Cress found an Italian market that sold backyard vegetables—basil, dandelion greens, cardoons—and a cloudy green local olive oil. In a Mexican grocery, she found purple hominy and chipotle chiles, crusty lumps of piloncillo sugar.

She shopped at Younts, not only for Julie but also now for Brian Crittenden and Florence Orliss, who each paid her ten dollars per haul. *That* compensated for wear and tear on the Saab.

She delivered Sawzall blades and a new sledgehammer to Freddy and River Bob demo-ing the Streeters' kitchen. Nails and an expensive six-foot level went to the finish carpenters at the Rodinger place, where, if she was lucky, Caleb, the younger,

homely brother, answered the door. He always made a joke—
Where's the pizza and Coke? Doughnuts and coffee? And once he
said, "Wait, wait. I have a tip for you!" and gave her the perfectly formed pinecone that now served as the centerpiece of her
kitchen table. The older brother, Quinn, took the supplies Cress
delivered in silence and shut the door as she stood there. At her
parents' jobsite, Brian Crittenden unloaded the Saab's trunk.
Hefting a new router, he whispered, "Between you and me, I
have no idea what in hell this is."

Cress was surrounded by men. In that respect, living at the
Meadows was not unlike grad school in economics.

One day, in the Younts checkout line, the woman behind her
said, "I know you." Cress turned to see the fat, grouchy, middle-
aged lodge waitress with her puff of almost colorless bleached
hair. DeeDee. Cress had heard Jakey call her Princess, Blondie,
and, in a hissy mood, DumDum. Of course, DeeDee called
him Bossy, like a cow. Close up, Cress had a shock: DeeDee was
her age.

Here in the provinces, as in all provinces, something happened to women. Lovely in their smooth-skinned, shiny-haired
bloom, they married, had a kid or two, and off went the starch
bomb. Looks faded and the pounds rolled on, thirty, forty, fifty
of them.

"I've heard all about you," DeeDee said. "Jakey goes on and
on. Cressida this, Cressida that."

"All good, I hope."

"Let's just say that you don't bug him yet."

"Gee," said Cress.

"The others bug him pretty quick. Though you can't blame
him. They sit at the lodge, all moony. Cleavage hanging out.
Hey, want a coffee?" Younts had a coffee shop attached.

First, Cress took seven bags of groceries out to her car, lining
them on the backseat like seven small brothers. The sun was

warm; she shouldn't stay long. And she had qualms: DeeDee was so brash. But Cress was curious to hear what she had to say.

DeeDee had ordered coffee for both of them. "You're the only one Jakey's never called a bim," she said.

"Is that short for *bimbo?*"

A peroxided eyebrow—with dark roots—arched.

DeeDee was twenty-nine, divorced with three boys and, apparently, Jakey's great confidante. A thin gold cross swung over her cup as she leaned forward. "That voice mail you left? He sure got a bang out of it! God knows how many times he made me listen. *Don't heat the oven if you've got nothing to bake!*"

"You heard that?"

"Me and everyone else who came into the lodge—for weeks!"

DeeDee wasn't out to embarrass her—not exclusively, anyway. She wanted something more—a confidante of her own. A friend. Swearing Cress to secrecy, she confessed: she was in love with Jakey's youngest son, Kevin, the nineteen-year-old. "Well, maybe not *love* love," she went on in a rapid whisper, "but we are sleeping together. Uh, constantly. It's like God's little gift to me after the worst divorce in history; best sex ever. But it is a sin, so I'll probably go to hell. I pray to stop. Every night I tell myself I'm going to stop. The mind is willing, but the flesh—"

"You're kidding, right?" said Cress. "About the God and hell stuff."

"No. No. Not at all."

DeeDee was a born again. "Bathed in the spirit, reborn in faith. Tulare First Presbo. Evangelical!" Her tone was so light as to seem self-mocking.

"Does that mean you had a whole conversion deal?" Cress asked. "Blinding flash and all?"

"Sure," DeeDee said. "Only it was less a flash and more like a huge wave of relief. That I didn't have to do it all anymore. That Jesus was driving the bus and I could sit back, relax, and enjoy the ride."

The waitress poured more coffee. She wore a spongy white uniform just like Cress had worn at the Dinner Plate.

"Jakey's very proud of you," DeeDee said. "Your intelligence and education. You really are the only one that hasn't gotten on his nerves."

Five

Her father came up alone and spent an afternoon at the jobsite, searching the ground and stooping to pick up nails that had been bent or simply dropped during framing. He summoned all the carpenters and spilled the collected nails onto a stack of plywood. "These represent real money," he said. "That's money just lying on the ground. Someone have a hammer I could use?" He banged the bent nails straight on a sawhorse and handed them around to the carpenters.

The head carpenter, Don Darrington, later told Cress that he and the others had taken the nails and, laughing a little among themselves, gone on working.

Her father's purpose in coming was to discuss costs with Rick Garsh. Before construction began, Sam and Sylvia had paid an architect's fee (for the plans) and a thousand-dollar contractor's fee to get things under way. Now Rick's first construction bill had come and he had charged, as agreed, the cost of time and materials plus 10 percent. Sam showed Cress the invoice: Rick had charged for the crew's wages and all materials, plus 10 percent. He'd also charged for the services of a bookkeeper (Julie) plus 10 percent and a gofer (Cress) plus 10 percent. Those fill-ups at Jakey's gas pumps Cress so liberally used? Sam was billed for a third of them, plus 10 percent. Rick also included five hours a week for "consulting," plus 10 percent.

Sam pointed to this item. "If Rick's the contractor," he said, "and the 10 percent is his fee, what is this *consulting* charge?"

"I don't know, Dad."

"And the bookkeeping! Do doctors, dry cleaners, and mechanics charge for bookkeeping? Let alone tack on 10 percent? Isn't that just part of doing business?"

"I don't really know how cost-plus works in construction," Cress said.

"It doesn't work like this, I'll tell you that much. And your pay," he said, pointing to another line item. "I'm charged for a third of your trips. Do our supplies constitute a fair third of your purchases?"

The last trip was exclusively electrical supplies for the Streeters' remodel. But she wouldn't fan her father's fury. "It all works out," she said.

"And look at the gasoline charge! At the lodge! The highest gas price in California, plus 10 percent. Rick should really gas up down below."

"He's hardly incentivized to do that," said Cress. "The way you two have set it up, the more he spends, the more he makes."

"That's where trust comes in," Sam said. "I trust him to keep costs low. As he promised to. And he probably gets a contractor's discount on materials."

He did. Cress had signed invoices: 40 percent off on lumber, 30 on hardware. "So?" she said. "The cost is the same to you whether you buy from the retailers or through Rick."

"But that's double-dipping!" said Sam. "He's honorbound to pass at least some of those savings on to me."

"He's not incentivized to do that, either. Given your arrangement."

Her father's face twitched. "Is *incentivize* really a word?" he said.

"To me it is."

He gazed at her typewriter, the stacked files, the thick ream of white paper. "Tell me, Cress—what would incentivize you?"

—

Her father had brought up a letter to her from her sister, Sharon. On the back of the envelope Sharon had written over the seal: *SNOOPERS BEWARE!!!*

Dear Cress,

Greetings from Hampstead! I hope Mom and Dad give you this. I didn't know how to send it to the cabin, so I just enclosed it with their letter—(hahaha, Mom, you old snooper, I'm onto you). I have left Cairo (that HELL-HOLE!!!) and am back living in London. You have to come visit! I'm hoping to buy a flat, but in the meantime, I've rented a tiny bedsit on a picturesque square—you can almost imagine horses and carriages parked on the street. I bought a not-too-lumpy old couch just for you and anyone else I can lure here.

I couldn't believe it when Mom said you were living at the cabin—I thought you hated it up there!!! I sure did. (Sorry, old snoop, but it's the truth! Captives have few fond memories of prison, Frau Warden.) I remember how every Saturday I'd walk down to the lodge and buy the big package of Hydrox cookies, then walk out to the Crags or Globe Rock and sit under a tree and read Irving Stone novels, and eat each cookie in three stages, wafer-filling-wafer, until they were all gone. I'd stay out till the sun set. Nobody ever, ever asked me where I went. (No, Snoopy, you never did. Not once.) (Sorry for all the asides, Cressie. Mom used to read my diaries so I just assume she'll read this.) Luckily, I wasn't eaten by a mountain lion or raped by Big Foot. Anyway, good luck up there.

Once you get your thesis written, you can celebrate with . . . a London vacation! So hurry up.

Cheerio, old chap,

Sharon

Alone again, Cress drew trees, rocks, and dirt and thought in long, circular whorls. (Rocks were hard; the more she looked at them, the more specific *and* abstract they became.) The plaint of country music fed a thickening strand of yearning. Now that she saw him less often—and wondered if she'd ever see him again—Jakey looped constantly through her thoughts. She wanted, or thought she wanted, what any lover does: access on demand to that cozy furnace of a body and centrality in his life—unlike now, when she ranged, wineglass in hand, while 1.2 miles away he roared at strangers and knee-nudged his neighbors.

"Call him," said Tillie. "Better yet, go get him. How does he know you're interested if you play it so cool?"

How interested was she, really? More than their prospects merited. She'd never marry or even live with him, but the thought of him bearing down on her in his cheap white shirt, the whole hot juicy weight of him, stopped her breath.

Two glasses of burgundy and what the hell, she phoned the lodge, ready to leave a message. Jakey picked up. The background music and laughter were loud for a weeknight. "It's me," she said. "Feel like coming up?"

"You bet!" he barked. "Soon as I can get away."

She put away her pastels. She drank another glass of wine. She fed the fire and walked outside onto the front deck. The Milky Way, that big galactic smudge, hogged the black sky. The wind gathered, heaved, and ceased; gathered, heaved, and ceased. Headlights flashed through the trees and did not turn up her driveway. It was fall, the world was dusty, pinched, dying back. She was not really writing or drawing, or even steeping herself in the beauty of the natural world. She was waiting for Jakey. She was waiting all the time now, suspended in the hours, poised, nose quivering in the air. Another car rounded the curve and relief rushed in. But that car, and all the others passing by that night, never turned her way.

She went a little frantic then and fought an almost constant urge to go to the lodge, to call Jakey, to locate him. *So this is what he did to the bims.* She held off, for pride's sake. She used the back way into the Meadows—a narrow road half a mile west of the lodge—so he wouldn't see her come and go. She avoided walking or driving past his house. She avoided the phone, and the A-frame itself, so that she wouldn't know if he called or came by—or didn't. Avoidance was her only power. She carried a falling-apart copy of *David Copperfield* to her old spot, the bench on the porch of the Bauer cabin, and read it belly down while woodpeckers bored into the trees all around her.

The A-frame's sliding glass door shuddered on its tracks after nine on a Sunday night. "Hullo, hullo?" He came in steaming and stamping. "I miss you something fierce. Where have I been? Goddamn, it's good to bite your gorgeous white neck." The next Thursday, she was walking by the pond when he drove up alongside. He sweet-talked her over to his house, then hurried her back into his truck post-sex. A week after that, he found her by the back entrance and unlocked a nearby cabin. They used a bed, helped themselves to a brandy bottle.

This intermittency generated a nervous, involuntary hope.

"Just talk to him," said Tillie. "Ask him what he wants from you!"

But she couldn't ask, because she knew: the slightest pressure, the least demand, and Jakey would vanish for good.

Julie Garsh said, "He's acting out. Which is perfectly predictable. After a long, failed marriage, he's in a lot of pain and grief. Then he meets someone he adores, and it scares him to death. Loss and love are equivalent to him."

"Where does that leave me?" Cress asked.

"Just be there for him. He'll see that you're steady and come around."

No reasonable future contained him, Cress knew. But how to

relinquish the great crush of his body, the tidal pleasure when he roared her name?

She walked farther now, one day even made it to Globe Rock, a vast granite dome with its own three-hundred-degree view of the Spearmint watershed and the northern Sierra range. The only vehicle in the small parking area was the white Toyota pickup belonging to Don Darrington—Don Dare, he was called, the lead carpenter on her parents' new place. Cress recognized his bumper sticker: SUPPORT SEARCH & RESCUE / GET LOST.

She climbed onto the broad bald rock. The sun sat low on Shale Mountain and the thick sideways light glinted with dust, buzzed with gnats. The forested hills were sunk in shadow. Her family had picnicked here on the rare occasions when it occurred to them to do something together. The brown wooden sign with white grooved letters still said:

DANGER

STAY BACK FROM EDGE

DO NOT THROW OR ROLL ROCKS—HIKERS BELOW

Once, a little boy had run too far out on the rock and, unable to stop, tumbled to his death—but this might have been an apocryphal story to frighten children, and make them cautious. Still, the lure of the edge was strong; visitors invariably inched as far down the rock face as they dared, often going farther than Cress could ever stomach. Today, she sat on the warm granite facing northwest, where the four white humps of Camel Crags quavered in the late light. The tiny glass lookout Jakey had once commandeered for their pleasure flashed red and blue like a diamond. All that—that frolic and dance—was over, but when and how it had ended, she could not say. The night she didn't go to Jakey, when her mother had called out as she'd been leaving the A-frame: that seemed a turning point. He had receded ever since.

Some yards below her, on the curving edge of rock, a whitened human hand clawed into view, followed by an arm, backlit blond hair, an entire, crawling man. Still twenty feet below her, he stood up, trailing bright yellow ropes: Don Dare. He raised a chalky hand to her, then whistled shrilly.

His fluffy Australian shepherd mix, white with black spots, bounded up from the side, almost colliding with Cress. "Easy there, Shim," Don said.

Cress walked with him and the gamboling dog back over the hump of the rock to the parking lot. Don had a narrow, pitted, handsome face and a slight limp. His carabiners clanked. He climbed rocks after work every day, he said. Globe Rock. The Crags. "Ever try climbing? Ever want to?"

"I don't really get the appeal," she said. "But I'd try it, just to see."

"Anytime," he said. "I'll give you lessons."

"I like your bumper sticker," she said at his truck. "Have you ever rescued anyone?"

"A few hikers lost near Sargent Grove. A girl with a twisted ankle." He slung his ropes into the truck bed. "Last week, we got a call here about an Irish setter. He was off leash, and you know how hyper they are. He ran too far down and gravity took over. I had to circumnavigate the base till I found him."

"Dead?"

"Fell about a hundred feet. Such a beautiful dog, but uncontrollable. The owners were a mess. You walked? Let me give you a lift."

She also let him buy her a beer at the lodge. DeeDee, all business, drew their drafts. "Oh come on, DeeDee," said Don. "Life ain't that bad."

"You don't know the half of it. Bossy calls from town to say he forgot a hunting party of twelve coming in tonight. And major bimbology all day long."

Cress understood this to mean that one (or more) of Jakey's old girlfriends had lingered at the bar or hogged a booth in hopes of seeing him—and they probably ran DeeDee ragged the whole time.

Don Dare said, "Anything we can do?"

"Watch the bar while I set up for the hunters?"

"No problem," said Don. "I've done my time tending bar."

He and Cress were the only ones in the lounge area, except for Ondine Streeter, who was at a table by the fireplace studying blueprints for her new kitchen and not even drinking.

He'd worked at the Rip Curl Tavern in Carlsbad after college, Don said. He'd been headed to law school, but took a year off to surf. He surfed all day and poured drinks at night until he broke his leg in a freak collision with his board. He kicked out his right shin. "Went through a tough little interlude with heroin then," he said. "Had a real hard time coming back from it. Lost a couple years. Then I found climbing. Climbing saved my life. When Rick hired me, I told him I needed a couple hours of light every day to climb, just to stay sane."

Cress hummed sympathetically and thought, First a murderer, now a heroin addict; the Meadows apparently was full of criminals walking around like ordinary people. Don's pitted face now brought to mind the word *ravaged*.

That face came in close, so close that she assumed he was going to kiss her. "I have to tell you . . ." His voice was husky, confiding. "I'm with someone. We're in love, and we've made a decision not to see other people."

"Oh. Okay." Was her white flash of shame for thinking otherwise?

"She's Donna, the singer? I know, I know," he went on. "Don and Donna . . . But you've seen her here at Family Night? Jerry calls her onstage."

"Not the Sawyer Songbird?"

"That's her! I met her last November, the first time I came to climb the Crags. She had a gig at the Sawyer Inn. It was love at first set. Anyway, Jakey's thinking of hiring her on a regular basis and giving ole embraceable Jer a break. She really needs it. As a teacher's aide in Sparkville, she makes, like, twenty cents more than minimum wage."

"That's nothing!"

"So maybe you'll put in a good word for her."

"Me? To Jakey? What makes you think he'd listen to me?"

"It's a tiny community, Cressida. Everybody knows you and Jakey . . ." Don clasped his hands and wagged them back and forth.

"It doesn't mean I have any sway," she said. "I'm not even sure if Jakey and I are still—" She imitated the wagging handclasp.

"Oh God, *love*." Don came in close and husky again. Why was it never easy? he said. Donna wouldn't even *talk* about moving in with him till they'd been together a year. She'd made him rent his own place in Sawyer, though every night he was there, he spent at her house. She constantly accused him of seeing other women—which was why he'd told Cress right off the bat that he was involved, unavailable. "So you know, if I'm flirty, it doesn't mean jack."

"Understood."

"You two would really like each other. You and Donna. Maybe we'll have you over to camp some night. I've got this big outfitter's tent set up by Spearmint Creek. I ordered it when Boots Stahl was buying them for his pack station. Donna's made it into this lush Bedouin-boudoir-bower sort of thing."

Cress had already enjoyed the Bedouin-boudoir-bower with Jakey, but she didn't admit that to Don Dare.

DeeDee phoned. "Bossy and Kevin have gone down the hill together, so we might as well keep each other company."

In DeeDee's smaller, darker A-frame, they made popcorn and vodka drinks, and turned on the television. DeeDee had a big antenna on her roof, hence reception. The *Million Dollar Movie* starred Peter Lorre, but she lowered the sound to talk.

"After Connie left? Jakey had two dates a night," DeeDee said. "At six and at ten. Every female who walked in the door, just about. Though he never made a pass at *me*. I finally said, 'Hey, do I have leprosy or something?' He said I was too valuable. He couldn't afford to make me mad."

DeeDee put in fifty hours a week at the lodge; she also cleaned cabins and ran Jakey's caretaking services. All things his wife had done.

"I should tell you," DeeDee said, "that he's been seeing Honor for years. You know her. Who owns Hapsaw Lodge?"

"Not that old gal with the pageboy?"

"Even before the dee-vorce," said DeeDee.

"I should give him up. I know I should," said Cress. "But I can't. I'm stuck. Every time he comes around, I succumb."

"Jakey's a jerk," said DeeDee. "But whenever my child support is late, he finds me extra work. And lets me and the boys eat at the lodge for free."

"If you're not getting your work done," Tillie said, "forget the old man of the mountain. Come back to Braithway."

"Not yet," Cress said weakly. "And I have to get off the phone now."

She had to get off because Jakey was at her door, brandishing a bottle of Yukon Jack.

"Bear with me, Hartley," he said. "Once the snow starts falling, things quiet down a lot. I'll be around more."

They were in bed. He held her flush against his baking chest. For the first time, she'd been glum, unresponsive.

"I just don't know what to think about us," she said.

"Me neither! No idea! Just hang on till winter. I'd hate for you to miss it. Once the snow comes, everything changes. We'll have a cozy time, you'll see."

DeeDee's October child support hadn't arrived by the tenth, so Jakey paid her to deep clean his house. She showed up afterward at Cress's sliding glass door. "I've brought the cure!" DeeDee held up a small blue book. "I found this stuck between his mattress and headboard." A diary. The cover was padded corduroy, with a plastic daisy on the hasp. The ex-wife's diary. Or rather, an evidentiary record, diligently kept, of the last twenty months of their marriage.

Connie Yates had crept up to windows. She put her ears to walls and doors. She came home early (or never actually left), noted whose car was parked down by the creek, in that spot hidden from the road. *He's so obvious and predictable*, she wrote. She lurked among the aspens to see whom her home disgorged. *I don't care if he catches me. What could he say?*

The goal was not to catch him, but to convince herself. She got so she could tell. The way he joked with the checker at Younts. The change of voice in a weekender wife she'd waited on for years. How a strange woman sat at the bar alone, nursing a glass of wine, surreptitiously eyeing the cook's window where Jakey manned the grill.

Connie Yates unscrolled the register's journal tape to see what he charged Sandi White for a dollar bag of spaghetti. Fifteen cents. Bottle of rosé, a dime.

Connie pined for the day her youngest would graduate. She harangued herself not to sink back into self-deceit. *My eyes have been opened and I have to keep them open . . . He's not going to change . . . Only I can change. He's mental and can't stop himself, and he doesn't even want to.*

"Oh, here you go." DeeDee pointed. "Look."

Cress looked. And saw her mother's name, *Sylvia Hartley.*

Cress's heart rate shot up and her vision blurred. A long moment passed before the cursive words shivered through: *Sylvia Hartley brought up a teacher friend last week—now she's back, renting the Fuller cabin. J's truck parked up on the spur behind.*

Cress trembled afterward from the scare.

Some pages later: *S. Hartley's friend (Elsa?) rented Fullers' again, moped around lodge all Saturday. J ignored—he's moved on. Poor thing.*

Elsa! Cress knew Elsa, Elsa Calderon, solemn, moon-faced, forty-ish Elsa, plain as a nun, who taught Spanish and pinned gardenias on her blouse.

Sitting thigh to thigh on the wicker love seat in the A-frame, the small book open on their knees, she and DeeDee read every entry.

"What shall we do?" Cress said. "Xerox it and pass it out at the lodge?"

"Yeah!" DeeDee laughed. "We should charge for it. The bims'd pay."

"Oh, they'd pay all right," Cress said.

Then they burned it in the fire. For Connie Yates's sake. The cure, indeed.

"You can come in." He'd shown up late one afternoon. "But I'm done." In the A-frame's kitchen, he body-pressed her against the refrigerator, sent magnets skidding. "No, Jakey." She slipped out from under him. "No more. It was fun for a while, but these un-predictable onslaughts make me crazy."

"Oh, now, Hartley," he said.

"I can't take it, Jakey. I want more of an everyday life with someone."

"And you expected that with me?" he said.

"I don't know what I expected."

"But no hard feelings, right?"

He deftly slid his arms around her and they both laughed, and she said, "No, Jakey," and "No" again. She squirmed loose, and he took it in good humor and didn't insist, and that was pretty much that.

Six

Her bones and muscles ached dully, sore from the whole wild ride. She was distressed, but at her own obtuseness. In the mornings, longing drew her awake, a claw of hope: only now, what did she long for? She lugged the card table and Selectric upstairs to her bedroom, away from the distractions of phone, refrigerator, and view. She drank a pot of coffee and quivering from caffeine pushed herself further into her second chapter, so she could finish that and move on to the next, and eventually into the rest of her life, post-diss.

Franny appeared with the Hoover: the harbinger of parents.

"So soon?" Cress would've liked more time to herself.

They showed up in time for her father to visit the carpenters on site. He came back grumbling. "That Crittenden kid just spent twenty minutes trying to change a router bit—it was like he'd never handled one before. Of course, Rick's paying him a full carpenter's wage! *And* charging me 10 percent on top of that!"

Later, while Cress helped her mother with the dinner dishes, her father slipped upstairs, read her new pages, then thumped down again. "Seeing as I invested in your education, I took a look at your progress. I have to admit, your writing does improve as you revise."

She and her mother exchanged bright, surprised looks. Sam Hartley praised so rarely, Cress decided on the spot to overlook his snooping.

"I, however, find that I never need to revise." Sam squatted to poke the fire. "Whatever I write comes out best in the first pass. But then I know what I'm going to say before I start." He spoke over his shoulder. "That way I don't waste paper. Think things through first and you'll save time *and* supplies." He stood and went outside to the porch.

"He begrudges me *paper*?"

"Oh dear," Sylvia whispered. "I don't know why he's like that."

Sam came back inside with an armload of wood. "And you haven't kept the temperature log."

"I know, Dad."

"I ask you to do one thing, and you can't be bothered?"

"It's your thing, Dad. Not mine."

"You live here rent-free, eat our food, burn the wood I chop—?"

"Now, Sam," said Sylvia.

"She's almost thirty! When will she be weaned?"

In a single swoop, Cress crossed the room, pulled her jacket from its peg. "I'll leave. I'm happy to leave. I'll leave tomorrow, first thing."

She loped down the porch steps and the driveway, then turned right, past the Orlisses', into the farthest, uninhabited loop of the subdivision. The moon was an ungainly oblong. How dare her father claim reading rights to her work when, in fact, she'd worked and gone into debt for graduate school, and had paid her own way since college, except for a few emergencies, like when her CETA job hadn't paid her on time. And she'd quit that job, which would have been so good to put on her résumé, to take a waitressing job in order to make her student-loan payments. Working at the Dinner Plate had been hateful, eight hours on that concrete floor, hounded by a boss who criticized her appearance and her job performance nonstop by day, then called her at home at night, drunk, to beg for sex. After her last shift at the Dinner Plate, Cress had unlaced her white orthopedics, stepped out of them by the front door, and walked to her car in her stocking feet.

She would leave the A-frame, too, as happily: good riddance to the Meadows and its denizens. But where would she go? To return to Pasadena felt like going backward. As for joining John Bird in Minneapolis—unthinkable!

So maybe she'd light out to parts unknown, like Bishop, Mammoth, or Tahoe; she could rent a room, work the breakfast shift in a coffee shop, type in secret all night. Or fly to London and Sharon's lumpy couch.

Leaking into her thoughts came a sound so mournful, so minimally tuneful, Cress mistook it for an animal's cry or the creaking of trees. Then came the first recognizable bit, a scrap of "House of the Rising Sun." Another scrap was possibly the yodeling riff in "Lovesick Blues." An accordion? No, wheezier. Bagpipe? The shreds of melody stayed so low and private, a step could take her out of range and she couldn't get a fix on it.

Back in the A-frame her mother was reading Simenon and nursing a plastic cup of bourbon. Her father had a flashlight in pieces on the table. Cress went upstairs without a word. Her mother came in and sat at the foot of her bed. "Don't let him get to you. Rick has him all upset. Nobody wants you to leave."

"Thanks, Mom."

"If you could only write down the temperature . . ."

"I can't, Mom. I just can't."

A long silence. Moonlight filled the room with blue.

"I'm glad you're getting your work done," Sylvia said.

"I am, more or less. And it's pretty up here."

Sylvia moved her hand over the bedspread to Cress's shin and squeezed. "Not such a concentration camp after all?"

Tillie said, "Are you meeting any new men up there?"

"Supply exceeds demand," said Cress.

Between the carpenters and a sheepish Jakey, she never had to pay for a drink. Being single on the mountain was a form of public service.

The flaps on Don Dare's tent were open. T-shirts hung on a clothesline strung between trees. The Sawyer Songbird was wringing out a cloth over in some bushes. "Hello? Hello?" Cress called. "Are you the famous Donna?"

The Songbird regarded her coolly. "Do I know you?"

"We've never officially met. I live in the Meadows? Don works on my folks' house? He said I should introduce myself. You *are* Donna?"

The Sawyer Songbird glared. Between them, on the heavy, government-issue picnic table, sat a coffee can stuffed with dry, fuzzy grasses. "I guess not!" Cress said brightly, and turned to leave. "Sorry!"

"Just what did Don say about me?"

Cress swung around. "That I should introduce myself."

Another long, scouring look. "You want some ice tea?"

Donna lowered a netted cooler—"The bear's piñata," she called it—and took a pick to the block of ice, filling two pint mason jars with large clear shards, then sun tea from a pitcher. They took seats across from each other at the picnic table.

"I love your tent. It's so exotic. And luxurious."

"You've been here before?" The coldness and suspicion were back.

"Jakey Yates showed it to me once—Jakey, who runs the lodge?"

"Are you the one seeing him?"

"*I was*," said Cress. "We split up."

"Probably for the best," Donna said. "For you, at least."

"Yeah—since he was seeing fifty other women at the same time."

"Jakey's a goat, all right," Donna said.

"And I thought he was just this sweet, lonely divorced guy."

"I know a goat when I see one," said Donna, " 'cause I used to be married to one. I know the signs."

"Like what?" said Cress. "What signs?"

"That spotlight of attention. The way they single you out, get you off by yourself. Jakey damn near irradiates a girl. And the sexual confidence!"

"Really? He just seemed so good-natured and easygoing to me."

"Yeah? Well, whatever you do, don't marry him," Donna said. "That'll really drive you crazy. Those goaty guys sneak and lie for the fun of it. Never a straight answer to your questions."

"Jakey and I didn't even get to the point where I could ask questions."

"God, I cross-examine Don so much, he thinks I'm a nut-case. But if he's got nothing to hide, he's got nothing to worry about, right?" Donna poured more tea. "Oh, another sign would be crabs. Or chlamydia. Warts."

"Yeesh," said Cress. "I probably should see a gyno." The evening breeze high up in the pines made the long needles hiss. Cress was struck, not for the first time, how women could go from hello to gynecology within minutes of meeting. "But Don's crazy about you," she said. "He told me right away that you two are exclusive."

"Why should that even come up?" said Donna. "Was he flirting?"

"Not at all." A small lie. But why get Don in trouble? Especially since she wasn't even attracted to him. He was too familiar, too passive. And surfers had never interested her. Nor, for that matter, had heroin addicts. Cress was too polite to spell this out to Donna; certainly more polite than Donna had been to her.

Donna stood and started rummaging through foodstuffs, pulling out onions and carrots, a package of stew meat. "You'll stay for dinner?"

"Oh no, no thanks," Cress said. "I've got to get home." The truth was, the Sawyer Songbird had worn her out.

—

Crossing Spearmint Creek on a log, Cress took the campers' shortcut to the lodge.

"Whoa now, Cressida Hartley!" Jakey hollered from the lodge's porch. "I need to talk to you." He held a clipboard, a coil of raffle tickets. "Help me out here," he said. "Up your ante in the snow pool, kid. I'm trying to break a record." He had sold over three hundred tickets and needed to sell forty more.

"Nothing left in October?" said Cress. "How 'bout November 4?"

Jakey perused the clipboard, lifting the pages. "I have November 7, noon through two—three tickets. Three bucks."

"Put it on my tab."

He made notes, scrawled the times on three tickets, handed them to her. "Come in, try my new invention. A Rustic Nail. Yukon Jack 'n' brandy on ice."

"No thanks, Jakey. Thanks, anyway."

The quaking aspens by Jakey's house were yellow and fluttering madly on their slender hitches. The sky had deepened to a soft twilight blue. Up ahead on the road, the older Morrow brother, Quinn, in his crimped hat, walked alone, his gait oddly graceful, as if he were crossing a narrow beam or tight rope. Cress trailed him for a mile. He didn't look back once.

Apparently she and this carpenter had the same walking schedule. Every day, he was up ahead or behind her. After having the woods largely to herself, Cress was acutely aware of his presence. She used to pee whenever she felt like it, barely bothering to step off the road—a man's freedom. Now she headed deep into the bushes, once literally stumbling over the carcass of a coyote, its back haunch eaten by yellow jackets so that the dark pink meat had brainlike whorls and crevices.

Once, she saw him crouched beside the oxbowed meadow stream, smoking and gazing into the narrow channel. As she watched, he lifted a hand over the water and a trout rose up after it as if by sorcery, gold twisting in the air.

Of course, he'd been fishing (out of season!) with just nylon line, no pole. Wetting his hands, he laid the wild fish on the grass and, after a long moment, he slipped the hook from its lip and pointed it back into the leather-brown water.

At Family Night, she sat with Don Dare, Brian, and Franny, and waited for the buffet to open. Honor of Hapsaw Lodge sipped wine at the bar. According to DeeDee, Honor had thought Jakey would marry her once his divorce was final, and she still held out hope. Perhaps Honor hadn't heard about the bims, or, as Cress once had, she'd dismissed them as a predictable post-divorce effusion, soon to pass.

"Look who's all gussied up," DeeDee whispered, nodding at the Morrow brothers, who had on leather vests, cowboy boots, and those scrunched leather hats with their hair wisping out, while their beards were freshly, meticulously trimmed. They looked like extras from *Gunsmoke*, Cress said. Or some spaghetti Western.

"But they're great craftsmen," said Don. "They usually work down south for movie stars, but no one's building. Rick got 'em for, like, half their rate."

Brian said that they'd worked for one famous movie star in particular.

In L.A., thought Cress, all that leather, the fetishized hats and manicured facial hair would be giggled at; or people would assume they were off a set. But up here on the mountain, manly affectations were exhaustively on parade, what with the hunters and fishermen, the snowmobilers and cross-country skiers, rock climbers, backpackers, and mountain man reenactors, all of whom arrived studiously geared up, mostly, so far as Cress could tell, to generate admiration and envy in other men.

The motive for the brothers' careful toilette soon became clear. Quinn's wife, Cress saw with a small shock, was beautiful. Dark, petite, and slim, she had long, curly, molasses-colored hair. A sudden dazzling smile. "Wow," Don whispered.

Caleb's wife, Cress was more interested to see, was not beautiful but snub-nosed and plump in her bulky pink sweatshirt and too-tight jeans. Her blond hair, pulled into a stubby ponytail, reminded Cress of her own mother's decree: *A ponytail is not a hairstyle.*

Donna, arriving with her guitar, hollered at the Morrows with the drawl she turned on and off. "What brings you paleface townies to bear country?"

Caleb's wife grinned. Her teeth were small, with spaces between, like baby teeth. "Just checkin' on the menfolk!" she bawled.

The buffet opened, featuring Jakey's sausage lasagna and the usual salad bar. Old Jerry crooned "Fly Me to the Moon," "Stranger in Paradise," "Embraceable You." The Garshes shared a booth with Tom Streeter and the pale, willowy Ondine. Every few minutes, a loud, ribald laugh rang through the room— Caleb's wife. Heads swung around to see what was so funny: something Caleb said.

"He found her in South Carolina," Donna whispered. "Caleb used to play harmonica with me. He's seriously talented, recorded with the Maddox Brothers and Rose, Vern Gosdin." Donna lowered her voice. "Then Candy got born again and hauled him in after her and he stopped playing in bars and never comes to music nights at my house anymore. I don't know if he plays at all now."

"He does," Cress said. A harmonica—that's what she'd heard that night when her parents were up.

DeeDee handed out bowls of homemade blackberry ice cream, and shortly, the young families and older couples headed home. Donna came onstage. "Love, oh love," she sang, "oh careless love."

Caleb and Candy slow-danced—apparently their religion allowed them that. Franny and Brian also rose to hug and sway on the square patch of parquet.

Jakey sat beside Cress, pushed his big hot friendly body against her, and hollered to DeeDee. "Another round for Mr. Darrington and the economics professor!" He spun Cress's empty bowl. "The ice cream—what'd you think?"

Compliments, it seemed, were what he was after; receiving them, he moved on. "You could still have him," Don said.

"No thanks." Besides, Jakey was zeroing in on a woman Cress had met in the campground earlier that day, a thirty-seven-year-old grandmother who was taking a year to travel across the country by herself. The old green truck would rattle out of the parking lot any minute now.

Quinn Morrow and his wife stopped by the table on their way out. Quinn's hard-bitten Western affect only emphasized his wife's delicate beauty. "Don, Cress," he said. "My wife, Sylvia."

Cress was surprised that Quinn knew her name. "That's easy to remember," she said to the wife. "My mother's Sylvia, too."

This Sylvia smiled, ducked her chin.

"A fox," whispered Don Dare when the Morrows moved on.

"So shy," said Cress.

A loud laugh rang through the room. Caleb's wife, out on the dance floor.

Seven

Long before she was slain in the spirit and bathed in the light, DeeDee was a dealer in a Tahoe card room. Surely God would look the other way if she dealt a few more hands to feed her boys. Word went out: a poker night.

DeeDee's cheaply built A-frame was tucked in a dense grove of small pines, a mucky hollow plagued in warmer months by gnats and in winter by icy patches. She and her husband had bought the place early in their marriage. "It reminded me of a gingerbread house," DeeDee told Cress. Indeed, along the eaves, the fascia boards were gaily scalloped and painted white.

During the divorce, DeeDee traded her share in their Visalia house to own this mountain home outright. She'd been living in the Meadows mortgage-free ever since, although a son's asthma, roof leaks, car problems, and chronically unpaid child support never allowed her any financial ease. Her three boys rode the school bus down to Sawyer every day, darkness to darkness. Tonight, she'd arranged to have them stay in town with friends.

Kevin Yates was in the living room when Cress arrived. Taller and burlier than Jakey, he had chapped-red cheeks and an easy blush. Shy, he kept busy, replenished the wood box, moved tables together, corralled extra chairs, always with a quick glance at DeeDee for approval.

She approved; she was softer with him than with Cress, or even her boys.

A rumble and stomping on the porch: Don Dare and his

crew—Freddy and River Bob—came in swinging six-packs, followed by Rick Garsh and then the Morrow brothers, all leathered up in hats and vests and hauling more beer.

DeeDee had made pot roast and an iceberg salad; Cress brought corn chowder with bacon, green beans, and homemade biscuits. The day had been cold. Everyone was hungry.

"Should bring you some of our bacon," Quinn told Cress over the chowder. "Buy a hog every year, have the belly smoked by this old boy over in Fountain Springs. Sliced thick."

"Where did you grow up?" Cress asked, as his accent was so backwoods.

"Orange County. Seal Beach, mostly," he said. "And Noah Mountain. These beans are good. Almonds, and is that lemon?"

"*Haricots amandine,*" said Don Dare.

"Hey—you cook French food?" said Caleb. "We should bring you some frog. Got a freezer full. Big uns, legs on 'em like drumsticks."

"*Frog?*" Cress said. "Where do you get frog?"

They hunted the fat amphibians along irrigation canals at night, with torches and gigs. Caleb said, "You *gig* frogs. Though I gigged Quinn once."

"I got the scar to prove it," Quinn said.

"We'd been out a few hours, bagged a dozen whoppers," said Caleb. "I slipped on the canal bank and accidentally poked Quinn on his calf. Turns out frog skin is toxic. Half hour later his leg's swole up like an oozing watermelon."

"Remember that emergency room doctor?" Quinn said. "He comes in reading the file and says, 'So. Which one's the gigger and which the giggee?'"

"Then, at the start of fishing season this year," Quinn went on, "I'm tying hooks on leaders and holding the finished leaders in my mouth. Slowly, I notice this *sensation.*" He touched his lower lip. "Three barbed treble hooks had worked into my lip. I couldn't see to snip 'em out and Sylvia was too squeamish to try.

So I went to the emergency room and who's on call? Same old sawbones. Took one look at me and said, 'Refresh my memory— gigger or giggee?' "

Plates were cleared, cards produced. When it came to her turn, DeeDee's dealing was hypnotic, swift; her shuffle a pretty flutter. She was a pro. She didn't cheat. But she knew the game.

The brothers grumbled and joked over their cards. "Well, lookee there," Caleb said, playing a straight. "A king *can* look at a cat."

Cress lost almost every hand, so kept her bets low; Rick and Quinn also tended to lose. Quinn bet more recklessly. "Read 'em and weep," he said, about a pair of tens—which cost him two tall stacks of quarters.

They played for four hours, until all the beer was gone. Luck surged and ebbed around the table. DeeDee won thirty-odd dollars, but so had Caleb.

Cress stayed to help clean up. "Get Jakey to give you a card room," she told DeeDee. "Upstairs, in the lodge. You could have a real game. Some of those hunters'd play big money."

"I'll stick to penny-ante stuff. And let's not invite Caleb next time."

"I like those guys. They're characters."

"Caleb cuts in on my take," said DeeDee.

"Yeah, but Quinn sure bolsters it."

"He was on some kind of a tilt, doubling with that weak hand." DeeDee shrugged. "Not that I minded."

"Economists call it loss aversion—when you compound losing like that."

"Dumb is what I call it," said DeeDee.

Clearing the table, Cress found a twenty folded under Caleb's glass.

"Well, three cheers for the gigger," said DeeDee.

"He is adorable," said Cress. "Too bad he's married."

"And his wife's such a bush-Okie," said DeeDee.

"I heard she's actually from South Carolina. And she's a born again, too."

"A backwoods Holy Roller type. All Pentecostal and writhing on the ground, speaking in tongues, yabba dabba doo."

"Your church doesn't go in for that."

"Please. I'm a good old-fashioned Presbyterian. None of that charismatic Foursquare hoo-haw."

"But aren't you evangelical? I thought you said . . ."

"Evangelical means we proclaim the Good News. Not ignorant superstition. Our ministers go to school, study the Bible in Greek and stuff. They're not self-appointed, tent-show revival, open-your-wallet-for-Jesus types."

"Sounds like there's a class divide as well," said Cress.

DeeDee plunged glasses into soapy water, scrubbed. "You mean, like who's middle-class and who's white trash?" Her blue eyes glittered with challenge.

"Something like that." Cress had to remind herself that DeeDee was indeed middle-class: she owned a home. She'd had some college—a community-college business course, one year. "Well, it's too bad for Caleb," she added. "He's so funny and sharp."

"Not so sharp he didn't dodge that bullet. Now go on home," DeeDee said. "Kevin's coming back any minute. If he sees your car's still here, he'll be too shy to come in."

Snow whirled through, floured the landscape, then vanished. The temperature dropped into the twenties at night. Days, the sun brought back T-shirt weather, although with dwindling conviction. On October 26, early in the afternoon, a gusting wind pushed the clouds together. The sky sealed shut. The temperature rose five degrees. The clouds darkened and started to churn, crowding in lower as if pressured from above until, from the ragged undersides, big wet flakes began to fall. Setting out on her walk, Cress caught them on her parka sleeve, their dainty white geometry dissolving into clear droplets on the black Gore-Tex. The snow thickened and fell faster, the largest, stickiest flakes she'd ever seen; they clumped in midair, landed with audible plops. The meadows whitened as she passed. The world shushed.

By the time she'd looped through the campground and made it to the lodge, the parking lot was full of badly parked vehicles. Jakey's snow pool had a winner and the party was under way. Rick's crews had abandoned their posts. People had driven up from Cloud Slope, Pine Corner, Hapsaw Camp. The snow pool kitty was $412. The woman who won lived fifty miles off in Tulare; she was on her way, too, but in the meantime, as per the rules—Jakey's rules—everyone drank on her tab until she walked through the door.

Cress stood by Caleb in the crush at the bar. Jakey, DeeDee, and the bartender were pouring and serving drinks as fast as they could. DeeDee took Caleb's order—Coke for him, beer for his brother. "And get her whatever she wants," he said, tapping Cress's shoulder.

"Thanks, big spender," she said, and ordered bourbon on ice.

"Hey, have two." Caleb's long hound-dog face, brightened by humor, became droll and appealing.

"I've been meaning to say—I hear your harmonica at night," said Cress. "It's so otherworldly, drifting up through the trees."

"Otherworldly?" he said. "As in caterwauling?"

"As in haunting. You're really good."

"Should've heard my dad and granddad. *That* was some harp playing."

DeeDee plunked down their drinks, waved off Caleb's bill, which he left on the bar.

"I hear you draw," he said.

"I muddle about."

"I spent a year at Cal Arts. Drawing and illustration."

"Just a year? Didn't you like it?"

He'd been fresh out of the Army, he said, on the GI Bill, with a kid on the way. He couldn't sit still. He was itchy to make a living, a life. When his father took a big job in Malibu with a lot of fine work, Caleb went with him.

Quinn, alone in a booth, twisted around to glower at them. Cress said, "Better take your brother his beer."

"Join us," said Caleb.

She slid in next to him. Quinn raised an eyebrow at her whiskey, then waved down a waitress and ordered one for himself. "Just one," he said quietly to Caleb.

"Hey, I have a question," said Cress, and asked if it was true, had they really worked for the movie star Brian named?

"Built him a couple of guesthouses," Caleb said. "And a picture gallery. Quinn made him doors out of these Frank Lloyd Wright windows."

"That must have been nerve-wracking."

"I was very, very careful."

Caleb said, "Have Sylvia bring up the photos to show her."

"Did you ever see *him*?" asked Cress.

"All the time," Caleb said. "Some mornings he'd come out, hair sticking up, eyes bloodshot, gut sagging in some dirty T-shirt, like he'd been rode hard and put away wet. He'd knock a few dozen golf balls into the canyon, all snarly, like he'd bite if you got near him. Then he'd go back in the house, and couple hours later, a long black car'd drive up, and out he'd come in these beautiful clothes, all slapped and polished into a movie star." Caleb stuck a thumb at his brother. "He liked Quinn."

"What's not to like?" said Quinn.

"He'd talk to Quinn for thirty, forty minutes at a stretch, Quinn working the whole time, nailing, sanding, whatever."

"Basketball," said Quinn. "He was obsessed."

Don Dare sat down next to Quinn. "That woman who won's not going to have anything left if she doesn't hurry up," he said. "Donna's on her way. We've been waiting for our first night of tenting in the snow. The world all muffled . . ."

"Let's hope it'll muffle the damn squirrels who use our

trailer as a freeway," said Quinn. "And bomb target. They wait till you're snoring—then *crack!* like a gunshot. A pinecone from thirty, fifty feet: now, that'll set you bug-eyed and bolt upright in a jiffy."

Another round of bourbons, then Caleb and Quinn drove her home, the truck making the first tracks on blank white roads.

"I got a job!" Tillie said. With Edgar so busy, she'd needed something to do—that wasn't having a kid. Once you're married, she told Cress, everyone assumes a kid's next on the docket. The pressure is really on. But she met a man at the Wickers' house who worked at the *Arcadia Crier*—just a local throwaway paper, but still . . . This man was the art director, and he needed someone part-time to paste up ads. Tillie volunteered. How hard could it be? The art director mailed her copies of the paper, and your average chimp could do a better job than the guy they had. The art director told her to put together a few ads and send them with her résumé. "Maddie taught me paste-up in less than a day, but the résumé was harder. I had to stretch a bit. Those courses I took in textile design in Tehran? I changed them to graphic design classes. With all the purges at the universities, nobody will ever see a transcript. And I got it. I got the job!"

"Congratulations," said Cress. "And long live the Ayatollah."

"We're about knocking off," Caleb said, taking the gallon of tung oil from Cress. "Seen the job here yet? Well, come on in."

The Rodinger house sat on steep ground. The living room had a vaulting, twenty-foot cathedral ceiling and vast expanses of dual glazed glass. Matching half-ton boulders anchored the rock fireplace. Today the brothers were nailing planks diagonally on either side of the chimney. The boards ran pale yellow to rusty brown. "This British Columbia cedar will tone down and age real good," said Quinn, switching boards around on the floor. "We want to avoid too much of a stripety, dark-light effect."

They'd already clad the high beams in cedar and built a long window seat overlooking the forest. "Nice little perch," said Caleb. "Try it out."

Cress sat where custom-made linen cushions would someday stretch. Doors to the storage space inside the bench had sculpted, recessed handles that welcomed a hand. Outside, sparrows zinged between the spruce.

"Is it beer-thirty yet?" said Quinn.

Caleb rummaged in a cooler, handed Quinn and Cress cold longnecks, and opened a Coke for himself. Quinn sat near her on an unopened box of nails.

"Smells like a thousand pencils in here," said Cress.

"Cedar," said Quinn. "Working with it always reminds me of Lew."

"I know," said Caleb, then to Cress: "Our dad."

"He's gone?" said Cress.

"A year," said Caleb.

"Ten months," said Quinn.

"I'm sorry," Cress said, and because her mother had had a lobe of her lung removed three years ago, she felt sufficiently initiated into parental sickness to ask, "Was it a long illness? Sudden?"

The two men exchanged a look.

"Ah, Pop killed himself," said Caleb.

"Oh God. I'm so sorry," Cress said. "I didn't mean to pry."

"You weren't prying," said Caleb. "It's all right. No, Pop went out to the barn one afternoon and shot himself."

"Jesus. That's terrible. So hard on you."

Quinn set his beer on the floor between his feet and hung there, elbows on his knees. "It's the meanest thing one person can do to another," he said.

A deep line creased his forehead. Cress reached over and

grasped his forearm. So—it was sadness that had sealed his surface. Sadness and fury. Up close, his pain was a steady, low sounding. She held on right above his wrist.

When she let go, Quinn picked up his beer and drank the rest of the bottle in fast, long gulps.

Eight

Over the weekend, the snow vanished except in shadows and on the north sides of hills. She was hunting for clean hiking socks when a knock thudded on the sliding glass door: Quinn Morrow in a red-and-black wool shirt. "I was hoping you hadn't gone out yet."

Coming in, he handed her a long, thin white package, *Bac* written on it in ballpoint scrawl. "From our hog," he said. "Had it smoked out in Fountain Springs. It'll wreck you for that store-bought stuff."

"So nice of you," she said, and briefly considered inviting him and Caleb for dinner. But she had little to cook in the house.

"I was just heading out," she said, pointing to her hiking boots by the door. "Or I'd offer you coffee."

"That's okay. I'm heading out myself."

He's too solitary and grumpy, Cress thought, to want company.

"You guys knock off early," she said.

"We work six to two or three," he said. "Sometimes we go back to it after dark. No point in being up here if you can't enjoy the country. I've been meaning to ask—I see you come down into the meadows. Is there a trail?"

They switchbacked down through young pines and snow patches to the top of the first meadow, green-gold in the pale fall sunlight. "This was my secret spot as a kid," she said. "It looks like a place where fairies frolic, until you try to walk across and find out it's a stinky bog."

Quinn, too, had come to the mountains constantly as a child. His grandparents and two uncles had cabins on Noah Mountain, along the North Fork of the Hapsaw. ("Maybe six, seven miles from here as the crow flies, but forty-some by car," he said.) He'd run in a clutch of cousins and neighbor boys. The men took them hunting and fishing, and every weekend included a music night, when half the mountain was at the house picking and singing.

"You never wanted to stay home in Seal Beach?"

He turned with such a shocked, sharp look, Cress stopped in her tracks. "Who said I was from Seal Beach?"

"You did. At poker night."

His face relaxed. "Oh, that's right."

And no. He'd only wanted to be on Noah Mountain. His friends were all there, and also everything he loved to do— hunting, fishing, exploring. Intermittently, his family moved to the ten acres his father inherited. Today his whole family lived in the area. His mom and siblings. Quinn was the oldest. Nine years after him came Caleb, and nine years after *him* came their sister, Rosie, who lived in Sawyer with a husband and new baby.

"Big gaps," said Cress.

"Same with my kids," he said. "Annette's seventeen and Evan's eight."

"Funny how those patterns come down through a family," Cress said, and calculated. "Does this mean we'll be welcoming a new little Morrow next year?"

"Hope not," he said. "I've changed enough diapers for one lifetime."

"And Caleb's kids? Same gaps?"

"Two years apart. More like their mom's side."

They had come around on the fire road to the far side of the first meadow and now passed through a small woodlot to the second. "I haven't officially met Caleb's wife," said Cress.

"Candy?" Quinn's face went hard.

He'd spent a lot of time with Candy, he told Cress, when Caleb first brought her home. Noah Mountain was too quiet for her. She was a town girl, always afraid she was missing out on life. Whenever Quinn ran to Sawyer or Sparkville, she had to come along. He'd try to slip away undetected, and there she was, *Oh, Quinn, cain't I run down the hill with you?* People started saying, Who's Quinn's new girl? He didn't mind her at first, he told Cress. She liked to laugh.

"Not so crazy about her anymore?"

"Not so much, no." Quinn gazed off into the woods.

"Well, maybe it won't last. The marriage, I mean."

"Morrows mate for life."

"And you? How long's it been?"

"Twenty-one years so far."

"Your wife is very pretty."

"Prom Queen," he said. "*And* Homecoming."

"You knew her then?"

"All through high school."

In the second meadow, the old log cabin, shuttered as usual, sat in the thin, yellowing light. "Perfect, isn't it?" said Cress.

"I'd like to put something like that up on Noah Mountain," said Quinn.

"I wish my parents were building something more like it for the new place. But Rick Garsh sold 'em his bill of goods, I guess."

"Rick Garsh." Quinn let the name hang there.

"Yeah, well, my dad's giving him a real run for his money."

She told Quinn about her father picking up the nails and saying, "This represents real money. Just lying on the ground."

"Hell, I'd hammer out nails for thirty bucks an hour," said Quinn. "If that's what he wanted."

The fire road crossed Spearmint Creek, then followed it. They walked in silence now, side by side. Quinn, in his distinctive way, placed one foot directly in front of the other: it was a hunter's walk, a silent, controlled prowl. When not talking,

Quinn pulled into himself; she felt his withdrawal like a receding wave. She'd always been good with quiet men, she knew when and how to draw them out. "Tell me about your daughter," she said. "What's she like?"

"Annette? She's a great girl," he said. Captain of her water polo team, and not because she was such a good player—she wasn't. But she was bighearted, enthusiastic, and so encouraging, she really fired up the team. She was graduating in May and had her sights set on either Fresno or Davis for college. She already had lists of pros 'n' cons. Smiling, Quinn showed a discolored incisor. "Now, if I could just get Sylvia to go back to school, find something she wants to do . . ." He glanced at Cress. "I was thinking you could talk to her."

"Me?" Cress said.

"Do her good to see what some people do with their lives."

"Like loaf in the mountains when they should be writing?"

"Yes, but we've been living in these parts so long," he said, "the place has had its way with us. We're turning into hicks."

Cress had walked almost to the lodge for Family Night when Quinn's truck drew up alongside her. He rolled down his window, and she saw Sylvia in the cab, sitting flush up against him, the way couples did in high school. "Lift?"

"Need the exercise," she said, not wanting to intrude in such a small space. "I'll meet you down there."

They sat in a booth as they had in the cab, close, pressed together. Cute, Cress thought, given those twenty-one years. She slid in across from them.

"Quinn says you're writing a book." Sylvia's voice was soft and childishly sweet. "What's it about?"

Cress checked the floor for DeeDee, or anyone else who could bring her a drink. "It's more like a long term paper," she said. "On the economics of art. How artwork accrues value in the marketplace."

"That sounds interesting."

"Not so much as one might hope."

Soft, dark curls framed Sylvia Morrow's face. Orange lace edged the neck of her peach-colored T-shirt. She was so petite and soft-spoken, Cress began to feel oversized and brash.

Don and Donna and Brian and Franny had their usual table by the fireplace. They waved to her, and Cress regretted having committed herself to this subdued marital pair, the twinge of resentment familiar: one more time, she couldn't be with her friends. She wished that Caleb and his loud, laughing wife would join them—they would have livened things up—but they were back at the trailer. Stayin' in, Quinn said.

"I hear you work downtown," Cress said.

"Just at Harvey's." Sylvia Morrow kept her movements close to her body, as if she were confined to a small area or trying to take up as little space as possible. Keeping her elbow by her ribs, she dipped her head to push her hair off her face. "And I really like it," she said. "Despite what the grouch here thinks." Her hand darted up then and gave Quinn's hat a playful downward tug.

Displeasure darkened his features. He turned away, corrected the tilt of the brim.

Cold, Cress thought, and a little mean. She spoke cheerfully to counter his moodiness. "I sent myself through grad school waitressing," she said. "I was a waitress till I moved up here. And unless I finish this project lickety-split"—she couldn't bring herself to say "dissertation" to Sylvia—"I'll be one again. Nothing's wrong with restaurant work. Just the tedium. And the physical exhaustion. The customers. Oh, and all the idiots you have to work with."

Quinn, still canted away, laughed low and grabbed the end of the table.

Sylvia said, "Oh, but the people I work with are really nice. And our customers are, too—"

Quinn stood. "You girls want anything?" he said, already moving toward the bar.

Sylvia spoke rapidly in his absence. "I don't know why he acts like my job's so awful. Have you been to Harvey's? It's not fancy, but the food's delish and everybody's friendly. Old Harvey was a grump, but he's been dead for years, and it's Mrs. Harvey who's made it a success. She's always there in a blue dress. She has a hundred blue dresses—she's famous for them."

"Blue dresses?" What Cress really wanted to say was *Adult voice, please!*

"Not like dressy ones. It's just a coffee shop. But we grind our own hamburger, and a woman comes in twice a week to make our pies."

Cress marveled at Sylvia's use of *we* and *our.* "I love pie."

"Stop by! The next time you're in Sparkville. I'll buy you a slice."

At the bar, in his leather outfit and battered hat, Quinn leaned on one elbow and surveyed the room like a lone gunslinger, new to town.

"His work has been so slow," Sylvia said softly. "I've helped out, I really have, even if he won't admit it. He's embarrassed he can't carry us. It's not his fault nobody's building. If I was smart like you, I'd go to nursing school or get a teaching credential, but I can't take tests. I get too nervous, and my hand shakes too much to write. Even the driver's test. I like Harvey's. I hope you come in."

Cress promised: on her next run to town, she'd stop by for pie.

Quinn came toward them with two brimming draft beers, one Coke.

"I can't drink," Sylvia said. "My Indian blood. Half a beer puts me out."

"Half a beer, we'll be pulling her up from under the table," said Quinn.

The buffet opened and they filled their plates with pork chops and sauerkraut. After they finished eating, Cress refused a ride home and stayed to hear Donna sing.

He'd stolen Sylvia from a letterman, a linebacker, a senior—
when he was a lowly sophomore, no less. He'd wooed her away—
better care, he said, had done the trick. Her mom had just died,
and her dad, a Nez Perce Indian, was sweet when sober, but a
nasty drunk. So Quinn moved Sylvia in with his family, where
she stayed even as he went to U.C.L.A. and lived in the dorms.
They married over Christmas break his freshman year. It was
too late to get into married-student housing so Quinn left school
then, after that one quarter, thinking that he'd make some
money so they could rent a little place together near campus.
"But that spring all of us, the whole family, moved up to the
mountains for good." His parents lived on the property; he and
Sylvia rented a little house on Sand Creek Road. He worked
with his father and brother, often down south.

Quinn and Cress were wending their way through a manzanita thicket, the round little leaves beaded with fat drops of
snowmelt. Quinn batted them as they walked, sending bright
sprays into the air. Cress had to hang back or be soaked.

"You never went back to college?"

"I took night courses. Sparkville Community College. Still
do. Spanish. Welding. Shakespeare. Structural engineering."

"Ever take an econ course?"

"Should I?"

"I'm the wrong person to ask."

"Now, you tell me something," he said. "I talk too much around
you. It's your turn."

She told him how she'd lost momentum in Pasadena, working crappy jobs and hanging out with friends at Braithway Court.
How she'd come here hoping to get work done.

"But then you made all new friends." He turned and cocked
an eyebrow: *Am I right?* "You'd make friends wherever you go."

They turned east and crossed Spearmint Creek, and stayed on the fire road so they could walk abreast as they talked.

She'd tell him something else, too, she said, but he couldn't use it against her. It would sound like a rationalization, and maybe it was. Her father thought so. But she'd come to hate economics. She'd stopped believing in it, she'd lost her faith. She now considered economics a pseudoscience, much closer to theology than to math.

He wasn't a bad listener. He slowed and frowned—in concentration, she was fairly sure, not disapproval.

"All economists, Keynesian or libertarian," she went on, "believe that the market economy works like a machine powered by self-interest. They believe it can be diagrammed and understood mathematically. But that's so demonstratively not true! It's more like a huge, sensitive, infinitely complex organic system subject to many more influences and interferences than self-interest alone. Of course, saying this in grad school is like announcing you're an atheist in a seminary!

"And God! The endless mathematical elaborations bored me to tears. I thought I could go through the charade, jump through all the hoops—take my orals, complete my classwork—and then work on something that actually interested me for my dissertation. I thought if I figured out how artists' work accrues value, it might help some of them shape their careers. But the whole subject was too squishy, and I had to limit limit limit myself until I was tracking just a small set of artists who were all pretty similar. I put so much time and work into research! Or rather, in trying to boil the subject down to something I *could* research. I spent two years just getting a handle on my topic. In the end, what I'm trying to write is so different from what I wanted to do, I don't have the heart, or whatever, to get it done. I had to ignore so much reality to seem at all systematic. To get any kind of model. And that's what most economists do—ignore everything that doesn't fit their model, whatever doesn't function as part of a machine. I don't know. Maybe I picked the wrong subject. Art!

Artists! What was I thinking? Why didn't my advisor stop me? It's way too late to start over. And I don't want to be that pathetic never-finished-her-dissertation person. But even that, the prospect of being a pathetic All-but-Disser doesn't inspire me.

"I know," Cress pushed on before Quinn could respond. "I should just shut up and do it. Jump through the hoops, like my advisor says, so I can mount my critique from the inside."

"Or just decide you're never going to write it, and that's fine," said Quinn. "Then move on to the next thing."

"Yeah, but what's the next thing?"

"Don't you want to draw or paint?"

"I'm a Sunday sketcher, at best. Even I know I'm not talented enough to make a living at it."

Sadly, the only field she'd shown a talent for was econ, and even that was thanks to her growing up with a traumatized victim of the Great Depression. Her father's fears and obsessions had imprinted her with thought patterns that, superficially at least, were indistinguishable from the mind-set of a trained economist: What is given up to get this? What is the true cost? Whose self-interest is going to prevail? What are the margins, the hidden costs?

Back in college, she'd relished the prospect of achievement in a largely male arena. Lady economists were scarce, scary. Even her father would be intimidated.

But the men—her classmates—wore her down, she told Quinn. She won fellowships—some, perhaps, through affirmative action. And she published far more than anyone else in her class. Her essays, which she submitted to quarterlies and journals under the name C. A. Hartley, were praised in peer review for their clarity and readability, the writing. She was the first woman to edit *The Midwest Economic Review*, a coveted job among the graduate students; she chose articles and wrote the monthly editorials. Except for John Bird, not one of her male classmates congratulated her or acknowledged any of her triumphs. They ignored her, excluded her. Luckily, in her first year, there was one other woman in the program, Joan, a thirty-seven-year-old actress who was planning a second career in academia. Cress and Joan had huddled together while the men in their program formed study groups, went drinking, ate meals en masse, and threw parties without ever inviting them. She and Joan had their own study group of two, their own long nights of talking and drinking. At the end of their first year, Joan quit. "If I wanted to be around so much sexism," she told Cress, "I would've stayed in Hollywood."

In Cress's second year, she and John Bird were assigned a project together and started dating, which somewhat lessened her isolation.

"If I had the least talent," Cress told Quinn, "I'd be a landscape painter. I'd love to look hard at the natural world all day and make my feeble facsimile. It's such a noble, old-fashioned profession, like writing novels. But it's a lot harder than it looks. And totally out of vogue."

"I'll tell you what's out of vogue," said Quinn. "Fine architectural woodworking is out of vogue. Nobody wants boiserie or inlay or sculptural ornament. I haven't had a decent job in eight, ten months now, and the last one was just a tiny plinth for the Getty."

"You've had a bad year," Cress said.

He turned with such a look of shock and anger, she stepped backward, stumbled. "I mean, with your dad and all," she said.

His anger receded. "I guess that's right."

She wanted to put her hand flat on his shoulder blade to soothe and reassure him, but didn't dare, out here when they were alone. She wouldn't want him to get the wrong idea. The bright, chiming sound of water running over rocks in Spearmint Creek filled the silence.

He stopped short, pointing to a scrap of red plastic embedded in the dirt. He crouched and dug out a Swiss Army knife. "Lookee here," he said. "This represents real money. Just lying on the ground."

He rubbed the pocketknife on his jeans, and gave it to her. In the red plastic, a tiny, smiling, thick-lipped fish was inlaid in steel. The toothpick was still in its slot. "You got to pay me for it," he said. "Or it's bad luck."

"Bad luck, how?"

"Give a knife, sever a friendship," he said.

She dug in her jeans pocket, handed over a nickel.

Nine

The Morrow brothers camped beside the Rodinger house in an older white travel trailer with a thick aqua stripe and, high up at the back, a pair of small, flat, useless yellow wings. Inside was an entire miniature home—kitchen, dining room, bedroom— paneled in yellowing teak. Cress, Don Dare, and the brothers played hearts at the tiny dinette, whose table and benches folded down nightly into Caleb's bed. ("Quinn gets the master suite." Caleb pointed to a platform in the rear of the trailer where a sleeping bag curled on a bare foam pad.)

Cress was winning. They called her *the smart one, the little cardsharp in the corner there,* and *the doctor;* but they didn't seem to mind her victory—unlike her Econ colleagues, who had taken her successes as personal affronts. The Morrow brothers made sure she had a drink, a pillow behind her. She felt happy, petted.

The brothers glowered and clucked over their cards. "Hate to send a boy out to do a man's work," Quinn said, playing a jack of diamonds.

Caleb dropped a two of diamonds on the trick. "And that's all she wrote." He raised an eyebrow her way, as if they shared a secret. He was droll with that elastic, hound-dog face. The more she was around him, the less ugly he was. She hoped his wife was smart. At least she was a laugher, if a loud one.

Quinn scooped up the next trick. "That's what I get for bringing a knife to a gunfight."

Caleb stood and said he was going out to have a look at the stars. Quinn called after him, "Fifty feet, please." When Cress got up to use the bathroom a few minutes later, they shooed her away from the tiny one inside the trailer ("You don't even want to *look* in there," said Caleb) and sent her out of doors, with Quinn calling, "Fifty feet, please."

Caleb said, "This morning I'm making coffee and who's looking in at me but some white-muzzled old bear."

"That's my guy!" said Cress. "But why isn't he asleep?"

Quinn said, "Sierra bears don't go into a true hibernation. It's not really cold enough. They get up and snack."

Caleb made popcorn and they opened more beer. A wind came up and shook the little trailer, but they were snug inside. At midnight, she and Don clambered down the steps and both brothers, silhouetted, waved from the door.

"Pop bid a remodel at that house seven, eight years ago." Quinn waved at one of Reggie Thornton's ranch-style log homes. "The kitchen was a dark, airless cubbyhole they wanted to open up. That was my one time at the Meadows before now. Pop came in at something like twice the nearest bid—he was never ever the lowest. Of course, he was worth every cent. But not everybody wants a work of art for a kitchen. Or can afford one. Nobody did work like Pop."

"You must miss him," said Cress.

"When I don't wish I'd killed him with my own bare hands," said Quinn. "Ah, Pop"—this with soft bitterness—"such an artist and such an infant. Completely irresponsible."

"You're an artist too."

"Oh no. I'm just a craftsman, thank God."

But Caleb, Quinn said, took after the old man. Every project, those two had to go through the whole agonizing creative process, A to Z, starting from scratch; never wanting to repeat, they lived in fear that the new job was too much like the old job. If the client had paid them for an original design, they wanted it to be entirely original, from the ground up. Then, at a certain point, they became afraid that they'd gone too far afield from the last job, the one that the client had admired. Each step of the way involved torture and self-doubt, the smallest thing that went wrong became a major crisis. "Though they usually made something even more imaginative and unusual from their mistakes," said Quinn. "I wish I could show you; their work was so clever and funny—if you think cabinets can be funny—little stowaway places for lids and bowls. Handles in the shapes of bones and pomegranates. One in-and-out china cupboard they built, you filled the shelves from the kitchen and pulled the plates out in the dining room—just a lovely, one-of-a-kind thing . . . but the amount of moaning and self-doubt, and the *naps*!"

Whenever something went wrong, his father hit the ground snoring. The owner would come home and there was his carpenter, asleep on the kitchen rug. Whether it was a famous producer's private theater on Mulholland Drive or some housewife in Sparkville having Sears cabinets installed, his father went at the job like it was the Sistine Chapel. "Me, I go in, build the kitchen, the home theater, the bookshelf, and move on," Quinn said. "Someone in this family had to get the job done. They got the talent, I got the clipboard."

"But you were picked to make the Frank Lloyd Wright doors."

"I picked me. Pop and Caleb'd still be dithering over those damn pieces of glass. I'm a good woodworker, but Pop and Caleb, they're gifted—in music, too. They each learned like ten instruments. I'm the only Morrow who doesn't play at all."

His father played guitar, mandolin, fiddle, and banjo interchangeably. The bass, too, upright, and guitarrón. One night, just four years ago, all the instruments had been claimed, so Lew played percussion on a little plastic ice chest. At his memorial, Quinn said, a good half-dozen people talked about that—the night Lew played the Igloo.

—

She showed Quinn the back road to Globe Rock. On their way home, they bought a to-go cup of bourbon from the lodge and shared it while walking.

Quinn swished the liquor around in his mouth. His dad, he said, had loved bourbon. Not that Lew was a big drinker. Except when he gambled. Then all bets were off. Once Lew started gambling, Quinn said, he went headlong into devastation. He'd lose tools, cars, wedding rings, his clothes. He'd get into fights, black out, get sick, wake up in the middle of nowhere in boxers. He owed money everywhere, to everyone.

"I feel the tug when I play poker," said Quinn. "To throw it all away. But Pop—he was gone from the first shuffle. He bet on anything, gambled every penny that came his way. He had this stamina. He could ignore bills for months and brush off creditors like gnats." The gas, the electricity, the water, the phone were routinely disconnected. When Quinn was eleven, Lew parked the family on Noah Mountain and took disaster-relief jobs out of state. At first, his checks came home. Then they stopped, and for most of that year, the family lived on charity, until he came back with a big sack of cash, and they moved down south again.

"How did your mom put up with that?" Cress asked.

"Pop was terribly charming, and clever. You would have loved him. Everyone did. And talented? *Man.*"

His father had once built a library with carved wood paneling for Armand Hammer. He'd made the plain wood benches at the Arcadia arboretum and vitrines for the Getty. His whittling won prizes at the state fair. "But he had trouble finishing. He lost interest once the artistic decisions were made. He'd get within days, sometimes even hours, of being done—and vanish. Caleb and I called him the unfinish carpenter. What is that, not finishing?"

"You're asking me?" said Cress.

"Your case is different. In contracting, you don't finish, you don't get paid," Quinn said. "The last checks are what you take home free and clear."

As soon as he was old enough, thirteen, fourteen, whenever his father started to fade on a job, Quinn stepped in; he filled nail holes. Slapped on the last coat of varnish. Worked his way down the punch list. Swept. Coiled extension cords. Phoned inspectors. Wrote invoices, whatever it took.

"God, I wonder if there's an equivalent for you in economics," said Cress. "I could really use a finisher."

Out by Globe Rock, they came upon Jakey's green truck parked off the fire road in a stand of elderberries. The cab was empty, the windows half down. Around the next curve, there was Jakey having sex with a woman against a ponderosa pine, his usual checked cook's pants hobbling his ankles. Those strong solid legs shone pale pink in the late-afternoon light. His partner's eyes were shut, her straight, faded-blond hair familiar. Why, that was Ondine Streeter! Cress grabbed Quinn's arm, spun them around. "We don't need to see that."

Redness crept up Quinn's neck, flared over his jaw.

"You disapprove," Cress said.

"Who says I disapprove?"

"Aren't you the mated-for-life school?"

"I don't know about any school," he said. "And it doesn't mean I like it."

She wondered what, exactly, he didn't like: adultery in general, this adultery in particular, or being mated for life. She was too shy to ask.

"We had our first fire of the season tonight!" Tillie said. "We did a raclette-like thing using kebab skewers and a cookie sheet. We really missed you, everyone sitting on the rug, drinking rosé like old times."

"You should come up here," Cress said, sounding like her mother. "I have fires all day long."

But Tillie had her job now at the little newspaper, pasting up ads and contributing the occasional drawing and cartoon. And Edgar worked twelve-hour days at the Jet Propulsion Laboratory. They wouldn't have vacation time until December. "We'll come for a few days between Christmas and New Year," Tillie said. "A bunch of us. You wait."

"Why don't I like Candy?" Quinn took off his battered leather hat and eyed its unevenly curled brim. "Let me count the ways."

They were sitting on the bench on the Bauers' cabin porch, the meadow spread out before them. The pale afternoon light was going fast. The deep, narrow channel of water made its satisfying low chortle. Small birds, black in silhouette, swooped past.

His mother, Quinn said, somehow had set aside a few old family valuables: some guns, Lew's whittling collection, a steel box with two gold pocket watches, rings, gold coins from the 1870s, a locket holding a dark curl. After the memorial service, his mom gave everything to Quinn to distribute or keep, as he saw fit.

They were all living up on the Noah Mountain property then. Quinn and his family were in a double-wide trailer—he was about to build a new house for them on the land. Caleb and his family had just come back from South Carolina and were living with the parents until they saved enough to rent a place of their own.

Quinn brought out the heirlooms and went through them with Caleb. The women came in and out; Candy examined every item. For starters, the brothers each took a gun and divided the coins, then decided the rest could wait. A month later, Quinn took out a garnet ring and gave it to Annette for her seventeenth birthday. Apparently Candy had set her sights on the ring; when she saw it on Annette's hand, she blew up. "She accused me of hogging the booty," Quinn told Cress. "Said I was cheating Caleb out of his birthright."

"Birthright! That sounds so biblical."

"Oh, she's biblical, all right. Born again and more righteous than God."

Quinn refused to take the ring away from Annette. Voices were raised. Things were said that should never be said. Quinn had bought a little house in Sparkville at auction thinking to fix it up, flip it, or rent it out. At that moment, it was sitting empty, so overnight, he moved his family there.

Not long afterward, Caleb moved his family to a small rental in Sawyer.

"Mom wouldn't put up with Candy, either," said Quinn.

"You guys all seem on good terms now," said Cress.

Good enough. But they hadn't spoken for six months, during which time Quinn felt as if he'd lost both father and brother. "And there was no damn work to take my mind off what happened."

When Rick phoned with several large jobs, Quinn called Caleb.

"Caleb must have appreciated that," Cress said.

"Not sure anybody appreciates anything. They're too busy worrying about their share of the crap. Meanwhile, who scraped the hair and brains and eye jelly off the barn walls? Who shoveled out a ton of bloody mud? You know the first person who noticed I was hurting?"

"I'm sure Sylvia . . . Or no—your little boy?"

Sylvia? Sylvia had carried on worse than anybody. Couldn't sleep. Scared to death of death. Wept, moped, got the kids all wrought up. Quinn had to calm everyone down. No. Quinn pressed his finger to Cress's forearm. "You, Cress. In all the months since. You reached out. You held my arm." His hand closed around her wrist.

"Anybody would've," she said. "You were so obviously in pain."

"Not anybody. Nobody. Until you," he said.

The meadow simmered in the dusk, the air busy with birds. Cress wanted to hold him, soothe him, kiss his face. She didn't dare. He released her wrist. They stood and walked cross-country into the development. Before he split off from her by the Rodinger place, he said, "I talked too much back there."

"Not too much."

"But you're such a good listener. Maybe too good."

Back at the A-frame, Cress felt the impress of his hand around her wrist. She was all riled up. Oh, he was terribly appealing, or his sadness was. But he was married, mated for life, and to a woman far more beautiful than she.

Cress got going on her second chapter on a chilly overcast day—in that even, soft light, all the hours were the same. She worked until she couldn't see clearly, and then she saw why: dusk. She had forgotten to eat and walk. Months had gone by since she'd been so absorbed in writing that the clock hands twirled. These were the days that made work worthwhile, when concentration was absolute and time evaporated. You couldn't make it happen. You just got lucky. Something sucked you in, and held you, and you leaped over the hours, and dense, boxy paragraphs accumulated on the page.

The fire had gone out. She was cold. Snow, in small, glinting splinters, sifted down outside. She carried in logs, hatcheted a wedge of fatwood into kindling, crumpled newspaper. The resinous pine ignited, its heat instant, intense. She lowered the blinds, scrambled two eggs, and ate them, soft and buttery, from the pan. A good day's work transformed everything—how had she forgotten this? Snow now fell thickly. Finally, she was writing. Could she sustain it? Would the clock hands twirl tomorrow? The fire snapped cheerfully. Another sound bled through, footsteps crunching on the porch. There, in sideways-blowing flakes, Quinn stamped his boots.

A clench of fear. Then she walked over and opened the sliding glass door.

"Don't have much time. But I had to see you today."

Frost rimed his beard. He shouldered out of his coat, hung

that and his chewed-up hat on hooks. His hair was flattened, and creased where the band sat. She almost said, *Nice hat-do*, but his glower cut her short. She poured one bourbon and they sat on the wicker love seat, arms touching—So emotional! Cress thought—and passed the plastic cup back and forth, the room dark except for the lively fire.

"One other thing." He set the whiskey on the floor under the seat. "I wasn't ever going to tell anyone. But now I want you to know, so someone does.

"The day he died," Quinn said, "Pop borrowed my truck—his was in the shop—and he went into Sawyer. He had coffee at the café and mailed a letter—to me, it turned out. This was last December. December 14. He came back up with a bag of screws, a saw blade. In the middle of the afternoon, Mom knocked on our door and said, 'Lew just took his deer rifle to the barn,' and that very moment, we heard the shot.

"Merry Christmas, everyone.

"I hope nobody has to see what I did. Their own father. It never leaves your mind. I covered him up, called the cops, the mortuary. After all that, I scrubbed the walls and windows, shoveled out the floor. I wouldn't let anyone else in. I didn't want those pictures in their heads."

The letter addressed to Quinn arrived the next day. A balloon payment, his father wrote, was due on the Noah Mountain property December 31. He had tried every bank and loan shark, but he couldn't raise a cent, even at 25 percent. So he'd found a card game in Bakersfield. He was up 10K at first. But then he went in the hole. Lost his tools and his truck—it was not, as he'd said, in the shop.

Enclosed with the letter were three IOUs totaling more than thirty thousand dollars. This was on top of the balloon.

Quinn gulped the whiskey, handed Cress the empty plastic cup. She refilled it and returned. "What did you do?"

"I refi-ed the little Sparkville house at 19 percent," he said. "Nineteen percent! Thank you, Paul Volker. I took that and all the money I'd saved to build our new place to pay off the balloon, the 30K, and about ten more bills that come in. I didn't want them going after my mom."

Cress put her hand on his knee and he covered it with his.

"I'd have done it all, anyway," Quinn said, "if Pop'd just told me earlier what was going on. That's what gets me. If he'd of said something, he'd be alive today, all debts paid."

"I'm so sorry."

Quinn threaded his fingers through hers. Nobody knew about the letter, he said, or what it cost to get the land out of hock. His mom knew the property was in danger, but not to what extent. Sylvia had signed the mortgage papers on their little house without reading them. "I did what had to be done, only to hear I'm hogging the heirlooms."

Cress was silent. In her family, every cent spent on a person was trumpeted, with due gratitude extracted—often many times over.

"I know, I know," Quinn said. "No good deed goes unpunished." He bounced their interlaced fingers on his knee. "So now you know."

She was about to say, *You should tell your family what you did!* when his face loomed, dark and cramped with pain. With his hat-flattened hair, he looked big-eyed and wet, as if he'd just surfaced in a dark lake.

His kiss set off a whirr in her mind: What about Sylvia? And *mated for life?*

Does he know what he's doing? The kiss felt premeditated and deliberate—a decision he'd made. Given the choice, she would have preferred Caleb. But Quinn had chosen her. How had she never noticed his eyes were such a strange pale green? She checked herself for guilt, or at least compunction about kissing someone's husband, but nothing flared. He was the one who had made—and now was breaking—vows. Perhaps Sylvia should've paid him more attention. Been more sympathetic. Read those mortgage papers.

They kissed and murmured on the love seat, and then he suggested they go upstairs.

Later, as he stood to leave, Quinn said, "That is one damn hard bed."

Cress got up and put on her woolen bathrobe and her mother's ridiculous fluffy turquoise slippers and went downstairs to call Tillie.

First, she reclaimed the watery bourbon from under the wicker love seat. She sat and drank it staring into the fire. A married man. A man with a beautiful wife. A man willing to endanger his long marriage. For her. The compliment seemed enormous. Of course, Sylvia, with her heavy curls and little-girl voice, would never know. For all her loveliness, her flashing smile, Sylvia was a child. Who could blame Quinn for wanting intelligent conversation?

Cress could already imagine Tillie's vicarious excitement—*A married man! What's* that *like?*—but also her concern: *Aren't you afraid? Oh, be careful, Cress. Careful, careful.*

So maybe she wouldn't call Tillie. Not tonight, at any rate. Why not keep this moment close, close and sweet. Tillie could wait.

And Cress wasn't afraid. She'd handled Jakey when he turned out to be a compulsive philanderer. Once she knew the facts, a door had shut in her chest. The same grasp on reality would keep her safe with Quinn. If Caleb—so much funnier and more her style and closer to her age—had come after her, well, that might have been a different story. Cress glanced at the pinecone on her kitchen table, the perfect petalled symmetry, the jaunty outward curve of thorns. She could fall hard for Caleb. Quinn not so much. But she did feel for him. He cast sorrow and loneliness like trees cast shade. He was in dire need of comfort.

As it happened, she could use some companionship too.

Ten

Quinn had scars: a shiny white belly arc from an appendectomy at eleven. Under his right breast a puckering ridge of proud flesh and, on his back, a long slice over a shoulder blade where the skin, neatly parted, was imperfectly rejoined. Burn scars scalloped his forearms from years of feeding a wood-burning stove. "The word *scar* comes from the Greek for fireplace," he said.

"Now, how do you know that?"

"Built a kitchen for a classics professor in Claremont," he said.

"And this one?" Cress tapped the fat of his palm where a shiny white concavity the diameter of a pencil looked like an off-center stigmata, long healed.

He turned his hand over to show her the matching white dent below the pinky knuckle. "I was sanding a fir beam, bearing down, and before I knew it, a four-inch splinter'd went right through my hand. I'm screaming even as I'm trying to decide which way to pull it out."

"And this?" Cress traced the white, scapular line.

He caught her hand, pinned it to the pillow. "So many questions."

"So many scars. And I'm interested. Would you rather I wasn't?"

He was thirty-nine years old, ten and a half years older than she was—exactly the age gap between her parents, almost to the week. Quinn liked the slow drift of kissing, seemed at times to prefer it. He wasn't inclined to make love all over the forest, as was Jakey's wont. He preferred her too-firm bed, and darkness.

Afternoons, he came to walk smelling of sawdust and, faintly, sweat, the combination familiar from deep in her childhood, when her father was moonlighting as a carpenter and kissed her good night with sawdust in his eyebrows. At night, Quinn had washed and used a musky drugstore cologne— Matchabelli, he said. A gift. Cress didn't ask from whom. She was silently contemptuous of its cheap, chemical edge, although in time, one whiff launched a freefall of longing.

Although he was not an athletic or strenuous lover, or what she'd call an ecstatic lover (he did not tug and nudge her into odd positions, or hold back and go on forever like some virtuoso of intercourse), he was intense and attentive and profoundly well suited to her. He never had to ask (as John Bird had so often, it was like a tic) what she liked, what she wanted him to do that would make her happy. She and Quinn seemed to understand each other sexually. Currents of sympathy and intuition ran between them. Somehow she knew what pleased him. Or maybe everything pleased him. Maybe he was easy to please.

Her feelings for him seemed closest to the fierce allegiances she'd formed in elementary school with Jeff Dutro and Kathy Perrie: strong, unembarrassed attachments grounded in camaraderie, the joy of each other's company.

The day before Thanksgiving, Quinn came to tell her that he and Caleb were heading down the hill. His mother would be cooking turkey for twenty.

Her own parents, she said, were due up in a few hours.

Standing just inside the door, he took off his hat, rotated the brim in his hands. "And again. So you know. Ahh. To be clear. So there is no mistake," he said. "I'll never leave Sylvia."

Outside, the sky was flat, talc blue. "Yes, yes," she said

absently, having just noticed at eye level, on the sliding doors, all-new nose smears from the bear.

He came farther in and up to her. He set a fingertip over her heart, tapped. "I know why I'm doing this," he said. "But why are you?"

She was surprised by the force of his gaze. "You and I get along."

"That we do," he said. "We do get along."

The coming holiday must have stirred him up. She wanted to reassure him. "To me," she said, "we're like childhood friends. How we walk all around looking at things. Telling each other stuff. Liking each other best."

Quinn slid a hand around her neck, pulled her ear to his mouth. "You say things I feel but could never put into words."

Her parents brought a blue aerogram from London, dated a month ago.

Dear Cress,

How's it going up in those Meadows? How's things with the King of the Mountain?

Sorry for using this irritating postal gram—or what my friend James calls an aerogami-gram. At least they are snoop-proof, ergo Mom-proof. And also very cheap to send! (That's my Dad-side talking.)

Yes—indeed I do remember Jakey Yates. I used to see him those times Mom guilted me up to the cabin for Thanksgiving and Christmas. (You were so smart to go to college far away.) Jakey once sold me a large package of Hydrox for fifteen cents, a kindness I haven't forgotten—though this was only five or six years ago. Being up there with Mom and Dad, I had regressed right back to adolescent binge eating.

Forty-nine does seem a little old for you. My therapist says that anything more than fifteen years is probably a father thing—though that shouldn't be surprising to you, given our dim stingy doofus old dad. Of course we'd try, unconsciously or not, to improve on HIM. I'm given to foreign men, which my shrink points out is my way of escaping the culture of our family. Long live exogamy! (My friend James says that foreign men are the first stage of lesbianism, but he's gay and sees gayness everywhere.)

FYI, I'm in sort of a fight with Mom and Dad—just a warning because they'll probably try to draw you in. It all started because I figured out that Mom must have gotten another pretty good inheritance when Grandpa Abe died last year—I mean, they're building a new cabin, right? Where did the cash for that come from? Anyway, I asked if they would give (or lend) me a small down payment for a flat here. Dad wrote me back—six marginless pages that looked insane, like knitting or what madmen nail on trees in the park. Most of it was about how broke he was as a kid, and how hard he's worked for everything that has ever come his way (no mention of those big infusions of cash that Mom has inherited). But all that was just buildup to the real reason they couldn't give me money, which was "single women are notoriously bad lending risks," and if I lost my job and couldn't make my house payments, then their money would be gone. No credit for supporting myself for the last twelve years! I brought the letter in to my therapist, and while she was reading it, her hand kept reaching out for something on her little side table. This odd groping motion happened four or five times, and when she finally noticed what she was doing, she looked up at me and said, "I can't read this letter without reaching for a drink!"

After that letter, my therapist recommended that I try this process called "Rebirthing." She'd just finished training for it, and will take me through it at a cut rate, since I'm her first client. Basically, you work through all the events that added trauma or tension to your life, starting from the present, then going back to your birth, which is supposed to be one of the biggest traumas of all! I'm a long way from that happy day, however: I'm still processing Cairo—Hafez, his horrible parents, and their prehistoric view of women! I am so glad to be out of that roasting shitpile!

At least London is fantastic!!! Work is easy; I have about fifteen students, and then I teach teachers about ten hours a week. I have tons of free time, most of which I'm spending at the Victoria and Albert Museum. You must come! Your couch is calling!!!

Love,

Sharon

Sylvia Hartley spent the morning clattering around the kitchen—her pan-banging and cupboard-slamming expressed annoyance for every item Cress had shifted or misplaced. Cress pretended to work upstairs, then skiied in the afternoon, alone and sweetly melancholy in the silent woods. When she got back, Sylvia had dinner on the table: Cornish game hens, yam casserole, creamed peas and onions. The phone rang while they ate. Sam answered, clutching his napkin. "Hello? Hello?" he bellowed. "I can barely hear you with the static. Can you hear me?" He frowned at Cress and his wife. "Who?" he yelled. "Who do you want? Cressida or Sylvia? This connection is terrible. Was that Sylvia? Or Cressida?" Sam finally pointed the phone at Cress.

Static crackled in her ear. "Hello?" she said.

"Who the hell was that?" said Quinn.

"My dad."

"For a moment, I thought it was God."

He'd made a beer run to Sawyer, he said, so he could call her from a pay phone. "I wanted to hear your voice. And say I'm thinking of you."

She was pleased and surprised, although his call, she thought, crossed a line. She would never call him at his house when he was with his family.

Every night he was at the Meadows, Quinn walked first to the lodge's phone booth to call his wife and kids; then he walked to the A-frame. They either built up the fire and settled in or they drove out the back way, down to Family Night at Cloud Slope (Wednesday) or the Hapsaw Lodge (Tuesday), where they listened to live music and had a drink or two.

"Doesn't Caleb wonder where you are?" asked Cress.

"He's out, too, playing his harp where I can't complain about it."

"For as long as this?"

"He thinks I got to drinking beer and telling stories down at the lodge, or at the Garshes'. Like I used to. Before you. He doesn't know that's changed."

"You wouldn't ever tell him about us."

"He wouldn't want to know."

One too-bright dripping morning, Quinn stood at her glass door. "I'm on a tool run," he said. "Want to come along?"

They took the back way out of the development. As they switchbacked down the hill, he pulled her close. She gripped his thigh to keep from pitching about. Fishing poles in tubes rattled in his gun rack.

They drove down through the seasons. The old snow freighting the branches melted as in a time-lapse film until, at 5,000 feet, the trees were clean, with soiled white patches only in the shade. Quinn stopped to take off his jacket and opened the door for room. Hundreds of feet below, the Hapsaw roared its fatted winter roar.

The boulder-strewn hills around Sawyer had greened with new grass. The trunks of oaks were black with moisture, the leaves shiny-clean. They drove by the golf course and stark, manmade Glory Lake, where white houseboats cluttered the water like so many floating carports.

"I spent far too many hours on that lake," said Quinn. "Fishing. Skiing."

"But it's so ugly!"

"Nicer once you're out on it."

He needed certain router bits that he could only get at the big hardware store by the highway. Cress wandered aisles of power tools while he paid.

"Want to see the house? I'd like to pick up a sander there.

"Sylvia's at work," he added.

Behind long cinder-block walls, the subdivision had wide streets and small lots, with modest stucco homes from the fifties. "Good sturdy little postwar houses," Quinn said. "Wood-framed windows, oak floors." The land had previously been citrus groves; you could trace the old rows of lemon and orange trees yard to yard. Quinn's house was white, with a picture window. The front yard was bleached Bermuda grass, with a lone, shaggy lemon tree. "Sylvia loves it here," he said, as the garage door wobbled open. "But she's a city girl at heart."

Cress thought that she, too, was probably a city girl at heart— a true city girl, of the large metropolitan variety—Los Angeles or San Francisco, say—and not the trifling ag-town kind.

From the dark garage, they entered the house though a laundry room to a bright white kitchen. Not a dish sat in the sink, or a sponge or cloth. Even the dish rack was stowed out of sight. Quinn grabbed a brown vinyl chairback. "My coffee-drinking station," he said. The air here at sea level was heavy and thick with the false scents of lemon dish soap and Pine-Sol.

Cress recognized with a shock the maple living room set from the perennial sidewalk sale at Frank's Val U Mart downtown; on the upholstery, white water spilled from one quaint mill wheel to an identical mill wheel below in an infinite churning. Didn't they—Sylvia, but also Quinn—know that you could get beautiful and far more sturdy used sofas at countless thrift stores for a fraction of Frank's "rock-bottom" prices?

In the one bookcase, thick paperback best sellers took up one shelf; kids' sports trophies and school portraits filled the rest. The dark-haired girl and honey-haired boy both had their mother's dark eyes, their father's dark brow.

"She collects teacups!" At a rack of knickknacks, Cress feigned interest in faded gold rims and hand-painted pansies, the closest thing to art in the room.

Quinn beckoned her down the hall, past the boy's room with its Dodgers posters, then the girl's with her pink ruffled curtains, not a single toy or hairbrush or stray sock anywhere. "Here's this." Quinn opened a door at the end of the hall. "I know you want to see."

The bed was king-sized, its baby blue spread a shiny quilted synthetic, slightly pilled. Matching nightstands, also Val U Mart items, held small, matching yellow lamps with pleated yellow plastic shades.

Quinn's arm and hip grazed hers; one move, and they'd be on that bed. She held back, with distaste. They had their own places.

He crossed ahead of her. "In here's where I make my messes." He opened another door, to reveal a skinny bathroom with twin sinks, the faux-marble clear, unbesmirched by toothbrush or whisker.

A toothbrush or a whisker, Cress knew, was the mess he talked about. What the wife swept away.

"Satisfied?" he said.

No! She was not satisfied. Any insight into the daily texture of their lives—to say nothing of their marriage—had been thwarted by an obliterating, hotel-maid tidiness. How on earth did Quinn, who often looked as if he lived in a bark lean-to with a pet bear, emerge from this domestic nullity?

Back in the bright, disinfected kitchen, he stopped. "Listen. Hear that?"

The refrigerator purred. A car hummed on the street. The highway, farther off, produced a steady sound like wind. "No," she said.

"Exactly. That silence?" he said. "That's what I live with."

In the garage, as he rummaged for tools, Cress walked around idly. Above his workbench she found a row of small whittled animals: a swaybacked mountain lion, a coyote in a guilty skulk. A family of bears. The tallest piece was no more than three, three and a half inches. "Hey! Are these your dad's?"

Quinn came over. "Some his, some mine, some other people's."

"God, Quinn. They're fantastic! Why don't you have them out?"

"I do." He lifted his hand.

"I mean, in the house."

"Just more dustcatchers."

"No worse than teacups," said Cress. "You should build a vitrine for them! Put them where people can see them."

"They keep me company here," he said. "You can touch."

A beaver's rounded paddle had tiny scales; the narrow face, with its long, yellowed teeth bore a wry, comic expression. "I love him!" said Cress.

"That's my uncle Evan's. My dad's older brother."

"Who your son is named for?"

A sharp look. "Your memory!" he said. "He's who got us all whittling in the first place. He'd haul out a box of basswood chunks, we'd make piles of wood curls, tell each other lies. That was a long time ago."

"He's gone?"

"Kilt himself in '67."

"Jesus, Quinn."

"The Morrow solution to everything," he said.

And you named your son after him? she wanted to say. *Some legacy!* She picked up a two-inch squirrel, tail curled over its head.

"That's mine," he said. The bear family was also his: parents plus two cubs, a beguiling shagginess to their coats. A spiky porcupine, a detailed turkey.

"People should see these!" she said. "You could show them in a gallery. I'm not kidding. You could sell every last one in a second flat."

"Why would I sell them?"

"To distribute pleasure and delight! To make the world at large a little more beautiful! Why make art nobody sees? I can't believe you don't have them out where people can enjoy them. Doesn't Sylvia like them?"

"She does."

Cress touched the pink nose of the mountain lion. "They're so full of life. Don't they make you happy just looking at them?"

"Not so much anymore."

She wanted one, and hoped he'd offer.

"Let's get going," he said.

They drove across the valley floor, through orchards and sorghum fields, along canals with concrete banks, past packinghouses as large as airplane hangars. They slowed for the hamlets of Rooster Bend, Murdock, and Thompson's Corner, and stopped in Fountain Springs at a barnlike bar with an empty stage. "Open mikes here some Sundays," Quinn said. "Always a few Buckaroos or ex-Strangers on hand. Dad and Caleb used to get up with 'em. Some good music's played here. Some good times."

They sat on one side of a plywood booth, Quinn's hand on her knee. "That little beaver you liked? That was Uncle Evan's pet."

Hunters had killed the mother; Evan found the baby huddled by the skinned carcass. He took him home, named him Cump, after Tecumseh Sherman.

That Cump, Quinn said, was as smart, as affectionate as a dog. He lived in the house and followed Quinn's aunt Rose around all day. He slept on Evan's lap after dinner. His tail felt like a thick rubber mat. They had to trim his nails and give him wood to chew so his teeth wouldn't grow down into his chest. "We kids fed him carrots—he'd eat a willow stick like it was a stalk of celery."

"He didn't chew up the furniture?" said Cress.

"He got at the piano bench once and Uncle Evan had to turn a new leg."

And once, Evan and Rose came home to find the sofa pulled apart, the blankets dragged off the beds. Somehow, a bathtub tap was left on, or Cump somehow turned it on. Since every cell in a beaver's body is designed to stop the flow of water, that's what Cump set out to do. The first towel or rug plugged the drain, so everything after that served as a sponge. The bathroom and part of.the hall was a compacted, sodden mass of pillows and bedclothes. After that, whenever Evan and Rose left the house, they put Cump in an outside pen.

"How long did he live?"

"Oh God, they had him for years. After Uncle Evan passed, one of my cousins took him."

"And then?"

"Never cared to know more than that."

They ate Mexican food at a café overlooking the canal. "Won't Caleb be wondering where you are by now?"

"He'll forgive me anything for this." Quinn tapped a large combination plate in its Styrofoam container.

They returned through the Meadows' back entrance. Just inside, Quinn pulled over and shut off the engine. "I enjoyed today." His beard smelled of cumin and onion. "Being with you." She closed her eyes, slid a hand inside his jacket, around his ribs and staunchly beating heart; you could get closer to a lean man, she thought, nearer to his soul.

Even through her closed eyes, the flash registered. Quinn broke away. "Shit." She slid across the bench seat. When the beam bounced over them again, she'd flattened herself against the passenger door, the armrest gouging her ribs.

Quinn turned on the truck and in its headlights stood Rick and Julie Garsh. A box torch hung from Rick's hand. Hard to know what they'd seen.

Quinn drove up, rolled down his window. "Nice night," he said.

"Everything okay?" said Rick.

"Got them bevel bits I needed," Quinn said. "Found this one out walking after dark." He thumbed in Cress's direction.

Cress waved listlessly from the far side of the seat. Rick raised his chin. Julie stared, her small mouth curved downward.

"All right, then." Quinn lifted a palm, drove on.

Cress said, "That wasn't good."

"They don't care."

"Julie was bent."

Quinn patted her thigh. "Rick needs me even more than I need him."

Alone in the A-frame, Cress built a fire and sat down with a book, a thick popular history of the fourteenth century. She dozed off on the love seat. The phone made her jump. "Rick here," Rick Garsh said, and before she could say hello, he pushed on: "Think I'll be making the town runs from here on out. Appreciate your help this fall. I'll drop a check off tomorrow. I'll stick it under the mat if you're not home."

Eleven

She waited until after three, then walked alone. She did not mind at first. She liked to stick her nose in pine trees and had been too self-conscious to sniff them around Quinn. She lingered in the first meadow for a long time watching a rufous-sided woodpecker. How did it feel to bang your head so resoundingly against wood? To get in such a long, staccato, reverberative run?

A small sick feeling came over her at the Bauer cabin when he still had not materialized. Yesterday was a lot. Ten hours in each other's company. He probably needed a breather. Or he regretted putting his family's house on display. Or Rick Garsh had fired him, too. Or maybe—this cheered her up—he was working straight through to dinner, knowing he'd see her later, at poker.

Cress scalloped potatoes with chunks of ham and drove the hot casserole in her mother's silver-plated pan holder to DeeDee's, where Kevin was splitting logs on the porch with enviable ease. Inside, extra leaves were in the dining table, the poker chips and cards set out.

"You made so much," DeeDee said. "There's only seven tonight."

"Who bailed?"

"The brothers."

"What happened?"

"Who cares? I won't have to split the pot with Caleb for once."

"He leaves you half his winnings. More than half."

"I want all of them."

That sick sense came again, that Quinn probably regretted yesterday and now was pulling back. Because if anything else was wrong, he could've caught up with her on the trail or stopped by the A-frame to let her know. She'd been findable. Needing consolation, she turned to DeeDee. "Guess what, DeeDee? I'm seeing someone new. But it's a secret."

"Hardly," DeeDee said.

But she thought Cress meant Don Dare.

"Guess again," said Cress.

River Bob? Freddy? Boots Stahl?

"A hint," said Cress. "They couldn't come tonight."

"Not Caleb?"

"No, no. Not Caleb."

Cress expected a big DeeDee guffaw, incredulity, a hundred questions. Instead, DeeDee bent to take a chicken from the oven and clunked the roasting pan onto the stovetop. Keeping her back to Cress, she moved to the refrigerator, withdrew a head of iceberg. She set it on the cutting board, peeled off the outer leaves, and, picking up a large knife, split it with a juicy whack.

"What do you care?" said Cress.

"Must be a big-city thing."

"What's a big-city thing?"

"Sleeping with another woman's husband."

"DeeDee!" Cress cried out—and only then remembered that DeeDee's husband had left her for another woman.

"If you want approval for wrecking someone's marriage," DeeDee said, "you're barking up the wrong ponderosa pine."

"I'm not wrecking anyone's marriage," said Cress. "That's the last thing either of us wants. We're just friends. With a little sex thrown in. It's an interlude, like you and Kevin. Quinn's lonely here. And it's good for me, too, after Jakey."

As DeeDee carried the salad and Wishbone bottle out to the

table, Cress trailed her. "And I'm working like crazy, for the first time since school. This has helped in a weird way. Energized me. I've never had such a fertile burst."

"I'm sure Sylvia Morrow would be thrilled to know that."

"Since when are you all Moral Majority?"

"Since all along."

"It's not as if you don't have sex secrets."

"I keep Kevin secret," DeeDee said evenly, "so I don't get ribbed by my loudmouth boss for sleeping with his son. Who's single, like me."

Without really thinking about it, Cress realized, she had equated DeeDee's secret romance with her own; both seemed equally illicit and compromising. She saw now that they were not. Even so, DeeDee shouldn't come down so hard on her. She wasn't the adulterer. She'd broken no vows.

"You are older than Kevin," Cress said. "You have to admit, that's unconventional."

"Unconventional, maybe. But we're not hurting anyone."

"He is only nineteen."

"Eighteen's the age of consent."

"If you two are so guilt-free, why do you say you'll go to hell for it?"

"Because the only sanctified place for sex is within marriage."

"Then we're all evil!" Cress said. "Everyone on this mountain. Except the old folks. And the Garshes, God love 'em."

"Kevin and I may be fornicators, but we're not adulterers." DeeDee kept her broad back to Cress. "You're breaking a commandment."

"Is that what you say to Jakey about all his married bims?"

"Constantly."

"Oh, for God's sake." DeeDee's heathered blue cardigan presented an implacable expanse. "You know what? I'm not going to stay for poker," Cress said. "I'll get my pan tomorrow." The heathered shoulders shrugged.

She drove home past the Rodinger place. The windows of the small camp trailer glowed with their poignant yellow light. A blue Imperial with a white soft top sat in the driveway. Cress braked, rolled down her steamed-up window. A clank of dishes floated out to her on the frigid night air. A murmur of voices. Candy's trumpet bleat of a laugh.

Quinn intercepted her in the first meadow. She dodged his kiss.

The wives had surprised them with steaks and bakers. A boysenberry pie from Harvey's. On a whim, they'd parked the kids with Grandma, driven up.

No doubt they'd pulled on lacy underwear, too, Cress thought, and were extremely pleased with themselves. *Yoo-hoo! Guess who's here?*

"You're not mad at me," said Quinn. "Are you?"

She had no right to be angry—husbands and wives could see each other at will. "You might spare me the details."

"Hey—you think I liked them showing up unannounced?"

"What's not to like?"

"You think I liked spending a whole night within spitting distance of Candy? I didn't ask them to come. Why are you being like this?"

"I was looking forward to one kind of evening," Cress said quietly, "and I had a very different kind of evening. I was disappointed."

"I was, too." He put his arms around her waist.

She twisted away. "But you had company."

Franny told her to try the golf course, Beech Creek Country Club, which had a busy holiday banquet season. "The banquet manager's Dalia Oliveras."

Dalia told her to come in that very night. A waitress had quit.

"If we like each other," Dalia said, "I'll keep you busy through New Year's."

Cress drove down the mountain to serve dinner to a private party of golfers from San Diego. The six older retired couples drank ten bottles of wine and left for their rooms by nine-thirty. Cress was home by eleven. The next day, Saturday, she worked a wedding with a hundred guests; the dancing lasted until ten, the cleanup till midnight. On her way home, she stopped by the Sawyer Inn for Donna's last set.

"We just had a big fight," Don Dare whispered. "She says I can't go to Family Night without her, or poker."

"Her ex drove her crazy," said Cress.

"I am not him! I have never been like that," he said. "I don't have the time or the energy or the *interest* to have more than one woman at a time. Speaking of which—how long have you and Quinn Morrow been up the tubes?"

"What do you mean 'up the tubes'? Says who?"

"My supersuspicious, eagle-eyed girlfriend. And I see you two out walking from the Crags."

"It's probably over, anyway. But Donna must really hate me now."

"So long as you're not with me, she doesn't care."

Working at Beech Creek wasn't half as demoralizing as the Dinner Plate had been; her hours were varied, with banquets clustered around weekends and a few easy luncheons during the week. Dalia Oliveras was a competent and calm manager, and the head waitress, Lisette, the pretty blond wife of an apricot farmer, called Cress a godsend. The owner of Beech Creek was a golf-mad oilman who had made his fortune selling drilling equipment; Beech Creek Country Club was a tax write-off, a hobby, and a folly. Nobody expected profits, and a relaxed, carefree mood trickled down to the employees, who ate the same prime rib and chicken Kiev as the members. Shift drinks came in twenty-ounce to-go cups.

Cress worked the Kiwanis Club Christmas party, then the

Junior League's, Snap-on Tools', the Sparkville Boosters'. She didn't see Quinn all week, he didn't even know about her new job. This time apart, she thought, was practice for their ending, or possibly was the ending. Although nothing seemed over. Quinn's heavy-browed scowl floated before her as she wound in and out of the curves in the dappled sunlight of morning, and later, again, when she drove up the mountain in the star-strung freezing dark. Serving a martini or carrying out salads—she could carry five at once—a sudden shift of light, a twinge in her thoughts, and she knew: *He's thinking of me.*

"You *are* still here."

"Where else would I be?"

His gloominess made her playful. She danced away from him, or started to. It was eight o'clock, and for the first time in six nights, she wasn't working. He caught her wrist. "Ah, Cressida." He kissed her, pressed teeth on her lower lip.

"Let go," she said.

He freed her wrist and sat heavily on the wicker love seat. "I don't blame you," he said. "I've cost you a job, and for what?"

She stood away from him. "I've been working a new job. That's all."

"When I married," Quinn said, "I was only eighteen. I made decisions then that have to last my whole life—at Annette's age, basically. I've had to give myself some leeway. Or I'd be out of my mind."

"I'm not your first"—Cress considered how to say it— "outside interest?"

"I was married twelve years before the first time. When I started working away from home . . . But nothing ever counted before."

"You never fell in love."

"The last one, down south, we enjoyed each other, and she started wanting more. But I told her from the start, nothing could come of it."

"How long ago was this?" said Cress.

"Two, three years now."

"Do you ever talk to her or write?"

He looked away, shrugged: he'd reached his limit of disclosure.

"And now there's me." Cress spoke lightly.

"It's not the same. You must know that."

"I don't know anything," she said.

"I never talked to anybody like I talk to you."

Ah yes. Her talent. Men talked to her. Even men who didn't
talk, talked to her. It usually meant more to them than it did
to her.

She smiled, and grasping his head, she kissed the crinkles
by his eye. He caught her hand. She allowed this for a moment,
then sprang away.

"Look." She swung a plastic bag of fresh chestnuts from the
Italian grocery. He'd never eaten one and didn't know what they
were.

"Come," she said, and showed him how to prick the hard
shiny skins, nestle the nuts in the coals, turn them with tongs.
They burned their fingers peeling them and their tongues eating them. "Like apple-flavored potatoes," said Quinn.

A loud crack and an ashy burst made them jump. Quinn
shoved her behind him, and still partly crouching to hold her
down, he faced the door.

"Quinn!" Cress tugged at his pant leg and started to laugh.
"A chestnut exploded! Just a chestnut. Insufficiently pricked!"

He sat heavily on the love seat. She was still on the floor by
his knees. "I thought maybe we had a crime-of-passion deal going on," he said.

"But Sylvia'd never shoot—"

"She's a damn fine shot. Taught her myself."

Quinn refused any more chestnuts, as if they'd offended him.
Snow swept against the window. He slid a hand under Cress's
hair, squeezed the back of her neck. "Please," he said. "I'm beg-
ging, here."

Quinn and Caleb left the mountain three days before Christmas and wouldn't be back until after the first of the year. Cress's parents came up for two days, then went to Mazatlán. Cress barely saw them; she worked every night until Christmas, including Christmas Eve.

Twelve

She told Tillie and Edgar to bring chains, and of course they
didn't. They called from the lodge to say that their VW station
wagon was nose-first in a snowbank a mile down the hill. Some
travelers had given them a lift to the lodge, and now they needed
someone with a truck to pull them out. Cress told them to go
inside and ask for Jakey or Kevin. Tillie called back to say that
neither was around, so Cress called Abe Johnson and waited. An
hour later, their VW was spinning its wheels in the elbow of her
driveway.

With Tillie and Edgar were two more friends from Cressida's high-school days, Miriam and Dora, plus Dora's husband,
Lucca.

"The famous cabin," said Dora.

"You never came up in high school?" said Miriam. "I was up
twice."

"Just once for me," said Tillie.

"You could've come up more," said Cress.

"Except your mother hated me," said Tillie.

Dora said, "My parents wouldn't let me go so far away."

Edgar and Lucca hauled in grocery bags and duffels.

Three more women were on their way, Rochelle Boyer and
the Ellis sisters, Maddie and Lina. Cressida had not been sure
how many were coming, or who. She'd let Tillie do the arrang-
ing so as not to run up the phone bill. All the women were
friends from high-school art classes. Except for Tillie, Cress
hadn't spoken to any of them since her going-away party in late
July. She was a delinquent letter writer, too.

Edgar set to work frying spices for a lamb curry. Much was made of the snow; Cress found old sleds and saucers in the basement, and they took them right outside the cabin and slid down to the meadows between the trees, trudging back up again and again until the sun dunked behind Shale Mountain. Cress built a fire; they drank wine and waited for the curry.

Tillie demanded to see all of Cress's drawings and sketches and, paging through them, said, "Coming along, coming along . . . Can I have this one?" She stabbed a rock study with her finger.

"Take it," said Cress.

Miriam, a business major, had landed a job in the ad department of *City and State,* a glossy new monthly with offices in Westwood. "The publisher's this iconoclast, a journalist with an MBA who calls himself a publisher/editor," she told them at dinner. "He wants big investigative pieces, but also to make money. So ads and editorial work together. I get to suggest story ideas! Tillie's applying for a job in the art department. I'm trying to talk Maddie into coming on as an editor, and you should apply too, Cress. They need editors."

Cress doubted that her stint as the editor of an obscure university-published economics journal—no ads—would count for much at *City and State.*

"No thanks," said Maddie, who had a master's in journalism from Berkeley and was now interning at the *LA Weekly.* "I still believe in a firewall between editorial and publishing. Advertising shouldn't even *talk* to editorial."

"Doesn't hurt to throw advertisers a bone now and then," Miriam said. "Sure helps with ad sales. It's just for the front of the book: gizmos, fashion, decor. I wrote a fifty-word squib on a vertical chicken roaster—and got an ad!"

"But readers will think you liked the roaster," cried Maddie.

"The roaster's fantastic! It cooks the chicken upright, so all the skin gets crisp," said Miriam. "Seriously, Maddie, you know subscriptions and newsstand sales can't pay for a magazine."

"That's no excuse for sneaking in ads posing as articles."

"Look at it this way," said Miriam. "The guy wants his writers to make a living. And why shouldn't he make a profit?"

"Not that kind of profit," said Maddie. "God, you sound like Milton Friedman. I just saw him on PBS extolling the virtues of sweatshops!"

Cress kept quiet; her friends were all out there making headway in the wild-and-woolly marketplace. She could join them, once the damn diss was done.

After dinner, they walked to the lodge in the moonlight. Tillie was keen to meet Jakey, but he was still not around. Waiting for the bathroom, Tillie did befriend a pretty thirty-two-year-old veterinary assistant from Encino and brought her over to their table.

"But she's a bim!" Cress hissed in Tillie's ear.

"I know!" said Tillie. "She came up to spend a week with him—rented a whole cabin! And then he had to go down the hill on family business."

"That just means the bull is tending his lower pastures. The poor thing."

The next day, they sledded and lolled around the A-frame, reading and drawing. Cress had to work a dinner dance at the club, so she sent her friends to eat dinner at the lodge. By the time she came home, the house was dark. She filled the percolator with water. Tillie wandered in, wearing Cress's robe. "Who's Quinn?"

Cress counted six spoons of coffee into the percolator's filter. Come morning, the first one up could just plug it in. "A carpenter up here. Why?"

"He called a few minutes ago."

"What'd he want?"

"To talk to you. Is this someone I should know about? Another one of your virile working guys?"

If Tillie hadn't taken such a taunting, lascivious tone, Cress might have been more frank. But she wouldn't sacrifice Quinn for Tillie's amusement. Best keep that sweet small corner of her life to herself. "He and his brother work up here. Both married, by the way."

"Why is he calling so late?"

Cress put the coffee can back in the cupboard. "People know when I get home from work. Did he want me to check his trailer? Hand me that sponge, would you?"

"He didn't say." Tillie reached into the sink. "But God, what a low, sexy voice. You should make him read you to sleep."

Breakfast the next morning was complicated by an old waffle iron and a breaker thrown when someone turned on the bathroom wall heater at the same time. Then the women sat around the kitchen table and made monoprints with art supplies Tillie had brought up. They inked glass plates, laid paper over the ink, drew trees, rocks, each other, and peeled off the images. They talked about Jakey, who'd finally shown up—"So adorable! So appealing!" He'd bought them all drinks, then cozied up to the women in turn, and chatted with Edgar for half an hour. "He ignored the poor vet tech for the longest time," Tillie said. "But he finally made his way over to her."

"We've unanimously decided," Miriam said to Cress, "that Don Dare should dump that hick folksinger and get together with you."

"He's so not my type! And Donna's not a folksinger, actually."

"Well, he's definitely my type," said Miriam, who was single and looking. "I like Jakey, too. Which makes me think I should widen my sights to include more working-class guys. Carpenters, small businessmen, like that."

"Neither Don nor Jakey is exactly working-class," said Cress.
Miriam said, "Well you'd hardly call them professionals!"

Cress had the day off, so they drove in two cars to Globe Rock for
its view of snow-choked forests and Camel Crags frosted like
cupcakes. A fast, furious snowball fight broke out on the big bald
pate of the rock, the teams random, this side versus that. Cress
stood up to warn everyone again about running too far down
the rock—"You could start sliding and never stop!"—and took a
ball right in her eye, a big red shock that stopped the game.

For dinner, Tillie had braised a rump roast all day with ten
onions and two cans of beer. Cress made coleslaw and biscuits;
after such gamboling in cold fresh air, their hunger was shock-
ing. They stayed in and drank wine and played charades and
one by one drifted off to bed. As she had for three nights now,
Cress slept downstairs, on the window seat, that unforgiving,
narrow little shelf.

After the beds were stripped and the duffels and totes and grocery sacks hauled down to the cars, her friends departed. It was
December 31, everyone had a party to get to. Cress herself was
scheduled to work at the country club's New Year's Eve bash.
Her eye, at first faintly blackened from the snowball, grew more
colorful by the hour. The morning was bright, the roads clear,
the thermometer read sixty-three. Nobody would skid into snow-
banks today. Cress waved her friends off without regret. She'd
spent her high school years yearning to be with them; she'd
moved to Braithway Court to do so. But she could only take so
much. The years of childhood exile up here had trained her to
solitude after all.

The world clicked with the sound of water dripping off trees
and eaves onto the softening snow.

"Another perfect day in paradise!" Don Dare called from the
new house.

Cress went upstairs and took a nap—she'd be up late tonight. Jakey woke her with a phone call at two. "Big boulder and mudslide on the highway just below the back entrance," he said. "Nobody's getting in or out till Monday, which is as soon as the state can get up here." It was Thursday.

Cress phoned Beech Creek, told Dalia about the rock, then walked down to see it. Elephant-gray fine-grained granite with veins of white quartz, the oblong boulder sat high on a bulging skid of mud: God's shrug. Cress sketched it from two different angles; the surging shape suggested her grandmother's old swamp-green Hudson Hornet. When she tried to climb over the slide for another perspective, she sank to her thigh in pebbly mud.

Her friends had chipped in money to pay for a housekeeper so Cress wouldn't have to do all the cleaning and laundry. Franny arrived at four-thirty. "Who popped you one?" she said, lightly touching Cress's eye.

They made the beds together. "Brian's stuck down in Sawyer. Donna was the last person to make it up before the rock," Franny said, "which is good, since she's singing tonight. DeeDee and the boys are down, so I told Jakey I'd work her shift tonight, although it won't be many people at the party now, with the rock. Jakey's doing a six-buck steak for everyone stuck up here for New Year's."

Franny shuffled through the loose stack of monoprints and drawings left behind on the kitchen table—portraits the friends had made of each other, a few snowscapes. Cress pointed out Tillie's portrait of Edgar. "That's my favorite. I like her line, how playful it is."

Franny looked hard at the drawing, traced the line with her finger.

Strands of yellow crepe paper looped from the beams. Reggie Thornton pinch-hit as bartender. Jakey served forty-some steaks, with black-eyed peas and greens. Cress, Franny, and Donna sat with the carpenters. Donna spoke softly in Cress's ear: "At the

Sawyer Inn, Saturday night, Quinn and Caleb came in with their wives to hear me sing. They were really living it up—cocktails, steaks, more cocktails. Sylvia only had one greyhound and she literally slid under the table."

"That's exactly what Quinn said would happen if she drank."

"They kept dragging her up, and she kept slipping down again. It was kind of weird. I mean, why didn't he take her home?"

When Donna went onstage, Jakey took her seat. "Dr. Hartley!" He crushed into Cress. "Helluva shiner there! Hey, that friend of yours, Tillie, she's a live wire: 'You can't put one over on me, Jakey Yates, I've heard *allll* about you.' "

"Oh dear."

"I liked her. And all your friends. Nice people. That climatologist, Edgar, the Paki? Interesting guy."

The vet tech was sipping a green drink at the bar and giving Cress evil green looks. When Jakey moved on, Cress stood, stretched, and said her good nights. Happy New Year, Happy New Year, everyone! It was ten o'clock.

Cress was home only a few minutes and still fiddling with the fire when she heard drumming on the glass door.

"What are you doing here?" she said, sliding it open. "Why aren't you with that nice, pretty animal handler? Seeing how she came up to see you and rented that whole place and all."

"She told me she came up to cross-country ski." Jakey handed Cress a bottle of champagne, shrugged out of his coat.

"Can we drink this out of plastic?" she said, reading the label. "Not that we have any choice."

As she peeled off the lead seal, Jakey gathered her up. "I'm crazy about you, Hartley, you know that," he said into her neck. "Always will be."

"I know, Jakey," she said. "But . . ."

"It's New Year's Eve," he said. "Who wants to be with strangers! Auld lang syne, Hartley!"

She laughed and relaxed. She too could do what she wanted. She too could really live it up.

The phone rang sometime after midnight, waking her. Jakey rolled over, went back to sleep. Cress padded downstairs, lifted the receiver. "I wanted to hear your voice," Quinn whispered. "I'm in my mom's bedroom again. Can't really talk. We'll have a happy new year, Cressida, once I get back."

Or that's what she thought he said, or hoped he said, but he was whispering and there was static and she was half asleep.

During the boulder's siege, the days were sunny and short. Snow melted. Nights bristled with frost. Mornings loosed sprays of diamonds. The clack of water dripping into snow was continuous. Cress worked on a chapter, but mostly she drifted, read about the Black Death, and made herself small bits to eat: cinnamon toast, a sliced apple with cheddar cheese. By Saturday, the snow was mostly gone, and she walked her full loop, the world re-revealed, saturated and darker, spongy underfoot.

She felt delicately buoyed by her discovery that she preferred, even required, long stretches of her own company. She was pleased, too, that she hadn't offered her most recent love life to Tillie or the others as a topic of conversation. She'd kept Quinn for herself.

Monday morning a series of concussions rattled the A-frame's plate glass. A strand of white smoke spiraled above the trees to the south. Later, on her walk, she visited where the boulder once sat, now a mud-colored stain on the black road, a scattering of fist-sized gray rocks swept off to the shoulder.

The brothers returned on black roads bathed in snowmelt.

She ran into Caleb at the lodge; he was buying Bisquick.

"With the cats away, the mice wreaked havoc," he said. "What's with the eye?"

"Snowball," said Cress. "Enjoy your holidays?"

"A lot of eating. Took the kids out to the drags."

"The drags?"

"Drag races," he said.

She'd never known anyone who went to drag races. Dubious, she said, "Was that fun?"

"Had a ball," he said. "How's the drawing?"

"I've been sketching a lot of rocks."

"I'd like to see your work sometime."

"Anytime." She didn't ask about Quinn, and Caleb didn't mention him, either.

Something threw her: a new hat. Dark leather, handmade, stiff: the new version of his old one. She could see now that the hat was something you'd buy at the kind of craft fair that sold quilted Bible covers, wind chimes, and finger puppets. She grieved for the broken-in, chewed-up old model with its coiled brim and distinctive, lopsided silhouette. No need to ask who'd replaced it.

Snow blew through the door as he came inside. Cress poured bourbon into her mother's plastic tumblers. He sat beside her on the wicker love seat. The low fire pulsed and flared. "God, it's been forever," he said.

He pulled a wad of gray-and-blue tissue paper from his jacket pocket. "For you."

She hadn't seen this small, perfect donkey in his garage. The mane was finely articulated and tinted dark, the hooves dainty, the eyes shiny and black. She turned it over: two tiny teats. A female. "Hard picking out the right one for you," he said. "Singling them out, they start getting symbolic. I know you liked the beaver . . ."

"But you settled on the ass."

"I used black onyx beads for the eyes," he said.

"I love it," she said. They clicked glasses and he put his down. Taking her face in his hands, he examined her eye, now yellowish, with green-and-purple tints. He kissed it, then her mouth. She inhaled his ferny cologne, tasted his finely pebbled tongue, received the brush of his thick trimmed beard. He kissed her for a long time, through the first exuberant swells of emotion to a shining calm. Any minute, Cress thought, they would rise and climb the stairs and shed their clothes. But Quinn kept kissing her, his patience exquisite. In time, her lips grew numb and her desire receded; she opened her eyes and read the faded spines of books on the shelf and watched the long spiderwebs hanging from the rafters; thickened by dust, the strands swung slowly in the updrafts of heat from the stove. And still, he kissed her.

Each adjustment to their embrace caused the wicker to drily creak—never was a love seat less conducive to lovemaking than this wobbly pine-and-straw scaffold. She shut her eyes again and drifted languidly, daydreamed a blur of yellow meadows, blue snowfields. The fire sputtered; logs crumbled into coals with a sigh, and out of nowhere, it seemed, desire slammed back into her. Her womb twanged, the pain sharp, clarifying, and eye-opening, literally.

Over Quinn's shoulder, she saw a snow-dusted figure at the sliding glass door. Bundled, behatted, he'd raised a hand to knock. She shut her eyes and wished the apparition away, to never-have-been. She kissed Quinn with new determination—to distract. When she checked again, the visitor was gone.

Quinn stood, and led her up the stairs.

Thirteen

Snow fell and stayed, and more snow fell on top of that, and more yet. The world quieted, lost detail, shadows turned blue. Cress found skis in the basement, wooden Nordic skis, her parents' apparently, but hardly used. John Bird had taught her how, and they had skied cross-country over Midwestern fields, in leafless woods. She fit into her mother's pair and quickly picked up the old rhythms; Quinn, with thick socks, could use her father's set and, with his unusual sense of balance, he skied gracefully his first time out. For a scant hour and a half of light in the late afternoons they looped in wide slaloms to the meadow, and across the meadows' open expanses, then followed fire roads. The only other tracks belonged to chipmunks, rabbits, and hopping jays. They met no other skiers until at dusk one day, out toward Camel Crags, they skied in someone else's grooves and met Jakey and Ondine coming back. Jakey was ruddy from exercise. Ondine, fair and lithe in an ivory snowsuit, glowed.

Beautiful, lovely, the four said. Perfect time to be out. So quiet.

Getting cold, though. Whoops! You okay? Falling's part of the sport.

The brothers hosted no more card games in the trailer. Nor were there poker nights at DeeDee's.

Cress saw DeeDee only at the lodge. They were civil but not friendly. And then Cress stopped seeing her at the lodge, too.

"Hey, where's DeeDee?" she asked Jakey.

"Quit on me," he said. "The boys were missing too much school. Rented her house out to River Bob and Freddy. Went to live with her mom in Visalia. Took a job at the trophy factory."

Sylvia and Candy, he said, were bringing the kids up Saturday morning to play in the snow. "So you know," he said. "Arriving Saturday, leaving Sunday."

"You can't all fit in the trailer," Cress said.

Caleb's family would be camping in the Rodinger house, in sleeping bags. Sylvia and Evan would be in the trailer, with him.

"Did you invite them?"

"It was their idea."

"Will I see you tonight?" she said.

"Got the trailer to clean. Some deep bachelor squalor to dispatch."

"Have fun," she said.

"Don't be like that," he said.

"Like what?"

"Sarcasm doesn't suit you," he said.

She drove down the hill with Don Dare to see Donna sing. The Sawyer Inn was a two-story wood-sided building at the edge of town. The restaurant was in front, the lounge in the back, a dozen hotel rooms upstairs. Donna packed the place: in among the hotel guests and various locals, Cress recognized Beech Creek Country Club members and a famous painter from Los Angeles with his glamorous young wife. ("They have a place up on Noah Mountain," Don said.) Donna sang "Blue Bayou," then "Okie from Muskogee," which provoked stomping and hollering from the cowboys and loggers at the bar. She called a mandolin-playing sheriff onstage, then Mason the banjo player, and finally a dentist. "I see Felton the Extractor's brought his fancy Martin ghee-tar tonight—" Donna said. "Well, pull it out, Dr. F., show us how you do!"

Afterward—it was past one o'clock!—the banjo and mando-lin players came over to Donna's house. She lived on the river south of Sawyer in a raffish neighborhood of old vacation shacks. Her roommate, a cheerful, very large young woman named Norma, had baked chocolate chip cookies. Don built a fire in the woodstove, and there was another hour of music and enough drinking so that even Cress sang the choruses.

In a sleeping bag on Donna's sofa, Cress thought of another sleeping bag—and Evan only a few feet away.

Later still, she was awakened by faint swipes of a guitar chord and bawled words—*Donna! Donna! Please, baby. Let me in!* Felton the Extractor was serenading! Don Dare emerged from Donna's bedroom buttoning his jeans. "Occupational hazard," he told Cress. "Half the guys in any audience fall in love with her." Don went out, talked to Felton. Got the expen-sive Martin back in its case, the lovelorn dentist back behind the wheel.

In the morning, Cress and Donna drank coffee at a picnic table while Don reinforced Donna's deck railing. The Hapsaw gurgled and gushed just beyond the back gate. "Quinn's wife is sure around a lot with her pies and snow dates," said Donna. "I mean, how bad could their marriage be?"

"He never said it was bad."

"I wouldn't put up with it," said Donna. "The Meadows is your territory. He has no right to bring her there. That's disre-spectful to you."

Cress and Don drove back up the mountain around one. Just above the Hapsaw Lodge, they passed the blue Imperial heading down, dark-haired Sylvia at the wheel, the plump sister-in-law sitting shotgun, the children vague silhouettes in the backseat.

"Day shift heading home," said Don Dare. "Night shift on the way."

—

"Any coffee made?" he asked, hat in hand.

She hadn't expected him so soon, with the flush of family still on him. "I could make some. Or shall we ski?"

It was their time to ski, three in the afternoon, the shadows long and blue. "Not today," he said.

"There's bourbon, too."

"I really shouldn't drink," he said. "I stopped for years. I thought I could manage a little. But I can tell. I'm tapering back on."

His gaze was frank and direct. As he came inside, she saw a change in how he carried himself: he seemed unburdened, easier, much more adult. Where had all that pain gone?

"Coffee it is," she chirped, and busied herself with the kettle, the tap, the Yuban can. He poked the fire, added a log. They sat, finally, side by side, on their usual wicker perch, curled over cups.

"This probably isn't any good for you." He leaned into her for a moment.

"Probably not," said Cress. "Or for you."

"It has been," he said. "In ways I wouldn't expect you to understand."

"Try me."

He glowered at the fire. "Last night Sylvia wanted me to come up and get you to have dinner with us."

"And you said . . ."

"I didn't think you were home."

"I wasn't."

"Would you have come?" he said.

"Are you kidding?"

"She knows we're friends," he said.

"One look at us together and she'd know a lot more." Cress stood. "What were you thinking?"

"I saw it as a way we could keep on. After I come off the mountain."

"I'd say that the family-friend option expired long about Thanksgiving."

They drank coffee. The plate glass made its cooling, cracking noise.

He said, "The longer this goes on, the harder it's going to be."

"I know."

"I really don't want to hurt you," he said.

"Good."

"But if we keep going, that's what's going to happen."

"I know."

He hunched now, with his elbows on his knees, face in his hands.

"Louder," said Cress.

"I said, We should probably shut this thing down."

She had been expecting some sort of announcement like this from the start. She'd imagined it as a blow, a shove into sadness, but in fact, it gave her a small lift. Here was a way over the fence. They could part, and do so more easily than she'd thought possible. She scanned herself for disappointment or pain and found only agreement. Yes! Be done now! Why not stop before feelings grew unmanageable? "I think that's best," she said.

His trademark sharp, shocked glance hit with a sexual pang. But she wasn't frightened off. "I really do," she said.

"I'm sorry," he said. "I didn't want it to end like this."

She tapped his knee. "This isn't a bad ending."

She gathered their plastic coffee cups and washed them in hot water with a big squirt of soap. The water up here was naturally soft, so the suds were dense and not easily dispersed. She dried her hands and dialed Donna's number—Donna would so approve!—but the line was busy. On second thought, she didn't want to dissipate her resolve with talk. She felt strong, clear. She paged through *New Yorkers* till dark, then made herself a toasted cheese sandwich and read about excessive consumerism during the Black Death. She closed the screen on the fireplace, the two small chain-link curtains that made the fire seem like a play on a stage. She went up to bed, her mood steady, sturdy. For weeks now, this break had glimmered, a faint gray streak on the horizon. Better to have it over and done, when the cost was only a manageable, almost pleasurable ache.

There was something off, something unformed in what he'd proposed, an immaturity or denseness: Did he really think she'd be a family friend?

Later, drifting toward sleep, she came again to the old dogged confusions and crisscrossed tracks of her future. John Bird would take her back, no doubt, as unaffectedly as he had let her go. *You're a bit of a pilgrim,* he'd said when she announced she was moving alone to Pasadena and not to Minneapolis with him. Actually, it was worse than that: he'd said: *There's still some Gypsy in you.* Yipes. Never mind. She could visit Sharon in London or her old drawing teacher in Tucson. An idea would take hold—as one did when she'd moved to California, and another did when she'd moved up here. She need only keep an open mind, and wait. At least, here at the Meadows, she'd had adventures. Adventures in love: the phrase made her smile.

In the morning, still in bed, she tentatively probed yesterday's events. She found a general, faintly fluish ache. She'd miss his low voice, the reliable pleasure of his physical presence. His own tincture of sawdust and bad cologne.

But Quinn was a dope. As if she'd sit on the cheap ugly couch with the ever-flowing mill wheel and chat! *What lovely teacups, Sylvia. What clean counters and floors. Congrats on the sports trophies, kids. So when's your dad getting home?*

She skied alone in the silent, radiant white world. Out near Camel Crags a coyote with a thick reddish coat trotted amiably alongside her for a full minute before he struck off into the woods. Another day, she watched an enormous pinecone lurch across the snowy road, its invisible engine a gray squirrel. Omens, good ones, she thought. She'd made the right decision.

By Spearmint Creek, in fading light, she met another skier. Tom Streeter had a rifle on his back, a pistol in a shoulder holster, a sheathed knife on his belt. A pair of binoculars swung from his neck. "Seen that six-pointer come through here?" he asked, studying the tracks. Cress had a hard time speaking; she wasn't used to encountering heavily armed men when alone in the woods. Tom's flat gray eyes flickered at her. "Seen anything else I should know about?"

Cress waved vaguely upstream. "I saw a deer eat a fish once, over there."

Her parents came up for a meeting with Rick Garsh and the finish carpenters to choose cabinet doors, banister styles, hardware, and tile. Cress retreated to her loft bedroom under the pretext of working. She sat at her desk and read the file for Chapter Three until she had to take a nap. She sprawled on the bed, then jerked awake to see her mother standing down at the foot.

"Sorry, I thought you were working."

"I bored myself to sleep," said Cress. "It's part of the drill."

"Will you be done soon?" her mother asked.

"Sure hope so." She did hope.

"And what will you do then?"

"I don't know, Mom. Find a job."

"From here?"

"I'll move somewhere. Soon as I save up enough."

"With the phone bills you've racked up, that won't be easy."

"I said I'd pay. How much?" Cress swung her legs off the bed. "I'll write you a check right now."

"I'll look at the bills and let you know. Will you go back to Pasadena?"

"I don't know, Mom."

"But you're on track."

Mmmm. The track: degree, job, husband, babies, PTA president—or, given her credentials, treasurer.

Cress heard her parents talking before they left for the meeting with Rick. Her mother was leaning toward one of the more expensive knob styles. Don't forget, her father said, to add 10 percent to the price. Sylvia said that she could never forget, not so long as she was married to him; just as she could never forget the price of gas or postage stamps, a gallon of milk. Just this once, though, she would like to own something because it was pretty and felt good to touch, something that wouldn't tarnish or break overnight, something appealing for reasons other than it was the cheapest one available.

Sam said that Rick Garsh would be more than happy to provide her with all manner of fancy knobs and cabinet doors, large and small appliances. If she liked, Rick could spend all her money in no time flat.

Cress stayed in bed until they left the house.

Her mother returned alone from the meeting. "I have to say, the new place is more beautiful than anywhere we've ever lived. Though your father is fit to be tied that it's costing so much more than he thought. He and Rick are over there going through the line items on the invoice, one by one. Way, way, *way* too much tension for me."

"Those two are giving each other a run for the money," Cress said.

"Neither had any idea what he was getting into!" Her mother gave a bark of laughter and hit her wedding ring on the table. "This new house will be luxurious, though it's nowhere near as extravagant as Rick would like it to be."

"You should have it exactly the way *you* want it."

"I pick my battles. It's so hard for your father to part with a penny. Now, Cress—have you met the finish carpenter yet?"

Cress stilled. "Which one?"

"The main guy, the older one. He has the most beautiful, deep voice. He should be on the radio with that voice."

"I sort of like the younger one better," said Cress.

"Homely as a mud fence!" her mother said.

"But smart and very funny. They're both pretty backwoods."

"Real diamonds in the rough!" said Sylvia. "Though the main one—his eyes are really quite remarkable. Such an unusual light green."

"I thought you liked his voice."

"Oh, that voice . . . you should hear it, Cress."

"I've heard it. You know he's married, Mom."

"Oh honey, I wasn't suggesting anything like that. I just want you to hear that basso profundo. I wonder if he sings."

Plump drops of condensation rolled down the lodge windows. On her plate: a slab of gravied roast beef, a shoe-sized baked potato, broccoli with fluorescent-orange cheese sauce. Family Night again. She was at a long table with Don, Brian and Franny, River Bob, and Freddy. Onstage, Donna sang "Coal Miner's Daughter." Quinn and Caleb, leathered up in vests, hats, and boots, sat with Rick and Julie Garsh. How dare he drink beer, laugh, eat with them! Cress hadn't spoken to him in twelve days.

"Where're you going?" Franny said.

She'd stood up without knowing it. "Home."

She slammed around the A-frame for a pen, a pad of paper, bourbon, ice. She sat to write in ink the final imprecations, the words that could never be rescinded, that eliminated any chance of reconciliation—or goodwill. *The Garshes, Quinn— really? Are you so whorish?* Too ad hominem: he wouldn't read past that. She crumpled the paper, tossed it (aim perfect) into the fire. *Dear Quinn, I thought our time together was something to hold close. But seeing you suck up to Rick and Julie Garsh tonight—exuding all that phony mountain man bonhomie—made me sick to my stomach. How I ever let you . . .* The sliding glass door rumbled on its tracks. Her pen stopped. Quick! Crumple and toss. Aim perfect.

"I hated being at that table. With those awful people. And you so near."

"Don't." He'd reached to touch her face. "Why were you sitting with them?"

"Caleb and I met Rick to go over the supply list, then Julie showed up." He tried, and failed, to grab her wrist. "I can't be up here and not talk to you."

He had on his good leather jacket and hat. Cold air bloomed off him, and that faux-musk scent. "Talk away," she said.

"I miss our time together. Our hard bed."

"You'll live." She put the kitchen table between them. "What—you want to start again, only to stop in a few weeks? We've already come this far. Let's keep going."

"I haven't come an inch." Quinn took off his hat, raked his hair. "I am not in good shape. Every day gets a little worse."

Because of her? Cress wondered. How marvelous was she? "What makes you think it will be any easier later on?"

"It won't. But we'll be apart. Here, I can't bear it. Having you so close. Skiing out there without me."

She'd been stricter with herself, mostly. And maybe not as hard-hit.

"You can borrow the skis anytime you like," she said.

"Goddamn the skis."

From these few feet, she considered him anew: his aging, swarthy skin and rocky temper, the coarseness of his hair; his creased, darkening brow. All that sadness. Having him here, in her house again, was a relief, and gave her comfort, despite all qualms. His voice buzzed in her bones, quickened her heart. She yearned to touch him. He lived so easily in his body, like a loping coyote or deer, graceful and keenly alert. But he didn't even pretend that he wanted her for the long haul, which, finally, made him not so interesting and allowed her some remove. "So what is it that you're after? Another night? Another month of hanging out, or however long you're here?"

One palm swiveled outward.

"It can't be like before," she said.

"I won't pester you so much," said Quinn.

"That's not it," said Cress. "I want to be clear about the future. When it's over, that's it. I won't be stopping by for pie or family chats."

"I get it."

"And she can't come up here again. Ever. This is my neck of the woods."

He moved with a soft ruck of leather. "Fair enough."

She thought that she would never again inhale that mix of soap and sawdust and tinny cologne, never clasp his work-muscled shoulders and arms, brace her forehead against that straight bar of collarbone. Never grab the coarse, black-brown hair wired with white or glimpse that roan tooth he so assiduously hid. Lovely to be flung over and around him again, his familiar, lived-in body.

Fourteen

They skied to the big rocks. They met again on the wicker love seat, passed a plastic cup of bourbon, climbed the stairs to the unyielding bed. He went home, as usual, with Caleb early Friday afternoon.

Over the weekend, Cress worked a Ducks Unlimited banquet, where one of the attendees set up a table to sell his tiny, elegant watercolors—his many attempts at duck stamp art. Cress spent her share of the pooled cash tip on a two-by-four-inch portrait in jewel tones of a floating red-breasted merganser. A belated Christmas present, it was small enough to keep hidden, and generic enough, should it be discovered, not to arouse suspicion. She wrapped it cleverly, in a kitchen match box, so he'd slide it open and see: quack, quack.

Only he didn't appear Sunday night at his usual time. Nor did he ski on Monday or stroll up later that night. Ditto Tuesday: no Quinn. Annoyed, yet determined not to stalk, Cress did ascertain that his truck was at the trailer. And the Rodinger house emitted the usual banging and sawing. When Wednesday passed with no sign of him, she didn't know what to think.

Thursday, she had to work a luncheon at Beech Creek. She'd pulled on green rubber boots to walk down her unplowed driveway when Quinn stepped inside the A-frame. His face was pinched, clayey. "What happened?" she said.

"Caleb's gone," he said.

"What do you mean *gone*?" She gargled it.

"He left. Took another job, down the hill."

She felt the blow. "I'll make some coffee," she said. "I have time."

She put the water on, then had trouble separating a filter from the stack, her hand trembling from the fright. "Will you go too?"

"I'll finish up here." He still stood by the door, as if unwilling to enter. "We did a big push to finish everything I needed him for. The rest, and your folks' house, I can manage. I haven't slept more'n three hours since Sunday."

"I was beginning to wonder . . ." Cress had made popcorn last night and the smell—the oil a little off—hung in the room. "I'm sorry," she added. "You two were having such a good time."

"For a while. Candy didn't like him being up here. Out of her clutches."

"And he knew," Cress said. "He came up one night and saw us."

"I wondered," said Quinn. "He got pretty tight-jawed when I started back skiing with you."

As if skiing was the issue.

Guilt drearied the air. "I'm sorry," she said again. Quinn looked drawn, old, bruised under his eyes. Her own face, she thought, so wide and flat and never beautiful in the gentlest light, must seem starkly plain. She was self-conscious, too, about her work clothes, the ivory polo shirt and dull navy skirt, the rubber boots.

"I don't want coffee," said Quinn. "I have to get some sleep."

He saw her to her car without touching her or kissing her goodbye.

Curling down the mountain to Beech Creek, she felt chastened and faintly ill with shame, as if she and Quinn had been on a long and merry drunk, then abruptly forced to sober up and see themselves in the harsh light of day. As Caleb saw them. Misbehaving. Incautious. Poised to cause real pain.

And she'd liked Caleb first, and more. He was sunnier, cleverer, so much closer to her age and sensibility. Whereas Quinn was like some sad old king who'd designated her for his own use.

She was glad then to be at the country club, to run for lemon slices and ice for the golf ladies, to tray out glass bowls of green sherbet that none of them would touch, to make and pour pot after pot of decaf coffee.

Heading back up the mountain through blue afternoon shadows, Cress was calmer and resigned. Love affairs, it seemed, had hidden components that, when removed, destabilized the whole. Caleb, she saw now, had served as an impediment; by being there, he'd limited the time they could spend together, which fueled their yearning but also kept them neatly in check. His defection had knocked the wind out of them; she doubted they could rally.

She trudged up her snow-choked driveway to find a folded note stuck on the glass door with blue masking tape: *Come to trailer for pork chops.*

Quinn had slept all day. He puttered at the stove, clattered pans, hummed. The word for him was *chipper.* She sat at the table and tried to catch up. But being in the trailer raised another specter: it was impossible not to think of Sylvia. The scanty, stiff brown-and-white gingham curtains might have been original to the trailer, but Sylvia had surely selected the Melmac plates, the flowered pillowcases, and maybe even the double-flannel sleeping bag. Who knew how many nights she'd slept encased in that crass American toile of pointing setters, gun-toting hunters, and flying mallards. Had Quinn spent so many nights alone here that he no longer registered Sylvia's claim? Cress would not jeopardize his chipperness by asking.

He fed her chops and eggs, crusty potatoes, bourbon-spiked coffee. She presented the merganser miniature, which he propped up against the salt shaker so he could admire it all evening. They played cribbage with competitive intensity—she won by a full length; he was truly lousy at games. Victory, finally, made her chipper too. He showed her how to light the little propane lamp by the bed and crank the window, "or we'll be found en-twined and asphyxiated in the morning."

Quinn rose when it was still dark. He turned on a shuddering little heater and brewed coffee in an aluminum drip pot, brought her a cup in bed. He fried bacon and made toast, hummed as he basted eggs, and called her to the table.

Such was their first full night together, and it became a favorite, often visited memory.

Late in January, snow fell a foot a day for a week. The webbed aluminum deck furniture—a chaise and two chairs—went from blanketed to overstuffed, and finally to wholly abstract, Brancusian. "Welcome to your first real Sierra dump," Don Dare called to her from the new house.

They awoke one morning to find footprints on both of the A-frame's porches; they looked almost human, but were larger and clawed. "Your bear." Quinn crouched to examine the prints. "Big fella." The bear had gone to every door, the sliders on the front and side porches, then around back to the never-opened door by the kitchen. He had paused, too, at each of the down-stairs bedroom windows.

He'd tried the basement door, as well, they discovered that afternoon when they went to put on their skis. Quinn said, "You know my mother once baited, killed, butchered, and canned a bear."

"Your mom?" said Cress.

They snapped down their boot toes and moved off, into the trees toward the meadow. The snow was soft and deep.

The first time his family moved up to Noah Mountain, Quinn said, his father took a disaster relief job in Mississippi. Before he left, Lew cleaned out all the bank accounts, even the one his wife kept secret from him, for emergencies.

"But that's criminal!" Cress said. "Robbing his own family!"

"He was going through Vegas. He thought he'd double or triple it."

One night after dinner, Quinn said, his mother took the compost bucket and tossed food scraps into the yard. She loaded two deer slugs in the twelve-gauge, opened the kitchen window, and sat on the counter with her feet in the sink, the barrels resting on her knees.

Outside, an icy snow was falling.

The boys could sit at the kitchen table, she said, but they had to be completely quiet. Quinn was around twelve then, Caleb three. The kitchen was soon freezing from the open window. Quinn crept off and brought their hats and heavy coats and helped his brother bundle up.

They dozed and woke, dozed and woke, and each time found themselves still in the cold silent kitchen. And then Quinn opened his eyes just as his mother lifted her gun. Without making a sound, he stood on his chair, and Caleb did too. They didn't see anything at first, then just a thickening in the sleet that grew darker and, coming into the barn light, became a bear.

This was an old trash-pillaging campsite marauder that Fish and Game had airlifted from Yosemite and deposited south of Mineral King. Eventually, his nose drew him to the small scattered community of Noah Mountain, where he resumed his old vocation. All summer, he'd raided smoke shacks, gardens, and henhouses.

In the cold mercury vapor glow, he glittered as if covered with glass beads. He entered the yard on all fours, but when he got twenty-five, thirty feet away, he rose up, stuck his blunt old snout in the air, sniffing and sniffing, his head in a bright cloud of steam from his own breath. They got a big whiff of him then—man! was he rank!—and Quinn's mother fired both barrels.

It was like a bomb went off. In such close quarters, the sound blasts right through your bones. All the dishes in the cupboards jumped. Caleb started howling. Quinn's ears rang so much he got dizzy and had to sit down. But his mother made him get up and help her drag the dead bear into the barn.

They could move him only a few inches at a time. Four

hundred pounds of dead weight. He smelled sour and rotten, like week-old garbage. Quinn's mother knew what to do, she was a librarian. She'd done research. She skinned him and dressed him out, hung him in the barn, and, after a couple days, butchered the whole carcass. She froze some meat, ground and canned the rest.

"Canned it? Canned bear? And you ate it?" said Cress.

"All year long."

"What did it taste like?"

Quinn shrugged. "Like meat in chili. Meat in spaghetti. Every so often I got a hint of that garbagey smell. Like with a pig raised on a small farm, you can sometimes taste barnyard in the meat? I could taste the trash scavenger in that bear. Or thought I could. Never had much taste for bear after that."

"Who could blame you."

Yeah. And maybe ten years after that night, Quinn said, he was in a hut up north of Whitney, with his dad and his uncle Evan. They were in bed and heard the door scrape open, and in came that same hot sour stink. His uncle Evan shone a torch on him—he already had his nose in their supplies. "I got him," Quinn said, being the nearest, and the only one with a clear shot.

"I had this old Ruger pistol, and I shot six times at point-blank range and didn't hit him once. Unconsciously, I think I never wanted to eat bear again. Old guy finally did get the hint and lumbered out. Took his time, though. I never lived it down. Bear comes in and all but asks to be shot, and I couldn't oblige."

Cress, browning onions and chunks of pork, answered the phone.

"Cress? It's Julie, Julie Garsh. I'm wondering if I can stop by around eleven?"

They hadn't spoken for at least two months. In her surprise, Cress feigned enthusiasm. "Come for lunch! I'm making posole."

"No, no. I'll only have a minute."

Since it was the first week in February, Cress thought, her father must be contesting the latest invoice and Julie probably wanted to talk about that. The last time he was up, Sam Hartley had seen plans for Rick's next custom home, and although it lacked the Hartleys' glassed-in porch and there was a slight difference in scale, the two floor plans were identical. "I paid him a full architect's fee and not for a set of rescalable plans," Sam said and, for the first time, used the word *lawsuit*. Perhaps Julie wanted to talk about that, too.

In Sparkville, Cress had bought yellow and purple hominy and chipotle peppers from the Mexican grocery. The posole was simmering when Julie came in huffing from her climb up the driveway. "Sure I can't interest you?" Cress lifted the lid, loosing a cloud of meaty steam.

Julie seemed startled. "I have to feed Rick lunch. I can only stay a sec."

"At least sit." Cress motioned to the love seat and pulled out a chair from the kitchen table for herself.

Neither sat. Julie had gained weight, her chin was now farther adrift in her softening neck—fond of her own cooking, as Jakey once said. Not enough time spent stretching her legs in God's grandeur. "How are you?" said Cress.

"Rick's got three more houses starting in the spring, so I'm up to my ears getting plans to the county." Julie gazed out the front window, where Shale Mountain presided over the whitened world. "This really is the best view . . . ," she said. "You know, Rick and I were so glad when you moved here, Cress. We were really hoping to be friends. We were as disappointed as you were that things didn't work out with you and Jakey . . ."

"No great tragedy," said Cress. "Considering—"

"And I can see that you were probably pretty lonely then—"

"Not so bad. But if anyone else you know falls for Jakey, you might warn her that he's a compulsive—"

"I can't speak to that—"

"I can," said Cress. "Take my word for it. He's got 'em coming and—"

Julie's voice rose. "I am not here to talk about Jakey, Cress."

"Oh. Okay." Cress waited.

Julie drew herself up and looked at Cress for the first time. "I just can't sit by while you destroy another woman's life."

Cress's mind went white, even before she fully grasped what Julie meant.

"Sylvia Morrow doesn't deserve this," Julie added.

"Sylvia who?" Cress decided on the spot to deny everything.

"Rick and I saw you two. And you're out every day, over hill and dale."

"I have no idea what you think is going on, but you are way off the mark." Cress's heart and thoughts thumped: *Over hill over dale we will hit the dusty trail . . .*

"I called her once already, way back before Christmas. I told her, I said, Sylvia, if you want to hold on to your marriage, you'd better hightail it up here."

"You *what?*"

"She was here the very next day. I'll call her again if I have to. And this time, I'll name names."

"Call her! Why should I care? She knows we're friends."

Julie's mouth snapped shut. Cress's heart was banging so hard, the whole high room pulsed and contracted.

Oh, right. The night the wives showed up with the pie and the panties.

"Rick won't stand for this behavior," Julie went on. "Clearly Caleb couldn't, either. His leaving put us behind schedule on two jobs. If your parents complain, I'll have to tell them why their construction is taking a month longer."

Cress's lips twitched and pressure bulged in her sinuses; she was about to cry. But she'd never give Julie the satisfaction.

"Rick and I sometimes wish we'd never met any of you Hartleys." Julie lifted her coat off the hook. "But as someone who was once your friend, Cress, let me give you some advice. You should get into therapy ASAP."

"I've been in therapy."

"Then think about going back. You're—you're out of control!" Julie slid open the door. "Rick and I will be civil to you," she said. "Obviously, you have free run of your parents' place. But you are not to set foot on our other jobsites."

When the door shut, fat drops sprang from Cress's eyes. She disliked rebuke—who doesn't? Yes, yes, there was something wrong with her: she was insufficiently moved by—in fact, oddly impervious to—Sylvia Morrow's plight. But why should she be, when Sylvia was the one protected, the one in perpetual ascendance, whose rights and needs would always trump hers. Cress, in fact, had no rights! No protection!

How had she given the Garshes the benefit of the doubt? They'd repelled her from the start: Rick's finicky eating, fussy fires, and sly swindles; Julie's fringe and feathers, her too-rich cooking and sidling, peremptory intimacy.

Julie would never dare browbeat Ondine Streeter for cheating on Tom.

And this alleged solidarity of married people—did it extend only to wives? Did Julie scold Jakey about the husbands he cuckolded? Did she threaten to tell his parents? And hey—wasn't Rick married when Julie met him? Hadn't Julie demanded a divorce lawyer before their first date?

Hypocrisy always surprised Cress. Its transparency, its guilelessness. As if no one would ever notice.

"Julie says she'll call Sylvia about us."

"She wouldn't dare," said Quinn. "She knows I'd quit. Rick's already months behind and the Rodingers are in a swivet."

Fifteen

Once the sky cleared and the plow pushed through, the berms rose high as hedgerows and the development was newly devoid of landmarks. Houses, now windowed white humps, had lost all distinguishing characteristics. Distance became elastic. Walking from the lodge, Cress thought she was almost home, only to find herself on the main highway, which she recognized by the few yards of broken yellow line scraped clear. Kevin, passing by in his truck, picked her up and, after numerous wrong turns, finally dropped her off at the A-frame. Jakey himself walked to check on a cabin and ended up at the Orlisses', two miles northwest of his destination.

Marvelous, this reconfigured, swallowed-up world: the cold, the glowing snow, the deep planetary blues of twilight. Stars, reflected, shed enough ancient light to ski by. The full moon made night as bright as an overcast day. Snow muffled and absorbed all sound, except for wind soughing through trees and the occasional rumbling crash, more felt than heard, as great loads slid from high branches to the ground.

"Snow weighs nineteen pounds a square foot," Don Dare called to Cress as he shoveled off the roof of the new house. "Twenty-four pounds when it turns to ice. I now spend half my life raking it off the tent fly."

She and Quinn skied out to the Crags, and to Globe Rock, where they ran into Tom Streeter hunting rabbits with a crossbow and surveying the snowy ridges through his huge Nikon binoculars, which he offered to Cress. "Saw a big old bear a few minutes ago. Probably the same one as strews trash down my slope. I'd like to make a rug out of him."

Cress raised the binoculars. The near ridge jumped at her; trees bristled with fine needles, she saw the thorn tips of pinecones—those inwardly curved, she now knew, were ponderosas; outwardly, Jeffreys—and the jigsaw of bark. Tom was an optician, of course he'd have good binoculars.

No telling what else he'd seen with them.

Once out of earshot, Cress murmured to Quinn, "Let's hope he doesn't make a rug out of Jakey!"

He thought of her all day, he said. He loved to recall her slender fingers and long, strong neck. How happy she was when skiing. Her energy. Her strength. He had never seen a woman's back as well muscled.

Her soul, that long, dry lakebed, slowly filled, and in all the years afterward, she prized her fingers, neck, and strong back because he had.

Quinn drove down to the pay phone at the lodge and called home every night. Cress said, "Oh, just call from here," but he shook his head, and she didn't insist; why overhear endearments to the others? He went home every Friday afternoon in February and came back Sunday nights—ostensibly to get a head start on Monday mornings—straight to the A-frame.

A fire, a tumbler of bourbon, a lover's company. This was the heaven of her life.

Work was slow at Beech Creek; she was lucky to get a shift or two a week. She got out her dissertation again, but whole days passed when she didn't make it to the typewriter. Or easel. How much more gratifying it was to cut butter into flour, peel apples, pinch crust into pleasing points, and fill the A-frame with the aroma of baking sugar and cinnamon while Glenn Gould played the *Goldberg Variations* with his clear, chiming precision, or Lefty Frizzell sang his jaunty love-gone-wrong ballads. The pie cooled, and on the narrow window seat, Cress read *New Yorker*s from the 1970s, and waited for Quinn to stamp on the deck, rap on the thick glass. He'd offer to take her to the lodge, or to Hapsaw or Cloud Slope, so she wouldn't have to make dinner, but she liked the easy creativity of cooking, the immediate results. So he brought her bacon, steaks, and chops from his meat locker, and gave her money for beer or a bottle, then refused the change. She'd wonder, years down the road, what it was like for him, living in someone else's home with their directionless daughter playing housewife.

Quinn finished at the Rodinger house in the first week of March, then moved his tools and the trailer up to the Hartleys' new cabin. Cress brought him hot coffee mid-morning. "Inspector!" she called upon entering. He worked as he walked, skipcoating drywall or measuring a window bench with his usual grace and economy of movement. Did she want to help? He could use her, he said. So she hand-sanded and stained balustrades, took down measurements for a window seat as he rattled them off; she learned to use the chop saw and router. At three, they knocked off and skied into the woods.

He never bothered to level the little trailer in its new parking spot. They slept in the loft bedroom, on the unforgiving bed, with the window cracked for fresh air, the electric blanket humming.

On March 10, Don and Donna held a party at the tent to celebrate the syzygy. All the planets had lined up on the same side of the sun. "It's the most auspicious alignment for love," Donna said when she called to invite them. "When soul mates find each other. When eternal love takes hold."

"It better not take hold of me," said Cress.

She and Quinn skied over. Don had cut steps in the snow, and a glassy-walled chute led to the tent's opening. The snow had melted back a few inches from the tent and formed a hard wall around it. The woodstove kept the place warm—too warm; one front flap stayed up.

"Brian and Franny were going to come, but they went to Ensenada to thaw out," said Don. "So it's just us."

Donna wore a rabbit-fur vest, a long skirt, and shearling mukluks. Her hair was in looped braids. "Isn't she the adorable Laplander?" said Don.

The tiny potbellied woodstove was vented through the wall of the tent. Stew bubbled on the hob. Two propane lanterns hissed valiantly, producing a trembling pale light. The canvas swelled and contracted in the night breezes. They sat on folding canvas campstools around an old wooden folding table.

The tent's ceiling was beginning to sag, so the two men went out to rake the snow off the fly and to tighten the tension lines.

"You and Mr. Morrow are awfully thick," Donna whispered. "I was telling Don, it's too bad he's not single. I've never seen two people better suited. You brighten him, he sweetens you— you glow! He crazy-adores you."

"Really?"

"Completely gaga. Any plans to divorce the high-school sweetheart?"

"Oh God no," said Cress. "That's why it's so idyllic. With no future, you don't care about things that'd drive you nuts over the long haul."

"Like decades of wet towels on the floor?"

"For example." In fact, Quinn was tidier than Cress. She was thinking more of his past participles. Tonight he'd said, *Have you wrote much lately?*

"I still couldn't do what you're doing," said Donna. "I have to be the first and only. I get too mad at these guys just taking whatever they want."

"Quinn's not like that."

"They're all like that, deep down. I could kill Brian. Franny thinks he'll marry her. Not a chance. She's just his round-the-way girl."

"I think there's a chance."

"Not a whisper of a chance."

The men came back inside, finely frosted head-to-foot, as if pulled from a deep freeze.

In the A-frame, under the covers, in the cool blue darkness, Cress said, "Do you think Don and Donna will make it?"

"Make what?" said Quinn.

"You know. As a couple."

"I have no idea."

"Don't you wonder?" she said.

"Not about that."

"Well, I wouldn't bet on it," Cress said. "I've never gotten the feeling that she's too smitten with him. Have you?"

"Have I what?"

"Felt that Donna's really in love with Don."

"Never thought about it."

"You are no fun." Cress threw her leg over his and grabbed his arm. "I'm not even going to ask what you think about Franny and Brian. I mean, if you aren't interested in the people around you, what are you interested in?"

"Fly fishing," he said.

"Such a limited storyline!"

"Not if you do it right. It's very absorbing."

Cress snorted, and he drew her close, kissed her eye, her cheekbone, her lips. She drowsed and drifted, half-dreaming of fishing, of ripples, gnats, angles of the sun. She recalled the deer devouring the trout, the thrashing of the bushes, birds flushing, and hunters. She pulled back from Quinn. "I keep thinking about Tom Streeter and those binoculars."

"What about them?"

"I'm sure he's spying on Ondine," Cress said. "You don't think he would ever shoot Jakey, do you?"

Quinn grabbed her arm and flipped her onto her back, then stretched over her. "Does that big, busy mind of yours ever give you a moment's rest?"

"What's going on? Are you mad at me?" Tillie hadn't even said hello.

Guilt panged near Cress's heart. "Why would I be mad at you?"

"Maybe I didn't leave our room clean enough when we left at New Year's? Maybe I hurt your feelings about something? Or you hated my *boeuf carbonnade?*"

"I'm—uh—" Cress couldn't say busy. She wasn't busy. "Snowed in, I guess."

Tillie had a new job, at Maddie's magazine, *City and State.* Assistant art director. Full-time and a real salary. "And you? What's up? I've been calling and calling, all hours of the day, early, late."

Cress had heard the phone pealing downstairs. Three or four nights in a row.

"So what's his name?" Tillie said.

"Does it always have to be a guy?"

"What's her name?"

"The thing is, you won't approve," said Cress.

"I might surprise you," said Tillie.

But she didn't.

Franny made fish tacos at the Crittenden family's Swiss-style château. They were the first fish tacos the others had ever eaten; Franny and Brian had had them in Baja, and Franny had watched how they were made: chunks of red snapper floured and fried, onions chopped with cilantro, fresh limes squeezed over all. She'd bought salsa at Younts: "I hung around the Mexican food aisle to see what Mexicans liked—Herdez, mostly."

Brian patted Franny's hip as she served. She wore black stirrup pants and a crisp bright white shirt—new clothes, Cress saw. Good clothes. For the first time Franny's tiny body broadcast not a childhood of malnutrition but stylish, adult slenderness.

After dinner, Brian and Donna got out their guitars. "Come on, Fran," Brian said. "Sing for 'em." He winked at the others. "We've been practicing."

Franny stood by his chair and, swaying a little, sang "Satin Sheets" in a sweet, thin twang; then "Almost Persuaded."

"Dang girl, I'm gonna call you onstage next Family Night," said Donna.

"I won't do it," said Franny.

But she did, the next Thursday. Franny sang both songs again, plus she and Donna had worked out a duet, "Two More Bottles of Wine." Donna's capable alto provided a good foil for Franny's sweet, stubborn plaintiveness.

The next storm brought another four feet of snow. Don Dare's tent semicollapsed, and until he could dig it out, he moved in with Freddy and River Bob in DeeDee's old place.

During the days, the cold was not severe; once you got moving, you could ski as long as you wanted wearing a sweatshirt with a down vest.

At night, with Quinn asleep beside her, Cress listened to distant choruses endlessly singing, at a very high pitch, right on the edge of hearing.

They kissed on the creaky wicker love seat, the kissing a form of daydreaming, where she floated amid bright images. The white world, the golden meadow, a granular spew of stars. They stripped each other, layer after layer. His skin was supple but coarse; older and vaguely hide-like, just beginning to loosen at his wrists, knees, and elbows. Without cologne, he smelled faintly of wood and some days, not unpleasantly, of engines. They gazed calmly and at length into each other's eyes, inhaled each other's breath. She sat on the back of his thighs and pushed her thumbs up the trough of his spine—he claimed never to have been massaged before! She sat the other way and dug into his calves and thighs. "Do you think, in some far distant future, we'll ever see each other again?" she asked. "Like when you're old and I'm still relatively young?"

"I'll come see you in my wheelchair."

"And I'll tip you out of it. Onto my bed."

Cress's father came up for a night, long enough to have a yelling match with Rick Garsh over the inspection; since Rick wrote the inspector a check, he charged Sam Hartley 10 percent on top of the inspection fee. Sam called Rick a chiseler, a cheat, and a phony, and refused to pay. Both sides now spoke openly of lawyers and lawsuits.

Sometimes she wished that Quinn would just leave. Leave and get it over with, so she could stop being afraid of being alone on the mountain and just be alone on the mountain. She couldn't begin to get over him if he was still here.

At Beech Creek, Dalia announced that banquets would pick up mid-April and get incredibly busy come May, with weddings and graduation parties. Cress could work as much as she liked, six or seven days a week. The money was there to be made. So this became her plan: once Quinn left, she would make her nut (a thousand dollars was her goal) and leave. Where, she didn't know. London, maybe.

Donna said, "Hey! Rent a room from me, so you don't have to drive up and down the mountain every day. A hundred bucks a month. A good deal for you and a big help to me."

Cress hardly had to consider it. "Just don't tell Quinn. I don't want him to think that I followed him off the hill."

"I'm going to miss your gloomy mug, Quinn, man," Brian said at Family Night. "Now who's going to teach me how to use a router?"

"Cress can," Quinn said. "She's a pro with that thing."

At one point, when all the men had left the table—for the bathroom, the bar, the phone—Franny said, "Here's this, you guys," and pulled a chain out of her blouse. On the chain dangled a yellow-gold diamond ring.

Donna grabbed it, squinted. "Jeez, girl, that's a honker."

"Three carats," said Franny. "He proposed at Estero Beach. I'm wearing it round my neck till we get it sized."

Donna gave Cress a bright laughing look. "I knew it was going to happen, Franny. I told Cress just last week . . ."

"I wish you could be next, Cress," Franny said softly. "I see how he looks at you—it's like Brian looks at me. Like he'd curl up 'n' die without you."

Cress discreetly boxed up her woolens and hiking boots, her thrift-store ski pants. Her dissertation—or, full disclosure, two and a third chapters thereof—she filed in the box with her research notes. The Selectric went back in its case, and all of it went into the upstairs closet. She took an old plaid suitcase from the basement, filled it with Beech Creek uniforms and low-altitude clothes—jeans, T-shirts, light sweaters—and stowed it in the Saab's trunk.

Quinn finished her parents' cabin on a Wednesday. The next morning he cleaned and packed up his tools and secured the cupboards in the trailer. He and Cress skied for the last time to the meadows and the Bauer cabin.

The sky was an aching blue with two lenticular clouds, one large, one small, like enormous Frisbees tilted against the northern range. The sun was warm; they shed their sweatshirts and skied in T-shirts and open down vests. They pushed on, passing Don's tent, a hump in the snow, the fir ridgepole protruding like a bony elbow, and, deciding against a longer outing, turned back toward the lodge, where they stopped in for a drink—who cared what anyone thought now? The crowd was large for a late week-day afternoon, and a good-natured drunken hilarity gusted in loud laughter and shouts. Carpenters lined the bar, and a party of snowmobilers had pushed tables together; cross-country skiers dried their backsides at the fire. "Heya, Hartley!" Jakey yelled across the room from the register. "Your old boyfriend broke into the Mackenzie cabin last night, made a big damn mess! Kitchen looked like an eight-point earthquake—molasses, maple syrup, and pancake mix all over the floor."

Cress, confused, tried to smile, but she was socked by sudden guilt: What old boyfriend? Who was Jakey talking about? Himself? Had she lost track of someone? She tried to sound light and game. "Which old boyfriend is this?"

"Big old black guy with the white snout. The one who won't stay in bed."

"Oh, him!" She could've leaped with relief. "He's up again? Something's wrong. He's hungry all the time. Maybe he has worms."

They gave each other the same present: a silver flask from the locked knife case at the Sparkville hardware store. "The man told me he'd just sold one, and this was his last," said Cress. "Maybe it's a sign."

Quinn squinted at his elongated reflection. "I don't believe in signs."

He'd been intermittently gloomy and clingy all week. She'd been cooler, strict with herself. No fantasies of a future. No weepy moments.

"You'll be okay up here?" he said.

"I'll be at Beech Creek most of the time." She kept her tone light.

She couldn't say so, but she was glad to be leaving. The Meadows was too small, Julie and Rick Garsh too ubiquitous.

"I'll have a little something for you once Rick's check clears," he said. "For all the hours you put in. To add to the kitty."

A flare of anger: that he would give her money to send her on her way.

"If you can't get hold of me here, call me at Beech Creek," she said. "I plan to work double time."

In bed that last night, Quinn held her too tightly. He wanted to stare into her eyes, he was too squirmy and abrupt in his movements.

"These were the best months of my life, since I was a boy," he said.

"Me too." She wasn't certain yet that this was true—she'd have to think about it—but why not say so now and make their last hours together sweet? Best months, second- or third-best months: she hadn't allowed herself such formulations.

She had been calming and kind to him for so long. Now, impatience jolted through her. What more could be said? They'd reached their agreed-upon limit. She put her back to him, feigned sleep. At some far remove, her distant chorus sang.

This was the end, but not quite the very end—they had to meet in a few weeks so he could give her the "little something"— so she was not sad yet.

Friday morning, she followed him down the mountain in her Saab. She had a luncheon and a dinner banquet. Her plaid suitcase slid back and forth in the trunk on the curves.

The trailer looked ridiculous. Quinn had hitched it to his truck without clearing the accumulated snow off its roof. Five or six feet had compacted there, forming a concise history of snowfalls, glacial blue at the bottom, with compressed and stratified layers. The overall shape was a blunted trapezoid, like a scudding cloud or an enormous white pompadour. Quinn was charmed by its comical look. Evan, he said, would get a big kick out of it.

Eleven or twelve miles down the road, Quinn steered into a

tight inside curve, and Cress watched as the trailer-with-snowpack leaned to the right, and then leaned some more. As the truck began pulling out of the curve—to the left—the top-heavy trailer continued its rightward trajectory. In languid slow motion, twisting at the hitch, the trailer leaned farther and farther to the right, finally landing softly on its side in a turnout, where a spring flowed from a small pipe into a culvert. The truck dragged the trailer a few more feet and stopped.

Cress pulled over and met Quinn beside the trailer's exposed chassis and white aluminum belly, so wrongly revealed. The top wheel still spun. Quinn's hands rested on his hips.

"Hey!" Cress elbowed his elbow. "That's good money! Lying right there on the ground."

He touched her waist.

Two cars stopped. Men got out and closely examined the twisted hitch. A boxy green Forest Service vehicle drove up. The driver used a walkie-talkie to call for a tow truck. Quinn had to wait. Cress didn't want to be late, so she left him by the toppled trailer in a cluster of onlookers and went to work.

PART II

THE FOOTHILLS

Sixteen

Donna gave Cress a tiny bedroom off the dark, narrow front hall, between Norma, the established roommate, and a storage room. Cress's room was also half-relegated to storage; she could walk only partway around the bed before musical instruments in their cases, black speakers, and hatboxes blocked her way. Donna was an accumulator, a prodigious one. While Cress went to college and grad school, Donna had married, amassed the stuff of several households, then divorced with full custody of the goods.

Donna had cleared nine inches of clothes rod in the closet for Cress, enough for her work uniforms. The closet floor was a foot-deep jumble of shoes. Cress would have to live out of her plaid suitcase, and the only place for that was at the far foot of her bed. To draw the thin white curtain, Cress had to walk across the mattress and reach.

But this was only a way station; she'd live here for ten weeks at most—and better here than driving daily down and up the coiled road. Better here, with roommates, than alone in the Meadows in noxious proximity to Julie Garsh.

That first morning, she found coffee made in the kitchen and joined Donna at the picnic table under a white-trunked sycamore swelling at its nubs. Up and down the riverbank, back-yard lawns and shade trees formed a lush green park. A black phoebe flew past, a long dirty string in her beak.

Here by the river, in her ruffled nightgown and slept-in braids, Donna looked romantic and slightly mad, Ophelian. "I didn't hear you come in last night. Sleep okay?"

"The Brotherhood of Masons partied hardy and late." Cress stretched, yawning. She wore only a light sweater over her T-shirt. "There's so much more oxygen down here," she said.

The Hapsaw, all forks united, gushed beyond Donna's back gate; flecks of foam from its eddies rode the air like tiny clouds. Donna said, "So. How'd you leave it with Quinn?"

"He's home," Cress said.

"That's it? Went back to the wife?"

"He didn't go *back*," Cress said. "He never left her."

"At least he didn't get your hopes up." Donna tucked her knees up under her gown. "I read that adultery's always about the primary couple, anyway. The third person's just a catalyst to shake things up."

Cress tried not to feel insulted, but who wants to be *just a catalyst?* "It wasn't like that with us," she said. "No shake-up."

"Good," said Donna. "Because even when men do leave their wives, they tend to bypass the mistress and move on to someone new, like 90 percent of the time. The mistress is the bus out of town, not the destination."

Cress didn't like being called a bus, either, or, particularly, a mistress. "That can't be right!" she said. "People are always leaving marriages for other people!" Her parents' close friends the Greens, had famously both ditched spouses to marry each other. "Look at Rick Garsh—he left his wife for Julie and they're still together. For what that's worth."

"I'm just saying what I read." Donna examined the tip of one braid. "Which was that adultery might even save more marriages than it destroys. Not that it saved mine. But with my husband, it wasn't one case of adultery—more like two or three hundred."

Cress pried a splinter off the table and used the sharp end to clean under her thumbnail. "I can see how, if people get their needs met discreetly, it can preserve the status quo at home."

Donna laughed her throaty laugh. "More like, when the truth comes out and everything blows sky high, the couple can finally get honest with each other—and rebuild their marriage from the ground up!"

Cress squashed an ant with the splinter. "Well. Nothing's blowing sky high with Quinn."

"Everything blew to pieces with Joe and me, but he never did get honest. You could hold a gun to his head and he couldn't tell the truth. That's 'cause he had no idea what the truth was!" Donna flung the braid over her shoulder. "At least you got out in one piece. Hey—want to walk into town for a doughnut?"

Roommates. Cress hadn't had them since sophomore year. Mostly, she tried to keep out of everyone's way, staying in her room until Donna and Norma left for work in the morning and using the common living area only when she had the house to herself. They shared a tiny pink bathroom. Bundling her hair into a ponytail before the mirror, Cress's elbow knocked Colgate, contact lens kits, and earrings off cluttered shelves into the sink.

Norma, a medical receptionist, could be chirpy and friendly, but Ike, her fiancé, a big, bearded, small-eyed lumberman, stared mistrustfully at Cress. The betrothed were in their mid-twenties and harmoniously overweight, her two hundred pounds to his two-seventy. They called each other Lovey and Sweetie interchangeably, relentlessly. After childhoods of schoolyard teasing, they'd taken on adulthood and their pending marriage with great self-importance. Every night, with the slow lumbering bustle of grandparents, they cooked large balanced meals: roasts or chops, mashed potatoes with gravy, frozen corn or green beans, pie or cobbler. They ate at the large table set with pitchers of ice water and milk, and never offered food to anyone else. If Cress went into the kitchen to make tea or toast, Ike growled, "We'll be done in twenty minutes."

"I wouldn't think that being obese was enough common ground," Cress whispered to Donna.

"Oh, they're very compatible," Donna said. "And besides,

I read that obese means a hundred pounds overweight, and they are not quite that."

Donna's expertise on this and all things human, Cress deduced, came from the well-thumbed supermarket glossies stacked in the bathroom, the living room, and under her own bed: the *Cosmopolitans*, *Mademoiselles*, *Redbooks*, and *Glamours* whose headlines Cress herself could not resist investigating:

Is Your Man Cheating? A Checklist
Twenty Ways to Keep HIM Happy
Wife or Lover—Which Are You? Take the Quiz!

A streetlamp shone all night through the filmy curtain, so Cress's room was never dark. She slept restlessly, queasy in transition's dim passageway. In her dreams, roads grew steep, then rocky, as narrow as game trails, and finally perilous—a single rotting plank over a gorge. She constantly tried to get back up the mountain. She tried, too, to reach Quinn, but people waylaid her with urgent requests, crevasses gaped in the road, or her car's steering wheel turned into a soggy wooden Popsicle stick.

Sternly, in daylight, she checked her yearnings. In the bright mornings, she drank coffee and read the newspaper under the leafing sycamore beside the lively river. Quinn, she imagined, was drinking coffee at the Formica table as his kids got ready for school and Sylvia scrubbed and swept around him.

He had said that their months on the mountain were the happiest of his life, that the memories would keep him going for a long time. They would see each other one last time, when he would pay her for the sanding, sawing, and routing she'd done. (She'd only done it to spend time with him.) They might meet after that, too, he'd said on their last night, from time to time. As friends. (They'd both smiled at this.) After a cooling-off period. How long a cooling-off period? she'd asked, and he shook his head, signaling an end to the discussion. Six months? she persisted. A year? He shrugged. A year, then. She imagined a key slid into a numbered door, the snub corner of an ugly bedspread. Thin towels. Small wafers of soap. Shyness after so much time.

But she might love someone else by then.

For now, she'd get some cash together and head back to civilization, wherever that might be.

She made the most money from large nighttime banquets, where 20 percent was added to the bills and divided equally among the servers. But Cress requested any shift Dalia could throw her way. Why not work as much as she could? Her boyfriend was back with his wife. Her dissertation was in a box in a closet at 7,300 feet. So Dalia duly gave Cress the small private luncheons that senior waitresses were only too happy to relinquish: the Junior Leaguers, the Sierra Wildflower Society, the Beech Creek Women's Golf Association, and its more casual subset, the Beech Creek Hackettes. These memberships overlapped, so Cress waited on the same women, aged forty-five to eighty-five, in varied configurations. They ran her hard. Some asked for their salad dressing or butter or mayo on the side; others demanded extra lemon in their ice water, or no ice, or a glassful of extra ice. Or they had Cress dump out a little water and add *just a splash* of lemonade or ice tea, but not so much that they would be charged for it. Some required their cottage cheese in a cup and not on a lettuce leaf; several had to have sliced tomatoes instead of French fries or, if it was the baked halibut entree, double vegetables in place of mashed potatoes. Together—and Cress saw them as a single many-headed organism, a sort of poloshirted, paste-pearled hydra—they had nosed out every possible cost-free adjustment to their meals. If Cress mentioned a surcharge—fruit substituted for fries, for example, was fifty cents, as was mixing half lemonade with ice tea—the request was immediately withdrawn. *Oh, just forget it!* The small banquet

room where these luncheons took place was on the far side of the
large banquet room, so that all the running to the kitchen and
the bar and back made it difficult for Cress to do her basic job of
serving and clearing plates in a timely fashion. The women, ir-
ritated by waiting first for their food and then for their places to
be cleared, left Cress negligible tips, quarters and dimes. Still,
the twenty, twenty-five dollars she earned each lunch shift was
that much more than nothing, and added up.

"Phone," Dalia said, as Cress served mousse cake at the Tulare
County sheriff's yearly fund-raiser. She took the call in the bar.
Quinn's voice sent a rogue current through her blood. He had
that little something for her. Would she meet him tomorrow at
the Staghorn bar out by the lake? She couldn't miss it. Four
o'clock?

Cress finished with the Wildflower Society by two-thirty. She
went back to the house, washed her hair, and dried it in the sun.
She helped herself to a daub of Donna's musk oil and to lip gloss
from a tiny tub on the bathroom shelf.

"I think he misses me," she told Donna, who'd just come
home.

"Of course he does. Back with his little mouse."

The Staghorn was a cinder-block box overlooking Glory
Lake. Quinn's white truck, with its chunky custom toolboxes,
already sat in the parking lot.

A pair of bleached, crooked antlers flanked the bar's front door.
His face was the color of clay. Clambering onto the barstool beside him, she almost made a joke—*I forgot how ancient you are!*
But she was cut short by his eyes, which searched hers as if
conducting a depth check of her affection. Again, she almost
joked—*Why the long face?*—and she was embarrassed on his
behalf, that he would look to her for anything. True, since fall

she'd supplied the attention he claimed to lack and sorely need; if he wanted a last top-off of that tonic, she could rally once more to the cause, muster fondness into her gaze for old times' sake—she'd missed him, too—but not without a prickle of irritation. Wasn't she the one without a home of her own, without a mate or affectionate children, or a fat final paycheck? The one who presently shared a bed with an ugly plaid suitcase in what was essentially a thin-walled storage closet? You didn't see her seeking reassurance or consolation or anything at all from him.

Oh, but a last dusting of sweetness: he craved it and she'd give it and have done, in honor of their time on the mountain.

"I know you can use this." He handed her a check. She read quickly before folding it in half: Pay to the order of *Cash*. Discreet. The wife would never know. He'd paid her more than minimum wage, too, but he hadn't been so generous as to be flagrant or to look as if he was paying for something else: it was a fair sum for fifty-odd hours of unskilled labor. (Though not, she couldn't help but note, as much as Brian *What's-a-Router?* Crittenden had been paid—she'd seen those invoices.) She slid the check into her purse. "Hey. Whatever happened with the trailer?"

"Had it towed to my mom's place," he said.

"And it's okay?"

"The hitch is shot and has to be replaced. Stuff came out of cupboards."

"How is it being home?"

"Busy." He'd had to rehang his mother's bathroom door. Take care of business at the bank. Caleb needed help installing cabinets on his job. "And all the time," Quinn said, "I'm wondering when I can see you."

Cress decided to ignore this. "And Sylvia? How's she?"

"She's at work," he said. "Till ten tonight. Come on. Let's go."

"Go where?" said Cress. "Do what?"

"Take a drive. Where we can talk."

They drove through citrus groves to the far-flung bars

they'd visited last fall. They sat pressed together in flimsy plywood booths, alone but for one or two dedicated drinkers at the
bar. Cress had gone to taverns and bars before, but always
in college towns, and they were not like these dim, shoddy
drinking stations with gritty floors, mewling jukeboxes, and
sparse liquor selections. The amenities were basic, utilitarian,
joyless. These were places to drink, or to meet someone you
shouldn't.

She assumed that what they had up the hill was officially
over. And maybe it was: he hadn't kissed her, and perhaps he
didn't intend to. Maybe this was some intermediate, post-
attachment stage, where touching arms and thighs when fully
clothed was allowed; it was already more than she'd expected.

He had a new, bad haircut, the top was thick and full, but
the sides were shaved, so his head was shaped like a mushroom:
a little boy's haircut.

"Sylvia must be glad you're home," Cress said.

"Her birthday was Saturday. We had twenty-two people to
Noah Mountain. I made my chili."

"Did she like that?"

"I think she did."

"And you? Are you glad to be home?"

"What do you think?"

"It must be nice to be back with your family."

"I hate every minute I'm not with you."

"You'll get over it," Cress said lightly, and perhaps heart-
lessly, but she had not indulged in such sentiments. She had
been strict with herself.

It was dark when they left the Murdock bar. Outside of
Sparkville, Quinn turned onto a farm road into an olive grove,
the headlights illuminating silvery slim leaves and gnarled,
vaguely human trunks. He parked and held on to her and shook
against her, and finally kissed her. She tasted tears in his beard,
and she knew then how tightly she, too, had been holding back
and wept hotly into his shoulder. They held each other until the

worst passed. Then he put the truck in reverse and drove back to the Staghorn where she'd left her car.

He followed her to Donna's house. Cress zipped the plaid suitcase and shoved it atop some speakers. They had to be extremely quiet; in the next room the fiancés were composing the guest list for their rehearsal dinner, every name audible through the plasterboard walls. Quinn left only at the last possible moment, when he could still make it home before Sylvia did.

Cress now had almost four hundred dollars, and a check coming Friday.

Tillie said, "Good. Make your nut, then get out of there. Don't you think it's high time you ended your little love affair with the working class?"

"I just have to figure out where to go next."

"There might be something for you to do at *City and State*."

"Moving back south just feels so regressive."

"Like waiting tables and dating a married man is progress?" Tillie said. "L.A.'s huge. You can't dismiss it out of hand. Things are picking up! There are jobs—and lots of *single* sad sacks to cheer up."

"Maybe I'll visit Sharon in London." Cress could use a vacation. Her stint on the mountain didn't count; it wasn't a vacation when you were under constant pressure to write your dissertation, even if you were blocked or avoiding it. She hadn't had a real vacation in years. The summer when she and John Bird went camping for a week in Wyoming, they'd drilled each other for their orals the whole time.

Up on the mountain it was snowing more than ever, blizzard after blizzard. Eighteen, then twenty, twenty-two feet accumulated.

You could hop over the power lines, Don Dare reported.

Cress could walk into her A-frame through the second-floor windows. The Simmses' roof had partially collapsed. The state plows hadn't made it up yet, which meant that homeowners had to park two miles below the lodge, where the county stopped plowing, and either snowshoe or ski the rest of the way in.

Cress missed the A-frame. She was sorry not to be there for all that snow.

She and Quinn now drove in aimless, perpendicular patterns past groves of Valencia orange trees simultaneously bearing fruit and blossoming, the perfume heavy, heady, cloying. One night, with no explanation, he took her to a bar in downtown Sparkville, the Coach 'n' 4, where a spoke-wheeled buggy hung from the rafters and harnesses and whips straggled along the walls. The clientele was older and dressier, the bar well stocked. They drank while, three blocks to the east, Sylvia served her regulars fried chicken and hamburger steaks.

Later yet, they sat at Donna's picnic table by the roaring Hapsaw.

"You face-suckers want some Ovaltine?" Donna called from the kitchen.

Owls hoo-hooed. Across the river, coyotes threw their voices to sound like fifty madcap laughers. "You'd better go on home," she said. "Aren't you afraid of being late? She'll wonder where you are."

He said, "That's not for you to worry about."

They slipped out Donna's back gate to lie on thick grass by the loud river, privacy courtesy of a lilac bush. In this way, they kicked loss farther down the road.

In the mornings, Cress woke to the jubilant jeers of mockingbirds. She ached all over from hauling dishes and tables at work, and the exertions of love. She carried her coffee and book outside. Spring was a clear flammable gas in the air. She was reading a novel whose cover showed a naked woman seated in a chair with her hair on fire, a literary novel that was borderline pornographic and seemed of a piece with the tremble of new leaves, the heavy orange perfume, the river's gush, her own sexual fog. (Years later she'd try to reread the book and was surprised that it was about the Holocaust, of which she had no recollection.)

She had not expected this coda with Quinn. This intoxicating encore.

In her spare time, when she wasn't at work or with him, she walked around Sawyer, to the small grocery store for beer or milk. She bought hand-hemmed antique handkerchiefs and embroidered pillowcases at the Ladies Auxiliary thrift store. One evening, she peered in at a storefront church and saw Candy Morrow with her stubby yellow ponytail; she was on her feet, singing and waving her plump arms toward the overhead fluorescents, eyes shut tight.

The days passed, dreamy and distracted. Quinn arranged to see her every day or so, for an hour or half a night, their lovemaking now urgent, intense, constant. She grew unclear where her own body left off and the bursting, efflorescing world began. She bumped into tables at work, rebruised old bruises. She knocked earrings, brushes, and makeup into the bathroom sink. "Sorry, sorry!" she whispered, fishing jewels from the drain.

Dalia asked to speak to Cress one night after the Valley Growers Cooperative Spring Fling. They carried their shift drinks to a table in the bar. "You seem so faraway lately," Dalia said. "I want to say, 'Come back, Cress, come back!'" Dalia clapped her hands in front of Cress's face. Dalia, who was quite tall and big-boned, had such calm authority and poise, she could clap her hands in your face and have it seem a generosity.

"I'm sorry," said Cress. "Am I screwing up?"

"Your work is good. You seem distracted, is all." In her pastel shirtdresses with belted waists and full skirts, Dalia looked like a mother from another generation. Her pale red hair was held off her face by a tortoiseshell band. Cress had heard bits: there had been a violent ex-husband, a protracted divorce, debt;

Dalia and her eight-year-old daughter had a tiny, immaculate house in Sparkville.

"Who's the man with the marvelous voice who calls here?" Dalia asked.

"This guy I know."

"The one you were with at the Coach 'n' 4 the other night?"

"I didn't see you," said Cress. "Why didn't you say hi?"

"His son's in the same class as my Hannah."

Oh.

"And I'm in the same boat." Whispering, Dalia named the white-haired district court judge who sat reading briefs for hours in the Beech Creek lounge. The judge's wife was bedridden with MS and had round-the-clock home care.

"Unfortunately, Quinn's wife is fully ambulatory," said Cress. "But I'll be gone soon enough."

"Just stay through June," Dalia said. "I really need you in June."

Seventeen

May brought the first hot days. Up at the Meadows, the temperature hit seventy-five. The Hapsaw promptly flooded, rising twenty feet: open Donna's back gate and you could step right into roiling coffee-with-cream-colored water. They watched from the picnic table as bushes and tree limbs sailed past, and the occasional whole tree, its tangled roots clutching skull-white rocks, its crown sporting new leaves and bird nests. A water-darkened pink sofa bobbed by, as did a bloated, stiff-legged cow. A small white refrigerator bounced along, jauntily upright. The dark currents twisted, revealed a blear of colored fabric—curtains? Sheets? A drowned woman's skirts?

After five days, the waters receded and black mire plastered the formerly grassy banks like a layer of tar. In two days, new grass poked through, a million bleached yellow needles.

Quinn wanted to show her Noah Mountain. Not the property that his father almost gambled away, where his mother still lived: he didn't dare take Cress there. His mother was always home, and she was an eagle-eyed old gal who knew him far too well. One look at the two of them, Quinn said, and his mother would know everything. He'd take Cress up the Hapsaw's north fork to his favorite hunting and fishing grounds, and Wanderwood.

The north fork was the Hapsaw's smallest tributary, a steeply falling trout stream in a narrow canyon. The water was fast and wild. They had to yell directly into each other's ears to be heard over its roar. They climbed through oaks and grassland into a belt of buckeyes—horse chestnuts—blooming early this year, their thick long white stamens upright in the trees like hundreds of candles. The valley below receded, became a series of rippling ridges. Mist erased all trace of human habitation; here was the primordial view.

Quinn leaped rock to rock soundlessly, his balance thrilling. Cress scrambled after him, grateful that the river's roar covered her stumbles. He'd told her to wear sneakers that could get wet, so she'd borrowed a pair of black Converse low-tops from Donna ("Take them, I never wear them, they're the wrong size, anyway!"), but these provided little traction on dry smooth river rocks and none at all on wet ones.

Startled doves flew off, chortling at their approach. They passed an abandoned apple orchard, the pink-edged blossoms tangled in the unpruned branches like clumps of lace. Quinn's pace was exhausting; she, a daily hiker, grew winded and whimpered freely, unheard over the river. She would not complain. After twenty-odd years of school, she recognized a test.

They stopped for lunch on a granite slab by a deep pool. On the sun-warmed rock, he tugged off her T-shirt, jeans, and under things, then his own, smoothing their clothes for a bed.

Water bashed against the rocks. Ferns unfurled with prehistoric vigor; mist sparkled the air. Quinn's darkening skin took on a glow. His hair had been growing in thicker than ever; it was shaggy now, like a wolf's fur, she thought, and, in this light, silvery. He kissed her collarbones, her breasts, spoke into her low belly words that sped her blood. He rose over her again, and by some trick in the radiant, moist air, his eyes grew darker and greener, until the green's intensity alarmed her: it was grass green, mint-jelly green, transparent and glowing like backlit stained glass. Encircling his irises were blazing amber-gold rings. She closed her eyes, and the gold rings floated like a photographic afterimage, pairs of them clustering in velvety darkness. The altitude and its pranks! They had to be at 5,000 feet.

She kept her eyes shut as they made love, the rings floating in that blackness, her skin oversensitized, so that sexual pleasure intensified to terror.

"We really shouldn't . . . ," she said into his neck.

His low, unintelligible murmur reverberated in her bones.

Afterward, as they sucked in lungfuls of air, she checked: his eyes still glowed that beautiful, insane green, and the gold rings burned into her vision again, then jerked across the ground and bushes when she blinked and looked away. Heightened visuals usually heralded a headache—the one coming promised to be a doozy. She tried to focus on a dogwood blossom, but it took on a strange, moonlike luminosity. An ordinary bush, a rotting tree trunk simmered and seethed, with gold circles lurching in clusters over everything.

"Hey," he said. "Where'd you go?"

She could not say. Light sensitivity could be a problem for her at any altitude, but nothing had ever been this vivid or persistent, not when she'd been stoned, or the two times she'd tried mescaline. Sexual intoxication, exhaustion, sunstroke—surely an explanation existed. Unless—and she suddenly knew this to be true—her own shameful need was manifesting in hallucination.

"You're very pale," he said. "Are you all right?"

She hoped speaking would break the spell. "It's so beautiful here. With you." Idiotic, paltry, but all she could manage. She curled on his chest, closed her eyes, ground a bare foot into granite for pain's clarifying sting. Long minutes passed. He dozed, and a green-gold glow seeped out under his lashes. She wondered if she should rouse him to scramble downstream, get her to an emergency room for a syringe of Thorazine—isn't that how they tranque hallucinators?

Quinn snored softly. His heart thumped beneath her ear, and the world pulsed in its beat. She dreaded the long, slippery stumble back to the car. Clouds massed overhead, sealed off the sun. Restless and chilled, she moved off his chest and, tugging her clothes out from under him, woke him. In this more muted light, his eyes had dimmed to a bluer alfalfa green—which meant at least some of her problem was atmospheric.

Dressed and shod, she expected them to turn back, but he led her farther upstream. Rocks clinked under her slipping feet with a weird, internal sound, like bones shifting in her head. The trees grew taller, the air colder and sharp. Winded, she breathed in gasps, and stayed far enough behind so he could not hear her. An ache thudded in the base of her skull. He paused on a sandbank, squinted into the woods, then took her inland on two faint wheel tracks with shin-high weeds in between. The river's thunder receded, eclipsed by birdsong and the angry chuttering of squirrels. The understory thinned, and they came alongside a small, clear, musical creek—Lizzy Creek, he said—and soon entered a roomy grove of giant sequoias.

He said, "My favorite place on earth."

Cinnamon-red, the columnar trees stood singly and in fraternal clumps, the branches began high up and were short, like pudgy, cartoonish arms, their greenery scant and feathery, and tipped in bright new growth. Among the living trees sat many stumps, twelve to twenty feet high and ten, twelve, fifteen feet in diameter; they seemed human-sized, habitable, like so many small hermitages—some, where lightning had burned out the core, were already hollow; you could move in, install a Dutch door, deep-silled windows, flower boxes.

He'd wanted to show her this: Wanderwood, the only privately owned sequoia grove left. Once, over a thousand giant sequoias had grown here, but there had been waves of logging, in the beginning of the twentieth century and again midcentury. The mountain had swarmed with men and oxen, saws, axes, log-moving chutes; a long, sturdy flume had floated roughcut lumber to the sawmill near Sawyer. All was still now, the buildings torn down, the machinery dismantled and hauled off. Nature had crept back and all that devastation was now a sparseness in the canopy, a few yards of cart track, an empty flume, those stumps and the lingering, stunned silence of an old battlefield where a massacre had taken place.

All the other redwood groves in the area had been incorporated into National Forest, Quinn said, but this one had not. The preservationists had run out of steam, or money, for a final fight. Luckily, the present owner was a man Cress's age, a liberal hippie sort, said Quinn, and he'd vowed to preserve the hundred or so remaining trees.

(In a few years, though, the owner's three children would be in private schools, with college looming. He'd begin by lumbering the stumps. The first two trees he'd fell would shatter when hitting the ground. Even then, each tree provided a year's extra salary, easy to get used to. But that day in May 1982, the stumps stood as they had for decades among trees older than Christendom.)

A cold gust brought a swirl of sharp, splintery snow. Suddenly snow hissed all around them. Quinn drew her inside a burned-out stump, the inner walls a quilted carbon blackness. She sat between his legs, against his chest; he produced a thermos of brandied coffee; they passed the thermal cup—the hot bitter liquid dulled the thudding in her skull. Snow collected in patches of bright green new grass like a great spill of sugar.

Warmed by their body heat, the stump's inside began to reek of urine. "Ready?" he said, and led her downhill on a passable dirt road through the trees. (They could've driven here!) Within minutes, they were out of the redwoods, back in the pines. The snow stopped, the temperature rose; clouds slid off the sun. Light bounced off droplets and puddles, reigniting her headache. For an hour, they trotted down the road. When wet, blue, slag-faced Noah Mountain loomed close on their right, Quinn drew her to the shoulder and pointed to the wide grassy saddle below where his mother's small white clapboard house sat across from the terrible barn and perpendicular to the double-wide trailer where he and his family lived before the war over heirlooms. By the barn, the small travel trailer tipped toward its tongue, its tiny, useless wings pointing up.

His eyes were almost normal now, the pale, soft blue-gray of sage.

It had taken them four hours to clamber upstream to the redwoods. By the road, they were back at Quinn's truck in an hour and ten minutes. "Sylvia never made it up that canyon," Quinn said. "She gets maybe a quarter of the way, sits, and refuses to take another step."

His admiration, so far as Cress could tell, went both ways: to Cress, for hiking all the way, and to Sylvia, for her flat refusal to proceed.

She went home and crawled into her bed. Pain swirled and crackled through her head, accompanied by sprays of small, whirling prisms and blue sparks, and the occasional reprise of rings, now ghostly white. Her feet were swollen and blistered, her calves and thighs sore to the touch. She spotted a bottle of aspirin in Donna's bathroom and helped herself.

After a golf lady luncheon—twenty-two women, eight dollars and seventy-five cents in tips—Cress drove into Sparkville for groceries: her turn had come to buy coffee, milk, and bread for the household. She called Donna from the wall-mounted pay phone outside the Younts coffee shop: "Do we need anything else?"

"Quinn called," Donna said. "He says it's urgent, call him back."

Cress didn't recognize the number. Then again, she'd never called Quinn at any number. Wanting more privacy than this public wall phone afforded, she crossed the parking lot to a dusty glass booth. A woman with a gruff, low voice answered, and when Cress asked for Quinn, the woman set down the phone without another word.

"Where are you?" Cress said.

"My mom's," said Quinn. "Look, Cress, I've made a decision."

"Okay," she said, and wondered what decision needed to be made.

"I'm going to get a divorce." This was the first time he'd

used the word to her. He said it the way DeeDee had. DEE. Dee-vorce.

In that instant, a new landscape unfurled in all directions: the very fields and precincts they'd vowed never to enter, where innocents would be hurt and she'd be implicated. Terror was her first reaction. Terror, then intense interest.

She echoed him, with her own pronunciation. "Divorce, Quinn? Really?" Who knew he'd ever consider it! But good. Maybe they could spend the night together again. Be together out in the open. Take trips. Santa Barbara, Mexico.

"It's been a long time coming," he said.

Yes, and the divorces she knew about—of her friends' parents and her parents' friends—took a long time to happen, too. Lawyers were involved, and hard-to-get signatures, court appearances, shouting and sobbing. Her mother spent hours with Francine Davis listening, soothing, advising. Francine's daughter Jennie was Cress's good friend, and the two had crouched in the hall to hear Francine weep in her bedroom. Cress recalled, too, a sleepover at the father's new apartment, the empty beige rooms and mothball smell.

Even if Quinn passed through all that tumult, who's to say that he and she would care for each other on the far side?

"Are you there, Cress?" said Quinn. "I tried being home. I was out of my mind. I drove up here today and talked to my mom. I told her everything."

His mother, who'd clonked the phone on some table just now? The bear-killing librarian? "That's good, Quinn, that you talked—"

"I'm going to dee-vorce Sylvia," he said, "and marry you."

"Oh now," she said. "I mean, one thing at a time. Let's not—"

"Even before I left the mountain, Cress, I knew."

She stood up straight, nose level with the punch pad on the pay phone. She had been disciplined. She had not allowed her affections to range so far afield. She'd held herself in check. Marry? She never let herself imagine it. Where would they live? And what about her friends—her Pasadena friends from childhood: What would they think of him, or he of them?

"If you will have me. Cress? Are you there?"

If you will have me. The tremble in his voice hit low, like sex. "If it ever comes to that," she said quickly, "yes, yes, of course," because it was urgent to reassure him. And to keep the matter open so she could think it over at leisure, in private, because the slightest hesitation here might frighten him off. She wanted, at the very least, to prolong the incredible flattery of his offer, for it was an offer, wasn't it? And who had ever wanted her so much? Saying yes to him, yes of course, in an easy, offhand, contingent way, bought her time. Also, she was stunned, perhaps even in shock, the way people are when they win a lottery; they have to sit down, and sometimes they keel right over. She sagged against the booth's scratched graffited glass wall, the greasy receiver pressed against her ear. "But so much has to happen before we can even really . . . I mean, you might change your mind a hundred—"

"I've never been more sure of anything in my life." His beautiful low voice coursed directly into her blood. "Or I never would of spoke of it."

"Okay." She was breathless. "Okay, Quinn." He would have to be sure for both of them then.

"And even if you won't have me, I can't stay married to Sylvia. That's over. I'm done."

The sun had dunked behind the industrial buildings across the street. Long shadows stretched over the asphalt. The sky was pale yellow. "What did your mom say?"

"That I have to do what I have to do. Whatever makes me happy."

"You told her about me?"

"She knows there's someone."

"And Sylvia? Have you talked to her?"

"I won't till Annette graduates," he said. "I won't take away from Annette's big day."

Oh. So nothing irrevocable had happened after all.

Except that he had asked her to marry him, and she had said yes.

She'd told him yes when he wasn't in any real position to ask. *Look me up after you've done all the hard stuff*—that's what she should've said. But it was too late. She'd already answered.

He was still talking. He was dying to see her. He wished they could meet right now. He wanted to hold her, to lay her down. His term: *lay her down.* It came from a country song, and his use of it embarrassed her, especially now. She didn't like to talk about sex. She preferred to be more oblique and private about it. But he couldn't see her, he was saying. Not tonight. He was tied up. There was a big family dinner at Caleb's house, Sylvia and the kids would be there, and he was taking his mother. He'd see Cress tomorrow, he'd phone her at work. They'd figure everything out. He loved her. She knew that, didn't she? He loved her more than anything else on earth. They'd have a long, happy life together.

"Okay," she whispered. "Okay, Quinn."

Walking back across the parking lot, exuberance, and something like triumph, welled in her chest. So much still had to happen, but who knew he'd come this far? He'd told his mother! Of course, telling Sylvia would make it real in a way he probably didn't anticipate. Even Cress knew this. Sylvia would not say, *Whatever makes you happy.* He really should not have proposed till he'd talked to Sylvia. And not over the phone. Cress had made a mistake, too, she thought, in answering him so quickly. She should have put him off. Or said something even more equivocal: *Let's talk about it when the time comes.* Or: *Let's not talk about it over the phone.* But what she'd said wasn't so terrible. *If it ever comes to that.*

Despite her trepidation, jubilance kept bursting through. He did love her! She'd known it, of course, but hadn't permitted the words to form. Her own reticence, the stringency with which she'd held herself back, those thick old leather harness straps, had loosened once they came off the mountain, and now had fallen away. She could let herself go—or could no longer hold back. Of course she loved him. Allowed, love rippled retrospectively through their time together like a frisky zephyr, ruffling memories, sweetening and brightening all that had passed between them. She had been so firm and practical, she had built barriers of his faults, never once imagining *marriage*. Somehow, she'd played it just right. She felt clever, and carefully ecstatic, as if she'd coaxed a bull elk to nuzzle corn from her palm.

She went back inside Younts and bought the food he liked: pork chops, thick tortillas, jack cheese, eggs, thin breakfast steaks. She'd cook for him again, when the jumbo roommates weren't hogging the kitchen. Back in the Saab, she bumped over the train tracks on the outskirts of town in the hazy blue dusk. Engaged. Spoken for. Her hand was taken. It was a secret engagement, true. And bound to be a long one. A marriage had to end. Divorce filed for. A year must pass from the date of filing, and the filing itself could be weeks, even months away. She had time, at least, to get used to the idea. Or find a way out.

Since she was a little girl, she'd wondered whom she would marry, and now, it seemed, she knew. Quinn Morrow—was that even possible? He was not any of the husbands she'd imagined— not a bearish professor, jolly and loquacious, who was also an improbably good dancer. Not an intense, thin intellectual, a philosopher or historian, curly-haired, complicated, and probably Jewish. Not an artist, either, masculine, laconic, and moody—though Quinn was closest to that. A gloomy whittler! A handsome father of two, a skilled outdoorsman. A fine architectural woodworker, smart and agile and sad. Her heart lunged recalling his sadness. She would be his companion, yes.

The sudden constriction of possibilities also kicked up whiffs of disappointment—but wouldn't it always? Doesn't every choice eliminate all others, including some quite appealing? But choosing also spawned a hundred new possibilities: Where would they live? Who would work? Would they stay in the area? Could she bear that? If so, would she even need to finish her dissertation? Would there be babies? Maybe they'd live in the A-frame again—why not move back up tomorrow? Or rather, the day after Annette graduated. When was that? Cress had seen something on the schedule at work, a high-school graduation party later in May.

She'd missed her turn east and found herself in a dusty neighborhood along the train tracks. Body shops and salvage yards alternated with the occasional old farmhouse. Cress pulled into a dirt driveway to turn around. A hand-lettered sign by the mailbox said, DATSIE PUPPIES FOR SALE. On the porch a large, older woman in a pale yellow housedress rose from her metal chair, perhaps taking Cress for a dog shopper.

Quinn had no right. He was in no position to ask her. Divorce was just an idea of his, fragile and untested, a pale flower in a pitch-dark cave that might shrivel when brought to light. When he told Sylvia.

And he'd proposed on the phone. When he was married to someone else.

She shouldn't have answered him. She should've put him off. Or, changed the subject. *Hey! Those buckeyes bloom long on Noah Mountain?* She could have been sterner: *Now is not the time or place to discuss it.* Well, she'd blown it. At the first provocation, all that she'd held in check for months and months had boiled up and out. Impossible now to stuff it all back inside.

Sylvia, the few times Cress had seen her, had not seemed like a woman at dire odds with her husband. What if she didn't let him go? Or worse, what if his leaving pushed her over some edge? Guilt sloshed up, a tepid, brackish bath. Better nip the whole thing in the bud, before anyone got hurt.

Quinn phoned again as Cress was wedging meat packs into Donna's crammed-to-capacity freezer. He was whispering—his extended family was in the other room. "Maybe don't tell your parents just yet," he said. "Let's wait till things are a little further along before we make any big announcements."

Eighteen

"I'll just get my degree and teach," she said. "That will give us a good base income. We can still live up here. I can commute."

He said, "I don't care where we live, so long as we're together."

She was more marvelous than she knew.

"I'd like a little log cabin, in a meadow," she said.

"Can do," he said. But there were college towns he liked, too. Claremont, in the orange groves up against the mountains would do. Davis—the Sacramento Delta had some appeal. Even New York City, if they lived on Long Island, or the Jersey Shore. She wouldn't have to take any old job. Or any job at all. He'd support her. That, frankly, was his dream. To give her all she wanted. To take on her well-being as his responsibility. He'd be honored. The economy was picking up. He'd find work. Cabinetry or, if worst came to worst, framing.

Tillie said, "That's all very romantic and stirring, Cress, especially for you, given your stingy dad. But let's be practical. You will have to work. Because by the time your guy's paid his alimony and child support, there won't be much left for the two of you."

"I don't care about all that," Cress said. "Any of it."

Sunday morning, Cress went with Donna to the Sparkville swap meet. In the dusty vacant lot across from Food King, she bought three big boxes of Limoges china, the pattern a simple rectilinear band in gold-on-white porcelain from the last century: platters, soup terrines, coffee and tea pots, plus place settings for twelve, all for sixty dollars—which was still the most she'd spent on any household item in her life. When she held a plate up to the sun, she could see the shadow of her fingers through the china. She imagined the gold rims drawing light on a long pine table within dark log walls. Once she hauled it back to Donna's, the china seemed presumptuous, ill-timed, and she was too shy to show it to Quinn, who didn't notice the boxes stacked atop all the other stuff in her room.

The next week, with Donna at the much larger Fresno swapper, a bearskin sprawled on the hood of a vendor's Chevy pickup, a large old pale-snouted black bear backed in billiard-green felt. A persistent slice of sunlight had striped one thick paw; otherwise, the fur was thick and shiny, the snarling head intact, the glass eyes a rich brown, the teeth yellowed with varnish, the tongue a genital-pink plaster hump. He—Cress assumed so large a specimen was male—could not have been her former hungry visitor; this skin was clearly old—but it might have been her fellow's grandpapa. She trembled, knowing she would buy it even before a price was named; this would be her engagement present to Quinn, handed over when he gave her a ring. (Engagement present! The very idea of an *engagement present* came to her at the exact moment she laid eyes on the bearskin—the term itself must have seeped up osmotically from the stacks of women's magazines beneath her bed.) The skin, she knew, would make him laugh. It would go, of course, in front of their fireplace. Their hearth. The vendor asked for three hundred dollars and took her check for two. He folded the skin ceremoniously into a tight package, felt side out, which he wrapped in heavy brown paper and tied with multiple loops of hairy twine. Cress and Donna carried it together, heaving it into the Saab's trunk. On the drive back to Sawyer, remorse set in for gutting her bank account. "Don't let me be so impulsive," she told Donna. She left the bundle in the Saab's trunk, pending its presentation.

That was the fourth Sunday in May. Annette was graduating on Wednesday.

Beech Creek Country Club counted nine graduating seniors among its member families. The party was set up for a hundred. Tri-tip roasts were grilled on a big drum barbecue wheeled to the ninth hole. Bartenders poured unlimited soft drinks, which the kids fortified in the parking lot. After dinner and a short ceremony, a local rock band launched into "We've Gotta Get Out of This Place," and the dance floor filled.

Cress watched this, as she did all such celebrations of provincial life, with a mixture of wonder and contempt. Her own high-school graduation had been marked by a long, boring commencement at the Rose Bowl—her mother left to finish dinner before Cress's name was called—and that night a lady's Timex in its clear plastic case appeared beside her place mat. The thin brushed-gold band was designed for another kind of girl, the sedate, pretty, jewelry-wearing daughter Sylvia Hartley would have preferred. The tiny watch face with its speck-like numerals was virtually unreadable. Cress feigned pleasure for the gift and never wore it. She noticed the watch was missing her sophomore year, no doubt stolen from her dorm room still twist-tied in its original packaging.

Dalia came up beside her by the dance floor. "See that big kid with the butch cut?" She nodded to a likely linebacker, a pale, thick teen clearly raised on tube biscuits and grease gravy.

"Good dancer," Cress said, for despite his bulk and self-satisfied smirk, the boy moved nimbly, even delicately.

"See her?" prodded Dalia. His partner was a buoyant, curly-maned girl who pranced and swiveled in patent-leather kitten heels. She made little come-hither motions with her hands, then scram-scram ones; she tossed her masses of hair and tottered away, only to mince backward and collapse laughing in her partner's arms.

"Cute," Cress said.

"That's your girl."

"Mine?" Then a comic sternness in the girl's brow recalled a broader, manlier brow, and the bright mischief in her eyes was altogether familiar. Annette. And Cress began to love.

"I told her," Quinn said in a low rasp.

Clutching the extension at the end of its spiraling cord in the dim hallway outside of her bedroom, Cress sat on the carpet. "Where are you now?"

"My mom's. I've moved out. We're getting divorced."

"You okay?"

"Not so much."

"You want me to come up? You want to come down?"

"You're sweet. I can't right now."

Cress said, "Sylvia took it hard."

"No idea it was coming." Sylvia knew he'd been unhappy, he said. But not that unhappy. And not unhappy with her.

"You didn't tell her about me."

"It's not about you."

"Good," she said.

It was weird, he said. He'd been so mad at Sylvia for so long, about so much, but now that he'd finally had it out with her, he couldn't recall what had made him so furious. He had some weird kind of amnesia. Or he was in shock.

(He shouldn't be telling me this, Cress thought. But she didn't stop him. She needed to hear whatever he might say in order to gauge her own position and relative safety.) He knew he wanted out of the marriage; he'd wanted out for months. Years, honestly. But he couldn't remember why. He was exhausted. His mind and emotions had shut down.

He didn't remember that Sylvia bored him? That she'd failed to console him after his father's terrible death? That twenty years of anxiety and timidity had worn him down until his last tie to her was pity, and even that pity had lost its grip, like old glue that dried and flaked away? Cress would not remind him, of course. It was not her place to remind him.

He didn't seem to remember that he loved her, either.

"I need a few days," he said. "To take it all in."

"Yes, yes." Cress got to her feet. "Of course you do. Take your time."

"We'll talk. When the coast clears a little."

Cress beelined past the large fiancés lounging in the living room. Outside, by the Hapsaw, in the warm humid dusk, she shivered as if cold. A soiled white mist crept upstream. She was frightened to think that she'd caused pain—even if Quinn hadn't named her. What if Sylvia did something drastic? Cress imagined her sprawled facedown on that shiny, baby-blue bedspread, dark curls fanned over a pillow.

Cress shuddered and looked around. The ever-trundling Hapsaw was a midsized roil of muddy water with suds along its banks. Crabgrass choked Donna's lawn, and lawns up and down the riverbanks. Even the towering, white-armed sycamore appeared lopsided and ungainly, devoid of enchantment.

In the morning, he had to see her. It was urgent. He missed her. No, he didn't need more time to think things through. He was sick of thinking. He needed to see her warm, wide-open face, feel her smooth long fingers on his skin, smell her hair, which always reminded him of sleeping in the grass in the sun. He should be suffering alone, he knew, yes, yes, in exile; spiraling down to some essential truth about himself and his marriage, but he just couldn't bear to be away from her.

It was Saturday, and Cress was working the 320-person Franklin–Gillette wedding reception, whose setup started at noon; the meal, toasts, and dancing would last deep into evening; she probably couldn't meet him till sometime after ten, and only then if Dalia let her off before the very end.

He'd been drinking when she got to the Staghorn. He looked ashen, walloped, ill. She nosed his neck; his hair felt damp and hot underneath, he'd bathed and perfumed himself for her. His body quaked as she held him. "Nobody is making you do this," she whispered. "You don't have to go through with it. I'll be fine no matter what." She meant to soothe, to remove pressure; never mind if, for the moment, she exaggerated her own emotional capacities.

They hurried to Donna's house, to the tiny close gray room where they could speak only in the lowest whispers. He yanked her clothes off, gasping and determined, and they made love in desperate silence. Yes, it was as always, their great comfort and relief. His color returned, he stroked her face, looked long into her eyes. On the other side of the thin wall, Norma and Ike debated between prime rib and baron of beef for their wedding dinner. Surf and turf—excitement amplified Norma's voice— was only a dollar twenty more per person. See? On the list? Murmuring, and then, "No, Ike, we *need* the cobbler. Wedding cake doesn't count as dessert."

In the morning Cress was carrying two cups of coffee down the hall when Norma emerged from her room in her white terrycloth robe. "Morning," Cress said softly. The robe brushed past, flattening Cress against the wall. Coffee slopped on her bare foot.

She and Quinn huddled in bed with their mugs, gazing at the blank white closet doors. "I'll talk to Annette this week," he said. "She'll know, of course. She's home with her mom. I really want her to meet you. Down the line."

"In due time," Cress said.

"Evan will be the hardest," said Quinn. "I'll have to be very careful how I tell him so he doesn't take it on himself."

She touched his hip under the covers. They both felt ill, feverish, here, mid-gauntlet, the numinous months on the mountain behind them, the future a blur. They were together right now, in bed, naked, the coffee strong and delicious: weren't these the very components of their previous bliss? Would these elements ever again coalesce into happiness?

Cress was grateful, later, for the mindless setting up and taking down of banquets. The waitresses unfolded heavy pipe-legged tables, arranged, clothed, and set them; they hauled out the parquet dance floor in plywood-sized pieces. Because Cress had a "good eye," Dalia assigned her boxing and skirting duties, which meant she created virginal, linen-wrapped head tables, gift tables, tables for the cake, for champagne-glass pyramids.

A few weeks of weddings had made the waitresses into experts and brutal, mocking critics. "Not another mauve-and-ice-blue color scheme!" one of them would cry across the hall as they set up. "Not another peach wedding!"

"Should I ever marry again, my color scheme will be plaid," declared one waitress. Lisette, the head waitress, claimed polka dots; another waitress gingham. Cress said, "Maybe I'll have a striped wedding—or make that a leather wedding— No! no! not black leather, you pervs. More like a tanned-hide wedding . . . Oh shut up, everyone!" They uniformly disdained dyed carnations and any silk flowers; Cress alone defended a red rose, pine bough, and pinecone centerpiece. They were ruthless on wedding dresses and anything-but-black on groomsmen. "More powder-blue poufters!" a waitress sang into the break room to announce the arrival of yet another wedding party.

Cress drove home at midnight, her shift drink sweating between her knees in a waxy, twenty-ounce to-go cup. When she awoke, her tiny room was humid and cloyed with the evaporate of undrunk bourbon.

Between her lunch and evening shifts, Cress sat in the sun in Donna's backyard. The river had clarified and darkened; the low tones in its juicy passage resonated with the ache in her chest. She'd given up on the semi-porn novel. Her mind clicked and calculated. She was not a cost-effective choice for Quinn. He'd lose daily access to his children, the house in town, not to mention a wife's beauty and faultless housekeeping. And for what? A broad-faced, homeless All-but-Disser with a bank account in the mid–three figures? (Four hundred and twenty-eight dollars to be exact, thanks to her swap-meet splurges.) Also, Quinn knew she'd lived with boyfriends; he knew—in the vaguest way—that she'd dated Jakey. Having had Sylvia exclusively to himself might mean more to him than he realized. His generation put a premium on that sort of thing, while hers considered virginity and, to some extent, the monogamous impulse itself, a liability.

He phoned her midday as she fed the lady golfers. Dalia let her take the call in her office, for privacy. Annette had been sweet, he said. She, too, had said, *Whatever makes you happy, Daddy.* Also, *If you don't love Mom anymore, you don't love her—and I hope you find someone you do.*

"I love you, Cress," he said. "I wish this part was over."

Sylvia was the hitch. Sylvia was why this part wasn't over. Sylvia was suffering. He hadn't been able to talk to her yet about the next steps: hiring lawyers, dividing accounts. She was weeping all the time, and calling in sick to work. Perhaps she was too timid and fragile to survive on her own.

"She managed well enough when Quinn was on the mountain," Donna said. "And why would she want to stay married to him? If I was her, I'd wash my hands of him. Once guys start tomcatting, it's a hard habit to break."

Cress was grateful that Donna had reminded her: Sylvia had a job. She worked, she could support herself. She'd be fine. She'd get the house, and alimony. She'd remarry, too. Men liked her: a fox.

Then Annette announced that she would put off college for a year and stay at home to see her mother through this patch. For both of them to leave at once, Annette told Quinn, was too hard on her mom. No big deal, Annette said, really. She'd take classes at Sparkville Community College, get a job. Of course, Quinn forbade Annette to do this, although how he planned to prevent her—Annette was eighteen now and free to do as she pleased—he didn't say. He was also proud, Cress could see, of his daughter's generosity.

Cress did not want Sylvia to be miserable. But Sylvia should accept reality. Quinn was unhappy, and had been for years. Did Sylvia expect him to stay around just to keep her unhappiness at bay?

Cress worried, of course, that Sylvia might commit suicide. How had Quinn put it? The meanest thing a person can do to someone else.

Sylvia didn't kill herself. On a tip, she asked her daughter's pale, burly boyfriend to drive her to the Staghorn, where Quinn's truck and Cress's Saab mingled openly in the parking lot. The boyfriend peered inside, reported back. Sylvia directed him then to Corky Ned's Liquor Stop by the lake, where, being too distraught to go inside, she sent him in for a flat pint of whiskey, which he purchased with his fake ID. Back at the Staghorn, they parked around on the side, passed the flat warm bottle, and waited. In half an hour, they caravanned unseen behind Quinn and Cress to Donna's house. Sylvia was slipping out from under her seat belt by then, and so the boyfriend drove her home.

The next morning, Sylvia awoke and drove herself through woolly Thule fog, visibility thirty feet, the ten miles back to

Donna's house, where Quinn's truck was still parked. She wasn't surprised, she'd told Quinn. On some level, she'd known all along.

"I'm sorry. She had a real bad night," Cress whispered into the phone at the Petrocchi–Evans reception. "I know you wanted to keep me out of it."

"That's because you are not the cause," said Quinn. "Our marriage has been dead for a long time."

"Does Sylvia agree that it's dead?"

"She had no idea I felt that way. Which tells you how little she knows me. How little she noticed."

Men, Cress knew, sometimes said that their marriage was dead when their wives lost interest in making love. Mustering her courage, she asked.

"No, no. That was always the one good thing between us," Quinn said. "I never got tired of her that way."

Cress had her lady golfers on Monday, and a small dinner for the Old Duffers, a seniors-only male golf club that night. By the time she walked into the Staghorn to meet Quinn, it was ten o'clock. She was the only woman in the room. Men, mostly older, clumped around the small wobbly tables, and a few more sat scattered along the bar. She took a stool at the far end, near the sink, where the bartender, who knew her now, could run interference should she need it. No, he said, Quinn had not been in yet. She ordered a beer and sipped it, and after ten minutes, she took out a scrap of paper and, to appear occupied, pretended to write a shopping list. *Coffee, pork chops, razors, heroin, hanging rope.* The bartender set down another beer even as she still had most of her first. "He says hello, is all," he said, when she tried to refuse it. Her benefactor—white-haired, sixty-ish, handsome— saluted her with a finger to his curly eyebrow. She slid off her stool. Let Quinn find her at Donna's; he could tap on her window or pitch a handful of gravel.

But he never did tap or pitch and it was her turn for a sleepless night. The streetlight cast its chilly violet glare through
the thin curtain. She forbade herself to get back into the Saab.
She wasn't a person who drove all over in the middle of the
night to spy on her boyfriend and his wife, even if an effort was
required not to be that person; even if speeding down dark high-
ways was far more alluring than tossing and turning in this
airless clutterbox of a room.

In the morning, the phone rang, and Norma hit the receiver
against her hollow-core door, three short, rude raps.

He was sorry. Sylvia had wanted to talk. She'd swapped shifts
with another waitress and driven up to Noah Mountain. She
stayed till midnight. He couldn't phone Cress with Sylvia there,
and it was too late after she left. They'd had to hash out everything. He owed her that much. Sylvia said if more attention was
what he needed, she would *love* to provide it. In fact, she told
him, she would do anything, anything he wanted, if he would
come back home.

"And you said . . . ," said Cress.

"The time for doing is past. What's done is done."

Cress slid down the wall and sat on the gritty hall runner.

He needed to see her. What time was she getting off work?

They made a plan and, stupid from the one-two punch of
terror and relief, Cress wandered into the kitchen for coffee. In
the living room, Donna and Norma sat on the boxy old-fashioned
maroon sofa. Cress lifted her cup in greeting. In her thick white
bathrobe, her hair turbanned in a towel, Norma stood and
steered herself out of the room. For days now, Cress realized,
whenever she'd entered a room, Norma left it.

Donna patted the sculpted mohair. "Cress, come sit for a
minute."

Norma's heat lingered on the cushion, and the air there
smelled of crème rinse. "Until the wedding," Donna said, "this
is Norma's home. You must see that it's hard for her to have you
and Quinn carrying on in the next room."

Carrying on? "But we're completely quiet! Never a peep."

"What you two are doing goes against everything Norma and Ike are moving toward."

"It's got nothing to do with them!"

"And I don't like it, either," Donna said quietly.

"I thought you liked Quinn. You knew that he and I . . ."

"I knew Quinn had gone back home to his family."

"I didn't expect it to blow up like this. I never dreamed—"

"Please don't bring him here anymore," Donna said. "And this—you being here—isn't working out, either. You can stay till June 14, which gives you time to find another place."

A week! "You're kicking me out? Why? What'd I do?"

"For one, I'd like you to stop wearing those black sneakers."

"Oh! But I thought you didn't . . ."

"I lent them to you for one hike. And you've been wearing them ever since. I'd also appreciate it if you stopped using my makeup and perfume. And I'd like you to replace that earring."

Cress gaped at Donna. "What earring?" she said.

"The gold one that's a jointed fish."

"I never borrowed any of your earrings," Cress said.

"Well, it's missing, and since you help yourself to things that don't belong to you, it's logical to assume you had something to do with it."

"A touch of lip gloss is hardly the same as stealing a gold earring."

Donna set her cup down and frowned. "There's a carelessness about you, Cress, and a blurriness about what's yours and what's not. That earring disappeared since you've been here . . ."

Cress did not know what to say. She'd assumed it was okay to wear the sneakers again. Given Donna's vast inventory of *stuff,* who knew that she closely monitored drugstore lip gloss, musk oil, and secondhand shoes that didn't fit her and she never wore? And yet, to hear Donna list her crimes, Cress had to admit: it did sound like thievery. Thievery and thoughtlessness.

"Ask Don if you can borrow his room here in town." Donna's

tone softened. "He never uses it. But Norma deserves to feel comfortable in her own home."

Rosellen, the day bartender at Beech Creek, was a humorless older woman with a gray beehive who'd been working there for more than twenty years. She motioned Cress up to the bar. "What's your whole name, Cress?"

"Cressida. Cressida Hartley."

"I thought so. Listen. I don't want to scare you, but you should know. Some people in this town are not your friends."

"Like who?"

"That little storefront church behind the market? My daughter goes to prayer circle there. She came home last night and said you were on the prayer list. They were trying to pray you out of town."

Her mother phoned from the Meadows, and asked Cress to meet them for breakfast at the Sawyer Inn. The three of them took a booth in the log-lined dining room. What were her plans, they wanted to know. Was she done with the A-frame? Could they start renting it out? "We sure can use the revenue," her father said. "After the bath we took from Rick Garsh."

Go ahead, rent it, Cress told them. She could move her boxes over to the new house. At any rate, she'd be driving up in the next few days to get her summer clothes. She was thinking of going to Pasadena for a while.

Her parents exchanged glances and mutually decided not to press her. She guessed then that they'd made a vow not to mention the diss. Grateful, she wished she had something more to offer them—and she did, a wisp: "So you know, I've been seeing somebody. Uh—a man. We might be getting married."

"Married?" her mother said. "May we ask this man's name?"

"I can't say yet. It might not happen."

"Why can't you say?"

"Can't say."

Her parents looked at each other. "Well, let us know when you can say," her father said.

"It won't be for at least a year. Probably a little longer than that."

"Does this fellow know he's marrying an heiress?" said her father.

"I'll be sure to tell him, Dad."

"Sam," her mother said, "will you do me a favor and get me a couple of aspirin out of the car? They're in the blue tote bag, behind the front seat."

Her father, sixty-six years old, stood. "Anything else while I'm up?"

"Pay," her mother said, and handed him the check on its little tray.

Her mother waited until he'd left the restaurant. "So let me guess," she said. "He's married, right?"

Cress dipped her head.

"The finish carpenter."

"How did you know?"

"A little bird. Is he getting a divorce?"

"Supposedly." Cress's eyes filled with tears. "I don't really know," she said. "I'm not sure he can go through with it. She's putting up a fight."

"Oh, Cress." Sylvia Hartley reached for her daughter's arm and searched out her eyes. "I can't believe this is happening. I vowed never to let anything like this happen to either of my daughters. It's the worst pain. I know."

She knew because something similar had happened to her, with her drama teacher at Penn, a man eighteen years her senior, who was married, with five children, a three-story house in Melrose Park, and tenure. They'd fallen in love her junior year during a production of *Two Gentlemen of Verona*—she'd played Julia—and that love hadn't gone away or lessened over time.

She'd had no choice but to stay on after graduating. He rented her a tiny furnished room downtown, where all she did was wait—for his visits, his phone calls, his divorce. At some point, his wife called her parents, who showed up, moved her out of the apartment, and shipped her across country to Aunt Shula in Hollywood.

Is that what happened? According to family myth, Cress's mother moved to Hollywood to further her acting career. "Did you ever see him again?"

"After your grandfather spoke to him, he wouldn't even answer my letters. It almost killed me. I suffered till I met your father, and even then . . . Your Quinn might have more courage. Does his wife know about you?"

"We tried to keep me out of it, but she spied on us. And now they're having these long talks."

"Some of the worst marriages have very deep roots," her mother said gently. "For your sake, Cress, I hope he doesn't pull it off. You don't want stepkids. And you'll never be shed of her, between the children and alimony."

"I don't care about all that," said Cress.

"I do," her mother said dryly. "I want so much more for you. But here. Before your father comes back."

Sylvia Hartley rummaged in her blue leatherette handbag, pulled out a checkbook, and scribbled intently. "Go away," she said, pushing the folded paper across the table. "Go see your sister. Take yourself out of the equation. It's your only chance. Let them sort it out. If he's serious, he'll come after you. If he doesn't, you're well rid of him."

Her father walked up, shaking a large bottle of aspirin. "Is the coast clear?"

"For God's sake, Sam," her mother said. "I only wanted a couple."

They left the restaurant together. Her parents climbed into the Jeep and drove off. Cress unfolded the check. Five hundred dollars.

"If you leave me," Quinn said, "I would still divorce her."

"I'm not leaving you," she said, now for the fourth or fifth time. She was just going out of town till the dust settled. How could Sylvia believe that Cress wasn't a factor if Quinn was with her all the time?

Besides, Donna had evicted her. And those prayers nipped at her heels, she could feel them. All signs pointed out of town. She'd only be in Pasadena, a hundred and sixty miles away. They'd talk every night. He could visit anytime. Once the coast was clear, she'd come back. He need only say the word.

She didn't mention London; London was her contingency plan.

"I don't know if I can bear your not being here," he said.

"We could always move to the A-frame," said Cress. "Nobody's rented it yet."

His face brightened, then he shook his head. That would only inflame the situation. No sense rushing into anything, when reason and gentleness might prevail. So. Hmm. Maybe her leaving town for a bit was a good idea.

"Tell Quinn to settle things with his wife in the next few days," Dalia said. "June is crazy busy, and if you leave now, I just don't know how I'll manage."

Nineteen

At six thousand feet, two inches of new undisturbed snow from a freak late storm blanketed the road. The Saab's tires held, and once Cress turned into the Meadows, the road was plowed. Smoke billowed from the lodge's stone chimney. Tire tracks corrugated the parking lot. She recognized Rick Garsh's work truck and Kevin's Toyota.

The A-frame was dark, the water and heat had been turned off. The fireplace held a match-ready fire, but she didn't feel entitled to light it. The macramé, the grocer's scale with its dusty pinecones had been restored to their former places. She had been gone for two months.

Seeing the wicker love seat and hard bed delivered shocks of pain. An ache lodged high in her chest, as if she'd swallowed a sharp pit. She pulled out her boxes and found the vintage rayon housedresses she'd worn all last summer in Pasadena and a pair of vintage red pedal pushers from the fifties with a side zipper. Here was the gingham shirt she wore last August; Jakey once tossed it through the air with hilarious abandon.

She called Tillie—to hell with the expense. "I'll be down Sunday afternoon," she said.

"Oh good—we're having a dinner for some guys Edgar works with and their wives. You can help me cook."

She hung up and clenched in pain.

Jakey was behind the bar, inventorying the liquor. "Saw you drive in," he said. "I was hoping you'd stop. How's my favorite economist?"

"Not so hot, Jakey." She pulled herself onto a barstool. "Love trouble."

"Your carpenter? I heard he left his wife."

"Of course you did. But I don't know if he can pull it off."

Jakey poured a generous bourbon-rocks and pushed it her way. "You're a great girl, Hartley. You deserve to be happy. I'm not sure this one's the one. What's the matter with Don Dare, or that Freddy—now there's someone who's going places. You know he got into Yale Law and Boalt?"

Really! "Good for him," she said. "But those guys don't do it for me."

"You don't give 'em a chance. Forget us old dogs," said Jakey. "We're secondhand goods, worn out and tattered. You need someone young, with juice."

"This one has juice, Jakey. He wants a divorce, but she doesn't."

"She wouldn't be single long, I guaran-damn-tee it," said Jakey. "Men go for that small dainty kind of gal."

"Hey! Why not help me out here," Cress said, not entirely joking. "Work your magic on her."

Jakey's eyes were bloodshot. He gazed out the window with his mouth open. A strange orange light flashed through the room, then again and again as the old Oshkosh plow growled into view. "You overestimate my powers," he said. "Someone like her would never give it over to a schmo like me."

"Sure she would. A friendly chat-up, a couple cozy nudges . . ."

"What if it worked? I'd have her on my hands. Then what would I do?"

"You didn't worry about that with me."

"Of course I did. But I knew you'd be okay. You're smart and tough."

"You're sweet, Jakey."

He came around the bar and sat beside her. "C'mon, Hartley." He crushed into her arm. "You're young. A lot of fun. A good damn lay. Don't waste your time on us has-beens. You should be out there cooking up economic theory, making a name for yourself. I'm telling you, a hundred guys'd love to scoop you up, give you all the babies you want, buy you a big old mansion in town and a place up here for the weekends. Give 'em a chance. Shit, man. Your leg's caught in a trap here, you gotta chew it off. Dump that hangdog nail-banger, Hartley. He's not hot enough or smart enough for you. Remember who you are. I hate seeing you like this. Take back your own damn life."

Jakey's words cleansed and energized her as she wound down through the snow zone. She'd move back to Los Angeles, get a decent job in a museum or some research firm, finish the damn dissertation, marry some smart, lively guy. Someone with money—what a good idea!—or at least excellent prospects.

At the Hapsaw Lodge, a truck in the parking lot looked exactly like Quinn's, and her teeth began to chatter. Her breath lost depth. Her heart flopped like a caught fish. She had to pull over to find a bag to breathe into. He'd never leave his wife. Cress knew this absolutely as she swung down the mountain. Although maybe he would. He'd come farther than she ever expected him to already, and if she didn't blow it, if she didn't spook him, if she played her own part just right, he might still come all the way.

"I wish you weren't leaving," Quinn said.

"You know I'd stay," she said. "If you want me to. Just say the word."

He was silent for a long time. "No," he said. "Let me clean up this mess I've made, then I'll come get you."

He stopped at a liquor store and demanded her flask. He filled both of their flasks with expensive bourbon. "Drink this and remember me."

"You're so skinny," said Tillie. "Not me."

Tillie looked the same to Cress. Short, cute, energetic. Frizzled black hair. She was cooking vegetarian Indian food, fluttering around the kitchen, frying spices, grating ginger, cubing home-made cheese for saag paneer. Tillie wiggled her fingers over onions simmering in oil; they became crisp, golden strands to scatter on dal.

"Cressida's fresh from the backwoods," Tillie announced at dinner. The Kalingas, two climate physicists, and the Prosser-Estephes, astrophysicist and meteorologist, turned to Cress with polite interest.

"I was trying to finish my dissertation."

"Up there among the bears," said Tillie.

"No, really?" said the female climatologist. "Actual bears?"

The conversation moved into a discussion of weather bal-loons and obscure atmospheric data-gathering methods that Cress couldn't follow. She was not in good shape. Here in Braith-way, it was as if she'd awakened from a dream or, more accu-rately, been dumped out of a fairy tale like the peasant girls who'd fallen down wells and found themselves in dark forests where animals talked and princes wandered disguised as beg-gars and you performed test after test until you woke up in your old bed, a silver flask the only proof of your ordeal. Cress felt her ribs. She was skinny, as if she'd been starved or ill.

Tillie gave her her old room on their sun porch, its many windows providing a bird's-eye view of the entire U-shaped court. Reaching to close the red silk curtains, she hardly recog-nized herself in the wavering old glass.

Applying for a passport took a few days; she had to get a copy of her birth certificate from the county offices in Norwalk, an en-tire morning's errand. She picked up passport forms at the post office, then found a small photography studio on Lake Avenue to take her photo. For hours post-flash, she blinked away a blazing lilac splotch edged in turquoise. Seeing her wide face and lank hair in black-and-white, she questioned her ability to command anyone's love.

The passport would come within six weeks, whether she needed it or not.

Cress walked around Pasadena with the idea of looking for a job. She could take her time. She'd made her nut and then some. The old places she loved to visit as a teenager—Rosa's Fabrics, the tiny French café with green-and-pink-striped awnings— had been razed for a huge, windowless, sand-colored indoor mall. Ten minutes within its buzzing fluorescent maw and panic flickered darkly in her vision. Outside again, she walked west to an older part of town, to the Disabled American Veterans thrift store. She clacked plastic hangers in a soothing rhythm and found a coral sweater from Italy from the forties that still smelled of cedar. A starched white cotton shell with scalloped eyelet at the neck brightened against her tanned skin, and was as close to lace as Cress would ever wear. She'd wear it for him. Everything she chose now, she chose for him.

June was cool during the mornings, heating up to the eighties by midafternoon. Nights, she and Tillie and Edgar sat in the living room with the windows open and drank chilled white wine. Maddie and the Ellis girls and other court denizens wandered in. They were finding jobs as production assistants, graphic designers. Maddie was on staff now at the *LA Weekly*. "Send them your quarterlies," Maddie said. "Maybe they'll take you on as an editor."

Quinn phoned her late, when his mother went to bed and the rates were low. They didn't talk long—both had to keep their voices down. He'd helped his mom put in tomato plants. He'd taken a small job, putting shelves in an office at the Sparkville library. He'd come see her next week, or the week after, whenever he finished. She wandered through the days to get to these few minutes; she curled around the comforting low burr of his voice.

"I went on a little spree," Tillie announced, bringing large shopping bags into Cress's room. "I need to class up at work. Shall I model?" She nimbly shed a vintage sheath, then pulled on taupe slacks, a linen blouse, and a brown damask jacket with enormous shoulder pads. "My power outfit," Tillie said, and with a lascivious giggle she confessed that the jacket alone was five hundred dollars. "Don't tell Edgar!" She swiveled for Cress, then paused. "Here comes the electrician." She pointed outside. "Only two days late."

A man in a baseball cap sauntered down the court. He wore a short-sleeved sport shirt, jeans, blaring white sneakers. He dropped something, a coin perhaps, and when he swooped over to pick it up, his grace set off a fast cross current in Cress's chest, not unlike fear. "No," she said. "That's Quinn."

They watched him search out Tillie's unit. Cress could have opened a window, called to him. But she was shy, and a little embarrassed—that he looked like an electrician—and her allegiances, to him and to Tillie seesawed. Then he was on the stairs, and knocking. Tillie's eyes were too bright, her interest too obvious; Cress wanted to ratchet her down or shoo her away.

Tillie flung open the door. "At last!" she rang out. "The Mighty Quinn!"

Cress had forgotten how he could hold himself back: with perfect poise, amused, hat in hand, he let Tillie's brashness hang in the air unclaimed.

In Tillie's dining room, he pivoted. "Pretty little complex. Like the built-ins. And those old alabaster sconces. They don't build 'em like this anymore."

He stood, swaying slightly, hands on his hips.

Tillie brought him a beer; poured wine for Cress and herself. They'd taken a sip when his bottle was emptied. He wagged it. "Got another one of these?" Cress went to the refrigerator. There were two more beers. Reaching in, she heard herself pant.

"Let's go buy another six-pack," she called to him. Anything to get him out of the apartment and alone. "We can walk."

Beyond Braithway's insular, manicured grounds, the traffic

surged and stalled up Los Robles Avenue. This was a transitional neighborhood, its fine old houses long since divided into small apartments into which crowded whole families or groups of men. The morning's marine layer hadn't burned off; with the afternoon heat and exhaust, it was a classic smoggy day. "A far cry from Noah Mountain, eh?" Cress said.

"You look like a teenager," he said. She was in pedal pushers and the white cropped shell, with its eyelet scallops at the neck. "I like that top."

His hand slid under it. He pinched her waist.

"Pretty little place, your court," he said. "I see why you like it."

She didn't like it! She was only there until he gave her the all-clear! "It's nice," she said.

"But hey! What's with your friend? She looks like a linebacker."

He meant the shoulder pads. They *were* excessive. "That's power-dressing," said Cress. "For her office."

"Power-dressing," Quinn muttered. And a little while later: "Power-dressing!"

A flash of annoyance, and allegiance to Tillie. "We all have our own affectations," she said.

How would they make it through the hours till bed?

Back in the apartment, he and Tillie talked for a long time about Braithway's architecture. Who knew that Quinn was so well-versed in the Arts and Crafts movement? He'd spent a year working here in Pasadena, he said, restoring a Greene and Greene house near the Rose Bowl. At dinner, he and Edgar discussed Lebanon, if there would be war, news that Cress hadn't followed.

She relaxed. She need not have worried. Quinn could hold his own. This was the Quinn she'd glimpsed in the Garshes' booth, the Quinn who met with Hollywood designers and their famous clients, Quinn the laconic craftsman who listened soberly and spoke seldom; his reticence, discretion, and rugged good looks were as desirable and necessary to that clientele as his craftsmanship.

"You never said—" Tillie seized Cress's arm in the kitchen,

whispered, "You never told me . . . He's such . . . He's such a *man!*"

In the morning, Tillie knocked and brought them cups of tea on a tray. "Coffee's coming, this is just to get you started," she told Quinn.

"I like this hotel," he said. "Book me indefinitely."

As a matter of fact, Tillie said, she had been thinking. Braithway's owner had long been talking about restoring the court to at least some of its former glory, with an eye to condo conversion. Perhaps Quinn could do the work. Many of the built-in cabinets needed repair or restoration, as did mantels and wainscoting, some of the columns and heavy oaken doors. Some cottages needed structural work—foundations were crumbling—but he knew about that, too, right? Braithway could keep him busy for months, if not years, unit after unit. Cress and Quinn could live there for free while he did it, as just a fraction of his pay. "Wouldn't that solve everything?" cried Tillie.

Quinn's eyes narrowed, and he made an obvious decision to humor her.

"Darn near everything," he said.

"Oh, and by the way . . ." Tillie stepped closer to the bed. That movie star Quinn had worked for? The one he made the Frank Lloyd Wright doors for? An editor at *City and State* wanted to do a profile of him, but the star's publicist wasn't returning her calls. Did Quinn have a home office number or remember the actor's address, or maybe know the name of his personal assistant?

Quinn's face darkened as Tillie rattled on. "No," he said. "And if I did, I couldn't give over that kind of information."

Tillie shrugged. "Worth a try." With a languid wave, she left them alone.

"Sorry." Cress patted Quinn's flank. "I didn't know all that was coming."

Quinn sat up, put his feet on the floor with his back to her. "Sometimes you talk too much."

"Me?" said Cress. "Because I told my best friend about your big job?"

"It's all over Sawyer about us, and I sure as hell didn't tell anybody, and neither has Sylvia. It's been hard enough on her without public humiliation."

"Why are you blaming me? Your sister-in-law had her church circle praying me out of town. And you should tell her—it worked."

"Not until everyone in Sawyer knew all about us."

"You've hardly been discreet. You took me to the Coach 'n' 4, the Staghorn. You parked your truck outside Donna's house all night long."

Of course Cress had confided in Donna. Don Dare. Dalia and her judge had seen them. Norma and Ike knew too. As did Jakey. Perhaps she was to blame, perhaps she *had* talked too much.

Quinn's fury, wherever it came from, relaxed in stages. She rubbed his back, and eventually, he swung his legs again into bed and finished his tea.

But when she returned from her shower, he'd found the passport documents on her dresser: instructions, a spare application, an extra photograph. "Going somewhere?" he said.

"My sister's in England," she said. "At some point I want to visit her."

"I put my whole life on the line for you and you're plotting a secret trip to England?"

"That's not how it is, Quinn."

"You can get rid of me with one word, Cress. You don't have to go halfway round the world."

"I don't want to get rid of you. That's the last thing I want to do."

Again, she had to calm him bit by bit; she was not going to England any time soon, she said. But her old passport had expired (a lie, she'd never had a passport before), and getting a new one seemed like something she could do here in town. She did not say that England was her contingency plan, if he went back to his wife. He was, she said, reading too much into a stray piece of paper.

As they dressed, she suggested they take a walk up the Arroyo Seco.

He said, "A short one. I pick Evan up at school at two."

This was the first she'd heard of it. "But today's not your day."

"I take him every day I can," he said.

"Where's Quinn?" said Tillie, coming in from work.

"He had to pick up his son today."

"I definitely get the draw. He has his own gravitational field. So sexy. But a little intimidating, don't you think?"

"I'm used to it," she said. "But maybe I shouldn't have left Sawyer. He's convinced I'm leaving him. I think I should go back up there, to be near him."

"Absolutely not," said Tillie. "Let him pine."

At dinner Edgar said, "He seems very American to me. Sad, in that cowboy way. What is the word? *Lonesome*."

Quinn didn't call her that night, or the next; he'd had Evan with him, he explained. But he phoned more sporadically now. Sometimes he sounded drunk. He was most affectionate then.

Twenty

On a Saturday afternoon Tillie was browning a roast in the Dutch oven and Cress was peeling potatoes for a dinner with scientists and high school friends. When the phone rang, Tillie grabbed it. "Quinn," she mouthed.

Cress went to the extension in Tillie's bedroom. She sat on the unmade king-sized bed. "It's me," Quinn said, and his voice bore only the faintest hint of the bass she knew. He was not drunk—the opposite: distant, businesslike. A stranger's voice, the voice of a servant sent to deliver an edict.

"Oh, Quinn." She spoke in a gush, urgent to delay. She'd just been thinking about him! How was he? What was he doing?

For eight months they'd loved each other. She had agreed to marry him. Would he really drop her in a phone call?

"Cress," he said. "I'm calling so you know. I moved back home today."

Of course. Of course he moved home. Theirs was too wispy a love, when weighed against children, houses, vehicles, decades.

"It's best," he said. "You may not think so now, but you'll see."

"What happened?" She fought to keep her voice neutral, reasonable, even kind.

"Sylvia and I have been talking more than we ever have. She thought I wanted to live in town. I thought she did. She thought I wanted to be left alone after my father died. I thought she wasn't reaching out to me."

Tillie's bedclothes were a rumpled mess of white sheets and a gray blanket edged in green silk. Cress, shivering, pulled the blanket to her chest. The closet door gaped open. Inside, the clothes were sloppily hung; even the five-hundred-dollar brown power jacket sagged unevenly on a wire hanger.

"Cress?" he said. "Are you there?"

"Donna always said you were just using me to shake up your marriage. Well. Glad to be of service."

"That's not how it was, and you know it."

"I don't know anything," Cress said. "Except that you asked me to marry you and I said yes." She stood abruptly and went to the windows and looked down at the court with its curving walkways. "You've already moved back? You're in the house? With her?" She shivered, and her teeth chattered softly.

"I really care about you, Cress," he said. "I will always care about you."

Care. What an ugly compensatory little word. *Care*, the downgrade from love. "Gee," she said. All down Braithway Court, she noted, every unit had its own flower bed and small, closely mowed patch of lawn.

"What will you do now?" he said. "Go to London?"

"That's hardly your business."

"This isn't easy for me, either," he said.

About halfway down the court, two tuxedoed cats sat on the grass by red geraniums. Pets were forbidden at Braithway, but cats abounded. Farther down, a fat white one slithered on its belly across another tiny lawn.

"If you're not going to talk to me, Cress, I'm going to say goodbye."

"Goodbye," she said.

"I wish you the best, Cress. I hope you do everything you dreamed of. I would of held you back. I'm too set in my ways. I couldn't change as much as you need me to. Your friends would never really like me."

"You've worked it all out, haven't you."

"Cress," he said.

Another silence. She said, "Goodbye," and set the phone in its cradle.

The large round planter in the heart of the courtyard had been a fishpond in Braithway's heyday as a tourist home. One tuxedoed brother leaped onto the concrete lip, followed by the other. The white cat had disappeared under a bush.

Of course Quinn would go back to his wife; he'd never mustered a convincing argument against her.

The kitchen smelled cool and green: Tillie was spooning yogurt into a bowl of sliced cucumbers.

"That was Quinn," Cress said. "He moved back home with his wife."

Tillie gave the bowl three sharp raps with the spoon. "The shit," she said.

She drank most of a bottle of red wine that night and woke up a few hours later aflame with thirst. In the morning, Tillie and Edgar said Cress could stay with them as long as she liked.

After they left the house, she took Tillie's dull old kitchen scissors and calmly cut—and partly tore—up the blouse he'd liked, the sleeveless white cotton shell with eyelet. She'd kept it unwashed because it smelled of him, that spicy musk with the chemical taint—and it still did, as a snarl of scraps and buttons and hairy threads; twice she pulled it from the wastebasket to inhale it. She emptied her flask in the sink and threw it down Tillie's back stairs, into the parking lot. Following, she kicked it, slid her foot on it, scratching and denting the silver before tossing it in a trash can. She retrieved it an hour later, filled it with water: no leaks. She wished she had the little donkey (she'd stored it at the A-frame, in her box of dissertation notes) so she could hammer it into dust.

The second day, there was a blare in the air and a weird edge around objects, as if the world were off-register. She didn't get out of bed or open the red curtains. She slept with the snarl of shredded blouse under her pillow.

On the third day, thinking that a vast body of water would

clear her head and allow her some perspective, she drove to the ocean. The beach was socked in with fog, but the sand was warm. Her mother always said that this was when you could get badly sunburned without knowing it. In her pedal pushers and T-shirt, Cress lay down on the old chenille spread Tillie had lent her and rolled up in it, covering even her head. She looked like any other homeless person sleeping in the sand. She wept until the warmth of the sun bled through and the thudding of the waves calmed her. She slept hard for an hour and woke up sweating. She stood, shook out the spread, and folded it.

A small crafts fair had set up along the boardwalk, and at a jeweler's table Cress chose a ring, a silver band with a green stone, to symbolize her own new beginning, one hundred dollars. Only after she got it home to the sun porch did she see the small peridot was the exact pale green of his eyes and that a thin bezel encircling the stone was made of yellow gold. Worse, at night, the stone seemed darker, greener, and the gold more pronounced, which frightened her, made her feel unhinged. The next day she drove back, thirty-seven miles, to return or exchange the ring, but the little fair was gone. Afraid now even to look at the stone, she waded into the surf, holding her skirt. The water was cold and prickling, churning with sand and fine pebbles; only children scampered in and out without wetsuits. When the receding tide tugged hard at her shins, she slid the ring off her finger and flung it into a gathering wave.

Back at Braithway, there was a note from her mother, who'd stopped by and dropped off a letter from Sharon.

13 June 1982

Dear Cress,

  I hope Mom and Dad deliver this letter intact! Did you check the seals?

How are you? Still enjoying wedding season? (Loved your last letter! So funny!) I hope all is well with the Dark and Handsome Woodsman. (Mom says you're somewhat engaged!!! Is that true??? Details, please!)

I know that I've been nagging you to come to London, and Mom wrote that you're waiting for your passport. If you haven't already bought your ticket (and even if you have), I'm afraid I have to withdraw my invitation. For the last few months, my rebirthing process has been very intense, and this week I made it back to the moment of my birth, and before, as well. I recalled in perfect detail the darkness (or really a kind of gray-blue dimness) of the womb, and how it split open (remember—you and I were both C-sections!) as if the night sky had been slit and peeled back. Light poured in, along with enormous fuzzy shapes that bobbed and loomed over me. What a shock! No surprise I carried that trauma all my life. You go from the dark lull of the womb straight to blinding light . . . and MONSTERS! You can't imagine how much better I feel having gone back with adult eyes and seen that those fuzzy giants were just nurses and a doctor and dumb old Dad in surgical caps and masks!!!

The whole basis of rebirthing is not only that you get to reenact the entire traumatic birth process, but you also get to go through a brand-new one, this time trauma-free! That's what I did this week, and it was so amazing and mind-clearing. Unfortunately, according to my rebirthing counselor, for the transformation to really take hold, I need to stay away from my original toxic family, which—I regret that I have to say, and no offense— includes you. (Not that you yourself are toxic [although my life did take a huge turn for the worse the day you were born and knocked me off center stage] [!!!]) But that's hardly your fault. Still, the old inherited family patterns are so strong and so deep, and the new ones are so fresh and fragile, that they really need time to get established. Please understand that it's nothing personal. For years now, I've been desperate to find a way out from under Dad's extreme narcissism and pathological stinginess, and Mom's hysteria and control, so much of which I seem to have absorbed into my own personality. Hopefully, that will change now.

I wish you would consider rebirthing for yourself. I'm sure there are rebirthing clinics and therapists in L.A.—it's a worldwide phenomenon. I can ask my counselor for referrals, if you'd like. It'll free you up, make you much more your own person and much less a product of Mom and Dad, who are bloody neurotic, you know.

In the meantime, best of luck with the dark handsome affianced. I'll let you know when I'm ready for a visit, but it might not be for a year—or longer, even!! (Though I'd never miss your wedding!) If you've already bought your ticket here, and you don't want to visit England without seeing me, and you can't get a refund, or can't get the ticket credited toward some future adventure, let me know, and I'll reimburse you whatever amount you're out. This brings

Love,
Sharon

P.S. Don't be mad at me!!!
P.P.S. Although I'm happy to hear about your life, I must ask you not to share any opinions you might have about mine. If you need a ticket refund, just say how much and I'll send an international money order.

Cress hadn't bought her ticket. She'd only shelled out thirty-five dollars for the passport fee, and she thought of making

Sharon pay that—for slamming the door, blocking her exit at the worst possible moment.

"I might go to Tucson to visit my old drawing teacher," Cress told Tillie and Edgar. "Then maybe on to Minneapolis to check out the road not taken." She meant John Bird with his finished diss, his job at the Fed.

On the seventh day after Quinn's call, twenty days since the last time she'd seen him, Cress kissed Tillie and Edgar as they left for work. She drank tea and read the newspaper at their dining room table until noon, and for an hour or so, she sat in a chair and watched cats gambol up and down Braithway Court. She rose and pulled the sheets off her bed and stuffed them into the washer. She packed the plaid suitcase, carried that and another box of her things to the Saab's backseat—the trunk was still filled with the bearskin rug—and drove north.

She had to see him one more time. She had things to say, face-to-face, words formed from ashes and fury, from which there was no going back.

Although she had been there only once, she had no trouble finding the bleak subdivision or his uncharming tract home. His truck sat in the driveway. The lawn was dead. The lemon tree, a shaggy, asymmetrical hump, was overloaded with undersized fruit. The living room's picture window reflected a metallic twilight sky, but she saw the television flicker within and shadowy human movements. He was in there with his wife, her teacups.

Cress drove down the block and turned into a cul-de-sac. Pulling to the curb, for want of a paper bag, she cupped her hands over her mouth to capture carbon dioxide.

He's home, Sylvia has surely told her friends—she must have friends she talks to, at least one, someone she works with, possibly Mrs. Harvey herself.

Quinn's back. Cress can hear her childlike tones. *And he seems relieved.*

Just a midlife crisis, after all. It started with his dad. Then, for the first time ever, he couldn't find work. I went out and got a job, but it went against his masculine pride. Then Annette graduated and was going away to college—so much change, it really knocked him for a loop. He did some dumb things. But he's back now.

Cress pictures a small smile tugging at the corners of Sylvia's pretty lips, a smile that means they are having sex. Always something he enjoyed. They enjoyed.

Sylvia will have to be careful, and not let her triumph show, especially around him. He won't tolerate smugness. She'll have to act as if nothing has happened, as if she bears no grudge. He won't tolerate reproach, either. He certainly won't like Sylvia to ever mention Cress.

What's done is done, he'd say.

Sylvia will have to be more loving and attentive, and a little smarter, if possible, and more intellectually alive now, since that is what he gave up when he moved back home.

Cress imagined Sylvia leaving work, stopping in at Longs drugstore for toothpaste and mascara. She lingers, reading *Redbook.* Then, maybe, she picks up *Harper's Magazine.* If the girl reads such brainy publications, Sylvia no doubt thinks, she should, too. But she is quickly bored. The Afghan War, Tanzania, the Bauhaus—must she really be conversant on these topics? Even he probably can't locate Dar es Salaam on a map.

In one arena, there was no competition. Sylvia was not plain. She did not have stringy hair or a flat face and thin lips. It was not hard to imagine Quinn stroking Sylvia's cheek. *I missed your beautiful face.*

Cress shook her head and twisted the key in the ignition, making a terrible grating noise: the engine was already running. She pulled away from the curb, turned around, and, passing his house again, drove out of the subdivision.

Don Darrington stood outside his little back house in Sawyer watching Shim paw at something in the grass. "You're back," he said.

"I don't know for how long. Quinn dumped me over the phone. I came up to have it out with him."

"Donna dumped me, too."

"No!" Cress hummed and sympathized, and asked Don if she could stay at his place overnight.

"There's only one bed, if you don't mind."

She took the plaid suitcase inside his converted garage. Then they walked over to the Sawyer Inn and drank bourbon. "After you left," Don said, "Quinn hit the bars. He felt guilty about his kids. He couldn't see his way clear."

"Sorry about Donna," said Cress.

Donna had met someone else, a pretty boy from L.A.: Orton Froelich's nephew, twenty-two years old, who'd come up to his uncle's ranch to kick cocaine. "Four hundred bucks a day, I heard," said Don. "Up his nose."

Scott Froelich had come into the Sawyer Inn when Donna was singing and she couldn't stop staring. Don was there and saw it all. True, beauty of that sort was rare in Sawyer, and Donna's capitulation was instant and public. Guys clapped Don on the back, muttered into his neck. *Sorry, man. There's the shits, bud. Too bad for you.*

Donna invited the kid over to dinner, Don told Cress. "Like she had me over two years ago. You go thinking it's a barbecue or dinner party, then realize that you're the only guest. She grills steaks, pours good wine, sings to you." Don smiled faintly. "Poor little cokehead had no choice in the matter."

The worst thing, Don said, what killed him, was that he and Donna had been house-hunting the very day the Froelich kid showed up. Remember Ondine Streeter? She had a little rental property on the north fork. He and Donna had driven over to see if it was a place where they could live together. The house was far too small, given Donna's accumulations. Still, how could she go from moving in with him to falling in love with Scott Froelich in less than eight hours?

"*Falling in love* may not be the most accurate term," said Cress.

Don Dare had no way of knowing that, in three months, he'd meet a young pediatrician out climbing the Crags. They'd marry within the year, and she'd put him through law school. In five years, they'd build a Tuscan-style villa on a hill outside of Fresno where they'd raise four boys and Labradoodles.

"I need to talk to you," she said.

"Where are you?"

"The Food King near your house."

"Stay right there," he said.

His truck pulled up alongside the Saab. He motioned her into the cab. He was in that same cotton-poly short-sleeved plaid shirt, but his beard was gone and he'd shaved his head. He looked like a convict or a penitent.

He smoothed his scalp. "My summer cut," he said. "Like it?"

What did it matter if she liked it? And why were his eyes so merry? From her side of the bench seat, she caught his scent—he must have slapped on his cheap green slosh a minute ago. For her. As the shock of his baldness ebbed, ions fluffed and resettled. There it was, even now: the instant abatement of pain.

His lips seemed thicker, well shaped without his beard, redder, naked. "Very bad form to give someone the heave-ho over the phone," she said. It came out like a joke.

"I have to try it at home," he said. "After twenty-one years of marriage, I owe Sylvia a chance to make things right."

"It's killing me," she said.

He slid an arm around her shoulder and drew her close. His

face pressed against hers, his shaved jaw a novelty. "I thought I would never see you again," he said into her temple. "I thought you were in England." He kissed her brow, her cheek, and finally her mouth, right there in the Food King parking lot.

He shouldn't say so, it wouldn't do anybody any good, but he still loved her, he said, as much as he ever had; she was his favorite living thing.

She ran her hand over his shorn scalp, a fine springy velvet.

Twenty-One

She found an iron bedstead at the Sparkville swap meet, forty bucks, and an old wooden dining table for a desk, twenty-five. She paid a man to deliver them, fifteen, to Ondine Streeter's rental on Dawkins Lane, eight miles up Noah Mountain Road. At the end of a long driveway, the small yellow house had a green metal roof and a dirt yard fenced in white planks and tunneled throughout with ground squirrel burrows. A path from the back gate led through a thicket of cottonwoods and willows to a swimming hole in the north fork of the Hapsaw. Noah Mountain's massive, slaggy blue face stared in the kitchen window. She was ten miles down the road from Quinn's old mountain home.

She drove to the Meadows and filled the Saab's seats with her boxes of clothes, books, and research notes—no room, still, in the trunk. "Don't spend the money I gave you on furniture," her mother called from the new house as Cress loaded the Saab. "You'll need it when you get tired of being number two."

Now that they were renting out the A-frame on weekends, her parents saw the need for furniture more comfortable than the wicker love seat, the unyielding upstairs bed, both of which Don Dare hauled down to Cress in his truck.

At Beech Creek, Dalia said, "I shouldn't take you back, you deserted me in the heat of battle, but I'm helpless in the face of a good waitress."

"You should have let Quinn fester," said Tillie. "He knew where to find you. Now he can have his cake and eat it, too."

"That's a meaningless cliché," said Cress. "There is no cake. It's not like that at all."

"What is it like then?"

"Quinn's not greedy. Or getting any pleasure from the situation. We're all just exhausted and need time to recover."

She was speaking for Sylvia as much as for herself and him.

"And then what?" said Tillie.

Cress closed her eyes. Pain lay in all directions, a black moat. Sooner or later, one (or more) of them would get up the courage and strength to plunge in and get away. "We'll see," she said.

His truck lumbered down the long dirt driveway; Cress knew by heart the engine's eight-cylinder rumble, and Quinn's schedule, which was the old one, based around Sylvia's work. They swam in the Hapsaw's waning north fork, stretched out in the sun on granite slabs, fingers and shins touching, restored to one another. He tapped her rib so she'd see the bobcat drinking at the river's edge, its tasseled ears flickering, its tongue the pale pink of a powder puff. Another day, as they approached, a pair of red snakes slid off into the water, their movement synchronized, bend-to-bend. Cress was afraid to swim after that, disturbed by what lived underwater, unseen.

They drove to their far-flung taverns, a beer here, a beer there. They ate T-bones at the Murdock Grill and steak and eggs at the Koffee Kup in town. He ordered his meat *charred raw.* Trained by a stingy father, Cress chose the chicken or burger, but Quinn overrode her, insisted she at least have the ladies' cut.

He took her partway up the Wanderwood Road to a berry patch. "My uncle Dalbert lived just down the way there. He raised sheep, and this one old ram would eat his way into these berry brambles and get stuck. Too stupid to back up, he'd bleat and bleat till one of us came to pull him out by his tail."

With two gallons of blackberries, they decided on the spot to make jam—Quinn ran to the grocery in Sawyer for mason jars while she boiled and stirred. He took a jar of warm jam with him when he left—he'd fib about where it came from. Cress envied the jar, how it could enter his home, sit on a table in the middle of his family life. She wished she'd sunk something into the ink-dark semisolids: an eavesdropping bug, a tiny camera, a bomb to detonate at will.

In the Sawyer post office, she ran into Donna. "Cress! Great to see you. I heard you were back. Sorry I was such a hard-ass, but Norma really put the squeeze on me," Donna said. "Come, let me buy you a doughnut."

At the bakery, they sat on cheap metal folding chairs at an old cable-spool table. Above them hung the taxidermied head of a wild boar with a cigarette dangling rakishly between tooth and tusk. Donna swung her head around to see who was behind her: "That's the old Sawyer backward glance—you never know who's listening," she said, keeping her voice low. "Quinn was out every night after you left. He stayed through all my sets. Drank the whole time. He was a wreck. He adores you. But he felt bad about his boy."

And rightfully so, Donna added. As an aide at Evan's school, she saw him on the playground. He was shy and quiet and terribly sweet. His classmates' offhand savagery—their loudness, shoving, and teasing—frightened him more of late, and he'd taken to parking himself by any adult who wouldn't shoo him off.

Cress was grateful for the information and wanted to hear more, but Donna's eyes had started to shine. "I have some news, too," she said.

"I heard a little something," Cress said.

"It's not little." Donna was in love. In love and mesmerized by twenty-two-year-old Scott. "Wait till you meet him, Cress. He's the most gorgeous man you've ever seen. I'm *dying* to have his babies."

In the fall, the Hapsaw's north fork shrank and stilled, and those channels cut off from the main flow stagnated. Cress caught whiffs of it when a breeze came up from the river as she drifted through her sparsely furnished house, drinking coffee, reading books, sometimes sitting at her typewriter. She was on her own here now most of the time. Two afternoons a week, she went down to serve her golf ladies lunch, and there was usually a banquet on weekends.

Reliably, Quinn came to her Tuesdays and Thursdays, and sometimes for a stray few hours when he could. As he walked through her door, a sandbag slid off her chest, her vision brightened, relief rushed in like a fast-acting drug, a shot of liquor knocked back. They cooked together: pork chops, biscuits, green salads. He browsed through her newspapers and magazines and offered up whatever might interest her. The situation in Lebanon was worsening. The actress turned princess was dead in a car wreck. People in Chicago had died from poisoned Tylenol. Oh, and Glenn Gould—wasn't he the pianist she liked so much, the hummer?—he too had died.

For days she listened to the *English Suites*, the *Well-Tempered Clavier*, setting the little record player's arm to automatically repeat.

Because she expressed an interest, Quinn brought over a fly-tying kit, clamped the tiny vise to the table, showed her how to wrap feathers and tufts of fluff onto gold hooks with black thread; a swarm of Royal Coachmen collected by her salt shaker. When he stood to make the pan gravy, Cress sat and tied a fly using her hair, some yellow straw from a place mat, the fuzz from her blue mohair sweater. "See what you catch with that," she said.

By late October, they were building fires in the ugly but efficient woodstove—it looked like a blackened fifty-five-gallon drum on its side, with a small isinglass window through which they watched the flames curl and lick from their usual creaky perch, the wicker love seat. Without fail, before he left, they went to bed. Their bodies still snapped together like magnets.

She stayed hopeful for a day or so after his visits, then dread and sadness gathered again, like beggars tugging at her hem, stealing into her rooms. Over the long weekend, the need to talk about him grew intense and constant, as if she had to conjure him in words, and discuss all he'd said and done that week in her search for clues to her future. ("I don't know how I thought I could live without you," he'd said. But then he and Sylvia drove to Sacramento for a weekend to see Annette at Davis—he'd been hundreds of miles away without Cress knowing, and she'd only learned about it afterward from a chance remark.)

She felt like a child, perhaps like Evan himself, in trying to fathom what the adults were up to, a blurred and fragmentary mystery, with rare hints offering only the most oblique, partial insight.

Tillie now greeted any mention of Quinn tersely. *What'd you expect, going back? You've lost any strategic advantage you had.* Don Dare heard her out, so he could have his turn, first to mourn Donna, and then to praise Elise, the long-limbed, gawky pediatrician with small, clear eyes and a managerial briskness, who had big plans for him.

At Beech Creek, over shift drinks, Cress found a confidante in generous, nonjudgmental Lisette, who took it in stride that Cress's boyfriend was married and could not be named.

She met him at the Staghorn on a Thursday afternoon—they needed to get out, drive around—and after a beer each at Murdock and Fountain Springs, they stopped at the Koffee Kup for a quick bite. Once, Quinn said, he'd been eating breakfast here with Caleb—steak and eggs, exactly what he was having now— only that time, when his food came, there were black flecks all over his plate—the eggs, the hash browns, the steak. Caleb's meal was fine. But his was not. He showed the waitress. Had the cook sprinkled on some spice? The waitress took his plate back to the kitchen. The cook was puzzled and prepared a new plate, which looked okay at first, but soon, Quinn saw the black flecks over everything.

He sent the plate back again, and around the time his third batch of eggs was sputtering on the grill, he remembered trimming his beard that morning. "I was too embarrassed to tell the waitress, but I left her a ten-dollar tip."

His stories, Cress realized, never involved Sylvia, Annette, or Evan. Had he set his family off-limits to her? Was he being polite, pretending that her rivals did not exist? Or had his marriage and family life been so uneventful that nothing amusing, nothing worth relating ever happened? Or was it Quinn's sense of balance and fair play: since they knew nothing of her, she'd know nothing of them?

In the dusty, dim Coach 'n' 4, Dalia waved from the door. The next day at Beech Creek, Cress apologized for not inviting Dalia and the judge to join them.

"It is odd," Dalia said, "how out in public Quinn is with you."

"He assumes everyone's as private and closemouthed as he is," said Cress. "Or maybe he wants to get caught and it's his way of forcing the issue."

"I'd bet on forcing the issue," said Dalia.

Thanksgiving came, and then Christmas, those times of deep family burrowing. He vanished for weeks. Cress worked long hours at the club, then roamed her small house, restless, furious, and bereft, until the calls came late at night, whispered, barely intelligible, from his mother's bedroom, or the wall phone in his own kitchen. *I'm thinking of you. I miss you. I hope you're having a wonderful holiday.*

She walked every morning to the top of Dawkins Lane, a steep mile up, then back. Every day, she passed a man with a chest-length beard and a long, faded red ponytail lunging small white spotted ponies in a ring. They began to wave to each other, and one day he walked down to the road and introduced himself.

("Oh I know Trey Kidman," Quinn said. "Pop and I put in his cabinets. He called us a month later to say the hardware failed on a drawer. We'd used high-quality German sliders, so we went to see if they'd got a defective set. We opened the drawer—a bottom drawer, more'n a foot deep—and they'd filled it with dried beans—fifty, seventy pounds of 'em. Drawer was *sagging* off its rails.")

Trey waved her down, gave her chard and onions. Mint, beets, pesto he'd made last summer. He hailed from the Pasadena area, too—Arcadia, he said. In the early seventies, the rocky, cheap land on Dawkins Lane enticed him and a few fellow city-bred trustafarians to try the country life. You could buy a four-bedroom farmhouse with a barn and thirty acres for the price of a one-bedroom condo in Duarte. He and his wife bought fifty acres and built their own glass-and-wood home. "Dawkins Lane had a great little communal vibe for a while," Trey said. The newcomers bought milk goats, pigs, ponies, laying hens, then sought their neighbors' expertise on animal husbandry and irrigation, which flattered the old-timers and subdued their mistrust. But the never-ending physical work, hot summers, snakes, unenlightened hill folk, and eternally tunneling ground squirrels eroded the novelty. Plus, years without a decent radio station, foreign movies, a bookstore, or—as time passed—Montessori or Waldorf or even private Catholic schools—sent most of Trey's comrades back to the suburbs. He and his wife stayed, but they had long given up on self-sufficiency. His wife had gone to work at the state hospital, and with her degree from Scripps College, she had risen swiftly through the ranks and was now a top administrator. Trey stayed home, did the cooking and the child care; he gardened, raised those spotted ponies, and generally led the life of a gentleman farmer, pot enhanced.

When Trey invited her in for a cup of tea, Cress followed him through the wood-walled house with its floor-to-ceiling windows and casual, layered dishevelment of books and papers, clothes and toys. In the kitchen, herbs and baskets hung from beams; a glass conservatory off to one side was filled by oily branching pot plants. While Trey puttered at the stove, Cress studied the cabinets, now dented and grubby around the handles. The cedar still glowed. "I like your cupboards," she said.

"Designed them myself, and found a local guy to make 'em. The wood's soft, so they've gotten a little battered."

"I like that," said Cress. "The lived-in look. Who made them?"

She could not pass up the chance to hear his name.

"Oh God. Lynn will remember. I wrote it down somewhere. A father-son outfit up the road. See that? Dog food's in there, and the dogs know it."

Long deep scratches had formed a furrowed concavity in one low door.

Trey sent her home with a spidery branch of marijuana. "Dry it for a week," he said. "That'll add a little sparkle to your day."

Quinn didn't like any of it: that Trey Kidman talked to her, that she'd gone inside his house, that he'd sent her home with pot, that the branch now hung by dental floss from the wall-mounted can opener by her kitchen sink.

"I haven't smoked for years," said Cress. "I thought maybe you and I . . ."

"I'm not going anywhere near it," said Quinn.

"Could be fun. Tillie swears it's an aphrodisiac—"

"Tillie has a lot of ideas."

"Hey! Have you ever even tried it?"

"Why would I try it?"

She had never seen this particular snarl on his face—for once, he forgot to hide that roan incisor. "Why, you're a prude!" She gave him a playful push. "An uptight stick-in-the-mud!"

He turned away. "Call it what you like."

"You're serious? You really don't approve?"

"You have to ask?"

"God, Quinn, it's no big deal." And to prove it, she fed that perfectly good hank of weed to the woodstove.

The banquet waitresses at Beech Creek had suggestions for Cress. She should perm her hair, get contacts, wear more makeup, curl her eyelashes. Did she or did she not have a boy-friend? How could she not know? Well, she should come with them into Sparkville when they partied after-hours. Do a few shots. Snort a little something. That'd get her up and running. Why not? Lots of men hung around, she'd meet someone. "Cress," said a twenty-year-old, "how come you're here, work-ing with us? After all your college and stuff. Can't you get a real job?"

"Quinn Morrow? That's who you've been talking about?" cried Lisette. "I know Quinn, *and* Sylvia."

Lisette's seven-year-old son had attended a summer science camp with Evan. "Really, Cress? I picture you with someone so much looser and funnier."

"He and I had a lot of fun up on the mountain."

"He did have a way with the kids," said Lisette. "They flocked to him. He just didn't have a lot to say to the rest of us."

Cress had noticed Quinn's affinity for children, and theirs for him. They were drawn to his hat, as to any costume. He'd wag just the top of his fingers to a child staring out a car window or peeking over a café booth and they'd never stop staring and wagging fingers back at him. Dogs, too. Dogs came up for a pat and watched Quinn intently, as if he would tell them what to do.

"*Her* I hardly know at all," Lisette said. "She's so shy. But always so well put together—especially for someone living in the hills. I remember, she made cupcakes as perfect as store-bought."

"I may not be faithful, but I am loyal," he said.

"Whatever that means." Cress pulled herself up by the iron bedstead.

"I may not be great at monogamy, but I am loyal. To my wife. To you."

"Ahh—the sophistry of the philanderer," said Cress.

"The who what of what?" He climbed on top of her, pinned her arms down, tangled his legs in hers. "Say that again?"

"You heard me the first time." And refused to repeat.

He rasped her cheek with his unshaven jaw. "Don't sour on me, Cress. Not now. Not yet."

He showed up at ten in the morning, a first. He had that gray face, that walloped stoop. She'd been dressing for work and only had a few minutes before she had to leave. She made coffee quickly, her hands shaking, scattering Yuban over the countertop.

He ran the flat of his thumb around the rim of his cup. He looked ill, unsteady, remote. "This is not how I wanted it to go," he said.

Someone had blabbed, and Sylvia moved out. She packed a suitcase, took the boy, and went to live with a girl friend some-where in Sparkville.

Cress checked a burst of excitement. "How would you want it to go?"

"You know," he said.

"I don't, actually."

"Then you haven't been listening to me."

She'd done nothing but listen to him!

"I'm listening now," she said.

"It can't have anything to do with you and me."

Oh that. Right. Yes. "So she has to say that the marriage is over for her, too," said Cress. "Or something to that effect."

"She says she loves me and wants to stay married, but that this"—Quinn lifted his hand and let it drop—"is unbearable."

"For everyone," said Cress.

"She won't see me again till I give you up."

"Is that why you're here?"

She stood against the kitchen sink with her back to Noah Mountain and steadied herself for the blow. Surely, that's why he had come, at this bright morning hour, to accomplish the final, necessary thing. He curled over his coffee, glowering, suffering. At least this time he wasn't doing it over the phone.

He shivered, as if coming awake. "I can't bear not to see you."

She stood straight in her Beech Creek–issue polo shirt and navy blue skirt. "Here I am," she said.

Twenty-Two

Quinn moved back to his mother's place so Sylvia could have the Sparkville house. Their old double-wide was full of boxes and furniture from his mother's remodel, so he set up in the little travel trailer. He picked Evan up from school twice a week and brought him to eat and watch TV with his grandmother before they bunked down in the trailer.

All the other nights, Quinn came to her. With no fanfare, a life together began. Almost a life. An offhand life. She couldn't look directly at it, for fear it would dissolve. She certainly couldn't speak of it, for fear that Quinn, hearing his actions turned into words, might recoil and repudiate them and her. Still, he showed up midafternoons, often with groceries. They cooked together, or they went out to bars and restaurants. They held on to each other on the hard bed and slept the whole night clasped.

In the morning, he left the house when she went for her walk, or before. He was opening his mother's kitchen and living room into a great room. Sometimes he helped Caleb on an addition in Sawyer. He rented hours at a wood shop to build cabinets for both jobs and began building furniture on spec. When Cress worked late, she met him afterward for a drink, or they caught Donna's last set at the Sawyer Inn.

He was never at her house when she was not. "Why would I want to be here without you?" he said.

She couldn't say, *Because you live here.* He didn't.

They drove up to the Hapsaw Lodge to have dinner with Don Dare and Elise, whose crisp, cool managerial manner wasn't easy to warm to. But she climbed rocks, and had plans for Don and the life they'd spend together. Dalia and Judge Crochet invited them for steaks at the Murdock Grill, and another time to see *Chariots of Fire*, followed by drinks at the Coach 'n' 4.

Quinn discovered that the small barn at Cress's house had a mechanic's bay, a concrete trough, three feet wide, ten feet long, where a person could stand up and work under a car. Quinn changed his truck's oil there, then showed Cress how to change the Saab's. He made her do each step. It took her forever to get the plug out. If she ever went into business, he said, she'd have to call it Poky Lube. Or All Day Oil Change.

A small coal of happiness lodged behind Cress's heart. She was working on the diss again, slowly getting back into it, a couple of hours every day. Better get that degree, she thought, or he'd be choosing between two waitresses.

If Quinn ever spoke to Sylvia or met with her, he didn't say. Cress didn't ask. She knew better than to force an outcome. He had to be with her of his own free will.

"Had a long talk with my mom yesterday," he said. "She wants to meet you."

They arranged for the next day, after Cress fed her lady golfers.

Running for lemon slices, cups of ice, and tiny pitchers of skim milk, Cress felt more tenderly toward the Hackettes; she saw them as practice for the mother.

"At the Staghorn?" said Dalia. "That's weird."

"You go to the Staghorn."

"Not to meet my future mother-in-law."

"We're just meeting there," Cress said. "Probably we'll go out after. For steaks or something." But she was ad-libbing.

In Beech Creek's ladies' room, she pulled on clean jeans and her fuzzy blue sweater. She shook her fine hair down over her shoulders, brushed it vigorously. Lipstick. Oh, but she had a flat, wide, ordinary face. Quinn didn't love *her* for her looks, that much was certain.

Men in work clothes lined the Staghorn bar. At the far end Quinn and his mother already grasped drinks. His mother was no beauty, either. Nor did she remotely resemble the golf ladies with their brightly colored golf skirts, lacquered coifs, and paste-pearl chokers. The mother had Caleb's long jowls and a smoker's leathery skin. Her straight, chin-length bob was a yellowed white.

"I'm so glad to meet you, Mrs. Morrow," Cress said.

"Elinor Morrow," the mother said simultaneously.

Her clear pink glasses were too wide for her narrow face. A man's gold-ocher cardigan sagged off her shoulders, the sleeves rolled into thick doughnuts at her wrists. She was fifty-eight years old, but she seemed elderly, dried out. Well beyond any possibility of love. Cress took the stool beside her. Clacking open a brass lighter, the mother lit a long, skinny cigarette.

"Quinn says you were a librarian," said Cress.

Elinor shifted toward Cress, exhaled smoke sideways. Her voice was low like Quinn's, and croupy.

"Pardon me?" said Cress, even as she understood.

"I said, I just wanted to see for myself what kind of a woman tries to take a man away from his family."

Cress checked to see if Quinn had heard. But he'd canted away to allow them room and she could not catch his eye. She was on her own here. The mother gazed straight ahead, fingering her lighter and inhaling the smoke released from her mouth back up into her nose. Sweater, skin, and hair: the mother was a yellowed old thing.

So this is how she wants to play it, Cress thought.

"What kind of man wants to leave his family?" Cress addressed the gold-ocher sleeve and vein-rumpled hand with its trembling cigarette. "A man who's happy at home? Who's getting his needs met?"

"A sad man," said Elinor. "An angry man. A man who's grieving, and seeking comfort from the wrong people."

"Is that what you think?"

"I know my son," Elinor said.

This time, when Cress checked, Quinn met her eye with a merry look and raised an eyebrow, as if to say, *Going pretty well?*

Cress frowned and gave a quick shake of her head: *Hell, no!*

"Mrs. Morrow," she said, leaning in, "I *would* entice Quinn away if I could. But he has a mind of his own, as you know. So it's really up to him."

The older woman snorted with a backward jerk, which set off a coughing fit, the coughs deep, rasping, alarming. She fumbled in her purse for a wad of tissue and wiped her mouth. She lifted her wineglass to drink, then paused. "Sylvia's like a daughter to me. Since she was fifteen."

"That wouldn't have to change," said Cress.

"Of course it would. After she took half of what's ours?"

Cress had only glimpsed the family compound from above, the sloped acres, the small white house; trailers large and small. The barn. When Quinn refinanced, he must have put the property in his own name. Or something. "Is that what would happen? She'd get half?"

"With California community property laws? You bet!"

"I don't know anything about that."

Out came another long cigarette. The lighter clacked again. The bartender brought them each a new drink—Quinn must have signaled.

"I heard you were an economist. Knew all about money."

"I studied economic theory, not household finance."

"Well then: What about supply side?" Elinor barked. "And trickle down? What's your opinion on that?"

Cress wanted to laugh loud, or whoop like a crazy person. "Well, it's never been shown that tax breaks for the rich actually result in more private sector jobs," she said. "Or that wealth trickles anywhere."

Elinor elbowed Quinn. "She and I agree on something." She gulped down the glass of wine, picked up her lighter and purse, and stood. "I'm ready, son."

"You should have warned me."

He'd come in laughing and sheepish later that night. "I had no idea. The other day, she was so anxious to know you. Maybe she was drunk."

"When you were driving down to meet me—she didn't say anything?"

"Not that I recall."

"What did you talk about?"

"I don't know. Flooring for her bathroom."

"What did she mean that Sylvia would take 'half of what's ours'?"

"I'm not sure," said Quinn.

"Would Sylvia get half the Noah Mountain property if you divorced? How did your names get on the deed?"

"That's not your concern."

"Of course it is. Would you really have to divide or sell off Noah Mountain in a divorce?"

"Let's worry about that when the time comes."

"That's not why you went back to her before, is it?" said Cress. "To keep Noah Mountain intact?"

"I went back because I owed it to her to try one more time."

"And so you did."

"For a minute. A week. Till you came back to town."

Tillie phoned Cress one afternoon. "I had lunch with the arts editor today and he wants a money piece on the local art market—how a gallery owner decides on prices, how prices work in today's crazy market, what percentage goes to the artist, all that. I said I knew just the person to write it."

"All my research was in Chicago. I know nothing about L.A."

"Yes, but you know how the market works. You'd talk to a couple of galleries here. Add your theories."

"Do I have theories? I've never written journalism."

"You can do it—you just make research entertaining. You have a good ear. Get some good quotes, then write a short, snappy piece about what drives prices in an up market. At least talk to the arts editor. His name is Silas. Will you call him?"

Cress wrote down Silas's number. "I wouldn't know how to make it snappy," she said. "Or remotely entertaining."

"We do," said Tillie.

The reporting—as Tillie had promised—consisted of a few phone calls. The writing took three weeks. At one point Cress had three thousand words, academic and turgid. She went at it with highlighters and a pencil, got it down by half, then whittled, compressed, sacrificed whole ideas. Tillie had her read it over the phone and unknotted her sentences. It was amazing, finally, how the whole thrust of her dissertation fit into eight hundred words. "Now I see," Cress said. "You leap over the boring parts, attribute nothing to anybody, quote a few experts, showcase the most sensationalistic facts, and voila! A magazine article." Two days before it was due, Cress mailed three typed, double-spaced pages at the Sawyer post office and went for a glazed doughnut to celebrate.

Caleb and his little boys sat at the counter by the register where she had to order and pay. Caleb! She hadn't seen him in a year. He looked just the same, jowly and droll, his shiny bald spot sunburned pink—just adorable! She turned slightly, preparing to greet him warmly, but he never once looked her way.

Lisette brought news. A friend of hers had seen Sylvia Morrow in City Park, by the duck pond, and not alone. That dentist whose wife died—who owned that big Spanish house out on the

Lindsay Road? You know, who played the guitar? Anyway, that's who Sylvia was with! And it was more than friendly. Definitely. Smoocherama—that's how the friend described it. "You know him, Cress. You pointed him out when he was here with the Kiwanis."

Felton the Extractor! Lisette's friend knew him from church. He'd been dating like mad since his wife died, starting less than a month afterward. He'd already gone through all the single women at his church. But with three young kids on his hands, who could blame him for being desperate?

"Good. I'm glad they found each other." To tell the truth, Cress was disappointed in Sylvia's choice. Felton the Extractor wasn't very good-looking, and also, he was a little pathetic. Serenading Donna as he had. Bawling her name in the wee hours. At least he earned a dentist's salary. So maybe Sylvia wouldn't want half the family compound.

"I know I didn't make such a great impression on your mom, but maybe we should have her over for dinner."

Quinn diced onions by the sink as Cress melted butter in cast iron.

"It's not that she didn't like you. But Sylvia's like a daughter to her."

"Do you guys pass around the same phrase book? You say the exact same things."

"That's just how it is," said Quinn. "She's been a mother to Sylvia for more'n twenty years. That's not a tie easily broke."

"What if Sylvia met someone else?"

"That's not going to happen."

"No?"

"She's not the kind to move from one man to the next. She'd never impose some stranger on her kids. Ready for these?" He lifted the cutting board.

"Oh please, Quinn." Cress stood back as he scraped onions

into the skillet. "Give Sylvia a little credit. She's not going to pine away for you for the rest of her life. I bet she gets married before we do."

"Don't count on it. I'm it for her. That's how she's made. Too devoted for her own good. She's stuck with me all these years and I've never been good for her. I'm too critical, always wanting her to be someone she's not. I'm too hard to please," Quinn said. "You'll find that too."

"You don't scare me," Cress said, thrilled by the future inferred.

Quinn, she decided, would not hear about Felton the Extractor from her. Let him shoot some other messenger—ideally, Sylvia herself.

Brian and Franny bustled into Cress's small kitchen with hydrangeas and sacks of groceries: cheeses, baguettes, two bottles of burgundy. Cress had always considered hydrangeas an old lady's flower, but these were dense hummocks of dark ivory blossoms blushing green and violet: How did Franny get that they were beautiful? And since when did Franny eat Gorgonzola and triple-cream Brie?

Brian was easing back to work at his investment firm; they'd just spent a week in his Encino apartment. He looked tanned, relaxed, and slimmer; his laugh had regained that old frat-boy cockiness Cress recalled from childhood. Franny had cut her hair short, with wisps at the neck; she looked sleek and wore thin, pointed black flats that were latticed over the toes so her red polish peeped out. And here was Cress, in lug-soled hiking boots.

"You guys *are* coming to the wedding," Brian said, handing wine around in Cress's pink water glasses.

"Donna's singing," said Franny.

"I'll be there," said Cress, and Quinn said something she didn't quite hear.

He wanted, he said, to read something about economics, something that would serve as a basic introduction. She went out to the small barn where her book boxes were stored and dug out copies of *The Worldly Philosophers* and, because it was so novelistic, *To the Finland Station*. He read a chapter in each.

He kept no clothes at her house. He used her toothbrush and comb. He had yet to set foot in her shower.

The *City and State* editor—Silas—phoned with only a few edits. Where Cress had written ". . . the price of Pierce's paintings rose 125 percent," Silas inserted an adjective, so it read ". . . a startling 125 percent."

Startling, then, was the snappy part.

What could she write about next? Silas asked. If her next piece was even half as good as the first, he'd give her a monthly column; they'd call it "Art Market." Wasn't there a law that gave artists a share of resale profits? How was that working out for the artists? Who tracked the sales? Who had actually collected any profits? She should write it up. He had many other ideas as well: she could profile an art consultant who bought art for entertainment industry execs who had no knowledge or taste. And there was a controversy up north, where redevelopment contractors had blithely bulldozed some public art: she might even get a full feature out of that.

The economy has turned, she thought. Without her even looking for it, work had come her way.

"They want me to write regularly for the magazine," she told Quinn.

"You're on your way!"

"I won't quit my day job yet. But who knows?"

As they were falling asleep, he said, "You should clear out, Cress. Go live your big exciting life. This isn't the place for you to shine."

"I'll go, but only if you come with me."

"I'd just be in your way. But you got to get out there, have your day."

"Let me write that second article before you get all valedictory," she said.

In the dark early-morning hours, she woke up to his murmuring. His legs wound around hers, his lips moved against her ear. "You're the great pleasure and comfort of my life. For the first time, I've known what it's like to have real company, real attention. Before you, I was always alone. Since that first walk together, I haven't wanted to go even a few hours without hearing your voice. I don't mean anything against Sylvia. She's a good person, an excellent mother. But she never knew me the way you do. She needs so much for herself just to get through every day. I was okay with giving her that for twenty-some years. But you showed up, and now I've gotten used to having something for myself. Your hand brushes my shoulder, my whole body surges toward it. You call up something deep. I'm not sure I can survive without you. When you come into the Staghorn, you look around the room—and the second you see me, your eyes change, they mass up with love, and humor. And sex. God. It kills me, every time. Who knew, but I've been waiting my whole life to be seen like that."

She lay in his arms, eyes open in the shadowy dark, and, keeping as still as possible, held her breath.

At Beech Creek, wedding season was starting; already, in mid-May, receptions were back to back. Cress had put in for a weekend off—for a busman's holiday: Franny and Brian's nuptials.

"You don't have to come," she said to Quinn. "I don't mind going alone."

"I said I'd go, I'll go."

Yet his reluctance was like a brake. He insisted on driving the Saab, and they crossed the valley floor, the orange and almond groves, the oil fields, at a constant speed, with almost no conversation. When she reminded him to take the California Street exit in Bakersfield—weren't they going to the Basque restaurant for lunch?—he shot her one of his darkest looks. She pretended not to notice and cheerfully directed him to the Woolgrowers, where old men in soiled long aprons thunked unlabeled bottles of red wine on the table, followed by iceberg salad, a plate of cold beef tongue, bowls of gamy lamb stew. Quinn wasn't fond of wine, but he drank some and his mood improved. Beef tongue, he muttered, wasn't half as tasty as elk tongue.

"Sorry," Quinn said, back in the car. "Not feeling real festive about the whole wedding deal."

Cress had made reservations at the Red Lion in Glendale and requested a room facing the San Gabriels, so he would see mountains and not city sprawl. They checked in, changed clothes, and drove to the Unitarian church in Burbank.

Quinn wore a vintage charcoal-gray pinstriped three-piece wool suit with a turquoise bolo tie and cowboy boots. She had forgotten about his sense of costume. The staginess—the corniness—of his outfit recalled how embarrassed she'd been for him when he'd arrived for Family Night at the Meadows all decked out in leather.

Her dress was ankle-length red rayon with tiny white flowers, worn with a lacy white shawl and white sandals, all thrift store finds.

About sixty people sat in the small sanctuary. Franny, tiny as a nine-year-old girl, stood perfectly still, with a serious, attentive look on her face. Her white sheath was short, simple, perfect. She clutched a spray of pink rosebuds in one hand, while Brian, red-faced in a dark suit, kneaded the fingers of her other.

A plump, flushed Donna sang "Some Enchanted Evening." She was five months pregnant and single. (Young Scott had flown the coop; she'd already filed a paternity suit.)

Quinn held Cress's left hand, but he had pulled in deep. It

was like sitting next to quicksand. During the vows, those nets of tenderness and promise, her eyes filled with tears, and she glanced at him.

"I shouldn't of come," he whispered.

After Franny and Brian walked back down the aisle to applause and the trays of champagne circulated, Cress went in search of a bathroom.

"Over here," Quinn said when she came out. He'd found a small side room with cribs in it and plastic toys in a box. Hangers and clothes were heaped about—here was where the bride had dressed. Quinn closed and locked both doors. A high transom allowed in a weak gray light, the distant hubbub and string quartet. "I can't force it, Cress," he said, and drew her down to the floor. "But we got what we got, too." He pushed her dress up, pulled off her panties.

"Nobody's forcing you, Quinn," she said gently.

His face was dark, his gaze inward. He took off only his coat and pulled his pants down just to his thighs; the coarse wool abraded the skin inside her legs, and his belt buckle tore her knee; the carpet burned her arms and backside. He held her forearms pressed against the floor, as if she were struggling. Maybe he wanted her to struggle. His shirt smelled musty, like old wool. His roughness neither frightened nor particularly excited her. She went along with him and didn't protest or resist, because he clearly had something to work out, and maybe he'd feel better once he had.

He collapsed finally, with all his hot itchy weight on top of her, and breathed hoarsely into her ear. Absently, she patted his shoulder.

The wedding party had moved into the shady, Spanish-style courtyard, where tables had been set up around a gurgling fountain. Cress wore her shawl over her chafed and burning upper arms. She found their name cards at a table with Don Dare and Elise, River Bob and Freddy, where the talk was all about how Rick Garsh was being sued by the Streeters; apparently he exceeded his estimate for their kitchen remodel by more than 100 percent. The wedding supper was salmon on soft herbed lettuces, with steamed asparagus and roasted potatoes. Crème brûlée, then cake. Cress's banquet crew would have found nothing to mock.

At the hotel, she took a cool bath and sent Quinn out for antibiotic cream. He came back with Neosporin and a bottle of Wild Turkey. He made love to her again, in the same intense, punishing manner, and afterward he thrashed in his sleep and would not tell her his dreams, except to say that they were tangled up and disturbing. She had wanted to drive over to Braithway in the morning to visit Tillie, but his mood stayed dark and distant, and she didn't suggest it. They drove home instead, stopping in Bakersfield for gas. He remained withdrawn, and after a few efforts to get him talking, she left him alone.

He carried in her bag and washed his hands at her sink. He refused coffee, beer, and whiskey. There were things he needed to do at his mom's, he said, before the week started. He couldn't stay the night. He kissed her lightly in the kitchen, touched the rug burn on her arm. She never clung to him when he left—he would've hated nothing more—but today she wanted to grab on, pull him from whatever rabbit hole he'd tumbled down. She walked him outside. She'd already turned back toward her house when his truck's engine caught. A dark vein branched through her vision, like lightning, only black.

She drove to Sparkville for supplies on Monday, and was home by early afternoon. She cut up beef and browned it, added onions with cumin and chipotle peppers. The beef toughened and, after an hour, grew tender. The house smelled wonderfully of smoke and meat. He didn't come. She wasn't surprised. She ladled a bowl for herself but had to put it aside untouched.

She sat at her desk and read the notes for her second column. She started writing and worked until she needed to consult a book stored in a box in the barn. She went out with a flashlight, and when she shone the beam into the box, there was a papery rasp, a dark scurry: a small snake sprang out, a squiggle in mid-air, then disappeared, leaving its shadow. She recoiled, and understood: that shadow was skin. He'd jumped out of his skin.

She laughed at her shivering self, and wished that Quinn was there to see. Everything she saw, she stored for him.

Twenty-Three

In the week before she saw him again, they all moved to Noah Mountain. Quinn, Sylvia, and Evan. The Sparkville house was up for rent.

"Had to do it," Quinn said. "Had to give it a real shot. I owe her that."

"Why will this time be any different?" said Cress.

"I have to try. As many times as it takes to give it a real go. See if we can get along. Or I can't live with myself."

"Haven't you tried that already, several times?"

His green eyes were dull and jumpy. "I could never give you up before."

"And now you can?"

"We'll see," he said.

"Get out," she said.

It was eleven-something, not even noon. He left a cup of coffee untouched on her kitchen table, and his fly-tying vise was still clamped to the corner.

She emptied his cup in the sink. As his truck trundled down her driveway, she poured herself half a tumbler of bourbon—from the bottle he'd bought in Glendale—and took it outside to the porch facing the river, where she sat in a chair and waited for the pain to start.

In the mornings, she had a moment of pure bright emptiness before the truth broke over her again: Quinn and his wife now lived up the road in a double-wide aluminum home.

On the days she didn't work, she stayed in bed, drifting and periodically nosing her sheets for any scent of him. Food didn't interest her. She tried to take her morning walks but never made it down the driveway before she had to turn around and go back to bed.

It was a dry, hot summer. The hills crisped to the color of lions. The high whine of insects bore steadily through the air. The river, low this year, receded; the swimming hole was stagnant at its edges by mid-July. A dark flickering appeared in the corners of her eyes, and at first she didn't know what it was, but every day it seemed closer, stronger, closing in. If you found the one person you loved, and you couldn't lick his neck or stick your nose up under his hair, or fall asleep tangled in his limbs, what did you do? Her tears ran without warning, sudden sobs made her chest jump. A new line trembled on the horizon, a fine dark fissure opened between objects: the abyss, beckoning. She tried to pray: *Look, whoever's listening. Let them finish. Send him back. We won't survive apart.*

She wasn't making specific plans, but that hairline crack, she knew, could widen instantly to accommodate her, and day by day, its thin blackness grew less frightening, more logical and familiar, as if she could now walk right up, touch it with her fingertips, and, with a quick last smile over her shoulder at the fading world, slip right in. She was sorry. If she ever did, he'd mistake it for the meanest thing imaginable. But the natural outcome of abandonment was a failure to thrive, to survive.

She didn't see how she could continue much longer. Eating seemed senseless. At Younts, she passed up the two-pound Yuban special; she couldn't imagine living long enough to drink it all.

The first time she passed Sylvia in her blue Imperial on Noah Mountain Road, Cress felt as if she'd been squeezed like a sponge.

She took a box of winter clothes to the barn and was drawn

into the old mechanic's bay, which was cool and smelled of dirt and oil. She crouched on the floor between oil spots, then sat for an hour. The next day, she swept it out, found carpet scraps that fit, and made a tiny, subterranean room. A thick round of cut pine served as a table. On this, she put a candle and the little donkey. She brought a pillow and her old down sleeping bag, and she would lie there, fingertips on each cool concrete wall. By remaining absolutely still, she could make an hour pass, then two hours, three. Any movement and the pain unfurled.

On Noah Mountain Road, a row of telephone poles planted in the left shoulder of a curve introduced themselves. All she'd have to do was not turn the steering wheel.

"If he was really going to leave her, he would've done it the first time round," said Donna. Cress had stopped by to see the sycamore tree, the Hapsaw, the lilac bush once more.

"Of adulterers who leave their spouses," Donna went on, "something like 95 percent do it in the first three months of the affair."

Somehow Cress went to work. She wouldn't desert Dalia and Lisette again, as she had last year. She clocked in and washed lettuce for the cook, hauled the tables around, flung starched white cloths over them, arranged silverware, built tall pyramids out of wide-mouth champagne glasses; she trayed out hors d'oeuvres, took cocktail orders. She spoke rarely and in a whisper. In this way, moment to moment, by turning to the next small task, by functioning as part of a larger mechanism, she kept on.

Dalia called her into the office. "Oh, Cress. We've all had our hearts broken, but you can't let it go on too long, and take it in too deep. You've got to save yourself—go see someone, try to meditate, *something*. Or you might never make it back."

Back to where? Back to what? Her old life—school, econ—no

longer existed. She could finish her dissertation, but where would that take her? There was no place she wanted to go, or could imagine ever wanting to go. She had to be where he could find her.

Somehow—perhaps because she was too polite and too intimidated by Silas not to return his calls or complete the next column she'd promised him (this one about art resale profits and commissions)—she did the research and wrote it. Her reporting was minimal; talking to people was the hardest part; she couldn't drum interest into her voice. She made do with a few meager facts and data she'd coaxed from a secretary at Sotheby's and one voluble gallery owner. *Of the eighty thousand dollars in increased value, the artist received 2 percent.*

Change that: *an* appalling *2 percent.*

She lost twelve pounds. She weighed what she had at fourteen. For her third column, Cress went south to interview an art consultant over lunch. She drove down the night before, to stay at Braithway. Tillie had promised to dress her.

Tillie said, "You may not see it right now, but it's really for the best. Also, Cress, you look like a model."

She sent Cress off in a pencil skirt and the big-shouldered power jacket.

The consultant purchased art for corporations and hospitals, and also for actors and movie execs who didn't have the time—or the eye—to shop. "After they buy the BMW and take the trekking vacation," the woman said, "these guys buy art." The consultant had selected the restaurant for their meeting, and their two pretty, clean-tasting, hand-built salads cost fifty dollars.

Cress went from lunch to the magazine offices, where she finally met Silas, a tall, soft-looking man her age. Taking the lunch receipt, he said, "Ooh la la! Now there's a woman who is good at spending other people's money!" Column three's lede: *Maude Sweeney has a talent for spending other people's money.*

Days passed. Work at Beech Creek slowed down. In the hot late afternoons after golf lady luncheons or the Rotarians, Cress took a glass of wine to the barn, into the cool trough. She lit a candle, drank the wine, and lay down on her sleeping bag. She counted her breaths backward from a hundred, a form of meditation she'd read about. She rarely remembered getting below the eighties. She woke up to a guttering flame, or utter darkness. That was when she knew it most keenly. He was coming back. He was on his way.

Cress drove south in early September for her fourth column, which was about an international art exposition at the convention center. Galleries from all over the world displayed paintings and sculptures in souklike warrens. The middle class had disposable income again, and goods were pouring in. Even Cress, whose arms felt like lead, who had no taste for life, was making money—not a lot, but more than she ever had: her own small share of the boom pot.

Driving to Los Angeles and back, always alone, her mind stayed busy with its own absorbing mix of memory and hope. She replayed their encounters, combing them for clues and meaning, as if their love was a great mystery or puzzle to be solved. Had he really gone back for good? She didn't believe it. He could no more give her up than she could forget him. He was struggling, too.

If only there was a way they could be together and not hurt anybody else.

She returned again and again to her little house in the tilted pasture: to her hard bed, her cool, tiny, secret room in the barn.

Trey Kidman, who hadn't seen her walking in weeks, came

by bringing brownies with *some sparkle*. Was she okay? She looked so pale and sad—did she want him to rub her back?

"No, no. That's all right, thanks," she said, moving away.

He left, and she threw the brownies in the trash.

Dalia and Lisette took her out for drinks after work, in hopes of cheering her up. They went to the Lakeview bar, the Sawyer Inn, and talked brightly, trying to interest Cress with confidences. Dalia told the story of her brutal five-year marriage. Lisette told them how she used to be the girlfriend of a famous rock star, but she'd hated that life and had to leave it. She was glad, because then she met her husband—after nine years they still made love every single day.

Touched by their company, Cress nodded and sipped her beer and asked questions to simulate interest and keep them talking.

"You don't know they're going to be physically abusive until they are," Dalia said.

"Oh yes, it's definitely mutual," said Lisette. "We both want to."

And, "No! But then, we vary it a lot, sometimes we draw it out with massage or toys, whatever, and sometimes it's a quickie."

At a hundred days, Cress lobbed his fly-tying vise into the swimming hole, but the smallish plunk and splash gave her no lift. Twenty-five days later, the silver flask flashed up in the water, like a trout's pale belly, then glugged water and sank. She couldn't bring herself to smash the donkey, whose black eyes shone. She could keep one memento. Something that, in thirty years, she could still admire. The finely delineated mane. The precise hoofs and tiny black teats.

Trey Kidman came again; this time she was in the barn, counting backward in the concrete bay. He called her name at the gate, then knocked on her door; she was afraid he'd try the barn next, but after a while he left.

In mid-October, rain came in daylong bursts, leaving the land sodden, the dry grasses beaten flat and mildewing. She retrieved her boxes of warm clothes from the barn. When she lifted the garments out, the wool and cashmere were full of holes, speckled with larval crumbs.

He couldn't bear this any more than she could. She was sure of it. But he was doing what needed to be done. Making a real attempt. The dark flickers persisted in her peripheral vision. She drove up the narrow logging road toward Wanderwood, until she was face-to-face with Noah Mountain's slag piles. She parked and got out; she could see right down into the family compound: the mother's white clapboard house, the trailers big and small. Sylvia's car parked at an angle. Stacks of wood, of rusty junk, an old water heater. A haphazard rural cluster: Would it ever be her home?

She tried to drive on to Wanderwood, to be, at least, in his favorite place. But the road was more treacherous than she'd remembered, and after scraping the bottom of the Saab on a rock, she lost heart and had to back up for most of a mile before she found a place to turn around.

She passed Quinn on the road. His fingers lifted off the steering wheel in a quick gallop that rippled through her, reset her heart to a mad bang.

"He's suffering, too." She was at Braithway again, having come down for a meeting at the magazine. She and Tillie drank wine in her kitchen. "I feel it."

"You know what? I can't talk to you about Quinn anymore.

He's gone back to his wife. It's over. You're obsessed. You should talk to a professional."

Cress was surprised, and somewhat flattered that her unhappiness might qualify her in Tillie's eyes for a therapist.

"And you need to start eating," Tillie added. "It's getting scary. Now you look like a junkie."

Cress's mother had never visited her in college or grad school. In Sylvia Hartley's worldview, children visited parents. Yet here she was, self-invited, at Cress's door, having driven up from Carpenteria that morning. She held a sack of groceries: a leg of lamb, bananas, V8 juice, food she remembered Cress liking as a child. There were more presents in the car: a polka-dot comforter, two Indian-print blouses, an electric popcorn popper, all Price Club bargains.

Sylvia Hartley stalked through the little house, which was too clean to fault. "Do you like living here?"

"It's the most beautiful place I've ever lived." Cress motioned toward the slanted fields, the ring of blue mountains.

"Many places are beautiful. *And* closer to your friends and the magazine!"

"I can't move south. It feels like going backwards."

Sylvia sighed loudly and sat on the couch. She extended her legs, examined the ring on her right hand, a sapphire sunk in yellow gold. "It's time to move on," she said. "Time to pull yourself up by your bootstraps."

"What if I don't have any bootstraps?" Cress said. "What are bootstraps, anyway?"

"What about your dissertation? Have you lost interest in that?"

"I don't know, Mom. Maybe."

"After all that time and work and money?" Sylvia surveyed the small living room with its pale carpet and random furniture. She frowned at the wicker love seat as if she could not quite place it. "What's going on, Cress, that your friends are calling me to say you're in terrible shape and they're afraid you might do something bad to yourself?"

"Who called you?"

"Never mind who."

"I'm just sad about Quinn."

"For crying out loud, Cress. It's not realistic, after all this time, to go on and on about him. He's a married man!"

"I'm not going on and on."

"I don't know what happened with you girls. Sharon only likes foreign men and you only like married ones."

"Not *ones*, Mom. One. One man. But maybe if you'd let us have a more normal social life in high school—"

"Here we go," her mother said.

"I'm just saying, maybe if I'd had more experience with guys when I was young—"

"I know what you're saying. The mother is always to blame."

Cress lacked the energy for this—or any—argument. She wept weakly.

Sylvia watched her. "What do you need? I'll help you with whatever it is. An apartment in San Francisco? Seattle? I think you should go away. Get out of this place. Take a long trip. If you'd done that back when I first suggested it, you'd be beyond all this by now. Europe? Japan? I'll buy your ticket."

Sylvia lowered her voice. "Of course, you can't tell your father. But I have a little nest egg. I can spend it however I want. If you need me to, I'll go with you. Wherever you want. Whatever it takes to pull you out of this."

"I don't want to go anywhere, Mom. I'm fine here."

"Do you really think he's going to leave his wife?"

"No." Cress shook her head, slinging tears. She no longer thought so grandly. Her hopes were more circumspect; she hoped to see and speak to him, to smell up under his hair again. To stop the pain for a minute here, a minute there.

"You wouldn't want him, anyway," her mother said. "Not for a husband. Not in the long run."

"I'd like to find that out for myself."

Her mother went to the kitchen and came back with two glasses of wine. "I'd like to take you to a hospital, Cress. I think you need to check yourself in."

"You mean like a nuthouse? A booby hatch?"

"You're not in good shape, Cress. You're way too skinny. You're talking at half speed. I can barely hear you."

"I'm fine, Mom."

"I can't help you if you don't let me."

"I'm okay, Mom. You don't need to do anything."

"I do. I do need to do something. I can't let you slip through my fingers."

"It's okay, Mom, I'm all right."

Sylvia looked at her for a long time, then stood and put the lamb in the oven, boiled the string beans, set the table.

Cress was moved by her mother's visit and sorry to be so frustrating. She choked down some lamb, ate a whole banana. She had to make many promises before her mother would leave: she promised to eat, to consider moving, to socialize, to raise her voice, to cut back on the wine. She promised to exercise, to try to forget Quinn, to revisit her dissertation. She accepted another check, for four hundred dollars, and never cashed it.

When she got into her Camry, Sylvia Hartley latched her seat belt, then rolled down her window, motioning Cress close. "I just want to say, you were right," she said, "the Meadows has been a mistake, from day one. What with Rick Garsh and what's happened to you, I wish I'd never heard of the place."

Watching the Camry drive off, Cress made a promise to herself: to put on a better front from here on out, and keep her problems to herself.

19 November 1983

Dear Cress,

Well. It has been a year and a half since I was born anew into this vale of tears, and things are looking up!

Life in London continues apace. I have more students than is ideal and am also teaching pedagogy to the London Cello Instructors Association. I'm down to a size 10 again (I'm back in OA—it's been like slogging through mud!!!). I'm getting restless and have been sniffing about for foreign teaching gigs—in China, Turkey (of course!—or haven't I told you about Ibrahim?), and even grotty old L.A.

I hear things are not so hot for you—and I've been given to understand that this is MY fault (source: Guess Who?). If I'd let you come to England to be properly distracted, I'm told, you'd be well over the hauntingly handsome husband-of-another by now, plus: Ph.D.'ed, AND gainfully employed at some well-compensated economic research post.

Seriously, though, I hear that you have been very sad, and I would like to make amends to you for the part I did play in adding to that sadness: i.e., for not being available to you when I might've helped you out. I was careening about in my own oblivious way (i.e., head up arse), without thinking much or at all about the impact I might be having on you or anyone else. I'm truly sorry for that, and I can say with confidence that I won't ever be so impervious to you again.

I HATE a rift, esp. between US!!! You are the one member of our family I can talk to . . . stand . . . adore. The one person on earth who knows what it was like being in a family with Those Two. I miss your letters and your news. If the alarms sounding across the pond are even the tiniest bit true, I'm also very worried about you, and would like to help in any way I can. I will happily buy you a ticket to my TLC, i.e., Thoroughly Lumpy Couch, or I can come and occupy yours—if my company might cheer and you will have me. Just say the word.

This brings love,

Your 144* pound sister,
Sharon

P.S. If you come, don't worry about what it costs me. The
Great Mother has offered to fund everything if I can just
pry you out of your mountain cave. Don't you think we
should take advantage of this once-in-a-lifetime offer???

*Down from 187!!!

A pale log building went up on the west side of Sawyer: a new
bar, BOB'S BAR, the sign said. After a Rotary luncheon, Dalia,
Cress, and Lisette decided to drive over for a look. They took
separate cars to the unpaved parking lot. The owner himself,
eponymous Bob, a square-headed, Hawaiian-shirted Visalia
man, bought their first round. Beautiful women, he said, passing out the draft beers, were a boon for business.

Only in the hustings with two better-looking women, Cress
thought, would she ever be called beautiful. She sat facing the
two new pool tables, the felt expanses unmarred, the triangles
of candy-colored balls poised to explode. The new log walls
looked wet, resinous, as if brushed with maple syrup.

Dalia said, "Don't look now, Cress, but your guy just came in."

She froze and didn't turn. She hadn't seen him for a hundred
and seventy-four days. Her heart started slamming around her
rib cage. She heated up. "Does he see me?"

"I would say he most definitely sees you."

"Let him look," she said.

He would have spotted her Saab in the lot. Had he been
looking for it, hoping to see it for a while now? Or had he turned
in on a momentary impulse? Still, he had to park, get out, lock
his truck, and walk inside: time enough to reconsider. She finished her beer. "Here I go," she said.

Dalia said, "Oh, don't. You really shouldn't."

"Oh no, Cress, no," said Lisette.

"I have to," Cress said. "I can't not."

Spine straight, blushing and trembling like a bride, she walked across the concrete floor, past the line of men drinking at the bar.

"What took you so long?" he said.

His voice crackled through her veins as through ice. "How've you been?" she whispered.

"Good, good," he said. "You?"

"Not so good."

"You still know how to cook a pork chop?"

Inexorably came the blear of amazement that he would catapult over his scruples and his wife's trust and once more turn to her.

"Leave first," she said. "Give me a twenty-minute lead."

She didn't want her friends to know how instantly she'd capitulated. As she walked back to them, their faces were upturned, like plates, saucers of light and hope. Cress pulled out her chair.

"Look at you blushing," said Lisette. "What did he say?"

She felt like a drunk trying to appear sober. "He's doing well."

"He's leaving," said Dalia.

"Good," Cress said. "Anybody else want another beer?"

She bought the round and drank hers quickly. The noisy new room with its forlorn music and now-colliding pool balls was glazed in a rosy-amber light. Long before she'd planned to, Cress stood.

"Oh don't," Dalia said. "Don't. Let's go out to dinner. My treat."

"It's not what you think," said Cress. "I'm going home."

"We know what you're doing," said Dalia.

"Plain as day," said Lisette. "You're straining at the gate. About to burst."

Cressida toed the ground, sipped air. "I can't not," she said. "I have to."

"You should stop yourself," said Dalia.

"Don't do it," said Lisette. "Just say no."

How easily the car steered. How light were her arms. The phone poles ticked past. Not today, guys. The pain had receded, coiled back to its depths. How soft were the darkening hills, how sweet the breeze.

He met her in the hall, by the washer.

She showed him the magazines, her name in print. He read three columns, right there in front of her. "If you can do this," he said, "why are you still here?"

"You have to ask?"

In bed, they both wept; his wet cheeks glistened in the dark room. His beard was back, his hair long again. He'd gained weight, having stopped all cigarettes and all booze but beer. She went over his body, touching each scar, poked his new belly, stuck her nose up behind his ear, inhaled.

"How is it at home?" she said.

"Better, now that we're back on the mountain."

"Then what are you doing here?"

"Exactly what you're doing."

"Not exactly," she said. He was there for the alleviation of pain. And she was still hoping to redeem what had been offered to her once, what seemed to sit there yet, waiting to be claimed, just out of reach.

Twenty-Four

She turned in whenever she saw his truck. He'd plant himself in her path and she couldn't pass him up. She'd perch on the stool beside him, and sometimes before they had one drink, they'd leave—he was more careful now about being seen with her in town. Once she came into Bob's Bar and he was talking to a man his own age, a trim tanned man in a blue sport shirt. The place was almost empty. She took her seat and waited while they continued their conversation. Quinn ignored her. She nursed a beer. His voice buzzed, but she couldn't quite hear what he and the blue sport shirt were talking about: who was building what in town, maybe. Who got county contracts. The man ordered another beer for himself and one for Quinn. Cress got up to leave then, and Quinn's hand shot out, touched her leg under the rim of the bar, and pushed her back into her seat.

In the Sawyer bakery on a crowded morning, the air hazed with coffee steam and vaporized grease from the doughnut fryer, he sat with Caleb and two other men at a coil table, while she and Donna occupied the next one. Neither brother looked at her. Leaving, he passed within inches without glancing down.

"You might have at least raised an eyebrow," she said later.

"Half of Sawyer was in there watching," he said. "To see what I'd do."

"Even so, you could've been polite and not acted like I didn't exist."

"When you're seeing a married man, you should expect that sort of thing."

He didn't mean it the way it sounded. In fact, she understood: they had to be discreet; he had to keep up appearances so that this time Sylvia would think he was making a real effort to make their marriage work.

They drove slowly, pressed together, on the purgatorial grid of roads and orange groves. They sat in their familiar completeness and comfort in those small bars in far-flung places where a lurid canned sadness leaked from the jukeboxes and old men drank diligently till dinnertime, then came back to drink some more till bedtime.

Quinn phoned and she met him down by the lake and drove with him to Bakersfield, where he looked at a job in a treeless new housing development. She read a novel in the car while he talked to the foreman. Afterward, they bought a bottle and rented a motel room. "Now, this really feels like adultery," she said.

Quinn winced, as she knew he would. "It's not like that," he said.

"It's exactly like that," she said.

"More like, I met the person I'm closest to twenty years after I handed my life over to someone else. When I'm not my own to give away."

"Oh, sure you are." She had less patience now for his formulations. "People get divorced every day."

"People you know," he said.

The next time, he went to bid finish work for an office complex in Visalia.

The hours together invigorated her. She learned to make use of this invigoration. She drove to L.A. for research. She sewed curtains, she read novels from the Sparkville public library, she wandered in the foothills, her morning walks lasting two or three hours. As the days passed, the effect of their last meeting wore off; she saddened and slowed; pain and the internal chatter built back up, quivering dark edges reappeared around objects, the telephone poles bled back into view. She spent afternoons in the barn again, in the cool trough, with a candle and wine, lying under the polka-dot comforter, counting backward, waking up to a leaping candle and radiant darkness.

He took a job in Redondo Beach and during the workweek stayed with his cousins there. Cress drove down to spend Wednesday nights with him at a motel. They ate at seafood restaurants, took walks on the sand. He'd told his cousins he had a weekly poker game in Glendale and drank too much beer to drive home. When she was leaving in the morning, he said, "Poker again next week?"

Three more times in the next three weeks, they met in Redondo, and then the job was finished.

Cress's body startled before she saw why: Sylvia Morrow was standing at the fish counter in Younts. She looked smaller than Cress remembered: a slight, petite woman in navy pants and a navy tunic—her work uniform. Her hair was dark and thick, a heavy pelt. Cress swiveled her own cart around and fled the width of the store, to the produce section, where she stood by the watermelons, four field boxes pushed together. Cress slapped a melon, the hollow smack satisfying, like the correct answer to a question. She wasn't afraid of a fight; Sylvia was too reserved and timid for any loud accusations, name-calling, nail-clawing. But why not spare them both the pain and embarrassment of a meeting? Cress shoved melons aside to thump the ones below. She'd thump until she calmed down and was sure Sylvia was out of the store.

A cart rolled up beside her. "Hello, Cress," Sylvia said.

The aisle was wide enough that their shopping carts fit side by side. Sylvia's hair *was* weirdly massive and curled, the crimped mane of a country-and-western singer or a cocktail waitress with aspirations.

"How are you?" Sylvia said.

"Fine," said Cress. "And you?"

Sylvia must have noticed Cress staring, because her hand rose to a clump of curls by her face. "I just got my hair done. I hate how she rats it up so poufy. I always get in the shower the second I get home to wash out all the spray."

Stupefied, Cress nodded. Would they really stand here and talk hair like friends?

Sylvia put a hand on Cress's cart and left it, fingers curling slightly around the chrome. "I've been wanting to talk to you, Cress. So I'm glad we ran into each other. I wanted to say . . ." Sylvia glanced quickly into Cress's face, then down. "Well, I hope you're not staying around up here because you think Quinn's going to leave me and marry you. Because that's not going to happen, Cress. It never was, and it never will." In her girlish tones twanged a wire of certainty. "Quinn and I are going to grow old together. We always were, and nothing's changed. If he got your hopes up for something else, he shouldn't of, and I'm sorry for that. I really am."

Cress kept her face still, even as her heart went wild. Sylvia's self-possession was marvelous, but those clichés!

Up ahead of them, symmetrical stacks of waxy purple and green cabbages bulged with veins. The misters went on, spraying them, and in that hissing, Cress missed some of what Sylvia was saying next. She heard ". . . miscarriage last month, but the doctor says we can start trying again next week."

So here was a real prisoners' dilemma, Cress thought. Should I continue to nod and simper? Or should I now tell Sylvia about the day before yesterday at the Motor Inn? The bottle of bourbon? The hours in bed?

But Quinn would never forgive her if she narc'ed.

—

"I'm glad she talked to you," said Dalia. "Maybe now you can be done."

Cress hoped so too. She would like to be done. Done and gone. But when she saw Quinn's truck at the Staghorn, she turned into the parking lot. His green eyes brightened at the sight of her; he was down at the end of the bar, where she'd met the yellow mother. His low voice sent a fast current through her system. He was hoping she'd come; he always felt better the moment he saw her warm, open face. Did she feel like a drive? A steak?

They drove and ate, and drowsy from meat and liquor, Cress, who had been trying to ascertain if Sylvia had reported their encounter, said, "Sylvia sees me around, on the road. Does she ever say anything? What does she think?"

"She thinks you have psychological problems."

"Oh my. I suppose I do. What do you think?"

"I do wonder why you're still here."

She saw then that they'd found a way to unite against her. That they'd agreed on a narrative: Quinn had made a mistake, opened a real can of worms. And now he was pursued by the mentally unstable.

On a recent trip to Pasadena, Tillie and Cress had gone to see a movie where a spurned mistress—who'd spent only one night with a married man—stalks the man relentlessly, tries all sorts of shenanigans to get his attention, and eventually boils his family's pet. Cress would never go a tenth that far, but her sympathies were definitely with the mistress, who was up against the blameless bland wife and family itself, that fortress of sanctified virtue. The pet boiler was truly deranged—but isn't it often the fringe, unhinged person who acts out the anger of her cohort? The pet boiler, Cress felt, had struck a blow for their kind. The discarded. The unchosen.

She did have psychological problems, Cress would be the first to admit it: obsession, depression, loss of affect, anhedonia. And—not to be melodramatic here—she couldn't quite locate herself anymore. She'd try to consult herself on matters large or small and she'd come up blank, except through the filter of him. She bought only the food that he might eat. When she shopped for clothes, she thought only in terms of his taste, or what she imagined his taste to be: lace at the neck, and tighter, tidier slacks. Upon entering any room full of men—a banquet, the magazine's newsroom, a bar—not one pricked her interest, they could all have been chairs or lamps, since none of them was Quinn. Although Cress duly researched and wrote the assignments Silas gave her—she was too afraid of displeasing him and Tillie to fail—she had no real interest in the magazine work, the stories about art and commerce. The single story she did pitch—one about clearcutting in the Spearmint watershed and the war between local loggers and environmentalists—was dismissed on the spot. ("Write it for the Sierra Club newsletter," Tillie said.) As for her dissertation—well, that was like a small handkerchief tied to a tree so far away Cress glimpsed its listless flutter intermittently, seasonally.

A dissertation on art in the marketplace would do nothing to draw him nearer.

She understood that he was no longer listing in her direction. He had found a way back into his old life. His grief, the sadness and fury that sent him to her, had subsided, leaving her stranded here in the middle of a pasture. She should get out. It was time. Past time. And she wanted out, she really did. At least part of her did. More and more, it seemed, she was in a civil war with herself, the side that had dug in versus the side that wanted out. The dug-in side was like a steel I-beam sunk deep in unconscious muck. The wanting-out side was like that sheep of his uncle's, tangled deep in the brambles, bleating weakly for someone, anyone, to come and yank her free.

A motel in Reseda had thin, slippery sheets and hourly rates.

"Don Dare's in law school," she told him.

"Caleb and Candy moved to South Carolina again; she wouldn't let Caleb take jobs away from home, and he couldn't find enough local work to keep them going."

Two months later, she saw his truck at the Staghorn.

"Did you hear? Brian and Franny have twins! A boy and a girl!"

"Annette's transferring to Cal for her junior year," he said.

"You remember my friend Tillie? She had a little girl and is now a features editor at *City and State*."

Another time, they started at the Staghorn and ended up at the Dairyman's Inn out on the highway.

"Do you think we'll ever be together more than this?" she said.

"We shouldn't even be together like this," he said.

On a warm May day, they drove once more through the cloying perfume of the blossoming orange groves. "If you and Sylvia had stayed split up from the start and we'd married a year later, we'd be nearing our second anniversary."

"We'd be divorced," he said flatly.

"What makes you say that?"

"We're too different," he said. "We couldn't of pulled it off."

But she would have adjusted, for better or worse, and made him a home, with log walls, plank floors, fine china, and a snarling bearskin—the one that still occupied the Saab's entire trunk. A moldering smell sometimes wafted into the car.

"One day you are going to know how terrible I've been, and you are going to get really angry," he said.

She patted his thigh. "I look forward to that day."

Two more months passed and she didn't see his truck parked anywhere. The next time she climbed into the cab beside him, she wept silently for two hours as he drove across the valley floor, past orange and lemon and olive groves; then farther west into sorghum, apricots, alfalfa. The tears plopped on her lap until her jeans were sodden.

He was working on a library down on Mulholland Drive for a television actor, he said. She should come down.

They rented a room at the Starlight Inn in Encino, four times in six weeks. The renewed frequency, their high humor, dinners at Jinky's, seemed a resurgence. Loving and close, they sat on the same side of booths. There was always news. Donna had finally won her paternity suit and had also become impregnated by and engaged to the Sparkville deputy marshal. Don Dare and Elise had two boys already—and Don was almost through law school on a two-year fast track. Tillie had moved over to the *Los Angeles Times*, where she was now second in command at the Sunday magazine.

Cress could never remember which time was the last time, because neither knew it would be the last. She saw him when the Mulholland job was almost done, and then he must have been done, because she passed him in his truck midweek on Noah Mountain Road. He waved.

His truck was never parked at the bars, at least not when she drove by. She saw him infrequently on the road (he always waved). More often, she passed Sylvia (no wave). So they were still around. Seeing either one set off her heart and made her hands shake.

She was spending more time down south, a week or two every month. She had a desk in the *City and State* offices now, and a title: contributing editor. Tillie and Edgar had bought a large house by the Arroyo in Pasadena, and she had her own room—and bath!—on the second floor there.

Her father retired; her parents sold both Meadows cabins in the upward-trending housing market. Cress thought, for a split second, she might want the A-frame; then she remembered the Garshes. Her parents wanted to travel now, and her father, working with a Realtor, invested in second mortgages.

Her sister, Sharon, was coming to town as a visiting lecturer at her alma mater, the USC School of Music.

Cress quit working at Beech Creek, although Dalia called her in for the large banquets, and Cress was happy to help.

Donna, with a swift backward glance in the Sawyer bakery, spoke softly over the top of two-year-old Ava's blond curls. "I still don't understand why Sylvia took him back. I mean, a one- or two-night stand is one thing; even a two- or three-month affair might be forgiven, but three-plus years, with all that lying? That amounts to a whole secret life!"

But Cress understood why Sylvia took him back. Given half a chance, she would, too.

She would always wish that some small scrap of self had reared up and saved her. But that is not what happened.

August 18, 1985

Dear Cress,

Greetings from USC! I am here in my new office, a long, skinny room with a view of an ivy-covered brick wall. I spent the morning at the Natural History Museum where I attached myself to a back room tour and saw many interesting things in glass jars: 2-foot-long centipedes, Siamese-twin pig fetuses, etc.). I am finally getting over my jet lag! Still, it is weird to be back in smog-socked ole So Cal.

I promise to visit as soon as I'm settled. I've already made great strides—I found a therapist and a good OA meeting that's not too full of anorexic actresses. AND I found a place to live, which is the main reason why I'm writing.

I told Mom and Dad that I'd consider staying permanently in the area if they'd give me the down payment for a house. They said . . . NO! (Big surprise!!!) (Dad did offer me a mortgage at 12%, which I can get from any bank. It's the 10% down I need help with.) All of which is to say, yesterday I signed a year lease on a funky little hillside house in Echo Park—on a clear day you can see the Hollywood sign *and* the ocean. The house has three bedrooms and two baths, a big deck, pretty yards, front and back, etc., but the rent is a little steep for one person (or I'm a little too cheap to pay it all). I'll have to get a roommate, and it occurred to me that maybe YOU would be that roommate. *DON'T* Just Say No! (I'm writing rather than calling so you'll have the leisure to overcome any knee-jerk resistance and think it over.) I figure we can get along, since I'll hardly ever be home and it's only for a year (the end is already in sight!), after which you can get another roommate or go back to the mountains, or pay the whole nut yourself, or burn the place down. I'll give you a great deal on your share of rent (to make up for past transgressions—I owe you!!! I also promise not to proselytize *too* much or be *too* much the big sister!).

I won't advertise for a roommate until you get back to me—but try to let me know in a week. We can move in on the first—I'm paid up here at the oatmeal-gray Oakwood till then.

Think about it. Then . . . Just Say YES!!!!

Love,

Sharon

Her father rented a U-Haul to move her. She was grateful for his offer to help—her mother was behind it, she was certain—but once he arrived, she regretted taking him up on it. Having her father, of all people, escort her south felt far too much like being led away in defeat, as if she was retreating to the bosom of her own family, the last place she wanted to be.

He hitched the Saab to a tow bar. "No sense wasting gas,"

he said. "Though the added drag will definitely use more gas than the truck alone, especially on inclines. But your load is light."

He insisted on stopping in Sparkville for coffee; she steered him to the Koffee Kup on the mad chance she might see Quinn one last time. If he was there, she thought, even if he was sitting with other men, or with Sylvia, she would go right up to him. She would tell him she was leaving, and she would watch the truth of it take hold in his pale green eyes.

Quinn was not at the Koffee Kup. She sipped ice water while Sam Hartley drank three cups of coffee. "Yes, please! Top her off! We have a long drive ahead of us! Whoa there! That's plenty, thanks! Got to save room for a little arf-'n'-arf!"

His term for half-and-half.

South of town, her father pulled off the road to buy honeydew melons at a rickety farmstand and again, near Bakersfield, he stopped for a crate of tomatoes. Cress waited in the hot cab while Sam engaged the vendor and other customers in a conversation about canning methods. This was beginning to seem like one of her dreams, when she was trying to get somewhere and one obstacle after another arose. Didn't he see that she was crawling out of her skin?

"That guy was selling figs for four dollars a basket." Her father climbed back in the truck. "Eight, ten figs in each. My tree has a thousand figs on it easily. A hundred baskets, let's say, leaving plenty for the birds. That's what? Four hundred dollars? And I've been giving them away!"

Behind them, the Sierras sank into the valley mist, the highway thrummed under the truck's tires. The U-Haul locked in at fifty-five miles an hour, and cars passed them incessantly.

She would be a glint of light, a shred of old cloth, a mote by the time they got to Los Angeles, and here her father was signaling again, prompted by a another farmstand at the foot of the next off-ramp. "Can we sit this one out, Dad?" Cress said. "And keep driving? I'm so anxious about this move. You're sweet to help me, and I appreciate it so much. But can we just get there?"

"Hunh," he said, braking as he veered onto the ramp. "Moving's never bothered me one way or the other, though it always put your mother in a tizzy. I'll be quick. I just want a sack of sweet onions. They're picked every morning, dirt still on 'em. Only two-fifty for twenty-five pounds."

Twenty-Five

Exercise could raise Cress's spirits, Sharon said. As would getting out more, or taking a class. She should ride a bicycle or bake bread. Therapy—regular, not even the rebirthing variety—could recharge her. She might also consider AA, or just stop drinking so much. Sharon frowned at Cress's second glass of burgundy. "I can't see how guzzling a depressant helps anything."

Amid this welter of advice—really, in self-defense—Cress took out her dissertation. How could Sharon nag or interrupt her when she was finally doing the necessary thing? She set up on the enclosed back porch, facing northwest toward the Hollywood sign. A few feet behind her, Sharon wrote lectures and graded papers at the dining room table. Once Cress got down to work, the diss proved no more onerous than several columns. She finished in six months.

With graphs, footnotes, and bibliography, the manuscript came to two hundred and ten pages and bore only a faint relation to her prospectus, which now seemed a naïve mix of exuberance and grandiosity. Cress had stopped caring if her premise was sound—far, *far* too late to worry about that!—and proceeded as if it were unimpeachable. She worried most about her margins, as a proctor would measure them for precision. (John Bird's margins had been off by a sixteenth of an inch, and his whole manuscript had to be retyped.)

Long distracted by other promising pupils, not to mention his own research, her advisor replied to her manuscript with an offhand note: *Looks good. Go ahead and set up your committee.* He appended a list of possible names.

She flew back a month later for the defense. Her committee consisted of three people from the Art Department and three from Econ. They spent a few minutes on each chapter, asking her to describe her major points. Every professor praised the soundness of the writing. For her journalism, she had developed a clear, amusing voice, and clear, amusing writing was so rare in econ dissertations, it passed for competence, even authority.

No one remarked on the thinness of her subject—essentially, she'd charted and theorized about the small leaps and setbacks in the careers of twenty artists. The painting professor (and only woman) said, "If I read this before starting out, I never would've become a painter." A sculpture professor Cress didn't know proved annoying: Did she think selling prices were the only measurement of value in art? Did art have no value if it never entered the marketplace?

Of course it did. But this was about art *in* the marketplace.

She was sent down the hall to a small lounge where she sat looking out at the lead-gray river flowing through the state university. The cloud cover was low and taut. The last patches of dirty snow melted into the dead grass. Crows gathered in the naked branches of trees and made a terrible racket. She tried not to take this as a bad omen. Her dissertation, however tenuous its findings, had taken months—years, counting all that procrastination and avoidance—and in the end contained real work, even if the final product was made of spiderwebs.

"Congratulations," her advisor whispered at the door, and brought her back into the seminar room.

Very good, the men and one woman murmured; a bit iconoclastic, but quite creative, and a pleasure to read. A few minor changes were needed—just enough so that, yes, the whole thing had to be repaginated and reprinted.

At least those years of resistance and delay had brought her into the era of personal computers and printers, so no massive retyping job was required.

She finished the revision in two weeks, and three weeks af-

ter that—six years and two months since she and John Bird
parted in front of their Church Street apartment—she received
a thin letter addressed to Dr. Cressida Hartley, Ph.D. Her parents drove down and took her and Sharon out to El Tepeyac to
celebrate. "Now that you have this expensive degree," her father
said, "what are you going to do with it?"

Returning from a walk in Elysian Park one afternoon, Cress
found Sharon in the driveway, the Saab's trunk open, and the
bundled bearskin sitting on the concrete. "I hesitate to ask," said
Sharon, who had needed a tire jack.

The brown paper was torn, revealing green felt.

"I was too afraid to look," said Cress.

Sharon went to the kitchen for a butcher knife and a broom.
The twine cut with a *pop!* and the bundle relaxed. They pulled
away the paper. The stiff green felt had molded into a clump.
Using the end of a broom handle, Sharon prodded it open, prying the folds apart, poking them flat, felt side up. She looked like
a warrior with a spear, or a gondolier. Centered on the green felt
was a dry lake of mold the color of cigarette ash. Sharon flung
aside the broom and, grabbing one front paw, pointed to the
other. "Turn him over."

The claws were still black and plastic-like. As they flipped
the rug right side up, fur fell out in a rain of bristles, and a brown
cloud arose. The sisters jumped back.

The nose had partly broken off from the skull, revealing
papier-mâché; pink paint peeled off the tongue and two teeth
dropped out on the pavement. On closer inspection, the fur
seethed with tiny, winged, brown insects. "How long's it been in
there, anyway?" said Sharon.

"Three, four years."

"Well, it's garbage now!" Sharon yelped.

Sharon sprayed the skin with Raid. Later, they stuffed it into
a trash barrel, leaving a bear-shaped shadow of bristles and dead

bugs on the driveway. Sharon took her broom, swept briskly, and in moments even the shadow was in the bin.

"I still wish there was a twelve-step program for you," Sharon said days before she flew back to London. "One of the biggest turning points in my life was when I made amends to everyone I'd hurt—except, of course, those people I'd only hurt again by contacting them."

"Like Sylvia Morrow," said Cress. "I could never make amends to her."

"Oh, sure you can. That's an easy one. You stay the hell away from *him!*"

So Cress did. She stayed the hell away from Quinn. She never called (even just to hear his voice and hang up); she never mailed a letter to him (she wrote several); she never sent him a message through friends, or contacted them for news of him. In time, she lost track of most of those friends—Donna, Dalia, even Brian and Franny—who could pass on such a message. The only person she stayed in touch with (they swapped cards at the holidays) was Don Dare, and he'd moved a hundred miles from Sawyer to Fresno.

Cress kept her phone number listed, in case Quinn needed to find her.

Once Sharon was no longer there to nag her, Cress began running in the hills; she cut way back on the wine, took a drawing class, and found a therapist.

At first she talked about Quinn. She described their time together with pleasure, even reverence—but she harbored no hope. She'd given up. Sylvia was triumphant. But Cress could not shake the feeling that part of her had been left behind, as if her soul were invisibly married to Quinn in some kind of alternate existence. When her therapist asked her to describe this other life, Cress saw log walls, a jagged peak through the window. A low voice coursed in the background. She imagined berry picking, padding through the tall woods, fishing—well, Quinn fishing and her nearby, reading.

"And do you feel whole and fulfilled there?" asked the therapist. "Would you be doing your life's work?"

"I don't have a life's work," said Cress.

In dreams, endlessly proliferating obstacles—importuning friends, chasms in the road, vehicular disintegration—prevented their meeting. Once, she made it to his house and was welcomed by Sylvia—a burly, forceful Sylvia, who was bustling half-a-dozen children into a station wagon. "Upstairs, far bedroom," this Sylvia called before driving off larkily, thrilled for a few hours of liberty. Quinn, when Cress found him, was a brain-damaged, mute invalid requiring constant supervision, which even an old rival could supply.

Only rarely did she meet him face-to-face in a dream. In one, Quinn appeared at her kitchen table, smiling and jaunty, wanting coffee. She asked him, "How much time do we have?" and he cheerfully replied, "Twenty minutes!" In another dream, they floated down a river together, fingers touching, their skin mottled, greenish and cool, like frogs'. She awoke to the faint, evaporating threads of exquisite, tender feelings, amazed that, by herself, she had conjured the nearly unbearable sweetness of being known and adored.

Cress wrote about art for Silas and about economic issues for Tillie at the *Times*. But the freelance life was wearing thin; she missed the camaraderie of Beech Creek. She applied for teaching jobs at two community colleges, but halfheartedly, never believing they'd want her, and indeed, nothing came of it. Tillie tried to give her more interesting assignments and sent her to write about an enormous steel plant in San Bernardino County whose owners *disastrously* filed for bankruptcy on the heels of a three-hundred-million-dollar expansion.

At the plant, among many government officials looking to salvage something from the wreckage, Cress ran into a man she knew from her college econ classes; while she'd been the class star, publishing a term paper in an academic journal, he had struggled to get Bs. Now he worked for the state's economic development agency and was here looking for ways to put the abandoned plant back to good use. After two lunches, he mentioned a job opening at his agency, an entry-level position—his position, in fact. He'd been promoted. Was she interested? They weren't necessarily looking for a Ph.D., but a trained economist would sure add to the team.

A civil servant. She'd had bigger, or at least different, ambitions back in grad school. But the pay was decent for government work, her coworkers proved diverse and intelligent, the work itself was environmentally protective, and she had to start somewhere. She spent her days reading, reviewing economic impact analyses and feasibility studies for proposed developments in the county. Never mind that her boss was Mr. B-minus himself.

She was aware now of the time she'd squandered, how much momentum she'd lost. Four years—and more!—she'd given to Quinn. What had held her there? Why hadn't she extracted herself earlier? And how little she had asked for in love! How little she'd been left with: one small, carved donkey with bright onyx eyes.

Years passed, and Cress met men, usually through friends: a studio musician (gamelan, xylophone), a ceramic artist, another carpenter; and with each one, she was excited at the start, but in eight, ten months, or a year, instead of her affections deepening, they began to recede, until she was alone again.

There was nothing wrong with any of these men, she admitted to her therapist, except she did not feel for them the way she had for Quinn. They didn't hold her attention. The connections weren't as close. "Maybe I'm essentially monogamous," Cress said. "Maybe I mated once, and that's it."

Emotional flexibility, the therapist pointed out carefully, was a desirable trait, one that Cress might cultivate. Would she consider letting go of certain closely held beliefs if they no longer served her? Perhaps she'd allow in some new ideas about love and happiness, and welcome different kinds of people into her life.

In her late thirties, it grew harder to meet single men. She agreed to the occasional fix-up, but nothing took. She went ahead— she needed the tax write-off—and bought a house in Pasadena on a pretty oak-shaded street overlooking the arroyo and right around the corner from Tillie's. ("At last, I have you where I want you," Tillie said.)

Cress was not unhappy. She took a new job at a private environmental consulting firm, and now she specialized in "mitigations," finding ways for companies to offset the environmental damage they caused. She arranged for a utility company, after a bad chlorine leak, to fund the town's new soccer field. She set it up so that a polluting refinery could purchase a thousand acres of protected habitat for the fringe-toed lizard. A commercial developer in Agoura funded a wildlife crossing under the freeway. She liked the practical and creative aspects of this work: nobody pretended that damage wasn't done, and ongoing—so what could balance it out, make up for it?

At home, Cress put in a large vegetable and flower garden, and walked every morning, starting out in the dark, up and down the arroyo with its steep rocky walls and shallow stream. One of her neighbors, a widower with three grown daughters, walked a little later than she did with his standard brown poodle, Mimi. Every day, around the time the sun was rising, they paused to chat. Eamon Cuddihy was fifty-three, an internist–turned–hospital director. A black-haired Black Irishman, born in County Cork, he spoke with a lovely lilt. His wife had been dead for four years.

To Eamon, Cress described her time in the mountains as *lost*. And because he had been companionably married for twenty-six years, she felt shame and trepidation in admitting that her longest romantic attachment had been with a married man.

"Ah, but you were young," Eamon said.

Twenty-eight wasn't *that* young, but Cress didn't argue the point.

A week before Cress and Eamon's wedding, her therapist said, "You know, you really should be grateful to Quinn."

"I should?" Cress gaped at the woman. Quinn's name still set off a systemwide alarm. "For what?"

"He got you started working through your father issues."

"He did?"

Really, said the therapist, it was no mystery: Cress had acted out the oldest story, Oedipus-for-girls, if you will: push the mother out of the way, so you can have the father's attention all to yourself. "You were hardly subtle, Cress," her therapist said. "Quinn's wife and your mom even had the same name. And didn't you say that your father, too, was at one time a carpenter?"

Cress covered her face with her hands, embarrassed by how obviously—how obliviously—she'd acted out the whole family romance.

From therapy and self-help books, she had learned many such terms: *family romance*, and also *attachment disorder, codependence, repetition compulsion, narcissistic wound*. But these were words, uttered or printed on a page, and no match—no match at all!—for the bright churning waves of memory.

Don Dare phoned her out of the blue. He was going climbing in Potrero Chico in Nuevo León and was coming down to Los Angeles the night before his flight. Would she and Eamon meet him for dinner out by the airport? Cress suggested a French Moroccan place in Culver City with a large patio. (Eamon tactfully bowed out: "You two catch up without me.")

They were seated beside a gnarled pomegranate tree where two yellow canaries hopped and trilled in a cage. They laughed and insisted the other hadn't changed in the last twelve years. Don had gained some weight through his middle, but he had the same handsome, narrow, pitted face, the same shock of surfer blondness, if somewhat receded.

"You ever go back to Sawyer or the Meadows?" Cress asked.

"Just last weekend," he said. "Elise and I took the boys climbing at the Crags."

They'd camped at Spearmint Creek, too, on the site of the old tent. They'd gone to the lodge for Family Night, as well, and nothing had changed there, either, not really. Jakey's kids ran the place now, but Jakey was still very present, roaring at customers and giving his kids unasked-for advice. And guess who was singing?

"How to put this kindly . . . ," said Don. "She has grown, uh, quite stout."

Over kebabs, he passed Cress photographs of four towheaded boys and the Tuscan-style villa he and Elise had built. One snapshot showed wooden cupboards and a rectangular white farm sink. "Quinn put in the kitchen for us."

Spoken so casually, the name was a shock. Her heart zigzagged around her chest. She tried to sound offhand. "And how is Quinn?"

"Well, you heard he remarried," Don said.

"I've heard nothing! What happened? Did Sylvia die?"

She left him, said Don Dare. She took the boy and moved to the coast. Long time ago. Right after Cress left.

"I assumed you knew all about it," said Don.

After Sylvia split, Don said, Quinn became a fixture in the bars. Quite the town drunk, in fact. Then he got together with Jill Jurgensen, and she took him in hand.

Louder than Cress intended: "*Who?*"

"You never met Jill?" Jill was a Sawyer girl, from an old, rich ranching family. "A friend of Donna's. That's when I first met her."

"Never heard of her!" Cress was still absorbing *Took the boy. Moved to the coast.*

A long, almost electrical chittering tone bore through her thoughts. One of the canaries singing.

"Jill must have moved back after you left," Don was saying. "She teaches biology at Sparkville High. And she's a real jock. Still. A triathlete. A bicycler and jogger and—what's the third thing?"

"Swimming," said Cress.

There were two little boys, too, Ace and Dalbert, Roman twins, nine months apart. "They must be six and seven now," said Don Dare. Jill had brought them up to the house when Quinn was working on the kitchen. They were only two and three then. "A couple of little scamps."

A plate of glass had gone up between Cress and the world beyond her. She could see and hear Don, but no longer take in what he was saying.

So there was no long shuffle *à deux* into old age. At least not with Sylvia.

But that alternate life Cress had tried to imagine was not so imaginary, after all: an energetic biology teacher named Jill Jurgensen was presently living it.

He had not come looking for her. She'd been waiting here with a listed number. For years. She'd made it easy for him to find her. But he must not have wanted to. Maybe it was never the same for him.

"To tell the truth," Don was saying, "Jill reminds us a lot of you. She's around your age. Her hair is long and straight like yours, only white-blond. She's got a really great sense of humor like you. And she's smart, too. Not as smart as you, but she has a lot more on the ball than that first wife of his."

A moth fluttered by, its wings ivory-white with ink-black dots. Cress's heart fluttered with it. With difficulty, she spoke over its frantic rhythm. "Did he ever—ahh—mention me?"

"Oh sure," said Don. "He read all your work in the *Times*. He and Jill were both big fans."

Don must have seen her paleness, her quivering lip. "Oh, Cress. I thought you were happy!" He waved a hand. "Your job, your husband."

She was happy, she assured him. But that had nothing to do with this.

"Don't feel bad," said Don. "Not about Quinn. I mean, I love the guy, but Jill puts up with a lot."

Quinn had never really quit the bars, Don said. He might sober up for a year or so, but then Jill would start getting calls to haul him out of Bob's or the Staghorn, or bail him out of the Sparkville tank. Each cycle was a little worse. "He vanished off our job for two whole weeks. We were about to hire someone else when he dragged in looking like ten miles of rough road."

So Cress was lucky, Don said. She'd dodged a bullet.

Yes, yes. Very lucky, no doubt.

But dodging a bullet, Cress thought, described a fleeting instant, as if she'd pulled her head aside in the nick of time when, in fact, no matter how often she'd put herself smack in the line of fire, she'd failed to get herself shot.

A sleepless night.

A constant ticking backward in time—to their last meetings at the Starlight Inn, where they had been so at ease and more cheerful than ever. Why hadn't he come back to that?

He'd probably needed money after Sylvia left. To buy her out. And along came a jolly, fit, rich girl.

Cress recalled something her own father said, way back when it was all starting. "Does he know you're an heiress?" Cress never had told Quinn that. Perhaps she should have. Perhaps it might have burrowed like a foxtail into Quinn's brain, so when Sylvia departed, he would have turned to her.

Cress would've loved to buy that land for him.

He'd probably been too afraid to call after so much cruel intermittency. Or he had moved on.

The memory of waiting—waiting to see him, waiting to touch him, waiting for him to make up his mind—was still visceral. Those years in Sawyer, she'd teetered on the edge, never knowing if she'd tip finally into exaltation or despair. Indeed, a part of her still waited like a girl sitting on a front stoop, watching the street for her love to arrive. Longing, that twisting needle, had been blunted by time and other happiness, but she felt it now, so painful and sweet and unendurable.

The young are better at withstanding such love.

By the time Sylvia finally left him, Quinn was probably ready for something novel and guilt-free, like a white-blond jock who could beat him up the mountain to Wanderwood and produce, in rapid succession, two small scamps.

Cress threw the covers off her shoulders, kicked at the tightness of the sheet down by her feet. Mimi, the cause of that tightness, raised her fluffy head, then decamped to the carpet.

Cress did have three stepchildren, two of them married and poised to reproduce. (So smart, Tillie said, to go straight for grandkids.)

Cress curled on her side. Eamon, possibly still asleep, sent a hand to her hip.

Their love was quieter, sturdier, nondizzying. Much more friendly and reliable. With a lot more laughter. But she rarely trembled. Nor did she wish to anymore.

———

In the morning, Cress plucked the donkey off her dresser. She wrapped it in tissue paper, then in bubble wrap; she sealed it in a padded envelope and mailed it on her way to work, to Quinn Morrow / Sawyer, California, with no note, no return address.

Acknowledgments

Friends give us the courage to go on, and I couldn't have written *Off Course* without Mona Simpson's conversation and hands-on writing help. Laurie Winer, Mary Corey, and Lily Tuck also read the novel in draft. I am deeply grateful.

The economists Cora and Jim Moyers, Julie A. Nelson, and Mark Maier graciously took the time to talk to me; particularly helpful was Julie A. Nelson's brave and clarifying book *Economics for Humans*.

Publication is a long collaboration; I am grateful to all who have helped *Off Course* along the way: agents Scott Moyers, Jin Auh, and Sarah Burnes; the team at FSG, including Dan Piepenbring, Oliver Munday, Jonathan Lippincott, Tobi Haslett, Rodrigo Corral, and especially my editor, Sarah Crichton.

I've benefitted immeasurably from Jim Potter's intelligence, patience, and steadying love. If he ever thought marrying a novelist was romantic, I have by now roundly disabused him of that notion.

A Note About the Author

Michelle Huneven is the author of three previous novels—*Blame*, which was a finalist for the National Book Critics Circle Award; *Jamesland*; and *Round Rock*. She lives in Altadena, California, with her husband, Jim Potter.